# Crossing Paths

## THE ROAD TO DESTINY

## NINA PURTEE

## PORTO BANUS
PUBLISHING

PORTO BANUS PUBLISHING 2024
St Pete Beach, FL

*Originally published by Newman Springs Publishing 2023*

ISBN 979-8-9898529-2-5 (Paperback)
ISBN 979-8-9898529-3-2 (Digital)

# Acknowledgments

*C*rossing Paths: The Road to Destiny unfolds as the captivating follow-up to *Beyond the Sea: Annie's Journey into the Extraordinary* and was inspired by the iconic group of multicultural characters introduced during Annie's original journey. Set against the vibrant backdrop of Mallorca, the actual Kings Cup Regatta, and Night of the Pilgrims overnight hike up to the sanctuary gave me quite a thought-provoking canvas to draw from. It allowed me to delve into those characters drawn into Annie's world to explore their individual strengths, weaknesses, and interactions with each other, inevitably embarking on journeys of their own.

The constant encouragement from my beta readers who have become immersed in Annie's initial journey was a much appreciated cheerleading team, because every day they wanted to know what would happen next. And, once again, to my friend and editor, Susan Schader...you're the best. Thank you!

*Paths charted, choices made...smooth sailing or turbulent sea awaits?*

# Chapter 1

Annie looked over at the strappingly handsome matador she had just agreed to marry. Hailed from generations of Spanish matadors, Ramone was legendary for his skill at facing the fiercest of bulls. However, there was so much more about him Annie found irresistible...his layers seemed to move from sheer strength and focus when fighting to achingly sweet gentleness filled with romance when they were alone together. Her mother had commented that perhaps it was his poet's soul that gave him the balance needed to offset his bold profession.

It was, in fact, his profession that almost made Annie turn down his proposal a mere day ago. On that day at the waterfall when she saw those wretched scars on his body from various goring injuries, all she wanted was to keep him safe. The closer they got and the stronger her feelings became, the deeper her debilitating fear of him facing that danger each time he entered the ring. After all, his brother Antonio, also a matador, was seriously injured and still remained in a wheelchair.

Ramone watched her studying him, then reached over to pull this woman he loved beyond words into his arms.

"*Querida*, I meant what I said. You and our unborn child are my world. If I must choose between you and what I do, I choose you. I can't fight knowing you will always live in fear."

Finally finding her voice, Annie answered, "As you know, my love, I have spent many months over the last year on a journey searching for inner peace, serenity, and balance. My mariner's spirit and endless restlessness took me to exotic countries and much time at sea for self-reflection and to expand my way of

1

thinking. What I found were people and countries immersed in history and tradition. Dingle in Ireland and Olympos in Greece both seriously maintain and preserve the traditions of the generations before them. In Spain, bullfighting is one of those traditions, and your skill and finesse makes you a hero to these people. I know I can't take that from you."

Shaking his head, he said, "I can't sit here, *querida*, and tell you it is not dangerous. I have seen many lives cut short or seriously changed in the ring. Antonio might never walk again, much less fight, but he puts himself through agonizing physical therapy to have the chance to fight again. My own grandfather was killed in the ring. It was his death that had such a life-changing impact on my father. Look at what happened to him, now held by the British authorities. All I can say is there is a rush after defeating the bull and defying death that day that is like no other."

Annie sighed. "Ramone, it is still hard for me to imagine that you betrayed your father to save me and my father from the Chinese renegades holding him captive. I have agreed to be your wife and to have your children. I love you from a depth of my heart I never knew existed. What if someday you do not come home to us? I don't think I could bear it."

"Do we ever know when our time will come?" Ramone reasoned. "There was no way I could let Papa's dire plan hurt you. We will find a way to make it work. Perhaps there is a compromise that will allow us to get past this obstacle."

"Yes. I do believe thoughts can transform into reality, so I know I must not overthink potential consequences. But, Ramone, you are so serious when you fight, or even preparing to fight. When we travel and explore, your whole demeanor changes. You relax and laugh...even become mischievous." Annie rolled her eyes and laughed, finally breaking the serious nature of their talk.

She studied her new blue diamond ring. "Tell me again the meaning of the blue diamond?"

Taking her hands, Ramone softly answered, "A blue diamond symbolizes eternity, truth, peace, and spirituality, as well as ensuring a safe journey."

Annie nodded. "That couldn't be more perfect!" Reaching into her pocket, she pulled out a brilliant yellow-green stone. "My grandfather gave me this peridot stone. He said it's beneficial in overcoming fear and instilling confidence in one's own abilities. Today, I am redirecting my focus. I feel certain we can get through this together! Let's go share the news!"

The journal that Don Marco, Annie's grandfather, had given her as she embarked upon her journey on his magnificent motor-sailing vessel, *Porto Banus*, had been a constant at her side throughout the unique experiences of the last year. A flip through the journal was a testament of how she had grown...learning gratitude for friends and family and to celebrate the opportunities each day brings. Her introspective nature reflected on the crossroads that entered her life and the consequences of the choices she made. She thought about the entry she would make about Ramone's proposal and her acceptance:

*It is hard to believe merely a year has gone by since the sailing accident with Sabine. In Boothbay, Maine, living with my mother, I left an amazing job with a prominent Portland architectural firm and was still mourning the military death of my college sweetheart, Jeffrey. The position in Boothbay at the Maritime Museum seemed right at the time but never made proper use of the talents I was taught and nurtured (and don't want to forget). My father was away far too long on one of his military missions, and I was so worried...I was stuck and sinking. Sabine, my beautiful cousin/sister/confidante, saw it first. She was even pestering me about it the day of the accident. But then it happened. Sabine was seriously injured, and I felt responsible. I was frozen with grief and unable to move forward. Thankfully, my grandparents invited me to their villa in Marbella, and once my mother literally pushed me out the door, my journey finally began... who knew how things would turn out and that now I would be engaged to a famous Spanish matador and pregnant with his child? So many memorable experiences along the way helped me grow and learn. Am I finally ready to take this leap of faith with this man who defied his own father to keep me and my father safe? God, I hope so.*

Hand in hand and newly engaged, Annie and Ramone took their first steps toward a life together. They were not just lovers; they were best friends and soul mates. Somehow the universe had led them to each other and the chance to find their destiny together. Annie still carried the short note Ramone wrote for her in Scotland so many months before.

*'Sailing maiden, thornless rose. Adventurous heart the sea best knows. The same love that draws me to you lets me set you free. Your journey's end waits next to me.'*

# Chapter 2

When Annie and Ramone approached Don Marco's villa, they noticed Sabine in the garden deep in conversation with Ramone's brother, Antonio. Sabine seemed to be managing Antonio's wheelchair easily as they maneuvered through the garden paths.

Glancing at Ramone, Annie smiled. "This is a good place to start, don't you think?"

Ramone smiled back and affectionately put his arm around Annie. "Yes, *querida*. These two mean so much to us."

About that time, Sabine noticed them. "We were wondering where you two were. Come join us!"

Ramone went over to pat his brother on the back, and Annie gave Sabine a giant hug. Sabine, trying to grasp this sentimental display, glanced back and forth between the two of them. It was then she noticed the brilliant sparkle coming from Annie's finger.

"What! You two?" Looking at Annie in wonder, she added, "You said yes? Oh, *mon Dieu*! I can't believe it!"

Antonio, knowing that Ramone planned to propose, literally beamed. "Well, brother, looks like you got the girl after all! And that ring! We should have a toast!"

Hearing all the excitement, Don Marco and Genevieve, Annie's grandparents fondly referred to as Dom and Gennie, came out to the garden.

Dom questioned, "What is this all about?"

Sabine jumped in. "It appears my cousin has gotten herself engaged!"

Gennie could not contain her excitement and opened her arms for Annie, her beautiful granddaughter, who such a short time ago had lost her way. Hugging her tightly, she said, "*Chérie*, you deserve this happiness. Let me see your ring!"

Annie glanced over at Ramone and asked, "Will you share with them the meaning of the blue diamond?"

After he did, everyone was impressed by Ramone's romantic gesture that carried with it such heartfelt emotion. Dom shook Ramone's hand and embraced him.

"Welcome to the family, son. We are proud to include you as one of our own."

The mood was festive out there in the garden, with hearts bursting with hope and joy for this couple and Annie's new journey ahead with a husband and child.

Annie and Ramone excused themselves to go call Annie's parents, Alex and Celeste, as well as Ramone's mother, Marguerite. They left the high-spirited group in the garden arm in arm to go make the calls.

Celeste answered on the second ring, but once Alex heard it was Annie, he quickly got on the phone with her. Annie told them about the proposal and Ramone's willingness to sacrifice his profession for her. She said, "I couldn't let him make such a sacrifice. We finally agreed to find a compromise in some way."

Ramone added, "Alex, when I was in Maine, I asked you if the right time came could I have your blessing to marry your daughter. I was honored you said yes. And, Celeste, trust me to hold Annie's heart close and to always do my best to protect her. I will never attempt to contain the spirit that urges her to travel and learn, as long as her heart remains with me."

Alex asked Annie, "Sweetheart, are you prepared to love this man despite the risks that he takes? Your mother has had to live with a similar life. It is not easy."

Annie sighed. "That has certainly been the biggest obstacle for me. But, Dad, I love him dearly and can't imagine a future without him." Ramone held her close.

Celeste chimed in, "I would never have chosen anything else. Have you thought about a wedding? Where or when?"

Annie reflected for a moment, then answered, "Tomás and Meghan just had the most beautiful and sentimental wedding. I would never want to rival that. They will be back from Ireland in a few days. My cousin and his bride are very dear to me. Ramone and I will talk about it. I think I would like to do something deeply spiritual and unique."

The conversation ended with well wishes and their agreement to be at the wedding, wherever they decided. Joyful tears were in Annie's eyes as they hung up. Next was Marguerite, Ramone's mother.

They were about to dial her number when Annie suggested, "She's not far. Why don't we tell her in person?"

Annie had not known Ramone's mother, Marguerite, long. In some ways, she reminded her of her own mother. Both women were strong, insightful, and nonjudgmental. It had been Marguerite who had wisely told Annie to make her choices today to avoid future regrets, but also to be aware of the impact her choices might have on those around her. Annie wanted to assure her that she would do her best to make the success of this marriage her priority.

Marguerite answered the door, and Annie was again struck by her natural warmth and welcome that made her already feel like family. Marguerite had been a talented flamenco dancer in Barcelona in her youth and had remained a Mediterranean beauty with her dark raven hair and a twinkle in her eyes. Even after Salvador, Ramone's father, left her alone raising their sons, she remained married to him hoping for a miracle someday. Her open arms received hugs from both Ramone and Annie.

"Such a surprise! Come in. Shall I make some tea?" Marguerite asked.

Glancing at Annie with a grin he couldn't hide, Ramone said, "Mother, we have some news!" Annie looked back at him, taking his hand, thereby showing Marguerite her ring.

"Oh, *hijo mío*, my son!" Showing the love she had for Ramone, Marguerite walked up to him for a deep embrace. Then, moving to Annie, another embrace followed by, "My darling girl, it gives me such pleasure to find in you the daughter I always prayed for. Your journey has led you to my son. Now your life will take on a new path. Hard as it might be to take those first steps, you are about to discover things you would never have known...a new husband and a child. My best advice to you is to enjoy the adventure and be amazed. It will be well worth the effort!"

Tears welling in Annie's eyes, she held this loving woman and said, "Ramone has captured my heart. I once thought love would be impossible to find, but somehow here it is with your son, and I am ready to move beyond my comfort to embrace a future together. Thank you for believing in me and trusting that I will respect and honor him, but most of all for accepting me into your family."

Ramone felt nothing but pride for this woman who had agreed to be his wife and bear his children. Watching her with his mother, he made a commitment to himself to ensure Annie's life was a good one, filled with love and happiness, and to keep fear to a minimum.

# Chapter 3

A few days later, Annie and Ramone were returning to the villa after a stroll along the shore discussing wedding possibilities. Gennie was happily pruning her flowers in the garden. She saw them and waved. "Tomás and Meghan have just arrived from Ireland! We waited for you to share the news!"

Ramone helped Gennie up, and Annie asked, "Where are they?"

"They are getting settled in the Carriage House," Gennie answered. "Why don't you go find them?"

The Carriage House was at the far corner of the villa property. Annie and her mother had lived there after she was born while her father was away in the British military. She was ten years old when her father arranged for them to move to Maine. The Carriage House had remained vacant, other than the occasional special guests, until Tomás took over Don Marco's business and moved into the house himself. Prior to that, he had lived in the villa with Dom and Gennie after his parents' death. He and Meghan decided before their family wedding in Maine to spend half their time here in Spain and the other in Meghan's hometown of Dingle, Ireland where they had been since their honeymoon.

Excited to see her cousin and his fiery red-headed bride, Annie quickly walked the distance to the house, pulling a laughing Ramone along with her, calling out, "Tomás! Meghan! Are you finally home?"

The door opened before she could knock, and the enthusiastic greetings took over. Tomás and Meghan had not seen Annie since then. Annie did not miss the wink Meghan gave Ramone. After all, she was the one who masterminded Ramone's surprise arrival in Maine at the wedding. If Meghan hadn't intervened after hearing about Annie's pregnancy, who knows what the couple's future might or might not have been? For that, Annie owed Meghan her deepest gratitude.

Tomás said they were famished and suggested they all go to a seaside taverna for lunch. Sitting around the waterfront table sharing a family-sized bowl of paella, Ramone seemed completely at ease and was enjoying the conversation. Annie took a few moments to study Tomás. There was a glow about him, and the love that showed in his eyes each time he looked at Meghan made Annie's heart swell with joy for him. He had not had an easy journey. Orphaned at age nine, Tomás moved in with Dom and Gennie. His father, Jorge, was Celeste's older brother. Jorge and his wife, Maria, had lived in Malaga, around sixty kilometers from Marbella. Don Marco had always expected Jorge to take over his business. When they tragically died in the sudden car accident, Dom determined he would raise Tomás to fill that position. Tomás, Sabine, and Annie were all only children with no siblings so the family decided early in their lives they should spend their summers in Maine together. It was the bonding during all those summers that made the three of them more like brother and sisters than cousins.

Annie knew Tomás had done well and how proud Dom was. Lost in her thoughts, Annie jumped when Meghan repeated her question a little louder. "Have you given any thought to a wedding?" All three of them were staring at her.

Blushing, Annie said, "Not yet. Your wedding was so special. We don't want to take anything away from that experience." Glancing at Ramone and reaching for his hand, she continued, "During my travels, there were many spiritual places that held an energy explained only by the presence of so many generations who lived and worshiped there before. I love the idea of finding a place like that."

Annie went on to share with them about Ayer's Rock in the outback of Australia. Named Uluru, it remained a living cultural landscape dating back sixty thousand years. She also spoke of Olympos, the traditional mountain village in Karpathos, which began a discussion of the similarities of Dingle, Ireland, and Olympos, Greece. They also recognized this child was conceived on the island of Karpathos, which gave it special meaning.

Tomás nodded and smiled at Ramone, then quietly said, "Annie is like a sister to Sabine and me. She was so fearful of your profession. How did you get past that?"

Ramone looked over at Annie and Meghan so animated in their conversation. He spoke softly to Tomás. "I was willing to give it up for her if that was what it would take. She and this unborn child are everything to me. I think that is why she wants such a spiritual ceremony. We haven't discovered just the right direction yet, but I feel we will know it when we find it."

Tomás's respect for Ramone was growing. When Annie and Meghan paused, Tomás asked, "What about a place to live?"

Annie heard the question and answered, "Ramone has to remain in the area to be relatively close to where he fights. All I know is the small apartment in Karpathos that looked out over the sea felt like home to us both. If there was somewhere that could replicate that for us, it would be a miracle!"

Thoughtful, Tomás's mind was running through the properties he oversaw for his grandfather. After a few moments, he lit up. "What about Mijas? It's only thirty minutes from here and would put you halfway between Marbella and the airport in Malaga. Dom doesn't have anything available, but you might get lucky."

Ramone enjoyed taking Annie on the scooter to the various whitewashed villages along the hills of the Costa del Sol, and they were both familiar with Mijas. As if dawning on them at the same time, they looked at each other, smiled, and simultaneously said, "Mijas? That is a great possibility!"

So beautiful with its dazzling white buildings, winding narrow streets, and spectacular views of the Mediterranean, Mijas held a lot of similarities to the village on the hill above the port

11

of Pigadia in Karpathos. Looking back at Tomás, Ramone asked, "Do you think anything might be available?"

"Why don't you go take a look?" Tomás reasoned.

Excitement building, Annie and Ramone decided to take the scooter to Mijas that very afternoon to see what they might find available for sale. Saying goodbye for now and thanking Tomás for the idea, they set off on a mission. As they approached the road up to the village then went through the white stone entrance of Mijas, Annie felt that warm sense of belonging. They rode up to the main square, parked and walked out to the terrace overlooking the village with a perfect view of the sea. Annie was soaking it in.

Ramone pulled her close. "What do you think?"

She hugged him back and smiled. "I love it!" Pointing, she added, "Look down there. Do you think that sign means it is for sale?" They started walking down the hill. Seeing the *Se Vende* sign out front, they took a chance that it would be open...and it was. The owner greeted them and recognized Ramone immediately. She was thrilled to have such a famous guest in her home! From the outside, tucked away at the end of the road, the house was very unassuming. A short driveway beside a walkway to the brilliant blue front door shaded by a trellised archway in full bloom with crimson bougainvillea...that was all you could see. But once inside, they knew immediately.

Across from the entrance was a full wall of floor-to-ceiling sliders giving the most spectacular panoramic view of the Mediterranean! Stepping down to the casual living area, they saw the sliders could open all the way to combine the outdoor terrace with the interior. The open terrace was potted with fragrant herbs and flowers. Built into the mountain, the living space moved through three levels at a meandering pace, each level with the same amazing view. The kitchen and two guest bedrooms were on the second level. The smaller one would serve perfectly as a nursery, and the other had such a pretty view, Annie couldn't wait to have visitors! Encouraged, they moved on to the sprawling suite on the bottom level that had a private wraparound terrace. They glanced at each other and smiled when they saw the dipping pool off to the side, so reminiscent of their apartment in Karpathos.

Had they indeed entered a charmed life? This villa built into a mountain overlooking the sea felt like home. Annie nodded when Ramone looked at her with the question. As he went back to speak with the owner, Annie wandered through, touching this and that, feeling a sense of peace that this place of wonder could possibly be theirs. After a brief discussion with the owner, Annie and Ramone made their way back to the square. Children playing along the way gave both a tug at their heartstrings, and Ramone stopped to pull Annie close.

"*Querida*, I believe this is one of those rare moments when the directions we take seem to come together in perfect harmony. Would you like to make this our home?"

Annie thoughtfully answered, "I felt a sense of true contentment inside the *casa* and with it an appreciation of earth and sea blended together like us."

Ramone kissed her gently, but the kiss deepened as he once more realized the treasure in his arms that would soon be his. "*Querida*, the villa will be yours. I felt it too. I know our children will as well, my love. I just need to work out the details in the coming days."

Words could not express the feelings that had come over Annie that prickled her skin. Was it too greedy to want it all? She dearly hoped not.

# Chapter 4

Annie returned to the villa alone to find Sabine packing. "Why are you packing, cuz? Where are you going?"

When Sabine looked up, Annie noticed she had been crying. "Annie, it's time for me to go back home to France. I haven't seen Maman and Papa in forever! It must be about time to harvest the grapes at the vineyard. There will be much to do. You have a new life to start with Ramone. Tomás and Meghan have now returned. You do not need me here and I can be of help at home."

Going over to hold her shoulders, Annie quietly added, "What is it, *chérie*? I thought you and Antonio were getting along so well. What does he think of you leaving?"

"*Incroyable*! He is such a stubborn man!" Sabine said angrily. "The doctors have told him to be patient. The physical therapy is working toward getting him on his feet to walk soon. But, no, that's not enough! These matadors, why do they seek the ring so intensely? Antonio is working six to eight hours a day with therapists to be strong enough not just to walk but to fight! His obsession is getting harder and harder to watch."

Annie understood the challenges of being with a matador and felt a pang of unease that Ramone in the same position might very well act the same way.

Looking closely at the cousin she so loved, Annie asked, "Sabine, there's something else. I know you. What is it?"

"I am so confused! It's Robert...I received a letter from him yesterday."

When Annie asked, "What did he say?" Sabine handed her the letter with a sniffle.

*'Dearest Sabine,*

*I was an idiot for letting you get on that plane in Maine. Life here in Boothbay is not the same without you, and I am furious with myself that I could not find adequate words to make you understand how I feel. You had such courage to work so hard to recover from the accident. Writing you all those letters afterward made me feel a closeness to you that I have never felt before. And when we had that time during Tomás and Meghan's wedding to spend together and get to know each other, I knew then, but the coward in me couldn't say the words. I think I am falling in love with you, Sabine. I am making a bold decision for once and taking two weeks off and would like to visit you in France to see if there could be a future for us. Please say yes.*

*Most fondly, Robert'*

"Robert? I never thought I would see the day! Wow, Sabine, what are you going to do? This was a big step for him."

"I know I should stay and help you with plans for the wedding, but I think I should explore the possibility with Robert. I never took him seriously because I assumed he was crazy about you. But I can't help wonder if it would cease to be impossible if I simply stopped thinking it was impossible, *n'est-ce pas?*" Sabine reasoned.

Annie crossed the room to give her cousin a giant hug. She was so proud of Sabine. "Perhaps there is a fine line between impossible and possible that can be crossed when the time is right? Go, *chérie*, give Robert a chance. Don't worry about the wedding. I have something incredibly special in mind, and now I just need to find where it is! It doesn't have to be a large spectacle, although with Ramone's fame and wide circle, it could get large. I think he would like to consider the Cathedral in Málaga. It is beautiful, of course, and naturally I love its traditional Renaissance archi-tecture. But I would like something more unique. Ramone has an exhibition bullfight in Barcelona next week where I will get my first test to subdue the overwhelming fear I have for his fight-ing. I thought it might be good to pay a visit to Montserrat while there. Its position high in the Catalonia Mountains is on one of the Camino pilgrimage routes, and its Benedictine monastery is home to the spiritual icon of the Black Madonna. This might be an interesting wedding possibility. The misty mountain setting there is supposed to be very spiritual."

"Annie, you will know the right place, and when you find it know that I will be there with you! Now let me pack and then give Robert a call. Maybe you could join us for a few days in Bayonne?"

Annie smiled. "No, *ma cousine*, this is a time for you to explore each other without our distraction!" Then, as an after-thought, "How will you explain your leaving to Antonio?"

"There is nothing really to explain. We have become friends, nothing more. He knows I have to return to France eventually. He is so focused on getting back in the ring he most likely won't even notice."

Annie smiled at her cousin's naive answer but left it alone. She wandered outside and found her grandparents having tea under the gazebo by the pool overlooking the sea. "*Hola*, what a beautiful day!" Annie said.

"Ah, Annie, come join us!" Gennie poured her a cup as she sat down.

"I never tire of this view! You both have been so good to Sabine, Tomás, and especially me. I practically dragged Captain Luis and the *Porto Banus* all over the world!"

Dom nodded with a knowing smile. "You three are our fam-ily and the future. Now, you and Ramone will bring the next gen-eration to us, and our hopes for Tomás and Meghan to follow are extremely high. Sabine will find her way. We liked what we saw of Robert at the wedding in Maine. Hopefully the three of you will have children who grow up to be as close as you cousins."

"That is a hope we all share...we feel more like siblings than cousins." Annie reflected.

Gennie added, "It has been quite the year, hasn't it? Annie, *chérie*, you have made the ultimate choice to marry Ramone and have his child. Are you ready to settle down and rein in that restless urge of yours to be at sea and explore the world? Did you have any luck finding a home you like?"

"I don't think I will ever lose the symbiotic relationship I have with the sea, Gennie. Luckily, Ramone and I found a villa built into the mountain in Mijas that has a beautiful view and such a peaceful energy about it. It will be a couple of months before we can move in, that is, if he can work out the details, but we should be settled in long before the baby arrives." Annie unconsciously moved her hand to her stomach.

Dom, always with a wisdom Annie so loved about him, said, "When the challenge you face feels insurmountable, whether it is the location of the wedding or your future home, just remember to take that first step. Through the years, I have found that if you work it through thoughtfully, you will find those challenges less overwhelming if you face them head on."

Annie was about to answer when Sabine came out to the patio. "Annie, there is a young man at the door. He handed me this long-stemmed red rose and said Ramone needed to see you urgently and that he would take you."

Looking at Dom, Annie said, "That is strange. Why wouldn't Ramone simply pick up the phone to call? He knows I'm here, but the rose?"

Dom got up and began walking to the door with Annie. "The last time someone you didn't know offered to take you somewhere, it was to your father, and you were kidnapped by Salvador. Let's find out what this is all about."

When the messenger saw Don Marco's stern questioning look, he ran. Looking at each other in disbelief, Dom said sharply, "Call Ramone. Let's get to the bottom of this."

# Chapter 5

With a tremble of reminiscence, Annie recalled the night in Ireland when Ramone's father, Salvador, supposedly her own father's best friend in their youth, emerged from the shadows to 'take her to her father.' Instead, she was kidnapped and used as a pawn to help take down her father.

Looking at Don Marco, Annie could tell he was worried too. Still holding the rose, Annie reached for the phone and dialed. Marguerite answered and immediately handed the phone to Ramone. When he heard about the messenger, Ramone somewhat stiffly said, "Stay there. We will come to you."

More confused than ever, Annie dropped the rose of such questionable origin. When she asked Dom, "What does it mean? Who would know Ramone gives me roses?" He shrugged.

Sabine and Gennie joined them to hear what had happened. Gennie reasonably said, "Ramone will be here soon. Hopefully, he can tell us who this messenger was."

Sabine went to Annie and gave her a hug of support. "Let's make some tea. It sounds like we have a mystery to solve." With that, Annie and Sabine went to the kitchen to prepare some adequate sustenance for the questions ahead.

Ramone arrived a half hour later, casually dressed in jeans and turtleneck. He was not alone and had brought Marguerite and Antonio with him. Gennie ushered them all outside to the gazebo. When Ramone looked at Marguerite and nodded, she was first to speak. "This morning, I received word that Salvador escaped the British confines where he was held the last two months. There is speculation Kung Li and his Chinese associates aided in his escape."

Before anyone could respond, the phone rang. Don Marco answered, then handed the phone to Annie, who heard her father's voice. "Sweetheart, the British authorities have informed me Salvador has escaped. They want him back and have reactivated my status. They want me there as quickly as possible."

"Marguerite just informed us she got a call from the British officer in charge telling her about Salvador's escape. Everyone is here at the villa. A messenger was sent for me with a rose saying Ramone needed me urgently." Ramone came closer, and she put the call on speaker.

Alex questioned, "What would Salvador do to seek the most revenge? Most certainly try to get to me, and with Ramone's betrayal, most likely him. Who could hurt both of us most but you?"

Ramone interjected, "Surely he would not harm her?"

"We don't know that. Secret Services wants me to urgently activate forces I trust to help find him and return him to prison. I have a message in to Ernest to wait to hear from me. With his former involvement, he could also be in danger. Annie needs to be in safekeeping. The messenger at the door no doubt means Salvador is close by."

Alex spoke directly to Ramone. "Son, you have a choice to make. Go with Annie and keep her safe, or join us to bring your father to justice. Think about it. I am booked on the next flight and am bringing Celeste with me. Tell Dom we need his help. I am calling El Amir next to ask him and his men to provide back up."

That last comment made Annie and Ramone share a glance... El Amir? Ramone knew the Moroccan had feelings for Annie. Turmoil showed across his face. Should he go with Annie or stay and face his father with Alex, Ernest, and El Amir?

Tomás and Meghan caught the end of the call as they joined the family. Without hesitation, Tomás said, "One of Don Marco's estates in Mallorca just had its tenants vacate. It is built like a formidable fortress, and it would get Annie off the mainland!"

Mentally calculating the location, Don Marco agreed. "The Mallorca property was a fortified estate in medieval times, around the thirteenth century, to protect the island, although it has been notably updated throughout the years to today's standards. It is not too far. I can arrange for Captain Luis and the *Porto Banus* to help with the transport and some extra security."

Nodding, Tomás added, "Are Alex and Celeste flying into Madrid? If so, I can meet Celeste and get her to Mallorca as well." Annie noticed the glance Meghan gave him but didn't say a word.

Once he knew Annie would be with Captain Luis and the security team, Ramone felt his answer and said to Alex, "I will be with you, sir."

Looking directly at Annie, he added, "If there is any moment you feel the need for help, please do not hesitate." What Ramone didn't realize was how strongly he was holding her hand.

From the side of the room, Meghan sounded in. "I am your family now, and I am going with Annie! There will be hell to pay if anyone messes with my new family!"

Ending the call, it seemed everyone was talking at once trying to formulate plans. What went unnoticed by all but one was the dejected look on Antonio's face as he maneuvered his wheelchair over to the garden wall.

Sabine quietly walked over to him. "Do you feel as helpless as I do?"

As Antonio turned to face her, Sabine noticed his glistening eyes and a single tear drop. There were great depths of turmoil in those eyes, and Sabine took his hand to comfort him. After a few long moments, Antonio tried to gather his thoughts and replied, "Even with the choices he has made and the harm that he has caused, I love my father. When Ramone and I were boys, he was such a good man. I try to understand why it was so hard for him to abide with our decision to follow the family tradition and fight the bulls. Was I the one wrong after all? Here I am confined to a wheelchair, unable to walk, much less fight, and certainly unable to defend my family."

Sitting on the wall next to his wheelchair, Sabine could hear the pain in his voice. "Antonio, the accident in the ring has taken its toll, but guess what? You made it though, *n'est-ce pas*? You have the chance to keep going, don't you? I know when I had bleak moments during the rehab from my sailing accident, it was the encouragement of my father that helped me push through."

She continued, "*Chéri*, the path may not be easy, but just suppose it turns out to be the best thing that's ever happened to you? Every one of these difficult days makes you stronger, and each challenge you can manage to work through enables you to handle even bigger challenges. You are here and alive today. Be grateful and don't waste the opportunity to stand up and make a difference."

The words struck a chord with Antonio, and he reached for Sabine to draw her into an embrace. "Thank you for sharing that sentiment. Your father must be a wise man. I need to determine how or if I can help. What are your plans?"

Sabine answered, "I was packing to return to France when all of this happened. I honestly miss my parents and my home-town of Bayonne. It is a town full of French charm and close to my family's vineyards in Bordeaux where I used to work. I mean nothing to Salvador so I should be safe to travel home by train. What about you, Antonio? Do you feel you should be part of all this intrigue?"

At the sound of Annie's raised voice, Sabine turned her attention toward the group involved in a heated conversation. Normally, Annie would not cross her grandfather, but the tone in her voice said this time she was a force to be reckoned with. Antonio was listening as well. Annie stared at Don Marco and continued, "I am not some helpless child to be tucked away in some 'fortress' with guards standing over me! I got through the kidnapping, not knowing Ernest, Ramone, and El Amir were there to help. All I knew was that I was being used as a pawn to get information from my father."

Don Marco chided, "Be reasonable, Annie. This is different. Salvador might be out for revenge that involves you, and he has no incentive to keep you safe this time."

Ramone added, "Don't you understand, *querida*, your safety is all that matters to me?"

With that, Annie raised her eyebrows at the irony of his statement since her fear of him being injured or killed inside the bullring was very real to her. He continued, "I know from experience my father's anger can be unpredictable. What we did made him lose face with Kung Li. He wouldn't take that lightly, and there will be no stopping his taste for revenge."

Antonio had rolled his chair over to the group and cleared his throat to get their attention. Looking at Ramone, he said, "Papa might trust me. I want to help." Almost as an afterthought, Antonio asked, "How would Papa know about the red rose? When he took Annie, there was no rose, right?" Ramone and Annie looked at each other and nodded.

Marguerite stared at her sons, understanding this difficult situation. She wisely knew there would be no way for Ramone not to be involved. But to think her injured younger son might also put himself in danger was horrifying. She reasoned, "Maybe it was not Salvador who tried to take Annie?"

Alex said he would call again once he had final instructions. While they waited, Gennie went to the kitchen to make tea and light tapas. Annie and Sabine were quick to join her and help. Sabine prepared a bowl of assorted Spanish olives while Annie was slicing leftover *tortilla de patatas*. Gennie added tea and an assortment of breads and cookies. The quiet was deafening. It was Annie who finally broke the silence. "I can't believe this is happening. When I was a child, I barely remember having to leave Marbella in the middle of the night to safely move to Maine. But when Salvador and Ernest kidnapped me in Ireland, of course I was frightened, but at least I had enough wits about me to give Captain Luis a clue in the note I had to write him."

Gennie came over to hug her precious granddaughter. "Yes, the captain immediately knew something wasn't right. The moment he showed the note to Dom, your grandfather went to Ramone. Look at the group of people in the garden, *cherie*. They have your back and each other's. Truly listen to what they say and try not to be distracted by your thoughts and how you think you should respond. It is all right for us to worry and want to keep you safe. Please don't let stubborn pride interfere and perhaps put someone else in jeopardy."

"She's right, *ma cousine*." Sabine looked straight into Annie's eyes. "Uncle Alex and Ramone, and even El Amir, need to think clearly. Didn't you tell me that Ramone said the two most dangerous things when fighting the bull were worry and distraction? You need to eliminate both of those as much as possible."

Annie closed her eyes and nodded. "I am so grateful for you two and this incredible family I love beyond words...and now Ramone and his family have become part of that circle. I suppose my recklessness comes from worry about these men I love and admire so much. Do you honestly think Salvador would harm Ramone, his own son, and my father, who used to be his best friend?"

Gennie answered, resigned to the truth. "Well, Salvador did try to kill Alex in Hong Kong and left him bleeding in the street."

"That's it! They will be safer if I get out of the way. I am going to Mallorca!" Annie didn't realize her fists were clenched.

# Chapter 6

Don Marco watched Annie as the ladies came back out to the terrace. He could see the look of determined resolution in her eyes and marveled at how far she had come in the last year. There was hardly a sign of the desolate young woman who arrived at his villa, filled with grief over the sudden death of her college friend, Jeffrey, and her devastating sense of guilt over the sailing accident that almost took Sabine's life. Annie had lost her sense of purpose, as well as direction. He was satisfied he had made the right decision when he gave her the use of his dear *Porto Banus* to readjust her self-worth and get her moving forward again. And quite the adventures she experienced! It was hard to imagine in such a short time new friends were made, her father was freed from his Chinese captor, Sabine was almost healed and back to her old self, Annie had found a deep love with Ramone, and there was a brand new life stirring within her. Yes, it had been quite a year. Dom took a deep breath and considered his family's current predicament. Lost in his reverie, he didn't hear the phone ring.

Tomás answered. It was Alex calling from the airport in Portland. On speaker, Alex said, "I understand you are all there. I don't have much time. I think it would be better if I spoke privately off-speaker with Dom." Don Marco took the phone into the library, leaving behind a group glancing around at each other with a feeling of helplessness.

After what seemed a long ten minutes, Dom came back outside with his notepad filled with notes. He had everyone's attention. "First, Alex wanted me to apologize for his not including you in that call. He had a lot to cover and not much time before his flight. He very much liked the idea of the Mallorca estate and sailing the *Porto Banus* (or by motor depending on the circumstance) to get there." Looking at his notes with a glance at Meghan, he continued, "Meghan, Alex asks that you accompany Annie to Mallorca along with two of my security detail. I was not going to let you two ladies go without me, and I was not about to leave my dear Gennie here alone at the villa, so we will be joining you. Tomás, Sabine is returning to France by train, and her route takes her through Madrid. You will take the train with her to Madrid, then Sabine will continue to Bayonne. It is all arranged for your train to arrive in time for you to meet Alex and Celeste's plane in Madrid."

The tension on the terrace was palpable. Taking a sip of water, Dom looked directly at Tomás and continued. "This part is important, and I need to be sure I get it right. Alex will deplane first. You are not to interact with him in any way. Understand? He wants to be sure you do not arouse suspicion." Tomás nodded with a glance at Meghan. "Alex will be watching from a distance. When Celeste exits the plane, you will be at the gate to meet her. She will be wearing a short blond wig and sunglasses. It is your job to get her and her bags on the flight to Mallorca. Alex will be close the entire time to be certain you are both on the plane prior to his own departure for Malaga." Making sure he hadn't left out anything important, Dom went on, "Ramone, you are to get to Malaga as quickly as possible. Ernest will be waiting for you at the Plaza de la Merced. You both are to remain there out of sight until Alex and El Amir arrive with some of their comrades. El Amir's plane will be flying them from the Madrid airport to Malaga."

When it appeared Don Marco was finished, Antonio spoke up. "What about me, sir?" He tried to get out of his wheelchair and stand. His foot hit the chair's footrest, and Antonio slid to the ground. Both Ramone and Sabine were at his side within seconds to help him up. Don Marco, assessing Antonio's emotions, answered, "Son, I am so sorry I didn't speak sooner. Your role is important in this. You and Marguerite will be the only ones left here in Marbella. There is every possibility that Salvador is in this area and might try to see you or your mother. As you mentioned earlier, he might trust you and seek safety. How you and Marguerite handle such a visit is of utmost importance."

Antonio nodded solemnly.

"Time is critical right now," Dom continued. "Everyone needs to proceed with their part of the plan. Gennie, call Captain Luis and have him ready the *Porto Banus* for immediate departure and pack a few things for me. Antonio, Marguerite, please join me in the library."

Ramone pulled Annie aside with a hard embrace. "I will go fill my backpack, but I will return to say goodbye before I leave." Annie looked at this man who was now such an important part of her life and her kiss let him know how she felt.

Tomás and Meghan headed to the Carriage House to get ready. Gennie made the call to Captain Luis and retired to their suite to pack. Annie watched Ramone leave and then joined Sabine in their room to quickly pack a few things she might need.

In the library, Don Marco spoke with an air of authority that was so natural to him after all these years. "Alex wanted me to speak with you both confidentially. Things appear to be heating up in Hong Kong. There is a huge exodus of residents racing to get foreign passports and leave Hong Kong prior to the takeover. There are activists everywhere. I told Alex about the rose, and he agrees the trap for Annie might not have been set by Salvador. He has every reason to think Salvador would be unaware of this and try to contact one or both of you. Antonio, stay close to your mother."

"Alex said his British liaison is still working on it, but he told him Kung Li might have arranged the escape not to bring him back to Hong Kong but rather to eliminate him. Supposedly Salvador shared some very sensitive information about Kung Li's ties to Beijing and their plans to suppress the resistance in Hong Kong to the British turnover. He didn't give any further details other than to make you aware that Salvador may, in fact, be in more danger from the Chinese rather than the British. Alex's job, despite Salvador's unpredictable plans, is to keep him alive and turn him back over to British intelligence. If Salvador shows up here, try to convince him Alex wants to help him. Tell him to get to Malaga and watch his back. Give him this number and have him contact Alex when he is on the way."

Antonio and Marguerite shared a look, and Antonio spoke first, putting the note with the number in his pocket. "Does Alex really think Papa will come here? Will he seek to harm us?"

Marguerite wisely answered, "No, my son. If Ramone is not with us, he will seek us out for protection. Salvador will not trust Ramone. But if what they think is true, we mustn't keep him long especially if the Chinese are after him."

Don Marco nodded, went over to his desk, pulled out his Ruger LCR revolver, and handed it, along with ammunition, to Antonio. "Conceal it well, son. Hopefully, you will never need it."

Turning the gun over in his hands, Antonio thought aloud, "It was my father who taught me to shoot a handgun."

# Chapter 7

Sabine closed her suitcase and looked over at Annie. "I am going to miss you, *ma cousine*. I must admit I was a bit jealous when Dom said all of you would take the *Porto Banus* to Mallorca! It has been forever since I have been on board."

Annie came over and hugged her, and without letting her go stopped for a moment to absorb all the gratitude she felt that Sabine was indeed standing there in front of her, healthy and strong. "You don't have to go back to France, *chérie*. I'm sure you could come with us. There's plenty of room on the *Porto Banus*."

"No, I need to go home," Sabine said. "I made a promise to Robert to give him a chance. He will be in Bayonne soon. And besides, I will be at your wedding once you decide where it will be. Since Celeste and Gennie will be with you in Mallorca, maybe you could take that time to plan the wedding. It will do you good to have something to think about rather than fretting over what Uncle Alex and Ramone are doing. And I am just a phone call away."

Annie went back to packing. "Sabine, any man would be lucky to have you. It seems just in the last few days, you and Antonio got closer." At Sabine's surprised look, Annie continued, "Ramone said the doctors are optimistic Antonio will walk again but question whether he will ever be able to reenter the ring."

Interrupted by a knock on the door, Annie opened it to Antonio. He looked straight at Sabine and asked, "Do you have a few minutes? I would like to speak with you before you leave."

Nodding, Sabine followed him as he wheeled past where his mother was seated under the gazebo to the boardwalk. They found a bench where she could sit next to his chair. "Why so serious, Antonio?"

Taking a few moments to gather his thoughts, he said, "I thought of myself as quite the Casanova for many years, seeing women as mere conquests to be made, with no thought of how they felt when I moved on. I am not proud of the way I behaved. Over the last months, something has changed. The injury alone I could handle but being wheelchair-bound has forced me to look at my own limitations. When I see my brother filled with love for Annie, I wonder if I will ever experience such emotion. Sabine, you have been kind to me and somehow see beyond my disability." Antonio reached for her hand and continued, "Is it true you are going home to see another man?"

Sabine looked into those endearing brown eyes and that serious face. All she wanted was to see the playful twinkle in his eyes and those irresistible dimples that only showed when he smiled. Tilting her head, letting her French nature come out with one of her sauciest smiles, she answered, "I do have a good friend coming to visit me. However, it would seem my cousin isn't the only one to be captivated by a matador, *n'est-ce pas?*"

There it was. Antonio's smile with those dimples and flirtatious eyes that warmed Sabine's heart. She continued, "Sometimes life can seem harsh or cruel, but you don't have to see yourself as a victim. I have learned that from experience. You're not here just to get by. You're here to be amazing! Remember that in the days ahead as your family deals with your father's escape. I will see you soon, Antonio. If not before, definitely at Annie and Ramone's wedding!"

They were almost back to the villa when they saw Tomás coming to meet them. "Let's go, Sabine. We can't miss the train!" With a last smile at Antonio, she ran to get her bag.

Tomás was kissing Meghan when Sabine reached the driveway. The couple understood they would see each other soon in Mallorca. Tomás will bring Celeste and should arrive first and have the estate opened and ready. Annie, Dom, and Gennie had all come outside to say goodbye. Hugs all around and with one final glance at Antonio, Sabine hopped in the sedan with Tomás for the ride to the train station.

Marguerite brought their car over to Antonio, and Don Marco was there to help get Antonio and his chair into the car. "Good luck to you both. Take care of each other and stay safe."

They both nodded, and Antonio patted the lump in his coat pocket. Marguerite and Antonio were hoping to see Ramone before they left, but he had not yet returned to the villa. Annie had also noticed his absence.

Dom looked at his watch. "It is time to go. Roff is on his way to pick up the baggage. Our driver will be here any minute. Did Ramone know what time we were leaving? Could he think he was to meet us at the port?"

Thinking back through Ramone's parting words, Annie didn't think so. Perhaps a quick phone call might settle any confusion. She went inside to call Ramone, but he didn't pick up. Although her rational mind told her there was no need to worry, considering their circumstances, anything could have happened. Don Marco came in to tell her Roff had their bags, and the driver was out front. Annie failed to keep the panic out of her voice. "Dom, where is he? He should have been back long before now! I can't leave without saying goodbye. Let me try calling one more time." Before she could pick up the phone, it began to ring. Looking at Dom relieved, she said, "Good. That must be him now."

Annie answered, but it was not Ramone's voice at the other end. It was Antonio on the line. "Annie, put me on speaker. You'd better sit down," Antonio said very seriously. Seeing the concern on Annie's face, Meghan and Gennie joined them. Once the speaker was on, Antonio continued. "Mother and I got home a little while ago and saw Ramone's car. At first, we were happy he was still here so we could say goodbye. But when we looked a little closer, we realized the door was ajar. Annie, Ramone's backpack was inside, along with two beautiful long-stemmed red roses."

The world stopped as shock set in, and Annie turned pale. With a halting voice, Annie uttered, "Ramone is missing?"

Don Marco took the phone and asked Antonio, "Was there any sign of struggle?" Mentally calculating that Alex and Celeste were in the air and Tomás and Sabine were on the train, he realized he and Antonio were the only men available for this family and they needed to think clearly. "Did you or Marguerite call the authorities?"

"Not yet. We wanted to call you first. It is like Ramone vanished into thin air. He should be well on his way to Malaga by now. We will hang up and call the authorities." The next thing everyone heard before the call abruptly ended was Antonio's surprised "Papa!" The phone connection went dead.

Stunned, the group at the villa absorbed what they had just heard. Salvador was there? Did he already have Ramone somewhere? Dom was confident Antonio knew what he needed to convey to Salvador, but with Ramone missing, should the plan remain the same? Where was Alex to advise them? Annie, shaking her head with determination, said, "Dom, we need to delay our departure. We can't leave Ramone and his family without trying to help them."

Meghan came forward. "I agree with Annie. The four of us should stay together. You said you had two of your security team ready to sail with us. What if they were to come stay here with us?"

"Let's get the authorities involved. We need to find out what is happening to Antonio and Marguerite," Dom said as he placed the call.

Meanwhile, Gennie said to Annie and Meghan, "We need to think. Alex and Tomás will be in Madrid, too far away to help." After a pause, she continued, "Annie, what about this man Ramone was supposed to meet in Malaga? Maybe he could help. Can you think of any way we might contact him?"

Annie tried to clear her head of the worry and fear she felt so she could remember any details. "I found out about Ernest from Colonel MacGregor in Scotland. They were in the same British military unit as Salvador and my father. Wilkes. I'm sure that is his last name...Ernest Wilkes. He is a saxophone player. I found him in London playing at the Dolphin Brasserie. Maybe someone there knows him? He is the closest one able to help us."

Meghan had written down the information, and when Dom hung up, she said, "I've got this. I'm part sleuth anyway. I'll call the Brasserie to see if there is anyone there who knows how to reach Ernest."

Dom filled everyone in on his call to the police. "The officer dispatched a team to Marguerite's house. They should be there within minutes and want us to stay in touch in case someone tries to contact us. There will be an officer patrolling nearby if we need him."

Annie's mind was moving in a thousand directions. "I just thought of something. Dom, do you remember if Dad said El Amir or his plane was meeting them in Madrid?"

Dom scratched his head. "Let me think. He did say he and El Amir would find Ramone and Ernest in Malaga. I am fairly certain Alex said El Amir's plane would meet them in Madrid. Maybe El Amir is on his way to Malaga to meet the plane and join Alex there. If that is the case, he is also close by."

Meghan was wrapping up her conversation thanking whomever she was speaking to. "I've got a number! The proprietor at the Brasserie remembered Ernest spent a lot of time with a certain waitress. As luck would have it, she was on her shift and came to the phone. When I explained we were urgently trying to reach Ernest, she gave me his number."

Annie was about to call it when there was a loud knock on the door. They all looked at each other, not knowing what to expect. Don Marco nodded at the security guard, who went to answer the door. There was a heated discussion at the door, but it just took a few seconds for Annie to recognize the voice. It was El Amir! *What is he doing here at the villa?*

"Let him in, let him in!"

There he was, as handsome as ever, dressed totally in black Moroccan garb with his headscarf tied over his hair in a side knot. Even with his stern look, those golden eyes were mesmerizing and always struck a chord in her. He did not wait to take the lead.

"Why are you all here! You should be on board and out of the port by now. When I saw the *Porto Banus* was still docked with no activity on board, I was so worried. What is this delay?" He spoke to them all, but his eyes were only on Annie, missing the glance and raised eyebrows between Meghan and Gennie.

Don Marco stepped toward him and rather coolly said, "El Amir, I presume? We were unaware anyone was watching us. We are seriously concerned. When Ramone's brother, Antonio, and his mother, Marguerite, returned home, they found Ramone's abandoned car with his bag inside." Don Marco saw no need to mention the roses. "Then, when we were on the phone with Antonio, he was about to hang up and call the authorities when we heard him exclaim, 'Papa!' The reality of this situation is there is much we don't know. We can possibly assume Salvador has Antonio and Marguerite, but we don't know if he might have taken Ramone. The question is how to move forward with the knowledge that we have."

# Chapter 8

El Amir studied this distinguished older gentleman and began to understand Annie's admiration of him. "Did the authorities agree to let you know what they found at Marguerite's home?" El Amir asked Don Marco. "From all that I have heard from Alex, I find it hard to believe Salvador would harm Marguerite. His feelings toward Ramone are no doubt quite different." The sharp intake of Annie's breath stopped him for a moment. He gave her a fleeting reassuring smile, which gave her some comfort. He then continued, "Ernest is waiting for Ramone in Malaga and should realize by now his delay might mean trouble. If Ernest follows protocol, he will go underground and try to contact either me or Alex."

Meghan interjected, "What about Tomás? He expects to pick up Celeste and escort her to the flight to Mallorca, and none of us will be there. Alex said he was deplaning first, but he was not going to have contact with Tomás at the airport. How do we redirect them? I'm sure Tomás has his phone with him."

Even while Meghan was speaking, Annie could feel the heat of El Amir's eyes on her. The turmoil of emotions causing havoc in her mind were centered around one thing, the safe return of the love of her life and father of her unborn child. She had learned through all the last year that in order to keep a level head and be able to function, she had to keep those emotions in check. Would El Amir help find Ramone? She had asked a favor of him once before, on his plane from Crete to Madrid. The result had caused Ramone both hurt and jealousy. Lost in her thoughts, she missed what El Amir was saying.

Refocusing her attention, Annie heard El Amir finish, "The knowledge of Salvador's whereabouts is most critical to where we start. We have three people in jeopardy."

To no one's surprise, the officer who called to report to Don Marco said his patrolmen did not find Antonio or Marguerite at the house. The wheelchair and Marguerite's car were gone. But Dom's revolver was found on the floor, and the front door was left unlocked.

El Amir's private phone rang. "It's Ernest." Walking toward the terrace, he answered in a low voice, "Hullo."

Ernest started with, "Salvador's son never made to Malaga. We have a problem. Our British contact got word Kung Li's men have taken him. They think Salvador has gone rogue and the Chinese are trying to lure him out into the open through his son. What they don't know is Ramone's part in his father's capture and that Salvador might not come running to his son's rescue. Kung Li found out we are looking for him as well, and his men are watching us, hoping we will lead them to Salvador if the kidnapping of his son doesn't succeed."

Annie could overhear some of the conversation and was digesting the information about Ramone's possible captors as she watched El Amir's reaction. "Is it possible Kung Li knows Alex's arrival flight information and that he is traveling with his wife?" El Amir asked, adding, "They might be walking into a trap."

Annie, now realizing her parents could be in danger, spoke up. "If Salvador found out about Ramone from Antonio and Marguerite, is it possible he might think they are in danger from the Chinese? Perhaps he took them to protect them?"

"Possibly," El Amir conjectured with a persistent twitch in his jaw. "If that is the case, where would he think them the safest?"

Simultaneously, they all answered, "With us!"

El Amir nodded. "Correct, but Antonio and Marguerite think you are all headed to Mallorca! What would be his second-best plan?" Back on the phone, he said to Ernest, "Salvador might seek you out in Malaga to find safety for his wife and son and help to free Ramone. Both Antonio and Marguerite know Ramone was to meet you at the Plaza de Merced. You should get back there and be prepared for either scenario. Be cautious. We do not know if we can trust Salvador. His past actions would indicate no. But he is well aware of the brutality these thugs are capable of. Keep me posted."

"Aye, boss." Ernest hung up.

After a short conversation with Meghan, El Amir stepped away from the group to try to contact Alex. Meghan was to call Tomás and tell him what was happening. He should follow the plan, have no contact with Alex, and get Celeste and her luggage. They were not to get on the flight to Mallorca but should wait to hear from them.

Annie's face had a look of sheer exhaustion. Worried too, Dom and Gennie went to Annie to provide a little comfort. As Dom held her in his arms, Annie allowed herself a moment to let her despair surface. "Oh, Dom, I have always been so afraid the bullring would take Ramone from me. And now this! How can I bear it if something happens to him? What about our child?"

Dom counseled, "Focus, Annie. Your matador is strong and brave, with impeccable timing. Believe in him. The two of you have a deep connection. Summon a ray of hope within you and give it the power to reach his heart. Let him feel that hope."

El Amir, watching this exchange, turned his head away resigned.

# Chapter 9

"Papa!" Antonio exclaimed as Salvador roughly yanked the phone from him and slammed down the receiver. It was clear his father was in a rage, and he glanced at his mother to silently tell her not to do anything that might anger him further.

With a low growl, Salvador barked, "You called the authorities? They are coming here? This is a trap! We must go. Now! Marguerite, I've got the boy. Bring his chair. We will take your car."

Antonio resisted as his father lifted him, and as he twisted, the gun he had so carefully hidden slipped soundlessly out of his pocket onto the carpet. Helpless to do anything to retrieve it, Antonio resigned himself to the fact that Salvador had the upper hand. He knew the only way to outsmart his father was to see his mobility limitation differently and find some way around it. He had a responsibility to keep himself and his mother safe but also to get to the bottom of what happened to Ramone and seek his safety. For now, Antonio's intuition told him to stay quiet.

Marguerite, in total contrast, was far from quiet. "Salvador, what do you mean coming to my house and putting your family in danger?" As she reluctantly got into the car, Antonio flinched as he heard the desperation in her voice. "Where are you taking us? What have you done with Ramone?"

Salvador had already turned on the ignition, but her last question made him pause and stare fiercely at her. "We need to get away from here now, but you will explain the meaning of that question as soon as I get you out of here."

At that moment, both Antonio and Marguerite understood Salvador did not have Ramone. Antonio acknowledged

Marguerite's knowing look and frantically tried to come up with a way to leave a clue behind them. Everyone would be long gone from the villa, but as soon as he thought that, he knew instinctively Annie would never leave with Ramone missing. As they drove away, they could hear the sirens of the police cars arriving at the house. They would find Don Marco's gun. What would they think?

Salvador was brooding silently at the wheel, so Antonio took time to observe his surroundings. They were off the highway, but Antonio recognized the back road route they were on. It looked like they were heading to the bullring on the outskirts of Malaga. Wasn't Ramone supposed to meet someone here in Malaga? He forced himself to remember. Yes! They were to meet at the Plaza de Merced! Thinking hard, he couldn't remember the man's name, only that he had been in the service with Alex and his father. Alex was supposed to come to Malaga! Did his father know that? Antonio reached into his pocket and retrieved the piece of paper Don Marco had given him with Alex's private phone number on it. He didn't have a phone, but he was sure his mother had hers. Fortunately, private wireless phones were gaining popularity in Spain, and Ramone had recently gotten one for his mother. Could he get the phone from his mother and try to reach Alex without Salvador's knowledge?

Salvador drove in through the back entrance of La Malagueta, one of Antonio's favorite bullrings right next to the Mediterranean Sea. It was a Sunday. Everything was closed except the museum in the front. The museum followed the history of La Malagueta since it was built in 1874 and had an inspirational memorial to Antonio's grandfather, who was killed in this ring. *Interesting that Papa chose to bring us here.*

Maneuvering into his chair, Antonio asked, "Papa, why did you bring us here where Grandpa died? What do you want from us?"

Entering the empty tack room where only the groomsmen were allowed. Antonio noticed the door which was always locked, was not. Inside, Salvador wasted no time getting back to Marguerite's question. "Why would you think I am involved with Ramone? He is no son to me after such betrayal!"

Marguerite, deflated, sat down, shook her head, and lamented. "That means someone else has him. Who would want to take him?"

Salvador tried to understand. "Has there been a note of ransom? How do you know he was taken?"

Silent tears were rolling down Marguerite's face. Antonio spoke up. "Ramone's car door was ajar when we got home, with his bag inside abandoned. He was supposed to leave for a meeting here in Malaga." He saw the confusion on Salvador's face and continued. "Since you have been gone, Ramone got engaged to Annie, and she is having his child. This morning, a messenger came to Don Marco's villa with a message for Annie asking her to come to Ramone. He carried Ramone's signature red rose, so she hesitated. Did you send that man for Annie?"

Salvador answered, "No, I don't know anything about a red rose except that he threw one to her from the ring that first day they met. I have tried to stay deep underground since I escaped. The British were moving me to Cambridgeshire, I think. They have tried to persuade me to rejoin their counterintelligence unit. During the transport, my guards most conveniently disappeared. When I looked around, it was evident escape was within reach, so I took the opportunity. It was obvious someone was helping me, but I had no idea whether the British purposely let me escape to lead them to Kung Li, or whether it was Kung Li's men who wanted to keep me from talking to counterintelligence. I did not stick around to find out."

Antonio knew this was the time to do as Don Marco instructed and said, "When Ramone learned of the attempt to take Annie, he immediately wanted to get to the villa. Mamà and I went with him for support. We had just learned of your escape. While we were there, Annie's father called with the same news." Salvador bristled at the mention of Alex.

Antonio continued, "Don Marco spoke to him confidentially, then asked to speak with Mamà and me alone. He mentioned Alex said you might reach out to us. He said if you did to let you know the resistance in Hong Kong is growing stronger among the people who are concerned that after the turnover, the financial freedoms they now enjoy will no longer be available. According to his contact, Kung Li wants you eliminated to keep from helping the British while they are negotiating with Beijing. Alex was contacted in Maine to travel over here to keep you safe and brought back into protective custody. Ramone was supposed to meet Alex here in Malaga. Their sources must have known you would come here! It was when Ramone went home to grab a few things to take with him that he disappeared."

"This sounds like a trap!" Salvador said angrily.

Marguerite shook her head. "No, Salvador, he is telling the truth! *¡Dios mío!* The Chinese have Ramone. What will they do? My son! You must help him! Do they also know you would come here to La Malagueta?"

Salvador began restlessly pacing as every one of his instincts was on full alert. Before he was captured, there was talk of an insider rebellion among Hong Kong business owners. Under British rule, they were free to run their businesses with a democratic leniency. They knew when Beijing took over, that freedom would no longer exist. A growing number of them were trying to force a delay of the turnover, but so far, Beijing would not allow it. Salvador continued his reflection. It was feasible Kung Li was feeling the pressure and became aware he was considering changing sides. *What had the British told Alex? Did he know about this possible turn of events? If he went to Alex for help, could he trust him, a man he himself had turned on and even tried to murder?* What he did know in his heart was that he could trust his wife and younger son. He also knew the way the Chinese treated their captives; they made no idle threats.

Salvador now told Antonio and Marguerite, "I believe you, and I will not walk away from my oldest son! I need to reach Alex as soon as possible. If they have Ramone, you both might be in danger too."

Antonio pulled the note out of his pocket and handed it to Salvador. "Don Marco gave me Alex's private number and asked me to give it to you. Mamà, give him your phone."

# Chapter 10

When the plane touched down at the Madrid airport, Alex turned on his phone to find three messages. The first was from his contact at British intelligence. "Intel claims that Salvador is somewhere in Malaga, probably with his wife and younger son. We think the Chinese may have the older son." *What? Ramone taken by the Chinese? What has happened while I was in the air?*

The second message was from El Amir. "My friend, a lot has happened! As you suggested, I watched for the *Porto Banus* to leave port, but it was still docked with no activity hours after the scheduled departure. I went immediately to the villa and found out Ramone has been abducted. Annie refused to leave without knowing he is safe. That girl has become quite headstrong. Please advise whether I am to leave them and meet you in Malaga. We told Tomás to wait to hear from us whether to board the flight to Mallorca." It brought a smile to Alex that his daughter had strengthened her backbone! Yes, it made sense that Kung Li would use Ramone as a pawn to lure Salvador into the open. They never saw Ramone's part in freeing Alex and capturing his own father. They did not know of the break in Ramone and Salvador's relationship. Now, what to do about Tomás?

The third message was from a number he didn't recognize. "They have my son, Alex, the father of our soon-to-be grandchild. Antonio told me the Chinese may have found out I am considering changing allegiance and using Ramone to bring me out into the open. He says I can trust you, but I don't see how. We are hidden, but I don't know for how long or if this spot has been compromised. Knowing these people, they will not be gentle with Ramone. Contact me as soon as you can." Alex knew from per-

sonal experience that the Chinese did not hesitate to use unorth-
odox means and hoped they would not harm Ramone thinking he
could lead them to Salvador.

Alex looked up and saw Celeste coming back from the
restroom with her wig in place and an unfamiliar expression. Only
Alex would notice the softening around her eyes, her silent way of
wishing him luck. She sat down without a word. Turning to grab
his bag, he took a moment to appreciate his wife's beauty, both
inside and out. He knew he would do anything for this woman.
Knowing their unborn grandchild's father was in danger, Alex
needed to do whatever it took to ensure Ramone's safety. With a
gentle nod and a movement hardly noticeable, he slipped a note
into Celeste's hand then got off the plane and casually strolled
over to a far corner where he could observe and watch as Tomás
greeted Celeste with a casual embrace, then the two headed off
together.

To avoid drawing unnecessary attention to himself, Alex
decided to text rather than call. To Salvador, he wrote,

*'Message received. Sending the* Porto Banus *to pick up
A & M for safety. We will ping this number when the*
Porto Banus *approaches the port. Be close by. My plane
to Malaga leaves in 45 minutes. Stay hidden until you
get the ping. Keep the phone with you. I will text you
when I arrive. We'll get him back. A'*

Alex took a moment to get to the baggage area where he could
observe Tomás and Celeste. He saw the note was in her hand and
they were talking. It seemed more a debate. Quickly, he pulled his
phone out and began a text to El Amir,

*'In baggage area Madrid airport. Have Meghan call
Tomás and tell him the original plan is in place. They
are to get on the flight to Mallorca. Have the family
board the* Porto Banus *and leave the port asap. One*

*stop at Malaga to pick up Antonio and Marguerite, then on to Mallorca. Salvador says he is with us for rescue. Possibly switching allegiance. Action going down in Malaga. After you see them off, meet me there. Will call once I board your plane. Make haste, my friend. Don't take no for an answer. A'*

Alex saw Tomás get the call and nod to Celeste. Once they got the luggage and headed toward the counter to check in for the flight to Mallorca, Alex was satisfied that part of the plan was moving forward. He took a quick moment to text Ernest,

*'Subject in Malaga with wife and younger son. Porto Banus will stop there to pick them up. Subject supposedly ready to help with rescue. Proceed with cautious optimism. Ping the following number when the Porto Banus approaches the port. Don't show yourself unless there is trouble boarding. I'll be in touch. A'*

Now to make his way to the private plane hangar.

# Chapter 11

El Amir looked around the room at the group watching him as he put down the phone. His first assignment was easy; he quickly told Meghan to let Tomás know to follow the original plan. She was already on the phone when he looked at Don Marco and said, "Sir, Alex wants the family on board the *Porto Banus* at once. He wants you to travel by motor with some haste and make a quick stop in Malaga. In Malaga, you will pick up Antonio and Marguerite. They will be near the port." The last sentence had them all starting with questions, but he raised his hand to quiet them and continued, "It appears Salvador had nothing to do with Ramone's disappearance. He has Antonio and Marguerite hidden in Malaga. They have convinced him of the danger Ramone is in, and he is willing to work with us to expedite his escape. Alex has offered Antonio and Marguerite safe passage on the *Porto Banus*. I am to ensure your hasty departure and make my way to Malaga." Still directing his conversation at Don Marco, El Amir paused, knowing what was coming next. He didn't have to wait long.

Annie burst out, "Well, I am certainly not going to run away while Ramone is being held against his will! I will go with you. Surely, I can be of some help. I know Ramone better than anyone. There must be some way I can communicate with him. He is everything to me and the father of this child." Annie placed her hand on her stomach with a sob.

El Amir saw the anguish on Annie's face. Knowing the intensity of her feelings toward the matador was like a knife cutting out a piece of his heart. He had no one to blame but himself since he had literally pushed her away toward Ramone. He had to be strong, even if it meant her hating him. "Annie, you are not going

45

with me, and you WILL be on the *Porto Banus* with your grandparents and Meghan." Before she could protest, he added, "If I need to throw you over my shoulder and carry you to the port, I will. What's it going to be?"

Don Marco saw the challenge being issued between them and intervened. "There, there. No need for all this. Annie, come with us. Think of the distraction your presence would cause. These men need to stay focused to bring Ramone home safely. The future hasn't happened yet, has it? How it unfolds will be influenced in some way by your attitude and your actions right now. You have a choice, dear. Try to choose to look forward with positive energy and expectations. Instead of dwelling on all that can go wrong, find inspiration in all that can go right. Stay focused on putting those positive thoughts in motion and allowing them to unfold."

His words struck a chord within Annie. She once again marveled at her grandfather's wisdom and reluctantly said, "All right, I'll go." She then turned to El Amir, with deep emotion in her voice. "Bring him back to me. Please."

Relieved she was going but still reeling from the raw jealousy simmering in his veins, El Amir ushered the ladies out the door while Don Marco locked up the villa. The arrival at the port was uneventful. Captain Luis told Don Marco they were ready to push off as soon as everything was stowed. The captain could feel the tension in the air, and he made a vow to himself that he would help any way he could. Roff brought in the last of the luggage, and Helene arranged some fresh sangria and tapas out in the salon.

Dom and Gennie would naturally have the master cabin. It had been quite a while since they had been on board, and, although the circumstances were dreadful, they planned to make the best of it. Annie would share a cabin with Meghan, and the two burly security guards would share a forward cabin. That would leave two cabins open for Marguerite and Antonio when they boarded.

Roff released the lines and jumped on board in time for the captain to maneuver the *Porto Banus* away from the dock, where El Amir stood watching their departure. Annie was out on the bow alone, staring at him with what looked like a prayer. Seeing her so serious, he allowed himself a moment to think about other happier times when he had been with her. He had loved watching her in Tanzania where he introduced her to his artist protégé, Sarah. He had known they would get along, but to see them grow together and become close friends was a delight. He knew it was good for Sarah too. Then there was the time in London preparing for Sarah's art exhibit. Although there was intensity in getting her father freed from Kung Li, the time in Paris afterward when he spent several days spoiling Annie and Sarah were some of his most favorite.

He gave one final look and caught her wave as they rounded the entrance to the east. El Amir shut away those memories and strengthened his resolve to get the matador back to Annie.

# Chapter 12

Annie stood at the bow waiting for that familiar exhilaration she always felt with the wind blowing her hair and the sound of the water rushing past the gleaming deep-blue hull of the *Porto Banus*. Don Marco walked up behind her, reflecting. "It never ceases to amaze me whenever I return to the sea on this exceptional vessel how it feels when we first hoist the sails and harness the wind. It's as though moments in time stand still when I can truly embrace nature's amazing gifts."

The soothing sound of Dom's voice blended with the subtle motion of the waves, bringing Annie a momentary sense of peace. She nodded. "There were times when I was traveling on the *Porto Banus* that I would look out at sea and write in my journal about that special feeling where the past and future cease to exist and only the present remains."

"I know it well," Dom commented.

Annie turned toward him. "I know this is Meghan's first time on board. I should be sharing stories of my adventures traveling from one dazzling location to another. But, Dom, with Ramone in trouble out there somewhere, I just can't. Would you sit with me and help me understand what is going on in Hong Kong?"

"Of course, sweetheart. I will do my best. Let's go back to the aft deck where it is more comfortable."

Meghan looked up from the book she was reading on the forward sundeck and waved as they passed. The aft deck was split into two areas: one with comfortable cushioned seating around a circular cherry-wood table, the other accommodating a large dining area. The retractable cover was extended over both areas to give shelter from the warm Mediterranean sun. Annie looked up at the well-appointed pilothouse to see Captain Luis checking his charts and navigating his way to Malaga. It should only take a few hours to get there.

Annie and Dom settled into two lounge chairs, and he began. "Annie, you are a history buff. Trade and trading rights have been issues between countries throughout the centuries. Britain and China were no exception in the late eighteenth and early nineteenth centuries. China offered porcelains, silks, and tea. Britain was trading silver. That created a trade imbalance between the two countries. The British East India Company soon began the cultivation of opium in its Indian territories. You see, the use of opium as a medicine had been around for hundreds of years, but the use of it to smoke was gaining widespread use and often leading to addiction. The Chinese emperor at the time banned the use of opium to protect his people, but the illegal trade of the drug expanded, and the British began selling to Chinese smugglers. To combat this, the emperor ordered the seizure of all opium in their free-trade area of Canton, enforcing a shutdown of all the factories that were producing it. The head of British Trade in China advised London to use military force to reopen trade avenues that had become highly lucrative."

"Ah," Annie said, "this is the Opium War I learned about in history."

"Correct. However, there were two Opium Wars. The second one occurred about twenty years later, but it was the first one that involved Hong Kong. One of Britain's first acts of war was to occupy Hong Kong, a sparsely inhabited but well-positioned island off the southeast coast of China. The war ended in the 1840s with a treaty in which China agreed to cede Hong Kong to the British. Britain's new colony flourished as a capitalist East-West trading center and commercial gateway. After many years of negotiations, Britain finally agreed to sign a formal joint declaration approving the 1997 turnover of the island in exchange for a Chinese pledge to preserve Hong Kong's capitalist system.

"The Chinese have waited a long time to take possession of Hong Kong, and there are many indications that Beijing does not plan to keep their part of the bargain. There are multiple factions within Hong Kong differing strongly about whether British rule should be extended."

Annie tried to digest the impact of such heated emotions about Hong Kong's future. What she struggled with was where her father, Salvador, and Kung Li fit into all this.

"Thank you for helping to clarify some of this for me. They must want Salvador badly to kidnap his son." She shook her head. "How is this going to end?"

# Chapter 13

The *Porto Banus* would enter the harbor soon. Both Alex and El Amir arrived in Malaga and located Ernest at Plaza de Merced as planned. The three men speculated on the supposed change of allegiance by Salvador. Alex started. "Salvador has every right to be furious with the three of us, as well as Ramone. How can we trust him?"

El Amir was first to answer. "Perhaps the best direction is not to trust. Give him rope, but be ready to reel him in, as necessary. Is there any new intel on the Chinese operatives and where they might be hiding Ramone?"

Alex replied, "There have been a number of Chinese nationals recently frequenting the Casa Fuénte. We don't know if Ramone is being held there. Our concern is the perfect view of the port they have from there. The *Porto Banus* is unique and massive. They will obviously notice it, but will they recognize its connection to all of us? How did they know about the rose? Could those on board be somehow stepping into an ambush? Our goal today is to rescue Ramone and bring Salvador back to the British alive."

Ernest was listening but letting Alex and El Amir figure out the details. However, it was he who spotted the *Porto Banus* entering the port of Malaga first. He pointed.

El Amir looked at Alex and said, "I need to be at the port. We don't know Don Marco's security men and whether they are any good. The yacht may be vulnerable, and both Marguerite and Antonio will be exposed as they board. Antonio's wheelchair will make it even harder for them to go unnoticed."

Alex quickly said to Ernest, "Text Salvador the *Porto Banus* is entering the port and to bring Antonio and Marguerite as close

51

as possible to the dock. El Amir will be waiting for them at the port. Once he has dropped them off, he is to proceed to Casa Fuénte to meet us."

As El Amir approached the port and the *Porto Banus* got closer, he regretfully realized there would be very few who did not notice such a vessel entering their port. At the last minute, he decided to watch from afar as they docked.

Captain Luis was a pro at docking, and he seamlessly and slowly moved to the dock with but a gentle bump. Roff jumped ashore and helped the dockmaster secure the ropes. Annie was so close to the gangway she gave thought to running ashore. Where would she go? How would she find him? From a distance, she could see Antonio in his wheelchair and Marguerite making their way to the *Porto Banus*. Salvador was nowhere in sight.

Suddenly, there was a movement from behind her, and one of the security officers grabbed Annie around the neck. He had her gridlocked and had pulled a gun. Trying to turn to tell him there was no need for this, she saw Don Marco and the other security guard warily stepping closer. At once, Annie knew this was real and that she needed to escape. As she started to struggle, they all noticed the activity on the dock.

Antonio and Marguerite were surrounded by four Chinese nationals. As they tried to board the *Porto Banus*, Antonio purposely flipped over his wheelchair to block their way. The noise had distracted Annie's captor, and both Dom and the other security guard rushed him. El Amir was there in a flash working on pure instinct. His martial art skills prevailed, and he quickly disabled the Chinese men surrounding them. He safely got the passengers on board and ensured the rogue security officer was detained. Glancing around on board, all looked in order, so he sprinted back off the gangway. It seemed important that the Chinese show a position of strength, so they paraded Ramone out into the open, with all the atrocities that had been done to him on full display, taunting Salvador to show himself. Salvador heard the disturbance and messaged Ernest while he circled back.

When their leader brought him out into the open, Ramone saw the *Porto Banus* and Annie being held captive on the top deck. That made him struggle harder. He was pistol-whipped once again. El Amir practically jumped off the gangway and found himself face-to-face with Ramone and the two men holding him. He tried to convince the Chinese that he was just trying to protect his friends on board. While he was speaking, Alex, Ernest, and Salvador got closer to where they had Ramone. They could see the wretched things that had been done to him. Salvador couldn't help himself. He ran into the midst of them yelling, "You bastards! Free my son!" The shot that downed Salvador resonated through all of them. Alex and Ernest wasted no time getting to Ramone's side and, between the three of them, subdued the Chinese and had Ramone released and secure.

Ramone was the first to hobble to his father's side. Ramone, as broken as he was, reached down for his father. "Don't leave us! Why were you so angry?"

Alex, convinced Salvador was dying, shook his head. Dom and the captain helped Antonio down the gangway, and he wheeled his chair to his father and brother. Salvador struggled to tell his sons what had happened. "I can't tell you the agony I felt when I saw my father die in the ring. And now I see my beautiful young son crippled from the ring. The bullfighting is pure ego and machismo." He haltingly finished as Marguerite reached his side. "I am so sorry for all of it. I love you." Looking at Alex, he knew it was a lot to ask. "Take care of them for me."

With emotion in his voice, Alex put his hand on his shoulder and answered, "I will."

Salvador took his last breath surrounded by all those he had treated so harshly but loved him anyway.

# Chapter 14

Annie could not get down the gangway fast enough to get to Ramone. Despite his swollen, cut, and bruised appearance, she ran to that man she so desperately loved. Her tight embrace caused Ramone to involuntarily flinch in pain, but nothing could stop him from cherishing his freedom and having the woman of his dreams in his arms. "*Querida*, I'm here. Thinking of you and our child kept me alive with these brutes." After a moment, he said, "Papa is gone."

Sirens were roaring as the Malaga police arrived on the scene. El Amir and Ernest rounded up the fallen Chinese and rogue security guard to turn over to them. The guard had been the one who disclosed the red-rose tradition. An ambulance was called for Salvador, and Alex helped the paramedics lift him onto the gurney and into the back. He somberly nodded to them as they closed the door and sped off directly to the morgue. Alex then went over to Marguerite, who was watching, silently crying. "He was such a good man who tragically took the wrong path. How sad we didn't have more time with him after his change of heart. In the end, he saved our son."

Alex hugged her tightly. "Yes, he came through in the end. Marguerite, you and your sons are family to us. I have pledged to always be here for you."

Alex then moved over to his daughter and Ramone. Embracing them both, he looked at Ramone and said, "Your father was a hero in the end. He gave his life for yours, son. Let this day spark a purpose in you that will motivate how you choose to move forward. The next step will become clear soon enough. For now, the authorities will want to question you about your abduction. We should have a doctor look at those cuts and bruises."

One of the paramedics from the second ambulance came over to check Ramone. The cuts above his eye and on his jaw would need stitches. It was decided he would go in the second ambulance directly to the hospital to get patched up, then meet Alex at the police station. There was no way Annie would leave his side. When the ambulance pulled away, she was right inside with him.

Alex moved over to where El Amir was speaking with Antonio. When he was close, he could hear El Amir say, "Antonio, you did well today! When you thought quickly enough to tip over the chair, not only did you keep those thugs from boarding the *Porto Banus*, you caused enough distraction so I could get in there and get the upper hand."

With a slap on El Amir's back, Alex said, "You both did well. But, Antonio, you did so much more. Getting your father to understand the danger Ramone faced was no easy feat. You worked through the challenges that faced you and made a difference in today's outcome. When we arrived, your chair was already flipped over. Did I see you get yourself up and right the chair?"

Antonio checked to be sure the lock was secure on the wheelchair, then pushed himself and slid to the ground. "It had to be the adrenalin I felt at the moment."

On impulse, Alex commented to Antonio and Marguerite, "You were both supposed to board the *Porto Banus* and travel with the family to Mallorca. Ramone needs some time to heal. Why don't you go?"

Marguerite couldn't help liking the chance to nurse her son, but she was conflicted about whether she should stay with Salvador and attend to the details of his death.

Alex put an arm around her and said, "Marguerite, he is gone now. There is nothing you can do. However, none of you obviously brought anything to wear. Ramone's bag was left behind."

Meghan was already down the gangway. "Did someone mention shopping? I can help!"

Alex wholeheartedly agreed. "It will take a while at the hospital, and the police will want to question Ramone." Looking up at Captain Luis, Alex asked, "Should the *Porto Banus* stay docked overnight and leave tomorrow at first light?" With the captain's nod, he continued, speaking to Marguerite and Antonio, "You will have plenty of time to pick up what you need. We can meet back here for dinner." Meghan began pushing Antonio's chair, and, although still reeling from Salvador's death, they took this offer to join the *Porto Banus* and left to pick up a few necessary items for themselves as well as Ramone.

Exchanging a glance with El Amir and Ernest, Alex knew these men would always have his back. "Thank you for today. I wish we had somehow been able to prevent Salvador's death. Perhaps one of the Chinese prisoners will be able to give the British intelligence what they need. They are on their way to pick them up. Would you at least like to stay the night and join us for dinner?"

Ernest quickly declined, saying he had to get back to London. El Amir hesitated. He still had feelings for Annie, and he did not want to cause any conflict. "Unless you need my help further, I will tidy up here, get to the plane, and head back to Morocco. Stay well, my friend. I am at your service any time." With a nod of understanding and shake of hands all around, they parted ways.

# Chapter 15

The adrenalin that had kept Alex going was starting to wane. Dom and Gennie could see how tired he was as they hugged him. Alex took time to shake Captain Luis's hand, as well as Roff's and Helene's. The security guard who helped Dom rush Annie's assailant had gone to the police station for questioning, most likely about the other guard. He would remain behind in Malaga. Alex knew he was due there soon. Helene brought out a charcuterie plate with cheeses, sausage, and mixed olives. Suddenly famished and jet-lagged, Alex dug in, realizing he hadn't eaten since the plane to Madrid. Gennie was already fussing about trying to figure out where everyone could bunk for the night. Alex saw the dilemma. "I need to pick up my bag that I stashed anyway. I can get a room. It is not a problem."

Gennie hastily said, "You will do no such thing! This has been a traumatic day for everyone, and we need to stay together. Don't you worry. And as for dinner, let's eat on board. Ramone will need tending, and you are exhausted."

Looking at Helene, Gennie was about to ask, but Helene beat her to it. "Roff and I have this. We will get to the market and set up a buffet for a casual dinner available as needed. We can easily adapt the sofas in the main salon into beds after we return." Helene grabbed her bag, and Roff led the way. Alex left for the police station shortly after to meet the British officers coming to question the prisoners and determine how they would be detained.

Gennie busied herself packing up Meghan's things to move to the stateroom that would have been Antonio's. Marguerite would have her own room. Alex and Antonio could take the two makeshift beds in the salon. If only she could convince Alex to go with them. She knew Celeste would want her to try.

Don Marco walked to the aft deck to his favorite lounge chair. Captain Luis appeared and asked, "May I join you, sir?"

With a smile, the answer was "Of course!" As he walked over to the glass-encased bar to pour two whiskeys and pull two cigars out of his special humidor reserved for extraordinary occasions. The two old friends sipped their whiskey and puffed on their cigars with an easy camaraderie built over two decades. At one point, Luis's manner turned serious. "You had me worried earlier. What were you thinking, rushing an armed gunman?"

To Dom, the answer was simple. "He had his hands on my granddaughter. Until my last breath, I will fight to protect my family."

Gennie emerged from the cabin area in time to overhear Dom's comment. She sat on the arm of his chair and caressed the back of his neck. "You were very brave, my dearest husband, but I honestly do not know what I would do if something were to happen to you."

Dom playfully smiled and gave her a pat on her bottom. "Let me pour you a whiskey, my dear. After today, I think we all need it!" The three of them sat congenially discussing the events of the day, the healing that would be needed, and the route they would take to Mallorca.

To the captain, Dom suggested, "Perhaps, with all the emotional drama that has unfolded, we should hoist the sails and sail across to the island rather than motor. Give everyone a chance to relax a while?"

Luis responded, "If the winds oblige, the sail will only take a few more hours than by motor. I believe we could be docked at Palma before sunset. Have you been to this property before?"

Gennie looked at Dom and shook her head. "I do love Mallorca, but it has been close to fifteen years since we have been there. I remember the island was lovely." To Dom, she added, "Do you think the villa will accommodate all of us?"

Dom reflected, "Tomás heard it was for sale and in huge need of repair. I gave him permission to purchase it on my behalf and oversee the renovation. I must admit, with everything I've heard, I am quite looking forward to visiting! A chef comes with the estate. There is a separate casita that should make good accommodation for you, Helene and Roff."

Agreeing, Luis thought aloud, "I will leave two crew members on board the *Porto Banus* for security and some standard maintenance. They have been with us for years, unlike the new hire security guard, whose credentials had us all fooled. How far is the estate from the port?"

"Tomás told me it was about fifteen minutes into the foothills with a distant view of the sea and spectacular view of the mountains. I will check with him to let him know how many of us will arrive and suggest he arrange transportation once we dock."

Helene and Roff arrived back on board with a cart full of groceries and Gennie joined them to help unpack and supervise preparation of the buffet. Soon after, Meghan returned with Antonio and Marguerite in tow. Roff saw them and came down the gangway to help Antonio and retrieve his chair. The captain was discussing the plans for Mallorca with two of the crewmen when he saw Alex return with Annie and Ramone further back, moving much slower.

The group on board gathered to hear Alex say quietly, "It's been a hard time for the boy. He appears to be quite shaken. Be aware, he might need some space."

They all tried to busy themselves as Ramone climbed aboard with Annie. He was almost unrecognizable and far from the dapper and confident matador they all knew. It was Marguerite who quietly approached and embraced him. "You are safe, my son." Ramone acknowledged her hug with an involuntary flinch of pain but couldn't answer.

It was Annie who spoke questioningly to her grandmother. "I would like to take him to my stateroom."

Gennie gently responded, "It is already handled. Meghan's things have been moved to the cabin next door. Would you like me to bring a plate of food and some hot tea? Some ice?"

Annie thanked her, nodding, and helped Ramone to her cabin. Marguerite had placed a bag on the bed with a few clothing items and toiletries she picked up that afternoon. Annie looked at this man whose strength seemed to have vanished. She would give anything to make that hurt go away, but what she realized was that although there were so many wounds on his body, it was the wounds to his spirit she was most worried about.

# Chapter 16

The hooded stare in Ramone's eyes gave Annie pause, but she moved to sit beside him on the bed, and he did not resist. She removed his shoes and slowly unbuttoned his shirt. The doctor in the hospital had checked for any internal injuries with several scans, and fortunately there were none. The bruises along his torso, however, were turning dark shades of yellow and purple. Annie was reminded of the first time she had seen him without a shirt. It was outside Marbella at a beautiful waterfall. She remembered how startled she was to see all the scars on his body due to many goring injuries from his bullfighting where the bull got too close. All she wanted to do was to soothe those scars. That day had led to her fear of him going in the ring and getting injured, perhaps fatally. Yet here he was. The physical injuries she was sure he could overcome. Somehow, she needed a pathway to comfort the mental anguish he was experiencing in seeing his father shot before him.

Carefully, with deliberate gentleness, Annie started to bathe Ramone's body with a wet cloth dampened with a mixture of water and arnica to help with the bruising. When she reached his belt, Ramone caught his breath. Unsure whether he wanted her to continue, she started to unbuckle the belt. When he placed his hand over hers to stop her, Annie had to clamp down her feeling of hurt in his rejection. To cover her disappointment, she helped him lie back on the bed and filled the cloth with ice for his face. "Get some rest, my love. I will be right outside." Ramone reached for her hand and held it an extra moment as if to plead, *please understand.*

The toll of worry on Annie's face was evident to all as she joined them. Helene brought her some ginseng tea and wafers as she sat in one of the lounge chairs next to Marguerite. She said to her future mother-in-law with a squeeze of her hand, "I hope he will get some rest. Thank you for getting the clothes."

Antonio overheard and asked what they all wanted to know. "How is my brother? What did the doctors say?"

This was the first chance Annie had been able to think about all the doctors said. "They ran a lot of tests. One doctor who did the physical exam said he had clearly been beaten, and it looked like several times. They were amazed there were no internal organ injuries, but the bruising is severe, especially around his ribs and abdomen. Because the facial injuries were so bad, the neurologist wanted to do a scan of his brain. There appeared to be a hairline fracture on his skull beneath the cut over his eye. Both doctors agreed he was lucky not to have lost sight in that eye. In all, they did twenty-seven stitches on his face. Because of the fracture, that one will cause the most pain. The doctors also agreed that as a healthy young man his physical injuries would heal. Their opinions differed on his mental reaction. Whether it was the trauma from the time he was held captive, or seeing his father shot in front of him, they just don't know. They want him to rest and heal for a couple of weeks. If he is not mentally stronger, they want him to seek therapy."

Alex thoughtfully added, "It is never easy to see another person killed. Having been in Special Forces as long as I have, I have learned everyone deals with it differently." To Marguerite and Antonio, he added, "You were both with Salvador and saw him have a change of heart about Ramone and the passion he felt to save him. Ramone never saw that coming. He only knew the father who was enraged with him and the world. I am certain he never expected to see his father readily give up his own life to save his son's."

Antonio agreed. "Yes, we did see the change in Papa. I knew he had many regrets. I had fallen from my chair, so I missed part of it. That does not change the deep sadness I feel losing him."

Marguerite began to share stories of Salvador as such a handsome young man, how they met in Barcelona, and how he had swept her off her feet. She was a well-known flamenco dancer at the time. Salvador and Alex were in the service together. They came in to watch her dance one evening when they were on leave. From the moment her eyes locked with Salvador's, he was relentless in his pursuit of her.

Their courtship was wildly passionate, and she did not hesitate to go with him when he got reassigned to Hong Kong. They eloped and bought a home within the community of Spanish ex-patriots. Soon Ramone and Antonio were born. Salvador was a good father...obsessed with his sons. However, once he was solicited by Kung Li, everything changed.

"At least he had the good sense to send us back to Marbella under the care of his brother, Pedro. I will never forget the fire that would light up in Ramone's eyes every time Pedro would mention their long lineage of star bullfighters." Looking at her younger son, she added, "You were slower to catch the fire, but once you started training at the bullfighting academy, you were hooked."

Continuing, "When Salvador learned both his sons were training to be matadors, he lost all control. All the anger he had suppressed since he saw his father perish broke through, aimed at his brother. Salvador blamed Pedro for his sons' decision. Pedro was very arrogant and dismissed Salvador like he was nothing. Instead, Pedro kept pushing the boys harder and attended every time one of them fought. Pedro died about five years ago under very mysterious circumstances. There was speculation Salvador was involved, but by the time of Pedro's death, we hadn't seen Salvador in years."

They had all gathered around to hear Marguerite. The conversation went on about Salvador until dinner was served. Annie fixed a light plate and excused herself early to go check on Ramone.

# Chapter 17

Annie entered the dimly lit cabin, with only the light from the bathroom for illumination. Gennie had asked Roff to switch the twin-bed arrangement that she and Meghan had to a queen bed. Now she wondered if that had been a good idea. He seemed asleep, and Annie didn't want to do anything to cause him pain. She began to undress and noticed his eyes slowly opened. She moved slower, allowing him to watch, but she self-consciously knew her stomach was beginning to show her pregnancy. She went to the other side of the bed and climbed in naked, seeking his warmth. Immediately she realized he still wore his pants and belt. Her question to him of whether she could get him anything went unanswered. The stress of the day combined with her condition had Annie asleep in mere minutes.

Somewhere in the early morning hours, Annie awoke trying to get her bearings. Ramone was naked. His hand lay possessively on her belly. Annie smiled inwardly and silently prayed this beautiful soul would come back to her soon. She snuggled as close as she could, trying to avoid hurting him, then fell back to sleep.

Annie, by instinct, knew the moment Captain Luis had released the ropes at the dock and was pulling away. She tried to rise with an urgent need to empty her bladder, but a certain matador had a firm grip on her. "Sir, if you don't unhand me, we will both be lying in a wet puddle." That brought a hint of a smile to Ramone's face, and he let her go. Annie quickly dressed. She didn't want to miss the hoisting of the sails. She quickly pleaded with Ramone, "Come on deck, my love. When they raise the sails in unison, it is like no other experience!" Her response was Ramone's groan rolling over into a sound sleep.

As Annie emerged on deck, the sun was just cresting over the horizon, offering a magnificent display of nature's beauty. Helene brought her a coffee, and Captain Luis smiled as he called out. "Ready to hoist!"

Dom didn't want to miss it either and came out on deck just in time. This was a moment that he could share with his granddaughter, who loved sailing and the sea almost as much as he did. He had so much pride in this young woman and how far she had come. He wrapped his arm around her. There it was...that moment when the sails caught the wind. *Whoomph!* Off they went. Dom was clear about one thing. This time in Mallorca would be healing for all of them. He would make sure of that.

Both Alex and Antonio, with their bunks in the salon, could not help but be awakened by all the activity. Alex commented, "Annie is so like her maternal grandfather. My parents were much more straitlaced. How can I help you this morning, Antonio?"

"My morning routine is not easy. I rely on my mother a great deal."

"Let me help. In the years I have spent in the military, I guess I have seen most of what is involved with recovering from an injury. I told your father as he was dying that I would bring you and your family into ours. I will keep that pledge. You can count on it, son."

Antonio was deeply touched. "My mother starts with a massage on both legs to get the blood circulating. If I have a chair in the shower, I can handle that part. Getting dressed is a little more difficult." Alex folded up his bed, got dressed, and was ready to help.

Alex followed instructions as he started massaging Antonio's legs. Meghan walked through the salon and saw what Alex was doing. "Use your thumbs to press a little harder on the inside."

"Like this?" Alex said. Meghan sat down to watch.

"Yes, that's right. Antonio, your legs found some strength yesterday. True, that could have been the adrenalin caused by the situation. On the other hand, your legs could be losing their atrophy or 'waking up.' Before I became a history buff back in Ireland, I worked at a physical therapist's office. They astounded me with what they could do! I used to watch in awe. Maybe we could try a few things while we are in Mallorca, then you can pursue serious therapy when you get home?"

Antonio was quick to answer. "After the accident, I was sure the injury was temporary and I would not just walk again but also fight back in the ring. It has been so long now. I feel I would be happy to simply be able to move about on my own. I hate being a burden. Yesterday, it felt good to be of help in some way."

Meghan gave it some thought. "I remember the therapist telling a teenage girl who had lost the use of her hand, 'Your injured hand is only a limitation if you see it that way. Choose to see it differently, and you'll find a way around it.' That's true throughout life, I imagine. If you wallow in disappointment whenever things don't work out the way you planned, as Annie would put it, you need to readjust your sails and see it as an opportunity to choose a different response to overcome whatever the challenge."

"Sometimes that is not so easy. Depression can carry with it a great deal of power. It takes tremendous strength to push through it. I am going to try hard to face this demon. My father finally faced his. I only hope Ramone can face his." Antonio looked down at Alex working his calf muscles and smiled. "Thank you...both of you. I think I'm ready for my shower now."

Meghan poured herself a cup of coffee from the pot Helene set out and went to find Annie.

# Chapter 18

Her first time on the *Porto Banus*, nothing had prepared Meghan for the excitement of experiencing this sleek sailing vessel under full sail with all four sails pulled taut. The wind and the speed of the water rushing past told her of their speed. When she reached the bow where Dom was pointing out some island to Annie, all Meghan could muster with the awe of it was "Wow!"

Dom saw the light in Meghan's eyes and smiled. "The crewmen have trimmed the sails perfectly and our captain is making great time! If we continue at this rate, we should approach the Balearic Islands sooner than scheduled. We will pass Ibiza on our port side on our way to the port at Palma de Mallorca. Tomás and Celeste should be there to meet us. Why don't we go aft and see if brunch is ready?"

Annie left them to check on Ramone and see if he would join them. The cabin was still dark. Annie went to the large picture window to pull back the drapes and saw that Ramone was awake. "Please don't," he said.

Sitting on the edge of the bed, Annie placed her hand on the side of his face to find him clammy and in a full sweat. "Have you slept?" Annie asked.

"No" was all the answer she got.

Annie took a deep breath, wondering what the right thing to say would be. She took his hand. "Why don't you take a shower, and we can change these sheets? Come up on deck and get some fresh air. All four sails are raised. It is a most beautiful day and a wonderful ride! Helene and Gennie have brunch ready. It will do you good to get out of this dark room."

Even though Ramone thought he could feel the touch of Annie's hand, she seemed so far away. Why couldn't she understand he didn't want to move? He had slept fitfully off and on until the nightmare would start again, and he couldn't stop it. She was still talking. What was she saying? She said he was sweating? He didn't notice. He gingerly reached up to touch the wounds where he got stitches. Yes, still there and swollen, but he couldn't feel anything. There should be pain, but nothing. *She is still talking. I need to focus. Why isn't she speaking more clearly?*

Annie felt a moment of panic that she could not get through to Ramone. He was so detached. If she couldn't reach him, she knew of only one other person who might have success, and she was right here on the *Porto Banus*.

Hastily, Annie went up on deck, her eyes searching for Marguerite. She found her deep in conversation with Meghan and Antonio. Pure instinct made Marguerite look up and meet Annie's eye. Immediately she saw the concern on her face and asked, "What is it, Annie? How is Ramone?"

"Marguerite, he is barely responsive, and I am not able to break through to him. Would you try? Please! He doesn't want the drapes open, and the sheets are drenched with his sweat. It is like he can't hear me, and his stare is frightening."

Within seconds, Marguerite was out of her chair on the way to Annie and Ramone's cabin. She marched right in and quickly pulled open the drapes, getting a flinch of Ramone's eyes. With a voice in Spanish he would know as his mother's, she said rather briskly, "*Escúchame, hijo mío!* Listen to me, my son. You are a strong man, and this detachment of yours has to stop. Your body is drenched, and you are in sore need of a shower so Annie can change these sheets. We will be docking in Mallorca soon to leave the *Porto Banus*. Son, get dressed, and I will be waiting for you up on deck."

When Ramone mumbled, "You don't understand," Marguerite lost her patience.

"Now!"

With a slow, resigned motion, Ramone made his way to the shower with hardly a glance toward Annie. When she heard the running water, she started to remove the sheets but found herself moving toward the sound of the shower. Annie removed her clothes and stepped into the shower, seeking the connection that had become second nature to them. She gently lathered both of them with body wash and pressed her breasts against his chest. He leaned into her like it was second nature, but there was no twinkle in his eyes or the friskiness he always displayed when she was naked in his arms. She brought his hands to her slightly rounded stomach, and finally there was a moment he was back with her. Annie dried both of them, taking particular care with his bruised and swollen body. She helped him dress and said, "Go up on deck and find your mother, my love. I will change these sheets and be up in time to see our approach into the port of Palma."

Ramone caught the fresh air as he emerged from the main salon where Antonio and Alex had slept. Antonio saw him first and mentioned how good it was to see him up. Although Ramone said no words, he rested his hand on Antonio's shoulder, appreciating his concern and sharing their grief. Seeking his mother, he found her with Don Marco who, when he saw Ramone approach, discreetly left them with, "Good to see you, son."

Marguerite reached up to hug her strong, but fragile, son and smiled. "Let's sit down for a while." Ramone had still not said a word, so Marguerite began, "You have chosen a life where you face challenges often when confronting a bull that weighs over a thousand pounds! You suffered cuts and bruises from those Chinese brutes. I understand there might be pain, but was it that bad?"

Ramone turned away and shook his head. "You really don't understand, Mamà."

Marguerite instinctively knew what the issue was but asked anyway. "It's your father's death, right, son?"

Knowing his mother would not give up her questioning, Ramone sought to describe the turmoil he was feeling. "When

Kung Li's men took me, I was not quick enough to leave a hint like Annie did. I thought they might ransom me or try to trade me for Papa, but they bound me and showed no mercy, leaving me unconscious a great deal of the time. You mentioned the challenge of facing a bull head-on. That is totally different. I am trained for the sport and know how to outwit the bull. But with these men, I had no training and no mobility to defend myself. I was not sure if anyone could find me, much less what they would find if they did. All I could think was how pathetically I failed and that I would be justifying Annie's fear. What if I weren't there to take care of her and the baby?

"I am not proud, Mamà. I felt self-pity and was at a particularly low moment when they brought me, stumbling, out into the open. First, I saw Annie being held at gunpoint on the deck. But nothing could have prepared me for the sudden outrage of Papa. It took a moment for me to comprehend that his outrage was not aimed at me but at my captors. Papa was less than fifteen feet from me when he took the bullet. Everything became a blur to me after that until I was released and could go to Papa. His last words were that he was sorry and that he loved us. I never had the chance to say it back. Why did I not have time with a father who cared about me?" Ramone didn't notice the tears that were trickling down from his eyes, but his mother did.

Grasping the reality of a mixture of helplessness, grief, and loss, Marguerite thought about how to respond. "It is true what you went through is unthinkable. I believe it is important for you to acknowledge and accept that reality. But there is also a way to deal with it from a different perspective. Your father was traumatized by the goring death of his father in the ring, yet he never dealt with that horrific emotion. For so many years, Salvador tucked that pain and grief deep inside. He was a good man. We married, and he was good to you boys. Perhaps it was the evil influence of his connection with Kung Li, or perhaps seeing the stronger impact his brother Pedro had over you than he did. But when you, and then Antonio, took the calling to be matadors, that brought the old wound to the surface and led him down the dark path he pursued."

She continued, "Antonio and I were with him when he realized you were in danger. In that moment, there was nothing he wouldn't do to save you. In the end, your father had the strength to turn his path around, and he died a hero. Do not let this get buried inside you and fester like an unhealable wound. Handle it differently than Salvador did by making the future for you and Annie and your children the best it can be. The secret to moving forward from here is not found in some clever technique. You just need to get up and go, be thankful you are alive and that your father made that possible. Appreciate him for his final sacrifice, learn from his mistakes, then move on."

Marguerite could see her words had the effect she hoped they would have. The others had respectfully given them privacy, but now she could hear Dom calling out that they were passing Ibiza portside, and they would be docking in Palma very soon. Ramone looked at his mother with deep appreciation and took her hand with a smile.

"Thank you, Mamà. I think I have a better understanding of how my grandfather's death affected him. Come on, let's go. I know Annie is worried."

# Chapter 19

Don Marco was pointing out the lighthouse at the entrance to the port of Ibiza. Annie was listening intently. She had dressed in a strappy aquamarine top that flowed over white shorts. With her hair pulled up in a high ponytail and wearing little makeup, she could be mistaken for a young girl. Ramone looked at her anew with pride and the sure knowledge she was all woman. He was overwhelmed with a possessive realization she was his, and he could not wait to be married to her. When Annie was instinctively drawn to his stare, she broke her attention from Dom and looked up. She warmed to the heat in his eyes, ever grateful that Marguerite had helped him find his way back to her.

The kiss Ramone took from her gave no heed to the others watching and, as it continued, got a loud cheer! Everyone was delighted to see a sign of Ramone's old spirit. A relieved atmosphere took over, and each gave their own support to Ramone with either a hug, handshake, or pat on the back. Don Marco continued, "If you look closely, you will see the port of Ibiza lies at the base of the fortified 'Old Town,' Dalt Vila, on the top of the hill. Meghan, you and Annie should like this example of classic Renaissance military architecture with many historical remnants of the various cultures that have called Ibiza home over thousands of years."

Meghan was first to react. "Perhaps we can come back here for a day trip during our time on Mallorca. I would be interested in doing a study on Dalt Vila. I think I read about it. Wasn't it a naval base for traders dating back to the seventh century BC?" Looking at Annie, Meghan continued, "I think there will be much history we can pull from this place. I am getting excited about the possibility we can turn a tragedy into something positive!"

Annie, in the arms of her soon-to-be husband, was reassured too and found her sense of adventure and love of history beckoning. "We should make a toast to Salvador." On cue, Helene arrived with a bottle of prosecco and sparkling water for Annie. Raising their glasses, they called out in unison, *"Salud!"*

Roff walked up to Don Marco as if to ask permission to speak. When he nodded, Roff continued, "The captain would like everyone seated. We are about to take down the sails and approach the entry of the port of Palma. We should anchor in about thirty minutes."

As they proceeded to the lounge area of the aft deck, everyone speculated on what to expect at the estate Tomás had arranged for them. Was it indeed the fortress he thought they might need for protection?

When the port of Palma could be seen off in the distance, Roff joined them to explain. "Since we will be staying in Mallorca for a time, the captain plans to anchor in the calm, enclosed area of the port. Our transom will lower our Zodiac to tender back and forth to the waterfront promenade near the Poniente Quays. The port is busier than usual this week, so Helene will be handing out life jackets for the tender ride."

Annie jumped up looking at all the sailboats in the harbor. "There are so many racing boats here! I know some of them! Is there some sailing event on the island while we are here?"

Roff answered, "The Copa del Rey, or King's Cup Regatta, starts the end of the week. Usually, the sailors come in early to practice here in the bay of Palma de Mallorca. It is a major cruiser class event. Since we will no longer be confined to the estate, you will likely meet many international sailors visiting while you are here, not to mention seeing a lot of world-class sailing."

Thinking aloud, Annie said, "I wonder whether any of them might need crew? It would be a once-in-a-lifetime experience to race with them!"

Ramone saw the excitement in Annie's eyes and thought he would try to find a way to make it happen for her. He was still dazed from the death of his father, but Marguerite's words had helped him resolve to accept it. He would always be overcome with the knowledge his father gave his life for him. He hoped the time here in Mallorca would be one of recovery for his family. With Alex's last promise to Salvador and his upcoming marriage to Annie, Ramone knew the lives of their two families would now be entwined. As for the wedding, it was time to decide where and when it would be held. He took Annie's hand to go gather their belongings from the cabin and go ashore with the others.

# Chapter 20

Roff lowered the transom with the Zodiac and tied it off aft. It was decided Annie and Ramone, Don Marco and Gennie, and Meghan and Marguerite would be first to go ashore. Captain Luis was giving final instructions to the crew remaining on board, and Alex wanted to stay to help Antonio maneuver the transport. The captain, Roff, and Helene would come with them on the second run and the crewman would return to the *Porto Banus* with the Zodiac. The bags and supplies were stacked under cover at the bow.

Annie couldn't help comparing all the times she had come ashore from the *Porto Banus* alone to this time, arriving surrounded by people she loved and could share the experience with. As the Zodiac approached the dock, Annie looked around at all the hustle and bustle in the marina. The air itself seemed to sizzle with anticipation and excitement. She marveled to herself: *this trip that started as an escape from danger might turn out to be an unexpected adventure!*

Nearing the dock, Annie spotted Tomás and her mom. She started waving and calling out, trying to jump up, but Dom with a chuckle said, "I suggest, young lady, that you sit down at once or you will tip us over and have all of us spilled into the sea!"

Ramone stifled a laugh and pulled her back to her seat. Although properly chagrined, Annie could not stop smiling at seeing Celeste. So much had happened since she left Maine, and the thought of how much she missed her mom and their special mother-daughter talks had her impatient to get to her. When she glanced over at Meghan, Annie realized she was not the only one excited. Meghan was glowing with happiness to see Tomás. To

Meghan, there was no one more dashing than this man smiling at her from the pier, her husband of just a little over a month.

Soon enough, they were at the dock. Don Marco blocked both girls as he allowed Gennie to step off first. Tomás was there to help her. Then it was time for Annie and Meghan, and they quickly jumped ashore to give huge hugs to Celeste and Tomás. Don Marco smiled as he gave Ramone a pat on the back. "I guess we're on our own, son. Tomás, lend a hand here. Our boy might need some help."

Celeste's eyes were misty looking at both her beautiful young daughter and her own loving mother. Alex had shared a little of what had happened in Malaga, and she studied Ramone as he approached to determine how he was. Don Marco could see the question in his daughter's eye and shared, "He has gone through quite an ordeal. His cuts and bruises will heal, but he has lost his father."

Ramone flinched at his words, and Celeste walked over to give him a warm embrace. "I am dearly sorry for your loss, Ramone. This must be horribly difficult for Marguerite and Antonio as well. Perhaps all of you can use this time to recover a little. The villa and the surrounding grounds are a spectacular haven!" Then, pulling Annie over, she continued to them both, "And we have a wedding to plan!"

They could see the second group approaching and began to gather at the dock. However, Tomás pulled Ramone aside to rest his hand on his shoulder. "Ramone, if there is anything I can do to help, please don't hesitate to ask. I lost my parents early in a tragic accident. Honestly, I don't know what I would have done without Dom and Gennie. Annie and Sabine are like sisters to me. Maybe this week will be a good chance for us to get to know each other better."

Ramone was touched by the genuine kindness of his new family-to-be. To Tomás, he said, "I would like that. It is not easy to talk about, but I appreciate all of you deeply."

The Zodiac arrived, and Roff climbed ashore first to receive Antonio's wheelchair. Alex and Captain Luis helped Antonio onto the dock, and Roff was there to assist with getting him settled in the chair. Marguerite was next, then Helene. When everyone was on the dock, Tomás cleared his throat to speak.

"Aunt Celeste and I had the privilege to arrive at the villa late yesterday, and I am pleased to say I think you will find it quite suitable. I have arranged two vans to take us about fifteen minutes from here, up into the hills. The accommodations are quite generous, so you should find each of your rooms unique and private, a perfect retreat from all that has happened. The baggage and supplies will follow. We have arranged with the staff a welcome dinner for tonight out on the veranda. Very casual, of course. For now, look around you. This shipping port that dates back to the tenth century was referred to as the Old Quay in the days of King James I in 1273. The island will be busy over the next two weeks with the Copa del Rey Regatta, but our villa is secluded and quiet. In light of what you have been through, it is your choice whether to enjoy the privacy or partake of the festivity. Considering most the issues that brought us here have been resolved, we will have more freedom to move about than we originally anticipated. For now, let's go, and let me introduce you to *Casa de Esperanza*— House of Hope!"

# Chapter 21

During the drive, the scenery was lush with tropical greenery, and the group in both vans could tell from Tomás's words they were in for something special. Don Marco, in particular, was most interested to see what Tomás had purchased and restored on his behalf. They arrived at the gate, which was certainly no ordinary gate. There was flagstone pavement out to the road. The stone walls were connected with a large oval entry that included a double wooden door and an elegant wrought iron piece above. Large potted palms flanked both sides.

Once inside the gate, the courtyard was breathtaking! The aromatic garden burst with color with seating areas specifically chosen for their locations for privacy and times of reflection. The entrance foyer clad in slick limestone, the bench made from the trunk of a zapote tree, and the soaring oval brick dome gave credence to its historical origins.

Entering the ancient walls surrounding the estate, Annie immediately felt the magic of this place. In the foyer, Yuba, the concierge, and the villa's staff awaited them. Yuba greeted them and introduced the staff members by name. As two of the staff began to escort Don Marco and Genevieve to the owner's suite, Tomás interjected, "This invitation came for you this morning, sir."

Don Marco opened it, read the invitation, then told the others, "It seems we have been invited to a party at the Real Club Náutico. It is tomorrow night and will host all the sailors racing in the Copa del Rey Regatta. It is Palma's royal sailing club that is hosting the regatta. Shall we accept?"

The entire atmosphere of the room lifted in anticipation of starting fresh, and they unanimously yelled "Yes!"

The ladies were first to realize their light packing had not prepared them for such entertainment. "Looks like tomorrow might require a little shopping!" Gennie exclaimed, looking at the excitement in the room. This was certainly a different mood from the one that started this sojourn. "Dom, I am going to check on the kitchen and what the chef will be preparing. Shall everyone meet back on the veranda in an hour?"

The group separated to seek out their rooms, each one with a unique flair. The three-bedroom casita with its own cooking facility was built into the stone wall adjacent to the stone firepit. It would be perfect for Captain Luis, Helene, and Roff. They left to settle in.

Tomás led the others to their rooms, explaining a little about the restorations along the way. "I am particularly happy with the flooring. The craftsmen I hired took the old standard Saltillo tile floor and replaced it with this design of mixed Rustico tiles in hexagon and octagon shapes in a Riviera pattern. You will find many of the walls in your suites are covered with conchuela stone brought all the way from Mexico and honed with ancient fossils and seashells." Pausing at a door, he added, "Each suite has been given a name. Antonio, this is the *Cascado Suite*. I think you will appreciate its convenient location on the main floor. Its décor exudes peace and tranquility, and its ensuite bathroom has a generous oversized shower." Antonio entered his room, and Ramone said to let him know if he needed help.

At the top of the stone staircase, there was a rounded foyer with an open railing looking over to the main floor living area. Annie, with the critical eye of an architect, sighed, "This is beautiful, Tomás! You have done an amazing job keeping the authenticity in the restoration." Taking Ramone's hand, she said, "We look forward to adding some of these touches to the house we found in Mijas." Her comment reminded Ramone he had not been able to finalize a deal on the house prior to their sudden departure. His head was pounding from his wounds and all that had happened. Somehow, the house in Mijas was not a priority for him.

Tomás stopped at the first wooden door. "Marguerite, I thought you would like the *Verano Suite*. You will find a four-poster bed made with rustic hardwood pillars and a small private balcony offering a sunrise view of the hills that reach to the sea, hence its name of 'summertime.'"

Moving to the next door, he said, "Uncle Alex and Aunt Celeste, this is the *El Ocaso Suite*. Its 180-degree view of the hills with its wraparound balcony offers magnificent sunset views! I hope you will particularly like the built-in, rounded, brick-and-river-rock headboard!" Both Alex and Celeste were delighted with their *sundown* room and agreed to meet out on the veranda after they unpacked.

Looking at Annie and Ramone, Tomás said, "That leaves the four of us. Meghan, *mi amor*, I chose the *Amorosa Suite* for us. It has wraparound windows and a soaring palapa ceiling, giving it an outdoor feel with a private outdoor shower. With its meaning of 'amorous,' an integrated handmade marble tub is featured inside the bedroom. Will this work?"

Blushing, Meghan looked at Annie and shrugged her shoulders. "I can't wait to see what he has in mind for you two!" There were no more suites on this level.

Ramone, suddenly exhausted, ventured, "I admit, Tomás, I am most intrigued at what our room might be."

Tomás smiled. "Follow me." He led the way up a rather hidden staircase to the third level. "This is the *Amànte Suite*, or 'lover.'"

Annie and Ramone began to explore. To the left, a door led to an outdoor garden covered by a bougainvillea-shaded trellis. Off to the side was an outdoor waterfall-fed tub for two. Looking at each other, they simultaneously remembered the island of Karpathos where their child was conceived. Ramone mumbled, "Perfect!" Back inside, in the center of the room, was a suspended king-size bed made of hardwood timbers and draped in colorful silks.

As Tomás backed out of the room, he said, "I thought you'd like it. By the way, Ramone, a package arrived for you this morning. It is over on the table. There is a note attached." Curious, they walked over and turned over the card. It was from El Amir!

Ramone's eye injury made it hard for him to read, so Annie picked up the note and read.

*'It is with heavy regret we were not able to save both you and your father. I am sorry I was not able to tell you personally, but I went to ensure the men that killed Salvador would suffer the consequences of their murder. In the meantime, please accept these bottles of Moroccan oils. Huile D'Argane, in particular, should help with healing the cuts and fading the bruises. They are all made from local Moroccan plants. Please accept my deepest condolences for your loss.*

*Sincerely, El Amir'*

Ramone couldn't help reflecting. "What an unusual man. I know he has had feelings for you, *querida*, yet he risks his life to save mine. I owe this man a large debt."

Annie nodded. "I have learned El Amir is not only an honorable man but also an extremely generous patron. I know my friend Sarah would not be as far along with her art if it were not for him. Perhaps at some point we can all be friends? I would like that."

Ramone looked around the room approvingly. He pulled Annie into a tight embrace and with words that caressed her very soul whispered, "Let's call it an early evening, *querida*. My body craves rest and I have plans for you in this room."

Meeting his eyes with a twinkle of flirtation, Annie picked up the oil and answered, "As a matter of fact, I also have plans. For now, however, shall we join the others on the veranda?"

# Chapter 22

Annie and Ramone walked outside into what could only be called an outdoor paradise. Annie's every sense was activated, and she tried to separate the different causes of her sensory overload. Structurally, the backyard was massive, but the way it was laid out felt intimate. The loggia closest to the house was separated from the rest of the yard and pool area by a perfectly trimmed dense evergreen hedge that looked like Portuguese laurel. It was separated into two areas. The lounging area rested on a slightly raised deck and had a vaulted wooden-beamed ceiling. The rattan furniture was thickly cushioned with large pillows that begged to be enjoyed.

To the side, a graveled area surrounded by a wide variety of potted plants and topped with a trellis of meandering grapevines accommodated a large teak dining table that could seat ten. Visually, with the greenery interspersed by so much floral color, it made perfect sense the furniture was neutral. But the aromas! Such a blend of herbs and a wide variety of flowers wafted amidst the breeze of the fresh air of the hills and the distant sea.

Everyone was seated and animatedly discussing their various rooms, but Annie was intoxicated with the beautiful simplicity of this place. It made her want to venture out beyond the hedge to see the rest of the design. It was intriguing to her to see that landscaping could have as strong of an architectural impact as the building itself!

The large pool was the primary focus. It was laid out in a moderate L-shape with a cinched corner where wide Roman steps with an accent tile trim was the focal point. This bend in the shape created a wide tiled area for a number of lounge chairs and a room-size umbrella. A separate, shorter hedge outlined the pool area with a line of olive trees behind, enhanced with an assortment of palm trees, a lily pond, and exotic plants in Grecian urns.

Annie came back to the veranda and said to Tomás, "Why have you been keeping this gem secret? It is stunning!"

Gennie added, "I agree. You should see the kitchen! The large open family-style *cocina* has a massive granite-top island and a breakfast bar with room for six stools. But the adjoining catering kitchen is a dream, whether for intimate service or large celebrations!"

Tomás warmed to all the praise over his purchase for Don Marco and replied, "A family from Barcelona was vacationing here and heard we were completing the restoration. They came by and rented it on the spot. That family has been in residence all this time until a couple of weeks ago when they were called back to the mainland on business. It was the perfect time for us to come!"

At that moment, Yuba came out to the veranda carrying two bottles of wine. Glasses were passed around, and even Annie took one. "This Rioja red wine is made right here on the property from these very grapes. Please, try it. I think you will enjoy its smooth flavor. The *tapenade* Maria is bringing out with the tapas is also made here. Plus, our chef uses all the herbs from the gardens."

It seemed as though a spell had been cast over the night providing a perfect respite from the last difficult days. But when a young musician came out and started to ply her soulful violin sonatas, all thoughts of an indifferent evening were forgotten.

The chef came out to the veranda to give them the menu for the evening. He began, "Mallorca is known for its gastronomy. As the Balearic capital, we have a passion for our seafood, whether it is prepared traditionally or as a fusion. I very much hope you will find this meal pleasing. For our appetizer, we will have chilled cucumber, olive oil, and pepper soup, followed by fresh basil crisp with grilled tomato. Our main course will be freshly caught sea bass over lemon-infused risotto, white asparagus, and citrus albedo. We will complete the dinner with our dessert of white chocolate mousse shaped liked coral intertwined by dark chocolate crisps. We kindly ask that you move to your seats at the dining table."

As they found seats at the table, Meghan pulled Annie aside. "You could totally get married here! It is beautiful!"

The evening progressed easily among these two families whose paths had interconnected on multiple levels. New friendships were formed, and old friendships renewed. Meghan promised to start working with Antonio on therapeutic physical exercises for his legs. Tomás agreed to teach him the card game of *conquian*. Celeste began the evening sympathetic to Marguerite concerning Salvador, but soon realized what a strong woman she was, and they settled into a comfortable camaraderie. Alex, pleased with Celeste's acceptance of Marguerite, entered into a insightful debate with Dom about what would unfold in Hong Kong as the turnover got closer.

That gave Gennie a chance to get to know Ramone better and discuss the upcoming wedding. Gennie started the conversation. "I overheard Meghan suggest this estate for your wedding venue. Is it something you would consider?"

Annie began to answer, but Ramone put his hand over hers in her lap to interrupt and answer himself. He had not spent much time with his soon-to-be grandmother-in-law. "May I call you Gennie?" When she smiled and nodded, he proceeded. "This place is magical, and I can tell Annie loves it. I want to marry your granddaughter as soon as possible. However, we have discussed it, and my *querida* has some pretty strong opinions about what she wants as a ceremony."

That caught the full attention of those at the table. Annie looked up at Ramone, who was still holding her hand, and said, "I was on a journey, filled with a mix of emotions, when I met this man. We have been through many ups and downs, including most recently. I came close to walking away from love because of my fear of his matches with the bull. Yet here he was, in real danger that had nothing to do with his being a matador. My dearest Tomás and Meghan, your wedding was lovely and an inspiration to all of us. I would never want to compete with such an experience!

"Throughout my journey, I was in many spiritual places that had an impact on my heart. It was the culmination of those experiences that has allowed me to open it to him for whatever might come. We have a child on the way who was conceived in one of the most beautiful places I have ever been. We have given thought to going back to that special Greek island of Karpathos to marry, but that doesn't feel quite right. I thought about Thailand and Bali, both of which would offer an abundance of wedding experiences. There was a place in Australia I went to with Mara and Jonathan McNamara. He took us to Ayers Rock in Uluru. It is a living cultural landscape dating back sixty thousand years, and it is said spirits of Aboriginal ancestral beings continue to reside in this sacred place!"

Meghan asked, "Annie, are you thinking of going back to this rock to marry?"

Annie thought for a moment and gave a soft chuckle at her calling it a rock. "It has the advantage of the fact that I have been there and know a little of what to expect. But there is another place I actually learned about at your wedding, Tomás. It was Emily Weston's friend, Deirdra, who spoke of her work in Peru."

Tomás nodded. "Ah, yes, Emily was a dear friend of my mother, and she remained close each summer when I was visiting you in Maine. I remember Deirdra. What a fascinating woman. Doesn't she live half the year in Maine and the other half in Peru?"

Meghan added, "Just like us living between Dingle and Marbella."

Annie answered, "Yes, exactly. The Andean people are quite remarkable, and they are descended from the ancient Incas. Deirdra told me about Machu Picchu as the 'Lost City of the Incas.' She told me there is a very spiritual wedding ceremony performed by an Andean Priest, or Shaman, with the help of all the Pachamama energies. It sounds fascinating."

Celeste quietly spoke up, "All those places sound amazing, dear, but they are quite far and remote."

Gennie said gently, "*Ma chérie*, these are not trips your grandfather and I could easily take at this time in our lives. But if this is what feels right to you, do it."

Annie, feeling a little defeated that she might not have those people she loved around her for such an important event, sighed.

Her mother immediately noticed her change of mood and said, "Let's sleep on it and see what ideas a new day brings!"

The evening had gone on longer than they had anticipated, and both Ramone and Annie were exhausted. With all the turmoil they had both been through the last few days, it was understandable. She was past the nausea part of her pregnancy, but she did tire more easily, increased by the worry of the last few days.

There was a gentle sway when Annie got in bed and realized the bed actually was suspended. Ramone got in beside her and cradled her in his arms. Annie was in a deep sleep within minutes, but Ramone's mind was too busy for sleep. Did he really want to get married at some Aboriginal rock or by some Andean shaman? Annie was much more spiritual than he was. Would he somehow disappoint her? Having his family at their wedding was important to him. It was not easy for Antonio to make a long trip with his infirmity. He definitely wanted his brother by his side. Instinctively, Ramone knew his response would be important to Annie. Seeking to ignore the pulsing of the wounds around his eye, he drew her closer and finally drifted off to sleep, determined he would find a compromise.

# Chapter 23

Annie awoke in the arms of her love who was sleeping soundly. Looking at his face, she was annoyed with herself for neglecting to tend to his wounds the night before. He would need the stitches removed soon. She had also been less than amorous. As if he could feel Annie studying him, Ramone slowly opened his eyes with a sly smile. "What do you see, *querida*? Does my wounded face offend you?"

Taking his hand to her heart, she said, "No, my love, I see your amazingly strong and loving soul. I am privileged that you share the love I feel. I should have tended to you better last night. Will you allow me to make it up to you? Come with me." Annie led them, both naked, to the outdoor garden area, shrouded in privacy by a wide variety of climbing vines. There was a wide lounging settee where she invited Ramone to rest while she started the waterfall that would fill their tub. He marveled at how her body was starting to hint at her condition and filling out in all the right places.

Their attraction to each other was intense, but sometimes the urge to stretch out the intensity was overwhelming. Walking over to the tub, Ramone helped Annie step in, then joined her amidst overflowing bubbles. Annie's eyes shut as she sat back against him careful of his bruises, and his hands casually roamed over her wet body. But urgency took over as the flame ignited Ramone's blood whenever Annie was naked in his arms. Her response urged him on, and soon she was straddling him, rocking in an age-old rhythm that moved harder and faster until they were both spent and fulfilled. The water had to cool until they were both shivering to make them move from this soothing solace.

The aromas of a country breakfast reaching all the way to the third floor tempted them to hurry to dress. They went downstairs to find Meghan and Tomás playing cards with Antonio. Marguerite was quietly reading on the veranda. Gennie and Celeste were busily helping Maria set the table.

When he saw Annie and Ramone, Dom put his newspaper down. Studying Ramone, he said, "You look much better today, son. What would you think about going to the Plaza de Toros today? Annie, you might like to see this bullring too. I hear the design is a feature of the old town and quite impressive with its ancient arena."

Annie quietly asked, "Is there a fight today? I seem to have developed a queasy stomach during this pregnancy."

Ramone shook his head. "I am not feeling up to a bullring today, sir. Perhaps something else?"

Dom studied his guide. "Gennie and I are going to tour the Santa Maria Cathedral today. It appears to be quite impressive. You young people might want to visit the *Coves del Drach* in the town of Porto Cristo. These 'Caves of the Dragon' hide inside a large underground lake, Lake Martel, which is considered one of the largest underground lakes in the world. They are covered with stalactites that drip from the ceiling."

Celeste called them to breakfast. "Why don't we discuss our plans over breakfast?"

After they sat down, Marguerite asked, "Does anyone know the attire for tonight's party? I know none of my family are prepared for it."

Celeste answered, "If it was in Maine, it would be easy...nautical navy and white would do. But European yacht clubs can be more formal, even stuffy at times. Dom, what do we know of this Real Club Náutico?"

Dom looked at his notes. "Here is what I know. It was founded in 1948 and remains among the elite yacht clubs in all of Europe. It is hosting the Copa del Rey regatta beginning Friday, so most likely an invitation is rare to come by. My guess would be leaning between semiformal and formal. My understanding is that the Spanish royal family will be in attendance. Tomás has arranged an account at the boutiques in Port D'Andratx. Your attire for tonight is my pleasure to provide. I do not expect my family to disappoint so be prepared to wear your finest!"

They spent the rest of breakfast deciding how to split up to shop. Although Celeste was drawn to shop with Meghan and Annie, she opted to go with Marguerite and Gennie with Annie's promise they would have that mother-daughter talk later in the afternoon. Remarkably, the men decided to stay together. Most probably, they wanted to ensure Don Marco's approval!

Roff declared himself the house chauffeur and agreed to take them in different groups wherever they wanted to go. With a quick kiss to their men, Annie and Meghan were the first to leave giggling over their outing together. And the shopping began.

Roff dropped the girls off at the end of the main street that was filled with boutiques and sidewalk cafés. Meghan suddenly suggested, "Why don't we stop for a coffee first and come up with a plan?"

Annie could tell Meghan had something to say. There was no hurry after all. Smiling, she answered, "Of course! Great idea."

In Meghan's typical forthright style, she jumped right into what was on her mind. "Annie, I have to admit I'm somewhat daunted and a bit intimidated by your grandfather. What exactly does he expect from us?"

Annie realized many people might feel that way. However, she knew the love, charity, and wisdom that lay beneath his public image. She wanted to explain that to Meghan, who was now an important part of their family. "Dom is a complex man. He is Don Marco to the public and Dom to his family. Over his life, he has traveled and entertained in high circles. He married the perfect woman in my grandmother with her French passion for social graces, culinary pursuits, and impeccable fashion. But she also grounds him and keeps his focus genuine. He has so many stories to tell. I never get tired of our walks and listening to him.

Usually there is much wisdom woven into the stories he tells. For tonight, the last-minute invitation is important for his position, not his vanity. We will be his ambassadors. It is his generosity, not his ego, that allows us to purchase something appropriate for this event."

Meghan nodded in understanding. "Ah, since no one had packed for an outing such as the Yacht Club gala, he didn't want anyone to feel pressured into spending unnecessarily."

"Exactly. He is not looking for your gratitude, but I always let him know how much I appreciate all they do. Both he and Gennie love Tomás, Sabine, and me equally. You are now part of that circle by marrying Tomás. Soon Ramone will be too. And then the baby."

Smiling, Meghan took her last sip of coffee. "Let's go make Dom proud!"

Annie nodded, genuinely happy that this spunky Irish woman was family to her. They stopped in at the first boutique but didn't see anything appropriate. At the next one, there were several nautical outfits but much too casual for this evening. Having no luck, by the fifth boutique they explained to the owner they were looking for a dress for the Copa del Rey gala at the yacht club. Understanding they would not find what they needed at her store, the owner sent them two blocks down and to the left on a side street. When they turned the corner, Annie suddenly stopped, her eyes glued to a dress in the storefront window. "It's gorgeous!"

Meghan looked at Annie, stunned. "I might not be an expert on what to wear to a party at an uppity yacht club, but I am fairly sure it is not a long ivory satin gown!

"Come on, Meghan. I have to try it on!" Annie was already halfway through the door. To the owner of the boutique, she pointed to the dress in the window. "May I try it?"

The dress was simple really. The off-the-shoulder style crisscrossed in the front with subtle draping across the middle. The back was a deep V-shape. When Annie walked out in it, tears were rolling down her checks. Meghan stared at her. "You look beautiful! The dress suits you perfectly!"

"I wanted simple. No ornamentation. It feels perfect," Annie commented.

It was then the owner said, "Yes, it is lovely on you. I see your condition and do not think this dress will fit you for long."

Meghan shrugged. "She's probably right. Why don't you think about it?" To the owner, she asked, "Ma'am, could you hold this dress for a couple of days?"

The owner replied, "Yes, of course. Will you please let me know if you decide against it?"

The previous store owner had indeed sent them to the right street; the boutiques there were abundant with choices for the evening. After trying on over a dozen dresses each, the girls finally made their selection. Meghan chose a sleeveless dress that was navy blue. The low V-neck front was alluring but not audacious. Fitted at the waist, it flared slightly over the hips, providing a most flattering silhouette. Annie thought she looked wonderful!

Annie's choice was a simple long black sheath that hung from spaghetti straps. However, that was where the simplicity stopped. Bold green fern leaves were hand-painted in a diagonal pattern, wrapping their way around the black silk. The hemline came to a point at the front and back. The boldness continued at the back neckline that plunged to her waist. Annie swirled once more, looking in the mirror, and with a grin thought to herself this might stir her matador a little. With shoes and bags to match and accessories in hand, they looked at the clock and realized it was almost time to meet Gennie, Celeste, and Marguerite for lunch. All of a sudden, they were starving! But as they walked by the familiar boutique, Annie couldn't help thinking about the simple ivory dress.

# Chapter 24

The ladies were already seated with a glass of prosecco in hand, setting the tone for a festive lunch. Annie and Meghan joined them for an animated discussion of their shopping success, as well as the plans for the evening. Celeste had heard from the men. Dom planned to meet Gennie at the cathedral after lunch for a tour. Alex was taking Ramone and Tomás to the caves. "Antonio will meet the rest of us back at the house."

Marguerite nodded, fully understanding her younger son would not be happy that he could not participate. It was Meghan who saw it as an opportunity. "That is perfect! It gives me a chance to work with him on his exercises."

Celeste added to Annie, "It sounds like this is a great time for our mother-daughter talk."

When Roff came for a pickup, Celeste and Annie offered to stay behind for a little stroll while he delivered the others.

While they were walking, Celeste asked, "How is Ramone? Really? Alex told me of his shock of seeing Salvador killed in front of him."

"Mom, it was horrible. He thought Salvador was charging forward to hurt him, but he was actually trying to save him. I think Ramone is suffering over not having more time with a father who had finally lost all the anger directed at him. He was frozen with the trauma of it. Marguerite was the one who was able to bring him out of it."

Annie loved how easy it was to talk to her mother. She was grateful that had never changed. Their conversation drifted from Mallorca to the party and the regatta, and eventually made its way around to the baby and the wedding. Celeste hesitated. Annie could sense it and encouraged her to speak honestly. "Sweetheart, do you realize how close your child came to not having a legal father? You are here in this special moment with a loving family all around you. Perhaps this is not the time to dream about someday? I do understand the desire to wish and dream and imagine. We all have that. Maybe the trick of it is to put your real life of today into those dreams. Every day you spend with Ramone is a priceless gift. My advice to you would be to explore this gift and jump all the way into it!"

Was it a twist of fate that brought them back to the boutique? "Mom, I want to show you something." The owner brought out the dress, and Annie tried it on for her mother. Once Celeste saw her daughter come out of the dressing room, tears sprang to her eyes. "Oh sweetheart, it is exquisite! It's as though it were made for you. Shall we get it? Whatever you decide about the wedding, I think this dress should be part of it." Annie's love for her mother at that moment had no bounds, and their embrace solidified their feelings.

Smiling at the encounter, the owner asked, "Shall I put it on the account?"

"No," Celeste said. "My husband and I would like to get this."

As the dress was carefully packed, and Celeste checked out, Roff appeared outside the boutique. Annie had a notion that Meghan had told him the address. Getting into the car, Celeste suggested, "Let's keep this in our room for now."

Suddenly a little apprehension rolled over Annie. "Mom, I love the dress, but I'm not sure how long I will be able to fit in it." She paused for a moment. "Let's get through the party and regatta, and I promise to make a decision about the wedding. You have given me a lot to think about!"

Celeste and Annie arrived back at the house to find Meghan and Marguerite guiding Antonio through some exercises. The villa was quiet since the others were still gone. Celeste went to her room to put away the dress with a questioning sideways glance and raised eyebrows from Meghan.

Annie's mind was racing, and for the first time in a long while, she longed for her journal. That journal had recorded her innermost thoughts, questions, and challenges during her journey that led her to the acceptance of Ramone's proposal. Somehow, since then, she had not felt that insatiable need to write, nor had she thought to bring it.

Meghan called over to her. "Annie, we are going to take Antonio to the pool. Would you like to join us?"

Annie replied, "No, I think I am going to take advantage of this alone time to relax out on the veranda. Maybe I'll join you later." Annie wandered outside to find a hammock nestled in a shady spot amidst the abundance of pleasant fragrances. As she lay back, letting her mind drift, she pondered about what she would write:

*Why is the memory of the old woman in the market in Bali resonating in my head? She looked at me and asked if I was happy. Such a seemingly random question. I remember smiling but not answering. Then she said directly to me, with the piercing eyes and wisdom of age, "The time to be happy is now." Can it be that I am building the idea of such a spiritual wedding ceremony into a faraway dream? Do I want this dream to exclude family or friends that I love? I spent a great deal of time traveling a unique and valuable path to get to this day. Perhaps now presents an unexpected opportunity to put even more positive purpose into my journey. What is more important...a spiritual ceremony or having loved ones at our side? Wouldn't it be possible to have both? And what about Ramone? Does he really want to travel to somewhere far for an ancient ritual, or is he merely going along with the idea to please me? We need to talk this through.*

# Chapter 25

Ramone came in with Alex and Tomás animatedly discussing their afternoon at the caves. They were debating about their tour through the four caves, each of which seemed bigger and more impressive than the last. The debate centered around how the caves were created millions of years ago. Annie watched, genuinely thrilled to see Ramone bonding with her father and cousin. It was feeling more and more like family every day. They asked Antonio about his exercises with Meghan, and he said he thought they might make a difference.

It was soon time to retire to their rooms to prepare for the evening's festivities. With Ramone finally in a lighthearted mood, Annie thought it best to wait for any talk of the wedding. She bathed and took extra care with her appearance. A simple carved emerald-green necklace was the perfect accent to the hand-painted leaves in her new dress. She created a hairstyle that was loosely swept up with purposeful tendrils escaping around her face. With a final spray of Ramone's favorite perfume, she was ready.

Ramone had already dressed and was waiting for her on the veranda. He was leaning against the column in conversation with Dom and Gennie, so Annie saw him first. He was so dazzlingly handsome even with the wounds on his face, her heart skipped a beat. Thankfully they seemed to be healing. His new formal attire fit him to perfection. He must have felt her near because he turned to face her. She melted as she saw his reaction. He didn't have to say a word. It was Dom who came over and said, "You are positively glowing, Annie. That dress is perfection on you!"

They all gathered, admiring the purchases of the day and exchanging compliments. It was the ching of the wineglass by Don Marco as a signal for a toast that had them all quiet. "To each of you! You make Gennie and me proud to show off our family tonight. Let us go enjoy the festivities!" He had hired two sedans to take them.

Their arrival at the Real Club Náutico did not go unnoticed. The normal highbrow group of locals were quite curious about these newcomers. As they entered, a gray-haired gentleman approached Don Marco. Wearing a dapper double-breasted navy sport coat over white linen pants and a navy-and-white striped shirt unbuttoned at the neck, he appeared quite the host.

"Good evening! You must be Don Marco of Marbella. I am Juan Carlos, the ambassador of the club. It is I who sent you the invitation. Please join us! You and your family are my guests. I heard you are the owner of Casa de Esperanza. Your recent tenants were members of our yacht club." Juan Carlos led them over to several tables, allowing Don Marco and Genevieve join him at his family table. The empty table for eight next to it would accommodate the rest of them.

Too excited to be amongst all these sailors, Annie could not sit down. She whispered to Ramone that she was going out to the dock to see if she could find the king's yacht that would be racing the next day. Realizing he had lost her attention, but happy to see her excitement, he took her hand and kissed it. "Come back soon, *querida*!"

The others wandered over to the spread of food that included a large Joselito Iberian ham platter with a wide assortment of national cheeses, red tuna tartar with avocado toast, a seafood medley, and a host of other gourmet treats that had everyone ready to fill a plate. Ramone glanced over to see Annie heading out the glass doors to the dock and smiled, but shortly the smile faded. A tall blond man was heading out right behind her. Angry at himself for his moment of jealousy, he realized many people were coming and going, checking on their yachts or simply viewing these magnificent vessels created for speed.

Annie looked around at the sleek polished sailboats waiting for their hulls to slice through the water with cunning and finesse. She did not hear him approach so the sound of his voice calling her name startled her. When she turned around, Annie was looking at the face of a man with such perfect angles they could have been chiseled by a sculptor. A closer look in the fading sunlight showed her a head full of slicked-back blond hair, a casual growth of facial hair, and a tall muscular body. He hadn't said a word after calling out her name, but his demeanor made quite an impression.

"Yes, I'm Annie. And you are?"

The man came closer as if scrutinizing her. "My name is Hans. I am captain of the crew scheduled to race the *Nautilus* in this year's regatta. One of my crewmen broke his arm and can't race with us. His role is quite important, and without him we could be disqualified from racing. The dockmaster mentioned you might have racing experience."

"It would be the dream of a lifetime to crew in the race. What is the position?" Annie asked.

"It is the key role of sail trimmer. It often requires climbing the mast heeled over at high speeds. I'm afraid you are quite slight of frame for such a role. We have been warming up on the *Nautilus* all week to get her rhythm aligned with ours. The accident just happened today."

Annie's mind was whirling. It was too bad Robert wasn't here. When they had raced in Maine, he had a natural talent for judging the best sail position for speed. Tomás could sail but had no racing experience. To Hans, Annie asked, "Where is the *Nautilus*? May I see her?"

"Of course! The *Nautilus* is tied up at the end of the dock. She is a sixty-four-foot foiling monohull designed for speed. We were able to get her up to fifty knots! There she is...the silver one with the black accents." Hans's pride in this vessel showed.

Annie felt comfortable talking with this sailor. It always amazed her how boat lovers never seemed to be strangers. She asked, "Do you mind if I go aboard? I would love to get the feel of her."

It was at that moment Ramone, impatiently waiting for her return, came outside in time to see another man giving Annie his hand to climb aboard his boat. Like the bull that he regularly challenged when it sees the wave of a red cape, Ramone's fury launched him forward.

Seeing the hulk of a man barreling down the dock toward him, Hans sheepishly stepped off the boat and muttered, "It appears your husband has found us out, love!" The sound of Annie's laughter at this man's obvious sense of humor, slowed down Ramone, suddenly unsure of the situation. Given the big smiles on both the man's and Annie's faces, Ramone realized she was not in any danger.

Facing Hans, Annie said loud enough for Ramone to hear, "Hans, I would like to introduce you to Ramone, a brilliant Spanish matador who happens to be my fiancé. Ramone, meet Hans. He lost one of his crewmen today, and the dockmaster told him I had racing experience."

Realizing his mistake, Ramone shrugged. "Oh, I might be the cause of that. I spoke with the dockmaster earlier today and gave him your name."

Annie stepped off the boat and took Ramone's arm. "Thank you, my love, but I was just about to decline. It is a rather strenuous position, and in my condition, I don't want to take any chances." Hans nodded, understanding she was with child. "However, I have an idea. Hans, come with us. I need to use my father's phone. Let's see if we can fill your empty spot!"

# Chapter 26

$A$nnie came back to the table with determination on her face. Meghan cast a knowing smile at Celeste as both of them loved seeing Annie when she was on a mission! "Dad, I need to use your phone. Ramone, will you make the introductions?" Alex knew better than to question his daughter and handed her the phone.

To Hans, she asked, "If I can get someone...when would you need him and for how long?"

Hans answered, "I would need him here at the dock no later than six o'clock tomorrow morning to take the *Nautilus* out as a crew to see if he fits in with us. The regatta goes on for several days unless you are eliminated. We would start Friday and count on four to five days."

Annie understood and started dialing as she walked out onto the terrace. Captain Luis picked up on the second ring. Annie quickly explained the Hans's dilemma and asked if Roff might be interested in the sails trimming position and if he had racing experience.

"Aye, lass. That he does. He crewed on one of the fastest boats in the Mediterranean before he came on board the *Porto Banus*. That is why he is so trustworthy to have on hand no matter what the sea conditions. I will ask him." Annie could hear the captain explaining the situation, and Roff heartily agreed to help. She was already smiling when Captain Luis told her, "As long as Don Marco approves this and agrees to wait for us to leave after the regatta, Roff would be honored to do it!"

"That is so great! I will handle Dom. Have Roff meet Hans on the dock at 6:00 a.m. sharp. The boat is the *Nautilus*."

Annie came back to the table to work her wiles on her grand-father. Hans had already had a chance to tell them about his need for a specialized crewman. It was Don Marco who was in the process of recommending Roff. "He is a highly skilled young man. My captain chose him thanks to his fortitude and skills racing throughout the Mediterranean."

Hans had to admit, "He sounds perfect."

Annie gave them her brightest smile. "That's a good thing because he will be here tomorrow morning at six ready to sail!"

Hans had pulled up a chair to join them for dinner. Celeste told Annie, "Did you know Hans is from Hamburg? When he is not sailing, he is the owner of a well-known art gallery. Isn't that interesting?"

"Well, yes, indeed it is." Annie digested this new piece of information and determined to get to know their new acquaintance better. Ramone and Hans seemed to be getting along well and were deep in conversation. Now that Hans had a crewman to fill in, he was markedly more relaxed. It turned out Ramone had spent time in Hamburg with his uncle and had loved it.

Alex got up to escort Celeste and Marguerite to the buffet. All of a sudden, Annie realized she was starving! She was about to join them when a lovely young woman came over to Antonio, who, bound to his wheelchair, was looking rather bored with all this sailing talk. She had long brown hair and a dazzling smile that was being flashed at Antonio. Her bright yellow sundress hinted of a voluptuous figure. Annie heard her say, "I could not help noticing you from across the room and wondered whether you might need a little assistance at the buffet. My name is Veronica." Annie smiled to see Antonio's posture straighten and his infamous rogue smile surface. Meghan and Tomás noticed too, and the entire mood of the group lifted even higher.

Ramone pulled up a chair for Veronica. They squeezed in two extra place settings, and before they knew it, they had made two new friends. Dom and Gennie seemed to thoroughly enjoy Juan Carlos and his wife, Carlotta.

The sailors had an early day scheduled for practice, so they were among the first to leave. Hans shook hands with Don Marco and hugged Annie, thanking them both profusely for providing Roff to round out his crew. The young people planned to meet at a waterfront restaurant the next night. Veronica's answer to an invitation by Antonio to join them was a quick "Yes!"

Arriving home, they all agreed it was a festive evening and decided to turn in. Once in their room, Ramone asked, "Are you terribly disappointed you will not be racing, *querida*? Maybe we can find a place to watch them once the regatta begins?"

Annie shook her head. "Each part a crewman plays is important to the overall synchronization. I could have filled in for several other positions, but I knew the one he needed was beyond my skill level. Hans mentioned most of the regatta routes are offshore, which unfortunately means we won't be able to see it for any length of time from land." With a sigh, she continued, "Do you have any thoughts of what you would like to do tomorrow? I would love to have some alone time with you. Does that sound like something we can arrange?"

"I love the idea. Let's go to the beach in the morning and maybe carry some shorts for a hike later. I heard Cala Varques is most beautiful and doesn't get the crowds some of the other beaches get. It is surrounded by rocks and cliffs with an ideal spot to jump or dive from the cliff. You have to hike a distance from the road to get there, or we could go by sea on a catamaran."

"You know I would like the catamaran!" Picking up the Moroccan oils, she suggested, "In the meantime, let me properly tend those wounds." She barely got the words out before Ramone's passionate kiss took over all thought. Annie's response ignited him further to explore the miraculous chemistry they shared. For the moment, the oils were forgotten.

# Chapter 27

Careful not to wake Ramone, Annie saw that dawn was about to break so she hurried to throw on some shorts and a T-shirt. Quietly, she let herself out the bedroom door and headed downstairs and outside toward the casita. Roff was just coming out, ready to get to the yacht club to meet Hans. "*Hola*, Roff. I wanted to wish you luck today! You know, I am very jealous, but I am so excited you get to do this. I know Hans will appreciate your skill as much as I do. I can't wait to hear about it!"

Roff smiled his smile that always seemed genuinely happy. "I admit I have missed racing and those adrenaline-pumping moments when you just edge out a victory. What is this Hans like? Captains who are arrogant and full of ego rarely allow the team to function together, often leading to mistakes. Then, of course, those mistakes are never his."

Annie tried to sum up what she had learned about Hans. "Roff, I was only around him for a short while and not when he was under stress. He seemed levelheaded, especially when a certain matador misunderstood the situation and came charging at him!"

Roff laughed at that. "I'd better be on my way. Wish me luck!"

Annie waved. "Ha! With your skill, Hans is the lucky one!" The shuttle was waiting, and Roff ran to catch it. Leaning against the stone wall, Annie closed her eyes, imagining all the early morning activity on the dock at the yacht club. It was still early. It would be a while before the others got up. She went to the kitchen, poured herself a cup of tea, then on impulse grabbed a pen and paper from the desk. She knew the day ahead meant having a conversation with Ramone about the wedding. After hearing her mother's thoughts, her ideas about the wedding and its venue, which just days before had felt so certain, were now wavering.

Sitting in what now Annie called her favorite chair on the veranda, sipping her tea, she picked up the pen and began to write.

'Dearest Sabine,

*It is early morning here in Mallorca. It is surreal how this adventure began under such dire circumstances. But here we are. The island is filled with sailors participating in the annual Copa del Rey regatta that begins Friday. I know you would love it! One of the captains was searching for a replacement for a crewman who was injured, and he was referred to me. It would have been the opportunity of a lifetime, but the position of sail trimmer was beyond my strength and experience. It worked out Roff could take his place. I so wish I could watch them, but they will be racing far offshore. Mom told me they got word to you about what happened to Salvador. Ramone took his captivity and the death of his father hard as you can imagine. Fortunately, he has come out of the deep depression he was in. By the way, has Robert gotten to France yet? How is that going? To be honest, chérie, I am missing you more than you can imagine! Everything that has happened the last week has delayed plans about the wedding. Now that I am here and understanding what a long-distance destination venue would sacrifice, I am not sure I can do it. Nothing seems to add up right now. I so wish you were here to talk it through! I am spending today with Ramone and am determined to uncover exactly how he feels about this wedding. Look forward to seeing that perky face of yours soon!*

*Love always, Annie'*

Annie finished the letter as Dom walked over with the paper to sit with her. "Something told me you might have seen Roff off. He will do great, and the *Nautilus* is lucky to have him on board." Looking at his granddaughter closer, he added, "Since you were a young girl, I have known from your face whenever you had some issue troubling you. What is it this time?"

Smiling at the luck of having these few moments with her grandfather she so respected, Annie answered, "It is the wedding, Dom. My desire for an ancient-ritual wedding in reality would take a long time to coordinate. Many of my friends, old and new, have lives of their own, and I am not sure I can ask them to drop everything for such an adventure. Plus, Gennie said you both would not be able to make such a trip. I do love this villa, but we need to get back for Salvador's service, and it still leaves the gathering of friends a mystery as to how to make it work."

Dom was listening. "So is it place, people, or logistics? Annie, sometimes if you break the problem into pieces, the answers will surprise you."

Quietly with her eyes down, Annie said, "I found a dress."

With a chuckle, Dom asserted, "Ah, that says it all! Go where the dress goes. Problem solved!"

"But this baby continues to grow every day, and the dress won't fit before long," Annie said sadly.

Dom got serious. "The others are stirring. Annie, if your mind is always jumping ahead to what you think is supposed to come next, perhaps you are missing something. Don't forget the opportunity to fully live in the present. Sometimes you have to be patient and allow life to unfold at its own pace."

Annie tried to absorb the words her grandfather said and once again had that longing for her journal. For this moment, she was determined to make the most of right now to assure the best of what was to come.

# Chapter 28

When Annie got back to the room, Ramone had already showered and was heading down to breakfast. He pulled her close for a sensual kiss. Holding her, he looked deep into her eyes. "Just a reminder of last night and what our life together holds, *querida*. It is a beautiful day! Hurry, I'll be downstairs." Delighted with Ramone's optimism, Annie quickly showered and threw a few things in her backpack, trying to be ready for whatever the day would bring.

Once back in the kitchen, Maria brought her a plate of some Spanish omelet, fresh sausage, and grilled tomato to carry out to the pool area, where she saw Ramone watching Antonio and Meghan. Antonio was sitting on the side of the pool with his legs dangling in the water. Meghan stood in the water in front of him. Wanting a better look, Annie sat on one of the lounge chairs to watch. Meghan was lifting one of Antonio's legs at a time bending each one upward to his chest.

She repeated the motion about four times for each leg, then Antonio called out, "Watch this!" He proceeded to lift both legs together about six inches several times. "Right now, I can only do it after Meghan does the exercises, but I can move them!"

Meghan laughed and turned to Ramone. "Your brother is working hard. Our goal on this one is to get him to be able to do the full motion of the exercise on his own, whether with one leg or both."

Annie walked over and asked Meghan, "Are you staying here at the house today?"

"Yes, at least for the morning. Tomás has some work to do and said he would finish in time for a late lunch. Where are you two off to?" Meghan hopped up onto the side of the pool.

Annie answered, "We're taking a catamaran tour from Palma over to Cala Varques. The colors of the water are said to be quite brilliant! Then perhaps a hike."

Meghan enthusiastically answered, "That sounds great! Depending on how the day goes, there is a wine tour later that sounds interesting. We are all meeting back here to go to the waterfront tonight, right?" Then, teasing Antonio with a splash, "Our boy here has a date!" That pulled a hint of that old smile to Antonio's face, and both Annie and Ramone were overjoyed to see it.

Ramone picked one of the scooters for he and Annie to make their way to Palma to find the catamaran. Once they were winding through the streets of the Old Town, they got close to the Plaza de Toros. Annie called over the sound of the scooter, "It is quite distinctive, don't you think? Shall we take a quick tour? Dom said it was very impressive."

Abruptly, without turning his head, Ramone answered, "No, there is no time!" Annie noted the tension that overcame his body at her suggestion of taking the tour. Perhaps there was yet another topic that needed exploration today. Determined not to have an agenda, and to follow Dom's advice to let the day unfold at its own pace, she simply squeezed him tighter.

The dock was less busy this morning since most of the sailors were out practicing for the regatta. Annie and Ramone found the catamaran, *Mar Turquesa* (turquoise sea), and were greeted by the first mate, José. "*Hola!* Welcome, please come aboard after you remove your shoes. There will be ten of you sailing today. Feel free to sit anywhere you'd like."

Annie looked around. There was a cushioned area up on the bow where they would be under the sails and have a perfect view, so they stashed their backpacks and settled into their spots. Also on board was an older couple, a couple with two grammar school-age children, and another couple around Annie and Ramone's age. It was a friendly atmosphere, and everyone greeted each other warmly. The other young couple got a similar spot on the bow close to Annie and Ramone but not so close as to be intrusive.

The captain finished his safety information and outlined their day. "The winds are favorable today for a good sail. We anticipate leaving the port to the southwest, going around the southern end of the island to make our way north to anchor at Cala Varques. There will be time for swimming, snorkeling, and even cliff diving for those of you inclined. After the water activities, lunch will be served on board. We plan to make a short stop on the way back to Palma at the small fishing village of Cala Figuera. It is quite charming. Any of you who want to hike back from there will be free to do so, or if you are not inclined to hike, the *Mar Turquesa* will sail back to the port."

Annie snuggled into Ramone as they motored out to open water. She was aware he didn't know much about sailing, so she explained, "Once we get beyond the protection of the harbor, the captain will turn the bow into the wind. Doing that allows him to get the sails raised without the pull of the wind making it harder. It is when the sails are up and he turns away from the wind that the sails are properly trimmed to catch the wind. Then we are off!"

Ramone had marveled over Annie's love of sailing ever since he met her and hoped he would share her enthusiasm. She smiled when his eyes lit up the moment the sails grew taut, filled with the force of the wind, and they lunged forward through the water. The tack they were on took them farther away from shore, and it wasn't long before they could see the sailors from the regatta practicing in the distance. Annie strained to see them, looking specifically for the *Nautilus*. When Ramone spotted some of the racing vessels heeled over almost sideways with the crew balancing on the top for weight to offset the pitch, he got a rush glimpsing what it might be like to wield such control between nature and machine. He shook his head and said, "This is amazing! We are going fast and are hardly tipped."

Annie quickly answered, "That is because our catamaran has two hulls. The second hull provides the counterweight and keeps us stabilized. The boats registered for the regatta are all mono-hulls. The less friction they have pushing against the water, the faster they will go."

Their captain called to "Come about," and they turned to a northeasterly direction heading for Cala Varques.

Sailing along the coastline, the view from the sea was remarkable. Annie and Ramone were enjoying the beautiful day without a cloud in the sky and the breeze from the sails offsetting the warm summer heat. Annie thought this would be a good time to broach one of the topics she wanted to discuss. Tentatively, she opened with "Weren't you scheduled for a fight when all this happened?"

Ramone had not come to terms with his new feelings about his profession. He quietly answered, "I have missed two fights, and another was on the schedule for this weekend."

Annie, somewhat alarmed, asked, "Why didn't you say something? Do you need to get back?"

Avoiding the depth of the question, he answered, "No, I am on leave until the stitches are removed. We inquired yesterday about a doctor who will remove the stitches in a week, and I have an appointment then."

"So you are okay staying through the regatta? Is there something else, *mi amor*? It is unlike you to not want to go see the local bullring." Annie was holding his hand, trying to somehow convey that whatever his answer, it would be all right.

"*Querida*, it is not easy for me to speak about. For the first time, I feel like I understand why Papa was so angry about Antonio and me accepting the calling to follow our family tradition of matadors. I now see the impact it had on him when, as a child, he saw his own father gored. Every day I watch Antonio struggle to find some semblance of a normal life. I know the fears you feel about what I do. I think about our children and how I would react if our son or sons decided to train for the tradition. I guess I have lost my passion. Can you understand that even saying these words makes me feel like a traitor to what I have worked so hard to accomplish?"

There it was, Annie realized. Now she understood what was going through his head. She cuddled close to him. "Maybe you need this break. Have you considered it might be okay not to know the path you'll eventually take? It reminds me of the conversation I had with Dom this morning. I think he would tell you it is better to admit you don't know the direction rather than pretend you do. Simply acknowledge that you don't know where these feelings will lead you. Then try to choose the path that leads you to your clear purpose." Annie paused, thinking through their individual struggles with indecision. "Follow your heart, my love. I have promised you my support, and you will have it. I, too, am facing a change in direction and don't know the answer."

"What is it, *querida*? You can always talk to me," Ramone said, pulling her close.

"Maybe I should just ask how you really feel about the wedding plans. I have been talking about us having a spiritual wedding steeped in ancient ritual, but now I'm not sure."

Ramone nodded in understanding. "Do you somehow think we will be any less married if we do not have this kind of ceremony you speak of? I know what I want is to be married to you as soon as possible, and it wouldn't matter to me if it was in a barn. The commitment I make to you and our unborn child is forever, *querida*. No time, place, or ceremony will change that."

"Of course, you are right. Who would you want at our wedding?" Annie wondered.

"My mother and brother are here with us. So are your parents and grandparents. I know it sounds crazy, but other than them, I would really like to have El Amir present. He has done so much for both of us, and I think it would mean a great deal. What about you? Who is not here that you would like?"

"Definitely Sabine. Tomás and Meghan are here. I agree about El Amir. It would be wonderful to have Sarah and Mara here, but they are so far away."

"They would be just as far away if we had the wedding in one of your remote locations, right?"

"True. Does that mean you would be good with a wedding here in Mallorca, or once we get back to Marbella? Would we be able to coordinate a wedding so quickly? Oh my! I think I have the dress!" Annie jumped up with excitement and pulled Ramone into a passionate kiss. The couple across the bow couldn't help but notice and smiled. At that moment, they rounded the corner to the most brilliant turquoise water that made the sailboat they were on feel like it was suspended in air.

Holding Annie close, Ramone huskily said, "I think we have our answer, *querida!*"

# Chapter 29

José was giving advice about how to spend the time here in Cala Varques. They could see the rock climbers reaching the summit to dive off. The couple walked over to Annie and Ramone. They introduced themselves as Stephan and Carmina and explained they were on vacation here from Barcelona to see the regatta and do some major mountain hiking. Stephan asked, "Are you planning to do the cliff dive?"

Annie answered, "I plan to take advantage of the clarity of this beautiful water and snorkel, but, Ramone, what about your stitches?"

"I would like to try the cliff. I'll protect my face."

Carmina noticed Annie's condition and Ramone's injuries. "Ramone, come with us. We can go up together. We heard there is a natural stone bridge around this hill. We will have our water shoes with us when we jump. Annie, why don't you take yours and meet us on the beach to go explore?"

Annie was quick to respond, pushing her worry aside. "That sounds great! I am taking my underwater camera. It takes good shots out of the water as well. I will get a photo of each of you diving."

With that, Carmina laughed. "I may be jumping! No promises on a dive."

They took the ladder down into the water. José recommended fins for Annie with straps so they could fit over her water shoes. "Just leave the snorkel equipment on the beach when you go walk. It will be fine." The group spread out. The older couple were taken to the beach by dinghy. The two boys were already halfway up the cliff with their father clamoring behind them. Their mother was snorkeling like Annie, but she never made an overture. Annie was content to swim alone with some time to think. The water was cool and refreshing, not too cold, so it felt good to meander about, following whatever fish interested her. She looked up to see Ramone climbing the rock and waved. He saw her and waved back.

She was relieved she and Ramone had both of the conversations she was hoping for. It looked like they had a wedding to plan. But, for now, Ramone's feelings about his role as a matador needed to be put aside and let time help him determine what course would be right. Captivated with the abundance of sea life during her snorkel, Annie took picture after picture. With a jolt, she finally lifted her head to see them waving at her to get her attention. They were ready to go and for her to photograph them as promised!

Carmina was first. Annie could see her hesitation, but she quickly overcame it and jumped far out away from the rock. Stephan was next with a one-and-a-half flip that got applause and whistles from the group watching. Annie found herself holding her breath when it was Ramone's turn. She knew he had loved cliff diving in Greece years before, but she had never seen him dive. He sprung out into a butterfly dive, and for a moment it seemed like he was flying. He then bent his body, touched his toes, and landed in a perfect dive. Annie got a photo while he was suspended and another as he hit the water perfectly straight.

The three of them were swimming toward the beach. Annie continued her snorkeling aimed in the direction of the golden sand, then began to speed up when she saw Ramone reach the shore. She looked a little closer at this beautiful man who was soon to be her husband. What was it? Ah...where was his usual stern demeanor? Ramone had never easily made friends and often distanced himself from strangers. That was one of the reasons she loved to explore his layers to find how sweet and loving he was to her. But here he was, deep in a congenial conversation with Stephan and Carmina. And just last night it was the same thing with Hans. Hmmm. Was it the harsh discipline required of him each time he fought the bull? Now that he was questioning that as his future, was he letting down his guard enough to allow potential friends in? Annie made friends easily and she often felt like an open book. This new development in her love's personality would be interesting to watch.

Ramone was there to help Annie with her equipment, and she was quick to check his face and say, "Your dive was so amazing! I got some great photos!" Looking at Stephan, she added, "And your flip was outstanding!"

Carmina was shaking her head but smiling. "Please don't say anything about my simple jump. But, hey, I did it!"

Annie looked at this pixie of a girl with a streak of red running through her short dark hair. "You were great! I can't believe you jumped so far out away from the rock!"

Annie was happy to see Ramone was in good spirits. "Stephan and Carmina are staying at an inn on the waterfront in Old Town. They have given me some ideas for a restaurant for tonight. They are planning to hike back from the fishing village."

Looking at Ramone, Annie asked, "Are we doing that?"

Before Ramone could answer, Stephan said, "It is a good distance from Cala Figuera to Palma. I am fairly certain you would not make it back in time to meet your friends." After a moment, he added, "See that pathway going around that hill? I think that is where the arched bridge is. Let's go!"

The rough path was carved into the rocky hillside among pine trees and low Mediterranean scrub. Looking down at the water, Annie marveled at all the colors of blue in the water. Aloud she said, "Look at the sea! Our catamaran looks like it is drifting in air. And this rock! It feels like we are walking on the moon!" Everyone laughed, enjoying the incredible views.

They crossed a small cove and around the next bend, there it was! The Pont de Cala Varques, or natural bridge, before them was huge and stood over a hundred feet high above the sea. It would have been formed millions of years ago from a combination of volcanic eruptions and erosion from rain and wind. What a sight! Annie asked someone on the path to take a photo of the four of them, dwarfed on top of this mammoth stone structure. They all agreed what a special place this was.

After lunch back on board filled with Mallorcan specialties like olive-oil-infused bread with garlic and tomato, *Sobrasada* spicy sausage, empanadas, and fish stew, the captain pulled up anchor and moved to Cala Figuera. Stephan explained to Ramone and Annie about the wide variety of hiking routes Mallorca is known for, particularly through the Tramuntana mountain ridge on the north part of the island. He spoke of the Dry Stone route that takes up to eight or nine days for the entire hike, but there were parts that connected charming little villages they planned to see and explore.

Carmina added with excitement, "One of the hikes we are most interested in doing is an annual event that will take place after the regatta has finished. It is the *Des Güell a Lluc a Peu*, the Night of the Pilgrims. It is a pilgrimage really, a challenging night hike up to the Santuari de Lluc. It is supposed to be one of the most inspiring and idyllic places on Mallorca. Roads are cut off to cars for the night, and thousands show up around 11:00 p.m. to start the long trek to the monastery, over twelve hundred feet above sea level in the middle of the mountains. Both young and old participate, but many won't make it."

Annie looked at Ramone, her curiosity piqued, then asked Carmina, "When is this pilgrimage?"

Carmina answered, "It is two weeks from tomorrow. We plan to stay long enough to do it before going back to Barcelona. We will be hiking other routes between now and then. Why don't you come join us on one of our hikes?"

# Chapter 30

The stop at Cala Figuera would be a short one of around thirty minutes. The awe-inspiring approach by boat was picturesque as they motored slowly over shimmering turquoise water surrounded by lush green fig trees growing everywhere among rocky low cliffs. The numerous fig trees were where the bay's name came from. Annie smiled at the fishermen's houses that came right down to the edge of the water, with the green color of many of the doors and shutters mimicking the color of the fig trees. Both sides of the harbor were lined with colorful wooden fishing boats. This appeared to be one of those rare villages where time seemed to have stood still.

Groups of fishermen sat in the harbor mending their nets, oblivious to the meandering boat's arrival. The most activity was around the local street market. Annie spoke up, "It is charming here!"

Carmina commented, "Yes. There is a natural park just northeast of the bay where we plan to hike. It goes through the town of Mondragó. Before we say goodbye, we should exchange contact information."

The girls were writing down the information when Stephen looked directly at Ramone and said, "I didn't see it at first with the wounds on your face, but you are Ramone Sanchez, the matador, right? I was supposed to be at your exhibition fight earlier this week. I am a big fan of yours. When it was canceled, they said your father was injured. But it looks like you were the one who was injured."

This was the last thing Ramone expected, and he was uncertain how to respond. Annie gently took his hand, encouraging him. Stephan sensed his uneasiness. "Hey, man, sorry. If you don't want to talk about it, that's fine."

Ramone shook his head. "Actually I was kidnapped and roughed up a bit. My father was killed saving me. Sorry I missed the expedition."

Stephan realized he had touched a nerve. "Ramone, I apologize. I had no business infringing upon your privacy. Do you know when you will fight again?"

"The stitches have to be removed first. The other wounds are superficial, but probably not until after our wedding," Ramone responded.

Not letting up, Stephan asked, "Have you considered seeing a fight while you're here? I heard there was a good matador in town for this weekend's festivities. I would love for you and Annie to be our guests."

Annie had watched a total reversal in Ramone's mood and quickly said their polite goodbyes and hoped they would see them again for a possible hike. No matter how Annie tried to start a conversation on the sail back, Ramone remained quiet.

Once they returned home, Ramone went to their room for a shower without any hint he might want company. Annie could feel a restless uncertainty about her that eluded mere words. She wondered at her hesitation to tell Gennie or her mother, or even Meghan, about the decision she and Ramone made about having the wedding here. Did he even feel the same way as earlier?

Wandering out to the veranda, Annie noticed a package wrapped in tissue with her name attached. Opening it, she found a new journal and pen. The journal had a leather cover with gold-leaf-beveled letters that spelled WANDERLUST. How did her grandfather continue to understand exactly what she needed?

Dom had been patiently waiting for Annie to return and find the gift; however, he strode nonchalantly out to the veranda with his book as if to read. Annie smiled, knowing Dom wanted to give her space, but she walked over to him and put her arms around him. "Thank you, Dom." Turning it over, she asked, "Why WANDERLUST?"

Dom settled into the chair beside her. "The goal is not to wander aimlessly. Instead wander with purpose. Remember, you can choose to be happy just as easily as you choose to be sad. The choice, my dear, no matter what the situation, is always up to you. Look ahead, Annie. Choose what you see as the best outcome for everyone involved. Your efforts can make a difference in making that happen. Your journey has already gained you much insight. Don't be afraid to pull from those experiences."

Annie tried to grasp the depth of what Dom was saying and how she could determine the best outcome for all of them, when Roff came bounding in somewhat out of breath. "*Hola!* I am so glad I found you both together!"

Annie was first to ask, "How did it go? Will the *Nautilus* be able to race in the regatta?"

Roff was quick to answer. "Yes, Captain Hans seemed pleased with my performance. The *Nautilus* will compete in the laser class, which means we will race against the king! The king's crew has been practicing, and he will join them at the helm tomorrow for the last practice day. Today, we actually outmaneuvered the fifty-foot Finland boat that is on loan to the Spanish navy! That is the boat the king will captain. There are over 150 boats from twenty-nine countries participating! It is all so exciting. But wait, Juan Carlos asked me to give you this." Roff handed a sealed envelope to Don Marco. Dom began to read aloud:

'Don Marco,

*I heard you loaned your firsthand to the Nautilus. We appreciate your help. If you intend to take the Porto Banus out as a spectator boat during the regatta, please allow me to loan you one of my crewmen to fill any void. There is an area close to an uninhab-*

*ited island where we get a good vantage point. If you anchor there, it would be our pleasure to host you for lunch on board our yacht. I look forward to hearing from you at your earliest convenience.*

*Sincerely, Juan Carlos'*

Looking at Annie, Dom could see the delight in her eyes about going and said, "Roff, tell Captain Luis to ready the *Porto Banus* to sail the day after tomorrow. We will go to the spectator area to watch the beginning of the first day's races and join Juan Carlos and his wife for lunch." Thinking for a moment, he added, "After lunch, we will be well positioned to sail over to Ibiza for the afternoon."

Roff left to deliver the message, and Annie's enthusiasm showed when she said to Dom, "Friday sounds fabulous! We seem to be here at the perfect time! Have you heard about the night hike up to the monastery in Lluc? It is an annual event, actually a pilgrimage, where thousands take over the roads and hike into the mountains overnight to reach the basilica. I'd like to learn more, but I think Ramone and I might do it. We met a couple today who told us about it. They are here for the regatta and the hiking. But, Dom, they recognized Ramone and had tickets to his exhibition fight in Barcelona. Ramone had been so upbeat until then. After that conversation, which included telling Stephan about Salvador, he withdrew into himself." Ramone came out in time to hear Annie's last remarks about him and was not happy.

*****

Annie took a deep breath and realized she was in one of those moments she had to make a choice how to react to him. She walked over to Ramone, took his arm, and said to Dom, "Please excuse us."

119

When they sat next to each other on the chaises by the pool, Ramone grumbled, "You were talking about me behind my back. None of that was anyone else's business."

Annie mentally crossed her fingers in hopes she would say the right thing; she knew her next words were important. Taking both his hands, she began, "Ramone, you are the world to me. It is inconceivable what you went through, and I can only imagine the grief you must feel about your father. I was not intentionally talking behind your back. Dom gave me this journal." Annie handed it to him. "I told him we learned about the Night of the Pilgrims hike to the monastery from a couple we met today. That led to sharing Stephan's recognition of you and the mention of the Barcelona exhibition. That is when all the good conversation we had earlier seemed to vanish. What you didn't hear is that I was about to say you have my total support no matter what you decide to do next. And please understand, every person here in this home feels the same."

"*Querida*, I do know that in my heart. The only way I can describe it is there is unbearable pain connected to fighting right now. For the last few days, I haven't had to think about a fight, and it has been like a breath of fresh air. For now, I do not want to be recognized for what I was but rather for who I am."

Quietly, Annie reasoned, "My love, you are a famous and, might I add, very handsome matador. It is inevitable that you will be recognized. Remember how we walked on the boardwalk in Marbella and people would stop to say hello? Their intentions are good. Maybe if you just react like you always did, with a friendly word and smile, then it's over."

Annie went to Ramone's lounger, and sat on his lap with her arm around him and head on his shoulder. "Always know you can trust me, but I have a favor to ask."

"Anything, *querida*," Ramone said, stoking her hair.

"I know there are big plans for tonight, but I am not feeling up to a large group."

Concerned, he asked, "Are you okay? Is it the baby?"

"No, we're fine. It was a long day, and I am tired. There is a part of me that would like to have a quiet dinner here at home. If a wedding here is feasible, we should be thinking about how to make it happen. It looks like we will be gone all day on Friday so there is not a lot of time to plan."

"We are bound together, *querida*. Just like you support me, I support you. Normally I would go to help with Antonio, but with Tomás and Meghan there, he will be fine. It is good to see them becoming friends. I think Meghan's exercises might be helping."

And just like that, a crisis was avoided. What a nice way to start her new journal. Annie left Ramone to tell the others they were staying home while she went upstairs to freshen up.

# Chapter 31

*How can I continue like this?* Antonio, still in his room, felt himself sliding into a depression. Always having to wait for someone to come help him get ready for the day or even get in and out of a vehicle made even the easiest tasks seem overwhelming. Here he was waiting for his mother, which annoyed him further. He had to be on her time frame to be ready for the evening. And here he was with a date. The thought of it was absurd. He had not been on a date since his accident. Sure, Sabine had been nice to him, probably out of pity, but he hadn't attempted a real date. All he could think of was all the things he couldn't do that he was an expert at in his previous life before the accident.

Marguerite knocked on his door, then walked in to find Antonio irritable and out of sorts. "What is it, son? You have planned a pleasant evening ahead, and Tomás and Meghan are happy to help however they can."

"What about Ramone?" Antonio practically growled.

Marguerite kept her tone matter of fact. "He and Annie are staying in tonight. Ramone says they had a strenuous day, and Annie is quite tired."

"That's it. I'm not going either," Antonio said with a challenge in his eyes.

Realizing what she saw was an abundance of self-pity, she tried to get to the root of it. "It will be a fun evening with friends, and you have a beautiful girl waiting for you! Is that it? Veronica?"

Antonio petulantly said, "What woman would want me like this? I can't open the door for her. I can't pull out her chair. I can't dance. And I can't even talk about all the other physical things I can't do!"

With a little exasperation in her voice, Marguerite answered, "Son, you are alive! You are devilishly handsome. Are you so intent on defining yourself by your infirmity? It sounds a little narrow-minded to me. Are you going to waste your days hiding when every moment is a gift? Maybe Veronica won't be able to handle your current limitation, and I mean current because no one has implied this is permanent. And if that is the case, let her go. It is her loss. Take a chance, Antonio! You are making progress with Meghan. Be determined to see it through and put your energy into it." Going to him to rub the back of his shoulders, she continued, "You're not a quitter, son. Keep going, keep moving, keep working. You've got this. Now let's get you ready!"

With a new sense of determination, Antonio absorbed his mother's words. In his heart, he knew he was a fighter, not a coward. Maybe he was still reeling from his father's death. He took a deep breath and resolved not to use this weakness as an excuse. He just needed to find a way around it.

When he was dressed, Antonio added a touch of hair gel to hold his brown hair slicked back as well as a dab of his favorite cologne. When he smiled at his mother, all she could say was, "Veronica will undoubtedly not be the only female eyeing you tonight!" And with a wink, she added, "Try to be kind." There was his devilish smile, and Marguerite couldn't resist a subtle shake of her head and roll of her eyes. To herself, she thought this might unfold to be quite an interesting evening for him.

Joining Tomás and Meghan, Antonio recognized their affection for him was real, no matter his infirmity, and he determined to move forward with gratitude rather than pity. Looking at both of them fondly, he said, "Let's go! I think there is a large mouth-watering sea bass waiting for me."

Tomás nudged Antonio on the arm. "Not to mention a lovely young lady!"

# Chapter 32

Annie saw Ramone having a drink with Dom and her dad when she came downstairs. Relieved he seemed in better spirits than earlier, she went to find her mom and Gennie. Not surprisingly, she found them in the kitchen speaking with Yuba. He was just leaving. Loving how comfortable she was with these two women she had loved her whole life, Annie hopped up on the counter and reached over for a handful of macadamia nuts.

Gennie was kneading dough. "We didn't expect you and Ramone for dinner, so we gave Yuba and the chef the night off. However, there is plenty of food, and this gives us a good chance to visit. Marguerite is changing and should be down soon."

"What can I do to help?" Annie asked.

"Why don't you slice some potatoes and onions? We will add your favorite *tortillas de patates*." Annie enthusiastically took over that job, wondering how she would bring up the topic of the wedding. This subject affected all of them, so she wanted to wait until they were together.

When dinner was finally served and they were seated, Ramone reached over for her hand in encouragement. Annie began, "There is no question none of us was expecting to have this time together on this island under these circumstances. But here we are. Fate has intervened, and it is time to rethink the wedding plans. Ramone and I discussed it this morning. Life is precious, and, as we all just saw, things can change in a moment." Looking at Ramone with love in her eyes, she continued. "The intensity of the love that we share made me want a deeply spiritual ceremony, so I was looking for ancient tribal ideas to bring into the wedding.

What I had neglected to see was that such a wedding would lose what is most important, the love and support of all those we love."

Celeste got up suddenly, and Alex asked, "Where are you going?"

"To get a pen and paper to take notes, of course. We have a wedding to plan!" Celeste answered rather sassily.

To which Alex responded, "Of course!" Everyone was smiling but Marguerite.

"Mamà, is something wrong?" Ramone asked.

Marguerite, obviously uncomfortable, said, "Son, I received word this morning that Salvador's body was released for transport back to Marbella. They will prepare him for the crematory. Then we need to hold his service."

The conversation moved throughout the table with thoughts and ideas. It came up that Marguerite, Ramone, and Antonio could go home for the service and come back, but Annie would not hear of letting Ramone go through that without her. Then it was suggested to have the ashes put in an urn and do the service when they got back after the wedding. That didn't totally satisfy Marguerite, but the idea did allow them to proceed with the discussion of what a wedding here would be like.

Celeste, careful to be sensitive to Marguerite's feelings, asked Annie, "Were you thinking of a wedding here at the villa? You know Sabine would want to come."

Ramone took the opportunity to step in. "Annie and I found out today about an annual tradition that is a pilgrimage up to the monastery in Lluc. It is in about two weeks, and we were thinking of going to the monastery tomorrow to see if it seemed like a good wedding venue. Perhaps we could somehow add the pilgrimage into the whole experience to give Annie a little of what she is looking for?"

Dom interjected, "I have heard about this event. Both young and old participate." Ignoring Gennie's raised eyebrows, he repeated, "Young and old make the hike together. Any who tire and can't complete the walk can take the shuttle back to Palma. It runs throughout the night. Annie, we have tomorrow free before the regatta begins. Why don't we make an outing of it and enjoy lunch in Lluc? We can tour the monastery and see what options there are on such short notice. I am happy to help any way I can. Juan Carlos might be a good connection as well."

Everyone seemed to like the idea. Celeste finished with the question, "Is there anyone else to invite who could get here on short notice?"

Annie and Ramone answered in unison, "El Amir."

It was Alex who nodded. "He is quite an amazing young man. He has the means to fly here. I am sure he would come if asked."

Gennie added, "If Sabine comes, perhaps Claudette can come with her. I haven't seen my sister in years, and I know she would love to share this. I doubt Francoise and Marta could get away from the vineyards with harvest so close."

Annie's eyes were glistening as she listened to them all. Having Sabine here would mean the world to her. If only there was a way for Sarah and Mara to join them too. The reality was that the idea was most likely impossible, but she wanted to ask anyway so they knew she wanted them.

Conversation was flowing about the possibilities and how they could all help. Marguerite brought up some of what Antonio was going through and how much she appreciated what Meghan was doing for him. Ramone overheard that and vowed to do as much as he could to help his brother get stronger. Inevitably, it came up that Ramone was recognized by Stephan.

Dom was the first one to respond, directly to Ramone. "Juan Carlos recognized you immediately, and spent most of last night trying to get me to convince you to do a fight here in Mallorca. I told him the timing was wrong. You needed to heal. He is not someone who takes no for an answer very often."

Suddenly wary, Ramone asked, "Will I be pressured on board his yacht Friday?"

Dom quickly said, "I have your back, son. I won't let that happen. The invitation is there only if you choose to accept it."

\*\*\*\*\*

Antonio was in the midst of a jovial debate with Tomás and Meghan when they arrived home and joined the group on the veranda. Their lively banter suggested there might be some interesting tales from their evening out. Meghan spoke up first. "It appears Antonio has quite the fan in Veronica!"

Tomás was laughing and patting Antonio on the back, then mimicking Veronica with a deliberate southern drawl. "I just want to hear all about bullfighting and what all you're planning to do on the island! All the men have been off sailing, and I've been bored to death!" That got a laugh from everyone listening.

Ramone smiled to see his brother blushing uncharacteristically. Showing a little mercy, he changed the subject. "Was Hans at dinner?"

Meghan answered, "Yes, and he could not stop raving about Roff's performance today! He actually said with Roff on board they had a good chance of placing in the top two or three overall in their category. He didn't stay long after dinner since he has an early start tomorrow. Hans said he was sorry to miss you and Annie tonight and hopes to run into you at some point during the week. He said he plans to stay for a few more days on the island to relax and do some hiking after all the sailing. It sounds like Mallorca is known for its many hiking trails on the island."

"I imagine the hiking trails are not wheelchair friendly." Antonio meant it as a joke, but there was no denying he resented not being able to participate with them. Annie and Ramone glanced at each other simultaneously, realizing the pilgrimage hike would leave Antonio out.

Ramone decided the best thing to do would be to at least bring the subject out on the table. "Annie and I are discussing having our wedding here in Mallorca. There is a night hike we heard about. It is an annual event where thousands come to make the ultimate effort to hike throughout the night up into the mountains to the monastery of Lluc. It is scheduled in about two weeks. We are thinking of going to Lluc tomorrow to explore and consider it as a possible wedding venue."

"So, you can get there by car? You don't have to hike?" Antonio asked.

Annie answered, "Yes, of course. There is a regular village around the basilica. We will know more about it after tomorrow." As an afterthought, she added, "Would any of you like to come with us?"

"We will be out all day Friday. Antonio and I have work to do here!" Antonio rolled his eyes at Meghan, but you could see the growing affection between them. Meghan seemed determined to get Antonio out of his chair.

Tomás was planning to work most of the day. Marguerite decided to stay home to lend her support to Antonio and Meghan.

Gennie got up to retire to her room. Before she left, she said to Annie and Ramone, "You can count on us, *chérie!*" Dom gave each of them a hug, nodding, then he followed Gennie.

Annie stifled a yawn herself. Her parents planned to go with them so there would be the six of them tomorrow. The only ones left on the veranda were Ramone and Antonio. Ramone seemed intent upon finding out more about Veronica. Annie didn't want to go to bed alone so she snuggled against Ramone's shoulder and promptly fell asleep.

Ramone pressed, "So, brother, tell me about this girl. Do you like her?"

"She's pretty enough, and she knows it. I'm fairly certain she's used to being the center of attention." Antonio gave a small laugh and continued. "She talks a lot! It is hard to get a word in. Veronica kept hinting to Meghan where I could hear that she would love to be invited to join us Friday on the *Porto Banus.*"

"Well, did you invite her?" Ramone chuckled as he asked. It had been a while since he and Antonio had enjoyed such an easy camaraderie.

He quickly got his answer. Antonio was emphatic. "No way! An entire day with her would wear me out!" Changing the subject, he asked, "What about you? How did tonight go?" Pointing quietly at Annie, he added, "Is everyone all right with doing the wedding here in Mallorca?"

"I think so. Tomorrow will tell us a great deal about whether we can accomplish the spiritual ceremony Annie wants for this wedding. We also want to be sure Sabine and El Amir can make it." Ramone immediately noticed the change in Antonio when he mentioned Sabine.

"I thought she went home to see some boyfriend?" Antonio tried to sound nonchalant, but he was listening closely.

"Yes, Robert is visiting from Maine, but he should be gone by the time we have the wedding."

"And what about El Amir? When did you change your mind about him?" Antonio asked.

"I suppose I was so busy fighting my own jealousy, I didn't stop to see all the good things he has done. He is an honorable man. I see that now. It's time I trust him."

# Chapter 33

The sun rising over the mountains illuminated the windows, giving a warm golden glow to the suspended bed. Annie was basking in it, lying naked next to Ramone, drifting between sleep and consciousness. "Ouch," she mumbled, thinking he had somehow bumped her stomach. She dozed again and snuggled closer. In his sleep, it was pure instinct to react by wrapping his arms tighter around her.

When she felt it a second time, she sat up suddenly awake. Ramone pulled at her to lie back down. Her body was tense, and Annie was obviously concerned. That put him on full alert. "What is it, *querida*? Are you all right?"

"I felt something. Oh no, what if something is happening with the baby? I couldn't stand it!"

Ramone put his hand possessively on her stomach and concentrated on keeping them both calm. Then, it was so slight he almost missed it. She felt it too. The smile on his face warmed her heart when he said, "It would seem someone is saying good morning and that today would be a great day to plan a wedding!"

Incredulous, Annie said, "He's *moving?*"

"Have you thought this child might be a 'she,' *querida*?" Ramone teased.

Annie took a moment to wonder if women throughout the ages formed this unique bond of love as they felt the first movements of their unborn child. The awareness of this treasure she carried came with awe and responsibility. To Ramone, she said, "*Mi amor*, it is time we get married!" The gaze in her eyes as she moved in to kiss him was enough to lead them into more intimate endeavors.

By the time they dressed and got downstairs, Meghan was already working with Antonio by the pool. Ramone ventured out to watch them while Annie went to the kitchen to fix them a plate of breakfast and hopefully run into her mom. When Gennie saw Annie, she took the two plates Maria had prepared earlier to warm them in the oven. Celeste sat at the counter working on her list. When she saw the glow on her daughter's face, she put the pen down. "What is it? Are you excited about our outing today?"

"Oh, Mom, I felt the baby move for the first time. At first, I was scared and didn't know what it was. Ramone felt it too. When I realized that our child was moving, I was overwhelmed with a feeling of love but also responsibility for this tiny person growing inside me!" Annie saw the knowing look her mom and Gennie shared and somehow knew she had joined womankind feeling this special gift. She hugged them both.

Celeste suggested, "Why don't you eat your breakfast so we can go check out Lluc?"

Nodding, Annie took the breakfast out to the pool. Fascinated, she watched Antonio seated on the side of the pool, this time with two weights around his ankles. Meghan told him, "Now lift your legs. It doesn't have to be far. Small movements are perfectly fine. Try to lift them together, but if you need to do it separately, that is okay too." Annie could see Antonio straining to move his legs beneath the surface of the water. Meghan then explained to Annie and Ramone, "We will be doing a series of exercises that might seem repetitive, but we are trying to strengthen both the leg muscles and awaken the part of the brain that controls them."

To Antonio, Ramone encouraged, "You are working hard, brother. You can do this!" He saw his mother come out in a swimsuit, obviously ready to help, and added, "Surrounded by two lovely ladies, you're a lucky fellow. Perhaps we should invite Veronica over as well?" The glare Antonio gave Ramone caused everyone to break out in laughter. Soon Antonio laughed too, then went back to concentrating on his exercises.

*****

The fact that Don Marco was prepared was no surprise to any of them, and they all awaited the stories he would tell. Alex drove so Dom could give his full attention to the city of Lluc and its monastery. The drive up into the *Serra de Tramuntana*, or Tramuntana Mountains, had steep inclines and hairpin curves, giving a preview of what an overnight hike to this place might be like. The higher they got, the more spectacular the views. They passed beautiful villages that could provide water, coffee, or fruit along the hike. Two in particular, Santa Maria and Binissalem, looked interesting as they passed through to come back at another time to explore a little further.

Dom showed them a map pointing to the northwest of the island. "This area, in the municipality of Escorca, has the highest mountains on the island. UNESCO has even made the Sierra de Tramuntana a World Heritage Site! Lluc is considered to be the most important pilgrimage site on Mallorca. Legend has it that in the thirteenth century, a Moorish shepherd named Lluc found a statue of a dark-skinned Virgin Mary in these mountains. Overjoyed by his discovery, the boy took the statue to the local priest, who gave it a place of honor in the church. However, the next day the statue disappeared from the church without any explanation. The priest searched and searched, then finally discovered it back up in the mountains where it was originally found. The priest and the locals were convinced this 'miracle' meant the Virgin Mary wanted to stay exactly on that spot, so they built a small chapel which became the origins of Santuari de Lluc."

Annie reflected, "It sounds similar to what happened at Monserrat."

"That is true. You might find it interesting that the architect, Antoni Gaudí, offered some significant embellishments on parts of the interior around the turn of the twentieth century. Gaudí actually participated in one of the annual Night of the Pilgrims walks you are considering. This morning, we have a curator meeting us to show us the sanctuary and the gardens." They arrived at the monastery to find what looked like a stoic stone fortress. Annie and Ramone exchanged a questioning look, simultaneously thinking, *get married at this place?*

The curator's tour took them through the entrance into the flagstone courtyard and along the arched walkway. She guided them past the star-shaped fountain and through the gardens. From the moment Annie saw the sprawling property, she knew this was not her wedding venue. However, the incredible basilica was exceptional with its ornate gold trimmings, and Annie could see the strong influences of Gaudí. She knew of Guillem Reinés, the architect who did most of the work under his mentor's direction. Studying more closely, she marveled at the baroque-style intricacy and appreciated that the basilica had been named "The Golden Room."

Annie took Ramone over to the blessing wall. People left hopes or dreams on a slip of paper with a prayer that the Madonna would grant the wish. "I would like to leave one for Antonio to recover quickly."

"Ah yes, *querida*, that is good. And I would like to leave one to ask that we find the right place to be married!"

Before the guide finished the tour, she told them a little more about the upcoming pilgrimage. "The distance along the country roads and steep inclines through the mountains is about fifty kilometers, so it is difficult for even the most fit without such inclines. It normally takes around ten or eleven hours, after a late-night start. There will be children holding lanterns and locals providing water, coffee, and fruit. It is a very spiritual sojourn. Many of the pilgrims like to push their endurance at this event to pay homage to the Virgin Mary."

Saying goodbye, she finished by suggesting lunch at the outdoor café on the property. In an effort to cover the frustration they all felt about not finding a wedding venue, lunch sounded like a great idea to regroup. The weather was perfect, not too hot with a pleasant breeze.

The waiter had just taken their order when Annie and Ramone noticed Stephan and Carmina crossing the courtyard. They both stood up to call them and wave. Annie explained, "This is the couple we met at Cala Varques yesterday, Stephan and Carmina. Great! They are coming over."

Alex quickly stood up and pulled over a couple of chairs. "Please join us! We have plenty to share."

Annie was quick to introduce them and gave them both a kiss hello on both cheeks. Carmina was full of enthusiasm to share some of their hiking stories. It was clear to Annie that Stephan was still worried he had somehow offended Ramone. When Annie kicked Ramone under the table, he got the message. He looked straight at Stephan with a reassuring smile and asked what they were doing in Lluc.

Stephan replied, "Lluc is one of the best starting and stopping points for the many hiking trails on the island. We walked from Valldemossa this morning. I think it might be the most picturesque town we have seen on the island so far. Carmina, what do you think?"

"I agree. If I could paint, there were so many areas to capture with its narrow cobblestone streets and the welcoming terra-cotta flowerpots hanging from the stone walls. You have to go there!" All Annie could think of was how special it might be to Sarah and Mara to paint such a place.

Stephan added, "Along the way, we passed mountain goats; farmers tending their olive, almond, or citrus trees; and views from the mountains down to the sea, where each one seemed to exceed the last!"

Don Marco was fascinated by this young couple. "Will you participate in the pilgrimage?"

It was Carmina who answered. "Yes, that and the regatta are the main reasons we are here. What about all of you? What brings you to Lluc?"

"My granddaughter and this young man are looking for a wedding venue. We thought this might be it. Unfortunately, it is not what we'd hoped."

Carmina looked at Stephan. "What about Vista Hermosa? The view from there is so inspiring! I think the property was owned by an Archduke in the 1800s. He built an open-air marble temple, more like a gazebo or pavilion, on the side of a cliff, and you can see amazing vistas literally in every direction! It is now a museum, so it might be worth considering."

Annie asked, "Is it far?" Then looking at Dom, "Perhaps we could stop there on the way home?"

While Carmina gave directions to Alex, Stephan pulled Ramone aside. "Hey, I want to apologize for yesterday. I can't imagine how hard what you're going through is. Hopefully, I can make it up to you. Why don't you join us for one of our hikes next week?" They agreed to stay in touch.

Both Stephan and Carmina wished them luck at Vista Hermosa. Carmina laughed and shared, "I have talked Stephan into a shorter hike to a spa this afternoon. With all this hiking, I need a little pampering!" Annie hugged them both and allowed herself a little hopeful anticipation about this new venue possibility.

# Chapter 34

The scenic road through the mountains was beautiful, but the closer they got to the sea, at this elevation, the views were breathtaking. They saw the sign for Vista Hermosa and pulled into a surprisingly empty parking area. At first glance, the building had some of the fortress features of the monastery that showed it was designed to defend in centuries past. The tower looked original with obvious signs of restoration through the years. The difference lay in the welcoming approach through the courtyard's open vestibule with the soothing sound of a fountain and arched wooden doors set into the most unusual stone walls. The sign beside the door showed the museum was closed; it did not reopen until 3:30 p.m.

Celeste suggested, "Why don't we see if we can look around the outside?"

Annie took Ramone's hand and quietly said, "I feel good about this place."

Alex found a path around to the right, so they followed it around the side. What they saw when they rounded the corner had them nodding in unanimous agreement. It was stunning. The original house was built into the side of the mountain; therefore, the property was terraced in layers, and nothing obstructed the view of the nearby mountains, brilliant blue sea and islands off in the distance. Marveling at the design of the structure and its gardens, Annie saw what Carmina spoke about. Projecting away from the mountain was a natural stone peninsula. At the end of it rested a pristine white marble pavilion in a neoclassical style. Annie tugged at Ramone. "Let's go out there."

Celeste, Alex, Gennie, and Dom wisely stayed behind to let the young couple experience this place, but there were tears in Celeste's eyes. She knew this was the place. Looking at the three people she loved as deeply as her daughter, she said, "We need to find a way to make this happen."

Annie and Ramone walked out the narrow walkway to the end where the temple-like structure with the dome ceiling and ionic columns awaited. There was a pedestal in the center that would be perfect for flowers. Standing in it so high in the air was surreal. Ramone reached for her and kissed her deeply. Huskily he said, "I could wait for you here, *querida*, and watch you come to me in this special place." Calculating their direction, he added, "I imagine at sunset the colors of all these surroundings will be magical."

"This feels so good to me." She gazed lovingly at him, and he kissed her once again. Annie waved at her mom to bring the others. "I want them to see this! It is a little like a very tall bow of a ship." When her parents and grandparents joined them, no one could stop talking about the mystical ambience that surrounded this gazebo.

Celeste handed Annie a couple of brochures she had gotten from the rack at the door of the museum. She said, "The terrace area also enjoys this view and would make the perfect place for a reception. Now we simply need to find out when it is available and when we can get the guests here."

Annie looked at her grandfather. "Do you think Juan Carlos can help us book Vista Hermosa? I think it is perfect. We will see him tomorrow for lunch on his yacht, right?"

Dom answered, "Yes, but I think I will go ahead and make the call to him when we get back to the villa to see if he can connect me to how I can reserve it. Are we aiming for two weeks from now?"

Ramone answered, "I think we could wait two weeks for my father's memorial. That would coincide with the Night of the

Pilgrims walk. As long as it is not on that night, it should be good. We like the idea of sunset." Annie heartily agreed.

*****

The drive home was filled with what-ifs. Most importantly, could they book the venue? Then, what about furniture, flowers, catering? How is this possible in two short weeks! Annie thought to herself, *I need Sabine here! Wow! This could be happening!*

Marguerite greeted them at the door. "I've been thinking about you all day! How was the monastery? Do you think it makes a good place for the wedding?"

Ramone smiled at Annie and interjected, "No, Mamà. We didn't care for it as a wedding venue. The funny thing is we ran into the couple from yesterday, and they suggested a place, Vista Hermosa. We went there, and the museum part was closed, but we were able to walk around and fell in love with it for our wedding!"

Dom slipped away to call Juan Carlos. Meghan joined them and wanted the details, so they all decided to go the veranda for an aperitif and discuss the possibility of a wedding. Annie handed Meghan the brochure while she talked about the pavilion and the views. Meghan shook her head in amazement after looking at the pamphlet. "You know who the owner of the property was, right?"

Annie glanced at Ramone and said, "Just that he was an archduke from Austria, I think."

Meghan said, "Archduke Ludwig Salvator of Austria. If I recall, he never lived in Austria. From what I just read, he came to Mallorca and fell in love with the island. He was a naturist and ethnographer. Annie, do you know what that means? He studied anthropology and the uniqueness of indigenous cultures. Just like us! And he was an early conservationist. It says here he bought many villas and estates between Deià and Valldemossa to help preserve the area in its natural state.

Vista Hermosa had his heart, and he built the pavilion structure at the end of the natural peninsula for people to enjoy the incredible surroundings. And what is even more ironic? His last name, Salvator, in Spanish is Salvador. Do you not think that is an omen?"

Annie thought about all the events and twists of fate that had brought her to this place. This was no accident. Even that she felt the first kick of her baby today. *He woke up to tell me: This is it, Mommy. Don't miss it.*

Dom came back from his conversation with Juan Carlos and said, "Juan Carlos knows the director of the museum at Vista Hermosa. He is placing a call to him now. Scheduling is the issue. Looking at the weekend two weeks from now, the Night of the Pilgrims is on Friday night. Saturdays they are booked for weddings up to a year in advance. I told him we were good with Sunday, Monday, or Tuesday, but we wanted sunset. Was I right? He also suggested we meet with a wedding planner as soon as possible to be able to accomplish this in such a short time. His recommendation was Veronica Ruiz. He said she was the best and that we might have met her at the yacht club party."

Looking at Antonio, Annie asked, "Is that your Veronica?" Back to Dom, she answered, "What day of the week doesn't matter." To Ramone, "What about your schedule?"

Ramone said matter-of-factly, "I'm open."

Annie immediately picked up his tone and asked where only he could hear her. "Did you take yourself off the fighting circuit?"

Ramone, equally quiet, responded, "For now, I am off indefinitely."

This was a topic Annie realized would need to be discussed later, but she put it aside for now to continue the topic of the wedding. Annie looked over at her mom and chuckled to see her list out and organizing already begun. Pulling her feet up under her to get comfortable and holding Ramone's hand, she was perfectly happy letting Celeste take charge. What a day! The baby, the venue, and she had her special dress!

Celeste got Annie's attention when she asked Meghan, "You met Veronica. Did she seem easy to work with? She has probably used Vista Hermosa as a venue before and should have a list of what we need. We are out all day tomorrow. Would you mind calling her to see if she can meet with us sometime Saturday?"

Meghan glanced at Antonio. "Did you know Veronica was a wedding planner?"

Antonio rolled his eyes. "To be honest, she talked so much I didn't listen to a lot of what she said."

Annie and Ramone chuckled, but that worried Celeste. "Do you think she will listen to what we want?"

Meghan laughed. "I'm sure she knows her business if Juan Carlos recommended her. If she gets out of hand, we'll dangle Antonio as a carrot to keep her straight!"

Antonio didn't care for being the brunt of this joke but summoned up his sense of humor and laughed along with the rest. "Yes, I will have to think hard how we can get her to focus." To Ramone and Marguerite, Antonio added, "So we decided to have Papa's service after the wedding?"

Marguerite reflected and answered, "The place you found high on the cliff sounds like the perfect setting to spread Salvador's ashes." To Ramone and Annie, "If we could get them here, what would you think about having him at your wedding and spreading his ashes after?"

Before her parents or grandparents could express any disapproval, Annie looked closely at Ramone before saying, "If it suits you, my love, I would love to have Salvador at our wedding. Without him, you might not be sitting with us right now."

Ramone closed his eyes for a moment to compose himself. "I love you, *querida*, for allowing this. Yes, Mamà, we will see if we can get Papa's ashes here."

# Chapter 35

The tone of the group on the veranda became more solemn, and Annie understood the wedding had before her eyes become more of the spiritual ceremony she wanted so badly. With an inner smile, she sent a silent thank-you to Archduke Salvator for providing this lovely place.

Meghan filled Tomás in when he came out to the veranda. He was thrilled his cousin had found the perfect location and knew Dom could somehow make it happen. Then an idea struck him. "If we have at least two weeks, I should go back to Marbella for at least several days to work. What if I went to the crematory and got Salvador's ashes to bring back with me?" Looking at Marguerite, he added, "You could write a letter giving me permission to pick them up."

Meghan smiled warmly at her husband. "You know I would love to go with you, but I would like to stay and help with the wedding details. After the wedding, I will need to return to Dingle for a while. Having our bags here would make it easier to go straight there from Mallorca."

The conversation soon turned to the guests. If Captain Luis, Roff, and Helene moved back to the *Porto Banus*, that would free up three bedrooms. Annie agreed she would call Sabine and Sarah. They debated whether Annie or Ramone, or even Alex, should call El Amir. In the end, Ramone felt he should make that call. They discussed Mara, but the chance of her coming all the way from Bali on such short notice was doubtful. Locally, naturally Juan Carlos and Carlotta should be included. If the date worked and they were still on the island, it would make sense to invite Stephan and Carmina. Meghan asked about Hans. Annie and Ramone hadn't been around him other than the night of the yacht club party. Naturally, Captain Luis, Roff, and Helene would come. Celeste was making her list and wanted to be sure they weren't missing anyone. She and Alex knew his parents were on an extended trip in the Philippines so Henry and Trudy would not be able to make it. Annie was relieved she had recently had a good visit with them but she assured Gennie she would invite her sister, Claudette. Meghan planned to call Veronica.

They were all waiting to hear back from Juan Carlos to find out if and when Vista Hermosa was available so they could make their calls.

Maria brought out a platter of light tapas. Helene was right behind her. She had obviously heard the news. As an explanation for the day ahead aboard the *Porto Banus*, Helene gave them the plan. "It will be an early morning for the start of the regatta, so Roff is staying with the crew of the *Nautilus* tonight. We heard from him a little while ago and he seems to have a great deal of respect for Hans as a captain."

Tomás was the first to ask. "Does he think they have a chance of winning?"

Helene answered, "He seems to think so. The captain and I are about to leave to go to the *Porto Banus* overnight to be ready for our outing tomorrow. Roff said he would keep an eye out for us. The captain did hear from the first mate who is joining us. I think his name is Simon. He will be on board early tomorrow." Looking at Don Marco, she asked, "What time would you like to get started, sir?"

"We will have a light breakfast then should be there around nine thirty." Looking around the group, he asked, "Does that work for everyone?"

"Yes, sir. We will be ready. According to Yuba, the chef is working on your dinner now. It should be ready in about an hour. I will see you all tomorrow."

The phone rang and Dom went to get it. They all held their breath to hear what Juan Carlos would say. All they could hear was Dom saying, "I see. Yes, I understand. That's fine."

The suspense was driving them crazy. Dom was so serious when he came back from the call, they were convinced they couldn't get the venue. Then, a tiny smile formed that grew very wide. Gennie said to him, "You rascal! Tell us!"

"As we thought, there is a wedding planned for Saturday night. Vista Hermosa is closed on Monday. That left Sunday or Tuesday. They have a concert on Tuesday, so Juan Carlos booked Sunday. Will that be satisfactory?"

Annie started jumping up and down, and the excitement on the veranda had everyone in high spirits. Ramone hugged Annie, and they set off to make their phone calls. Meghan went to call Veronica, leaving the others to discuss how to best make this wedding happen. They were also curious what tomorrow would bring.

# Chapter 36

Annie and Ramone wanted to remain outside, so they wandered over to the pool seating area to make their calls. Annie couldn't wait to hear Sabine's voice. "*Oui, bonjour.* Hello?"

"Sabine, it's Annie. I have Ramone right here with me. Did you get my letter?"

"*Non*, was it important?" Sabine asked.

"No, not anymore. So much has happened since we left Marbella."

"I heard. Ramone, I am so sorry about your father and what happened to you. *Mon Dieu*, it was *terrible!*"

Ramone answered Sabine, "It is still hard to talk about. Not sure I could have made it through without your incredible cousin. However, this call is about a wedding!"

"Really, you've decided?"

"It is a long story, but we found the perfect place today, and they have an opening two weeks from Sunday! It is so breathtaking. I can't wait for you to see it. Two weeks! Mallorca is beautiful. Can any of the family come?" Annie was so filled with excitement she was afraid she'd miss something. "Gennie would love to see Claudette and have her here for the wedding."

As Annie thought, Sabine said, "My parents are so close to harvest, I don't see how they could leave. Grandma has not been feeling well, so I would have to check on her. Annie, what about Robert?"

Putting her hand to her head, realizing she had forgotten about Robert, she glanced at Ramone, and he shrugged. "Is he there? Do you think he'd like to join us? The island is in a very festive time. The King's Cup regatta is going on, and the weekend of the wedding there is an important annual pilgrimage, which is an overnight walk up the mountains to the monastery in Lluc."

"Robert arrived yesterday so he might already be gone by the wedding. I want to be there with you! Let me speak with everyone on this end, and I will get back to you *très vite!*"

Ramone smiled when Annie asked, "How is everything going with Robert?" Realizing she didn't know Antonio and Marguerite were there, Annie added as nonchalantly as possible, "Antonio is here. Meghan used to assist a physical therapist, and she's been working with him. He seems to be making progress. By the way, Dom told me he would get your ticket. I can't do this without you!"

"You know I will be there as quickly as I can!" Sabine answered.

"Tomorrow, we will be out watching the regatta and spending the afternoon in Ibiza. If you can't reach me, leave a message." They promised to be in touch soon.

Annie was curious what Ramone thought of Sabine and Antonio. His answer was easy. "If he could walk, she wouldn't have a chance."

Annie, with a challenge in her voice, said, "So if he cannot walk, he will not pursue her, and neither one will have the chance to find out if they were meant to be."

Drawing her close, Ramone reminded her, "It wasn't easy for us either, *querida.*"

Annie nodded, ready to make another call. "True. Who's next? Sarah or El Amir?"

"I'll call El Amir," Ramone replied.

On the second ring, El Amir answered in his deep voice, "Hullo."

"El Amir, it's Ramone."

Immediately alert, El Amir quickly asked, "Is everything all right? Are you okay? Annie?"

Ramone reassured him, "Yes, everyone is fine. Annie is right here." She said hi, and Ramone continued. "First, I want to sincerely thank you for your note and the oils. You have given freely of your help time and again to us, and we are honored to have you as a friend. While we have been here, there has been a lot of discussion about where and when Annie and I would get married. Today, we found the perfect place, and the wedding is scheduled for two weeks from Sunday. We are hoping you can be here."

Mentally calculating his upcoming schedule, he answered, "That timing should work out perfectly. I leave for Barcelona the end of next week. Sarah is doing an exhibition on Las Ramblas. I will be there to help coordinate the details. We should be finished early the following week before the wedding. Were you planning to ask her?"

Annie got on the phone. "She is my next call. Could you bring her?"

"Of course. Are you okay if we get there a little early?" El Amir asked.

"That would be perfect! There is a village we heard that is so picturesque we think Sarah might enjoy painting it. Also, the weekend of the wedding, there is an overnight walk up into the mountains to the monastery here. It is supposed to be quite the pilgrimage." Annie then handed the phone back to Ramone.

To Ramone, El Amir asked, "How are you really doing? The Spanish papers have noticed your absence. There is much speculation."

Ramone turned slightly away from Annie and answered, "I know. I am not able to deal with that right now. For the moment, my concentration is on Annie and the baby."

"Well, if you think of anything you might need, call me."

"Thanks. I will. Goodbye." Ramone hung up. To Annie, "That went well, don't you think? Why don't you call Sarah? Do you need me here for that? If not, I'll go join the others."

"Sure, I won't be long." But Annie noticed the subtle shift of his mood when his bullfighting was brought up. She was hopeful this would pass in time. Putting those thoughts aside, she reached for the phone to call Sarah.

Sarah was delighted to hear from Annie and about the news of the wedding. They talked about her upcoming exhibition in Barcelona that she was preparing for. It was an entire collection of endangered birds of prey from her last stay in East Africa.

Annie told her about the wedding venue they found, the village she might enjoy painting, as well as the pilgrimage to the monastery. She also mentioned in passing she had met a man in the regatta who coincidentally owned an art gallery in Hamburg and that his name was Hans.

Sarah hesitated. "Hans Schuman? Blond, fairly handsome?"

Annie's curiosity piqued, she answered, "I don't know that I ever heard his last name, but his first name is definitely Hans, and he is blond. Fairly handsome? More like exceedingly handsome if you ask me. So, you know him?"

"If it is the same man, I've met him before. I think I remember he was an avid sailor." Quickly changing the subject, Sarah finished the conversation with "Unfortunately, I have to go now. We will be there Tuesday or Wednesday before the wedding. Can't wait to see you! Bye."

Annie went to rejoin the group. *Isn't that interesting. It seems I have a bit of a mystery to unravel.*

# Chapter 37

Over a mouth-watering chef's dinner of fresh grilled fish, *cour-gettes* (zucchini), peppers, garlic, and aubergines, they discussed the various phone calls. Meghan had spoken to Veronica, and scheduled to meet with her Saturday at eleven. It made sense for Celeste and Meghan to go with Annie. With that meeting scheduled, Ramone thought that might be a good time to catch up with Stephan and do a short hike. Alex and Dom arranged a game of golf, and Marguerite planned to take Antonio into the old town to look around.

As the conversation wound down, Annie asked Meghan, "Do you remember Hans's last name?"

"Ah, let me think. Schubert, Schuman...something like that. Why?" Meghan asked.

"Sarah might know him. Will he be around that weekend of the wedding?"

It was Antonio who answered. "Hans mentioned he was staying through the pilgrimage. I'm not sure after that. He seemed a little free spirited. Did she say where she met him?"

"No. What a strange coincidence." The phone rang, and Annie went to get it, hoping it was Sabine. Happily, it was!

"Annie, I have big news! We are all coming! My parents said they would not miss it and will let the foreman watch the vineyard while they are gone. Grandmama can't wait. Robert's ticket back to Maine is not until that weekend, and he is happy to change it to a return from Mallorca instead. I really want to come sooner. Is it all right for Robert to come too? Papa wants to speak with Tomás after we finish to arrange a rental close to your villa. We are thinking of coming in next weekend and staying through the wedding! I am so excited!"

Annie was caught up in Sabine's excitement and could not believe they were all going to be there for the wedding. She thought about it for a moment, then added, "It will be amazing to have Robert here as well. He is such a dear friend. I just didn't think it would be possible for him to get here."

Sabine told her, "Papa is arranging everything. Will you put Tomás on the phone?" Annie called Tomás to the phone and went to tell everyone the news.

"The whole family is coming! They are looking for a rental beginning next weekend." When Annie added, "They are even bringing Robert," it was Ramone who noticed the change in Antonio, but he said nothing. His brother had his demons to deal with in his own way. Ramone then realized he, too, had demons to overcome.

Celeste updated the guest list and asked, "Is there anyone else we might have forgotten?"

Annie thought aloud, "I would love Mara to be here and meet all of you, especially Ramone. But to come from Bali? I hate to even put that on her!"

Celeste shrugged with a smile. "Considering how your calls are going, you should probably try Mara."

Tomás was busy on his personal phone trying to arrange a rental for Sabine's family. With the popularity of the Night of the Pilgrims, few were available. Meanwhile, Dom was calculating where everyone would stay and suggested Tomás try for a slightly bigger villa.

Annie looked at her watch and noted the time difference in Bali. She hoped she wouldn't wake Mara with her call. When she answered, Annie said, "Mara, it's Annie. I hope I didn't wake you."

"No, are you okay?" Mara asked.

Annie replied, "Yes, this is all so sudden, and it is a long story. Ramone and I are in Mallorca with our families and are planning to get married in two weeks! I know it is outrageous to ask, but we were wondering if you might like to come here for the wedding. Ramone has heard so much about you. Is it a possibility?"

Trying to grasp the location of Mallorca, Mara asked, "Mallorca is an island south of Spain, right?"

"Yes, one of the Balearic Islands. I'm not sure what route you would take from Bali," Annie answered.

"Well, I would not be coming from Bali. Do you remember our friend Jonathan McNamara from Australia? He and I have been seeing each other off and on since our trip there."

"Really? How is Jonathan? Such a nice man. What was the name of his dog? That animal adored him and never left his side!"

Mara laughed. "Roscoe! Remember, I was so scared of him, but he's a big softy. So is his owner."

That got a raise of Annie's eyebrows. "Ooh! Do tell."

"Jonathan is on leave for three weeks, and we were planning to meet in Capri next weekend for a visit. I don't think Capri is that far from you. Maybe I could come from there?"

To resist was impossible. Annie had learned throughout her journey there really were no accidents. "Do you think Jonathan might come with you? It would be so good to see him again! And I would love to see you two together. I think he had a thing for you from the beginning. Sarah and El Amir will be here. They are coming from an art exhibition in Barcelona."

They left it that Mara would ask Jonathan and leave a message for her the next day about whether he would join her and what day she would arrive. Annie quickly told her about the pilgrimage and the village of Valldemossa. When they said their goodbyes, Mara emphatically assured her, "I will be there with or without him!"

# Chapter 38

Arriving at the Palma marina, Annie observed at once all the heightened activity surrounding the start of the regatta. They heard the echo of the horn marking the start of the first race all the way at the villa! As they walked toward the waiting Zodiac to tender them to the *Porto Banus*, Annie took Ramone's hand and quietly said to him, "So much has happened in the last week. Today should be a nice break to relax a little."

Ramone heartily agreed. "I'd like that, *querida*."

Simon, the new first mate, was at the dock ready to lend a hand to the ladies and to help with Antonio. It was hard not to notice the large, bulging muscles pressing against his white T-shirt. His wavy ash-blond hair was carelessly tied back in a ponytail. Annie and Meghan exchanged an *Oh My* look, but they were not who had his attention.

Annie caught him wink at Helene, who blushed furiously. *Oh, this is too good to be true!* Grabbing Meghan, they were like two schoolgirls surreptitiously watching Simon and Helene flirt, trying not to be noticed. The captain maneuvered the *Porto Banus* out of the marina and away from the charted courses of the regatta. When it was time to hoist the sail, Simon looked straight at Helene and pulled his T-shirt over his head, revealing all those muscles that tapered down to his narrow waist and low-riding pants. Helene, wide-eyed, couldn't stop staring. Annie and Meghan, watching all this unfold, could not restrain their giggles.

Seeing their women so taken with this young stud, Ramone and Tomás were none too pleased. Antonio thought the whole thing was hysterical, and the older generation simply rolled their eyes and focused their attention elsewhere.

Ramone pulled Annie to her feet. "Your husband-to-be does not take kindly to your wandering eye, *querida*. Do I need to take you below deck and teach you some manners?"

Annie, seeing the devilish look in his eyes that belied his stern words, said, dripping with sarcasm, "Oh, I have been bad, my love. I fully deserve whatever punishment you deem best."

Practically dragging her down to the cabin below, Ramone uttered, "You torment me beyond by endurance, *querida*!" Once inside the cabin, Ramone slammed the door shut and tossed Annie back on the bed. He removed his belt in long pull. For a moment, Annie's eyes widened, thinking he was going to use it on her. Seeing her alarm, Ramone quickly said, "No, *querida*, I will never harm you or our child. But I will make you forget any other man." Clothes flew in all directions until Ramone stressed his point with his first forceful thrust. Annie pressed against him, matching his rhythm, and together they climaxed with such passion there was no question of another man.

Afterward, content to lie close together entwined, they periodically heard cheers that would drift down from above. Presumably, they were cheering on racers as they swept across another's bow at lightning speed. Finally, curiosity took over, and after a quick shower, they emerged from below with quite satisfied looks on their faces.

Annie did covertly look around to see that Simon was wearing his T-shirt. Helene seemed to be hanging on his every word. Reflecting to Ramone, she said, "I have traveled all over on the *Porto Banus*. Roff and Helene are always together, so I assumed they were a couple." They were anchored next to Juan Carlos's yacht that rivaled the impression of the *Porto Banus*. Dom waved over to Juan Carlos, then Simon began to lower the transom, with Helene's help, to transfer everyone to the other yacht.

Lunch on board Juan Carlos and Carlotta's yacht proved to be quite festive. Tables were pushed together to form one large family-style dining table for all their guests. A huge TV was carrying the regatta live with commentary and aerial views, giving a much better perspective to the spectators. There was a comfortable lounge area that surrounded it for those who wanted to watch seriously. It looked like the *Nautilus* was maintaining a strong position.

Staff wandered through the guests, offering prosecco and freshly prepared hors d'oeuvres. Annie watched for a moment to approach Juan Carlos to personally thank him for his help in securing the wedding venue. "It would mean a great deal to Ramone and me if you and Carlotta would join us at the wedding."

Juan Carlos graciously replied, "We are delighted you have chosen to marry on our special island. Of course we will be there. And you can count on us if you need any help in these quick preparations. You meet with Veronica tomorrow, right?"

"Yes. Do you think she is up to pulling all this together so quickly? Especially with all the regatta events as well as the other activities leading up to the pilgrimage?" Annie asked.

"Veronica is very well connected. She is also extremely organized. Believe me, when she makes up her mind that she wants something, she gets it." Annie tucked this little piece of information away to think about later. Ramone was curious if Juan Carlos had participated in the Night of Pilgrims over the years.

"Ah, many times. In my youth, I always made it to the end." With a chuckle, he added, "Now I still like to go, but I don't mind sitting on the sidelines."

Lunch came out in large platters and served family style. An assortment of breads and olives was placed at each setting. There was a delicious fish stew with lots of herbs and fresh vegetables, a hearty salad, *costillas de cordero* (petite lamb chops), scalloped potatoes with onions, and a melt-in-your-mouth almond cake for dessert. When Annie tasted the almond cake, she looked at her mom. "Wouldn't this flavor make a wonderful wedding cake?"

Carlotta overheard her and smiled. "If anyone can do it, Greta can. Her bakery is on one of the side streets in Old Town. All the natural almonds growing on the island make this one of our specialties. Ask Veronica when you see her tomorrow."

# Chapter 39

The regatta had moved to another area, so they watched it on the big screen a little longer before heading back to the *Porto Banus*. Lunch had gone on a little longer than they had planned, but they all agreed it had been an enjoyable time.

Captain Luis was waiting for them back on board to present the options for the afternoon. "It sounds like everyone had a nice lunch. As you probably know, Ibiza is known for its nightclubs and all-night parties. Since we plan to be back at Palma tonight, here is what I would recommend. Depending on how active you want to be, we could anchor at a beach where you could choose a variety of water sports, or simply relax at a beach I know on the west side that is a brilliant shade of turquoise. There are beach bars where you can get snacks, or we are prepared to serve a light dinner on board. Then I thought we might go past Es Vedrà for sunset on the way back."

Don Marco asked, "Does anyone feel like water sports?"

Tomás responded with another question. "Can't we have both? I leave for Marbella tomorrow. I would love to Jet Ski."

Meghan piped in, "I would like to try paddle boarding."

Ramone added, looking at Antonio, "I could ride a Jet Ski and take you!"

Marguerite's reaction showed her doubt. "That would not be possible! If he fell, he would not be able to swim."

Antonio, feeling the first sense of normalcy in a long time was close at hand, interjected, "Mamà, let me try! I will have on a life jacket. Ramone will be right there."

Tomás added, "I will stay close to them." The support that grew within the group showed how strong the bond was becoming within this family to include Antonio.

Alex said, "Marguerite, I will Jet Ski too and be close by. Celeste, would you like to join me?"

Celeste, ever aware of her daughter's moods, declined. "I think I will paddle board with Meghan."

Hearing that, Annie piped in, "I'll go with you, Dad!"

Marguerite, realizing she was outnumbered and that Antonio would be well cared for, decided to paddle board as well.

Don Marco looked at Gennie for her answer. "I think I will be just fine on the beach under an umbrella with a glass of prosecco!"

That answer got a chuckle all around, but no one expected Dom to say, "If there is an extra Jet Ski, I think I will join you young people!" Gennie's look of surprise said volumes, but she was wise enough to stay quiet.

Giving his attention back to Captain Luis, Don Marco said, "I believe you have the consensus, Captain. Take us to a beach with water sports."

"I know just the one. *Talamanca* is a long stretch of beach with plenty of room for the Jet Skis to get good runs. It is situated between two headlands that give it protection and calm waters. I will call ahead. Six for Jet Skis and three for paddle boarding. One for a beach umbrella. For extra precaution, I can have Simon cruise around the bay in the Zodiac after he takes you ashore."

Helene had been listening from the galley. "I am an excellent swimmer. I could go with him." Ramone watched for a reaction from Annie. She now knew better and busied herself fluffing the pillow behind her. Inside, she couldn't help wondering what Roff would think about all this.

Captain Luis found an anchorage that was satisfactory. Simon and the other crewmen cast the anchor off the bow about two hundred yards off the shore. The plan was to spend about three hours here, then begin the sail back to Palma. It they timed it right, they would pass Es Vedrà around sunset.

155

Everyone changed into their swimsuits and packed their beach bags with all the essentials. Antonio could feel his rising excitement. Meghan's persistence with the exercises seemed to be making small steps forward, and he could not help but harbor hope that he would eventually make his way out of that chair. He made a vow to himself he would work even harder and push the limits of what he could do. For today, he wanted the wind in his hair and the exhilaration of speed across the water.

*****

Four Jet Skis were tied to the dock ready for them when they arrived. Gennie secured a spot on the beach where they could leave their towels and bags. Marguerite followed Celeste and Meghan to another part of the beach where the paddle boards were, but not before cautioning her sons, "Be careful...both of you." These two young men, both trained in such a daring profession, were each fighting limitations of their own. She was not certain she would see either of them in a bullring again. *Perhaps that is something we all have to live with.*

Fortunately, they were paid handsomely to do what they did, and both young men had made wise investments with the help of their uncle. She knew in her heart that her family was with good people, and they were fortunate to be able to call them family. She shook off her serious thoughts and looked forward to spending time with Celeste and Meghan.

On the dock, Alex and Ramone helped Antonio secure his life jacket, then put on their own. Ramone boarded his tandem Jet Ski and slid forward. Tomás and Alex helped Antonio get on board behind him. The attendant had an extra strap to secure Antonio's torso to Ramone's. Antonio used his arms to hold on to Ramone, and they started up to do a few circles close to the dock to get a feel of each other and the ski beneath them. Alex got Annie situated behind him, and they were next in the water. Tomás saw that Dom was getting some extra instruction and walked over to him.

"Are you sure you want to ride alone? Why don't you come with me?"

Dom smiled with a quick sigh of relief that his bravado could be salvaged. "I would love that!" Once they were settled, they joined the others and ventured out.

Ramone and Antonio were flanked by Alex and Annie on their left and Tomás and Dom on their right. Ramone gently accelerated, and they all kept pace. Antonio felt so close to normal, he wanted more. He yelled up to Ramone, "Faster, brother!"

Ramone yelled back, "Hold on!" He started to speed up, then he felt it. Antonio's knees were pressing against his hips. He let out the throttle more, and the knees pressed harder! They zoomed across the bay, and to Antonio it felt as if they were flying like the wind.

Ramone knew he had left the other Jet Skis behind and purposely headed in the direction of Simon and the Zodiac, closer to where the ladies were paddling. When they realized who it was going that fast, Marguerite about fainted, but Meghan yelled and screamed in excitement. Slowing down to let the others catch up, Ramone turned around. "Did you feel that?"

Antonio's ear-to-ear grin gave Ramone his answer. Emotion overtook him, and all he wanted was to hug his brother. "*O Dios Mío!*" Turning more, he came close to throwing them off-balance.

Simon was close enough to yell, "Don't turn so much! You'll capsize!"

Ramone, immediately chagrined, righted himself. Antonio, however, punched him in his side with his fist and yelled, "Again, please!" And off they went, realizing no one knew what had happened and were furious with them. They did twists and turns and let loose to full throttle.

Every maneuver got a stronger reaction from Antonio's knees. It felt to both of them that they had each outsmarted their demons that day. Alex and Annie had given up trying to chase them and, although they thought Ramone utterly foolhardy, they made the best of their ride and watched a little of the paddling.

Alex was particularly proud of the way Celeste was handling the board.

Tomás was closest to keeping up with Ramone, and Dom seemed to enjoy the ride immensely. He knew he could be at Ramone's side quickly if needed. At the rate Ramone was going, that seemed likely.

They saw the flag wave that signaled the end of the ride. Ramone held back to allow the others to disembark and to help Antonio onto the dock. While they were idled, Ramone asked, "Do you want to tell them, or should I?"

Antonio replied, "If it is okay, I would like to keep this our secret for the moment. I want to work really hard with Meghan's help over the next two weeks and see how far I get."

Ramone, realizing the wrath they would face about their ride, asked, "Can I at least share this moment with Annie? I don't really want to keep secrets from her or get married with her furious at me!"

Reluctantly, Antonio agreed but asked him to have her promise to keep it quiet. What a day! Both brothers understood the miraculous moments they had shared, and the bond between them soared to new heights.

# Chapter 40

The cold glares directed at Ramone told him how reckless the others thought he had been. Antonio was quick to come to his defense. "It was my doing. I kept asking him to go faster. I was secure. Fortunately, my arms continue to work, and I had a firm grip. Now let him be!"

Meghan equally came to Ramone's defense. "I thought it was exciting to see Antonio speeding across the water! For the moment—and, I repeat, *for the moment*—Antonio could not have done it without Ramone." Looking over at Antonio, she added, "Mark my word, there will come a time when you can do that on your own. Believe it!"

Back on board the *Porto Banus*, the sun was hanging low on the horizon. After changing out of their wet swimsuits, Captain Luis prepared to set sail. "Helene has prepared some refreshments for the sail back to port. It turns out Simon has lived in the Balearic Islands all his life. He has offered to tell you a little about Es Vedrà as we go by it."

They all gathered around the open-air salon. Annie was in Ramone's lap with her arm casually draped around his shoulder. She leaned in close and whispered, "It's a good thing you told me what happened today. Your actions are always so deliberate. I quite thought you'd lost your mind!"

Not wanting to draw attention to their topic, Ramone said, "Let's discuss this later, *querida*."

The sails caught the wind, and Captain Luis charted his course to pass on the east of Es Vedrà. Simon took a seat on one of the barstools and began his story. "When I was a young boy, my grandfather told me some of the tales about Es Vedrà." That made

159

Annie smile at her own grandfather, who had told her so many stories of faraway places throughout her life.

"He made it sound very mysterious and magical. Locals are convinced a special energy exists in this island and that it has a magnetic power that draws energy and even UFOs. Look carefully at sunset. The colors of the water and the sky somehow have a different hue as we pass. Over the years, Es Vedrà has been thought to be in a Bermuda triangle of sorts where electronics cease to work, perhaps because of its magnetic power?

"One of my favorites is that back around 110 BC, the Phoenicians were convinced this island was the birthplace of the goddess Tanit. They believed the island was a holy place, so every full moon they would make sacrifices to appease the lunar goddess. Later, she was declared the patron goddess of Ibiza. There have been many more stories about a monster who lurked there and preyed on passersby. For tonight, keep your eyes peeled. The island is a natural habitat and nature reserve with little human footprint. You might see wildlife such as Ibiza wall lizards, endangered gulls, and even wild falcons. Naturalists have counted over 160 rare plant species that are growing naturally on the island."

While the stories of Es Vedrà were absorbed by his listeners, Simon pulled out his guitar and started to strum some old Spanish folk songs. When he started to sing, no one was expecting the voice of an angel. His music affected all of them as they sailed along, past the island of his stories and through the farewell to the sun. Some of them sang along if they knew the songs. Others swayed to his rhythms.

It was Marguerite with her natural sense of dance who, caught up in the sounds, stood up and started to dance. Her talent was hypnotic, and Simon soon learned her rhythm. Her movements moved with his music, and as he would change the tempo, her dance moved with him. Entranced, he tried to slow the music down, then speed it up. She was brilliant in her talent to keep pace with his changes. Her sons had never seen their mother dance so exotically. It brought memories back for Alex and Celeste, who had watched her dance so long ago, mesmerized. Salvador was a lost cause the moment he saw her dance. Seeing her so naturally move to the music, no one could understand how she had never been with another man after Salvador.

They were approaching the port of Palma. Simon reluctantly put down his guitar to help lower the sails, but he could not stop thinking about this woman who could move like the wind with a rhythm that would make any man wild with passion.

Annie said to Ramone, "I had no idea she could dance like that!"

"Nor did I, *querida.*" Ramone had to admit he might have gotten his rhythm with the bulls from his mother.

"Do you think she might dance at the wedding?" Annie asked.

Ramone got her hand and pulled her over to his mother. "Mamà, your dance was beautiful. I have never seen you dance like that before. Annie and I would love for you to dance at our wedding."

Marguerite, warmed at the invitation to somehow contribute to this wedding, answered, "It is rare that I dance with abandon. Simon's music and voice beckoned me. I will dance at your wedding, but only if he agrees to accompany me with his music."

# Chapter 41

Annie went to her cabin below to retrieve her bag, so she was the last to disembark. She overheard Helene asking Simon if he wanted to go for a nightcap. His eyes were most definitely on Marguerite, but he turned and smiled at Helene. "Sure, that would be fun!"

Back at the villa, Ramone called Stephan to see if he could hike with them tomorrow. Carmina jumped at the chance to take a day off hiking to do a little beach and spa time. Ramone and Stephan agreed to a meeting place. Rejoining the others, he realized he didn't have any hiking shoes with him. Tomás checked Ramone's shoe size and agreed to loan him his for the hike.

Realizing they all had packed lightly, or not at all, Tomás offered, "I leave for Marbella tomorrow. Sabine and the family arrive on Sunday. I plan to be back here by Saturday to greet them. I will go get Salvador's ashes and also bring back Meghan's and my bags. If anyone else has items they would like me to bring back, make a list and I will do my best."

None of them were prepared with clothing for another two weeks, especially with all the company coming, and the wedding! Celeste and Alex were the only ones who had anything in Mallorca since they had packed in Maine, and Celeste had brought Alex's suitcase with her on the plane. But the rest were racing to get pen and paper, trying to think of all they needed for the week of the wedding.

List after list was handed to Tomás. Don Marco was proud of Tomás's offer but knew the task of bringing everything on these lists back with him was impossible. "I have an idea. The regatta ends Tuesday with the awards presented that evening. Roff will be available Wednesday. Why don't I send Captain Luis with the *Porto Banus* back to Marbella on Wednesday? Roff and Helene can help you gather everything needed, and you can sail back here with them to arrive Saturday."

Tomás was relieved to have some help with this task; he did still have to work. "I love the idea and would never pass up an opportunity to sail on the *Porto Banus!*"

Annie added to her list: some looser-fitting clothes, a pair of platinum satin sandals for the wedding, and a few jewelry pieces. Once they all finished, Tomás had a handful of lists, the keys to Marguerite's house and Ramone's car, where his bag was left, and a note from Marguerite to the crematory to release Salvador's ashes. "I think I have everything. I leave early tomorrow, so if I miss seeing you in the morning, I will see you Saturday."

Meghan agreed to meet Antonio at the pool for a round of exercises before dressing for the meeting with Veronica. Then she retired with Tomás to help him pack. At lunch earlier, Alex and Don Marco asked Juan Carlos to play golf with them. He accepted and offered to pick them up in the morning. Since Ramone planned to meet Stephan close to the golf course, they offered to give him a ride as well. All the plans finalized, they said good night after a long day.

Annie took a quick shower and was sound asleep by the time her head touched the pillow. Ramone got in beside her with a kiss on her forehead, cradling her in his arms. He took some time in the quiet to consider all the events that had led up to this day.

Salvador's death weighed heavily on him. On one hand, he was happy his father had reached out to him in love, not anger. On the other, he resented all the time wasted alienated from his father. Would their relationship have been different if he had not chosen to be a matador? Would that have changed the influence Kung Li had over him? Those answers would now remain a question. The strength of the movement in Antonio's knees on the Jet Ski gave Ramone a good sense of his potential recovery, but was this dance they did with the bulls and all the potential danger worth it? Did he want to risk that for Annie and his child? Should he get back in the ring and try it? Right now, he just felt numb about a fight. He had lost the passion, but the question was whether it was temporary or permanent. That was the question that invaded his dreams as he dozed off to sleep.

# Chapter 42

Ramone woke early and eased out of bed. Annie was sleeping so soundly he didn't want to wake her. He quickly dressed and slipped out of the bedroom carrying his borrowed boots. Meghan had brewed fresh coffee so he poured himself a cup. She had seen Tomás off a little earlier.

They sat at the counter sipping their coffee, both wondering what the day would bring. Ramone looked forward to spending time with Stephan. His work had kept him so busy he hadn't had much time for male friends who were not fellow matadors.

Meghan was thinking about what exercises she would have Antonio do and asked Ramone with a knowing look on her face, "Something happened out on the water yesterday, didn't it?"

"I promised I wouldn't say anything, but he should tell you of all people." Ramone poured a second cup and went to put on the boots.

"When is the last time you hiked? Anyone can see that you're fit, but hiking in the mountains can be a challenge for the most fit," Meghan said.

Ramone replied, "We have two weeks until the Night of the Pilgrims hike. I would like to attempt it. I know Annie wants to. So I thought I should start practicing."

Alex and Don Marco came into the kitchen, and Meghan poured them each a cup of coffee. Alex said, "We are having breakfast with Juan Carlos at the club before we tee off. Ramone, you should eat a hearty breakfast. We still have a little time before we get picked up."

Meghan began rummaging through the refrigerator. "I could make an omelet with mushrooms and mixed peppers. Maybe a little sausage? That won't take long."

Ramone continued to marvel at this family he was marrying into. To Meghan he said, "Thank you! That would be great."

The conversation had turned to the sunset sail back to Palma the night before and Marguerite's dance. Alex told stories of how he and Salvador met her at this club in Barcelona. They were both dazzled by her dancing, but it was love at first sight for Salvador. Alex asked Ramone, "She never divorced?"

Ramone took his first bite and gave a thumbs-up to Meghan, then answered, "She was asked many times. I always thought it was because she hoped in her heart my father would come back to her. I feel some comfort he will be at the wedding, even if it is his ashes."

While Ramone finished breakfast, Dom said to Meghan, "Do whatever it takes to make them do this wedding right. Even if it is a whim, try to make it happen and spare no expense."

Meghan assured him of her support, and Ramone, emotions running high, said, "Sir, you are far too generous, and I find it hard to accept. Please know I am humbly honored to join this family. I can see where Annie gets her adventuresome spirit with such an incredible sense of generosity."

Juan Carlos knocked on the door, and the men left. Meghan was left to clean up and prepare for round two. Maria came in to help, but Meghan liked doing it and let her focus on cleaning the rooms that were already vacated. But one thing she knew for sure: she would get to the bottom of what happened on that Jet Ski. Meghan rarely had a third cup of coffee; however, it seemed today was a day to splurge. Here she was, playing a key role with this family she had grown to love. Tomás had exceeded her every wish for a husband. Maybe he was not as outwardly passionate as Ramone, but behind closed doors, his passion raged, and hers equally met his. She liked it this way. It was like a secret they shared. It was not easy saying goodbye this morning. They hadn't gotten much sleep. He would be back Saturday, and for now she needed to focus on Annie and Antonio.

Gennie came in and together they created a feast of fresh fruit, custard, omelets, and sausage. Soon, Antonio showed up with Marguerite and Annie right behind him. Meghan had brewed a new pot of Mallorcan coffee, and the aroma permeated the air with a delectable fragrance that none could resist. However, she refrained from a fourth cup. Yuba soon arrived to check on everyone. Gennie assured him, "We are doing fine."

Annie tried to convince her grandmother to join them at the meeting, but Gennie adamantly said no. "*Chérie*, you do not need too many opinions. Marguerite and Antonio are going into town later. Maybe I will join them. Perhaps we can all meet for lunch?"

Antonio responded, "I love that idea. Meghan, what do you think about the restaurant we went to a few days ago? How long will you ladies need for your meeting? We could meet you there."

Meghan replied, "Perfect. Why don't you come by the shop?"

It was particularly hot this morning, so they all put on swimsuits to enjoy the pool while Antonio was exercising. Annie and Celeste were on their loungers getting some sun. Gennie got out her float and was quickly absorbed doing her water aerobics.

Meghan started with Antonio sitting on the side of the pool as usual trying to lift his legs. As she suspected, he was doing this with ease. When she added the weights, equally so. Watching him, her gut on full alert, she took a weight that was more like a buoy and put it between his knees. "Press as hard as you can."

As soon as she saw the pressure he exerted, she intuitively knew he had gripped with his knees. Looking at Gennie doing her aerobics, she had an idea. "Antonio, let's get these weights on your ankles. Good. Now the life jacket. Make your way down the stairs."

Antonio was waiting for someone to help him, but no one did. Marguerite was sitting on the other side of the pool watching Gennie. Celeste and Annie were nonchalantly watching. Meghan came around to the stairs and held his arms. "Antonio, the weights will keep your feet to the bottom, and the life jacket will keep you afloat. Watch Gennie. Follow her motions."

Soon Antonio was upright, as if standing, in the pool. Annie and Celeste came closer to observe. "Now watch Gennie. Start to bounce. Don't worry. We've got you."

He was doing it! Using his feet to bounce off the bottom of the pool. There were tears in Marguerite's eyes. "It's unbelievable!"

Antonio, for the first time since the accident, felt positive about his recovery. He owed all this to Meghan. She was so excited for him but also tough. "We are taking steps forward, but there are many more to your recovery. You have to continue to work hard. The good news is that it's coming. Breathe. Put your situation in perspective. Remind yourself of who you are, a proud and powerful matador. Right now, try not to do anything rash. Don't let the situation control you. Give yourself a minute, then do the work to make the future you wish unfold before you."

# Chapter 43

Ramone and Stephan crested the first foothill, and even the lower elevation view was spectacular out over the sea. He could even see Es Vedrà far in the distance! Stephan looked back at Ramone and asked, "You haven't hiked a lot, have you?"

Shaking his head, Ramone said, "It's that obvious?"

Stephan took a moment to explain. "I get it. You are used to looking at a bull who might charge at any moment. The adrenalin is high. A hike is more about finding your pace. If your pace is too aggressive, you most likely won't have the stamina to make it to the end. On the other hand, if your pace is too slow, you are missing opportunities to push yourself further. You want to develop a rhythm that keeps you moving but doesn't get you too winded."

"All right, I will follow your pace for the moment and see if I can find mine. How do you maneuver the steep inclines?" Ramone wanted to understand.

"A steep incline is nothing but a challenge. Step into an incline and back for a decline. Keep your balance and your pace." With a little chuckle, Stephan added, "I suppose it is a little like life itself. There will always be ups and downs, but you somehow find a way to strike a balance and keep going."

Ramone steadied his pace and followed Stephan's lead. He learned the technique of stepping into an incline and the reverse on a decline. In about an hour, they had reached the first mountain in the Tramuntana range.

Stephan called back, "There is a village not too far ahead where we can stop for a little rest. How are you holding up?"

Ramone had to admit he was loving the hike. The endurance, the fresh clean air, the views, all combined with the solitary quiet of putting one foot in front of the other seemed to bring some clarity to his jumbled feelings. To Stephan, he nodded. "Really good! Thank you for introducing me to hiking."

They walked through lush valleys and rocky gorges. Some of the ancient, cobbled footpaths had to date back centuries. On their approach to the village where they would stop, the paths wound between olive and fragrant orange trees with breathtaking views of the mountains. Such beauty and inspiration!

The stone village of Fornalutx was set high in the mountain range. The citrus scent grew even more intense with all the local lemon trees. Ramone had heard Annie and Meghan talk about villages that maintained their authentic culture so often, he felt like he had discovered one. He knew its stone buildings and red-tiled roofs with the traditional cobbled streets would resonate Old World charm to them both and determined he would bring them back here.

They sat at an outdoor café and ordered a beer and a platter of mussels and prawns. Stephan looked around the storybook village. "This is one of the things Carmina and I love most about hiking, especially here in Mallorca. The villages throughout the island are unique and offer great scenic stops along the way. If I recall, this village was originally an Arab farmstead!"

Ramone shared Annie and Meghan's love of authentic villages. "Meghan is from Dingle in Ireland and is a historian. In Dingle, they still wear the authentic clothing and speak Gaelic. Annie loves history. I will have to bring them here."

"What did you think of Vista Hermosa?" Stephan asked.

"Annie and I loved it! Thank you so much. We were able to reserve it with Juan Carlos's help for two weeks from tomorrow. We have friends and family coming in beginning next weekend. How long are you and Carmina planning to stay in Mallorca?"

"We planned to be here through the Night of the Pilgrims for sure. We can take the ferry back to Barcelona so we thought we would probably leave Sunday after the hike."

"Our wedding will be that Sunday night. If you can stay over, we would love to have you join us!"

With a wide grin, Stephan said, "We would certainly be the envy of our friends to be at the famous Ramone Sanchez's wedding!" Then Stephan immediately worried he should not have brought up Ramone's profession. "I didn't mean anything by it. Once you go back to the mainland, you know you will be hounded with questions." He paused to get a read of Ramone's mood, then continued, "I saw you fight once, you know. It was in Seville. Your timing and sense of what the bull would do next had me in awe and yelling with the rest of the audience at each pass of the bull."

Ramone thought about being in the ring. "There is something that happens when you face a bull for the first time. All the training kicks in, and you know you are facing possible injury or even death. The screams of support from the audience push me further. And when victory comes, the feeling of being invincible is so powerful it gives the satisfaction you managed to defy death that day."

Thinking it was good to let Ramone talk about it, Stephan remained quiet. Ramone continued, "I don't think I ever fully understood my father's anger at my accepting the family tradition. We were never close after that. It was only seeing him put himself in harm's way to protect me that I finally understood his reasoning. He had seen his father die in the ring and was afraid of that same thing happening to the sons that he loved. Annie almost said no to my proposal because of the danger of the sport. Like every matador, I have a lot of scars from close encounters with various bulls. When she saw those, it made her realize what could happen each time I fight. Seeing Antonio struggle after his injury that holds him to a wheelchair, I finally understand. Am I being selfish to cause such anguish to those around me? I don't let fear come near me in the ring. If I did, I would never survive. I guess I am having so many mixed feelings."

Stephan was touched by Ramone opening up to him and

reached within himself to find the right words to say. "You will find the answer, my friend. Maybe just let go of it for a while. Ignore the natural tendency to analyze, criticize, judge, and react hastily. Use this time that you have, and even these hikes, to explore the beauty of simply being in the present. You will be marrying a beautiful woman in two weeks! Don't waste one moment of this experience. Carmina and I will be there. You can count on us." Their embrace told Ramone he had made a new friend that day.

# Chapter 44

Annie and Celeste, like Meghan, were jubilant at Antonio's progress that morning. Celeste asked Meghan, "You have helped him gain not only strength but also confidence. Do you think it is possible Antonio will walk again?"

"I saw something while he was on the Jet Ski with Ramone that made me think he was stronger than he was letting on. I've seen it before. It could be lack of confidence, or possibly laziness. I don't really think Antonio is lazy, but there is no easy way out of this for him. The water spicket doesn't just turn back on by itself. It requires work, hard work, and lots of it. Do I think he can do it? Of course he can! Now he just has to do the work."

Veronica's shop was located on the same block as the Plaza de Toros, which would be filled with patrons later that evening. There were posters on the wall showing the various matadors to be featured that Saturday night. Annie acknowledged to the other two, "I never thought I would wonder if Ramone would fight again. Ever since Salvador was killed, he seems to have lost his spirit for it."

Looking down the street, she commented, "Isn't that Helene with Simon? I heard her ask him for a nightcap as we were leaving the boat last night."

Meghan mumbled, "Long nightcap!"

Celeste, realizing this was none of their business, changed the subject to their immediate project...meeting their wedding planner!

Veronica greeted them warmly at the door. "Come in! Make yourselves comfortable. We have a lot to accomplish, *está bien*?"

Celeste got out her notepad to take notes. Annie commented, "Veronica, when we met the other night at the yacht club, I never knew you were a wedding planner."

With a laugh, she responded, "Well, I don't usually go around passing out my cards, and I was a little preoccupied that evening!"

"Antonio?" Annie guessed.

"He is devastatingly handsome, don't you agree? And that smile just made me melt! But today is about you. Let's get to work. You have the venue for Sunday, two weeks from tomorrow. You will love Vista Hermosa! Sunset is so stunning as it captures the various golden hues against the surrounding mountains and the sea. The only issue is we have to have everything delivered. We can't take anything early because of the wedding the night before. Have you thought of a color theme?"

Annie thought and looked questioningly at her mother and Meghan. "Ramone used to always give me long-stemmed red roses."

Celeste gently said, "Red is not a typical color for a wedding, sweetheart. What colors move you the most?"

That was easy. "The changing colors of the sea, from the palest aquamarine to the deepest blues," Annie answered.

Veronica nodded. "We can work with that. My florist can create some ideas for you this week. Do we have a number of guests?"

Celeste looked at her notepad. "It looks like there will be somewhere between twenty to twenty-five."

Making her own notes, Veronica calculated. "Sunset should be around eight o'clock. We could set up the reception following the wedding on the lower mountainside terrace. Let's discuss whether you want a formal dinner, or more of a buffet like the other night at the yacht club."

Annie looked at both Meghan and Celeste, perplexed. "I honestly didn't think there would be this many people at the wedding. What do you think?"

Meghan responded, "There were about the same number of guests at our wedding, maybe a little less. We did the dinner with music and dancing. What did you think about that?"

"Meghan, your wedding was lovely and stands out as one of the most beautiful weddings I have ever been to. You both know I want something spiritual, which feels to me more fluid. Somehow, in that stunning place I can't envision a formal dinner. Veronica, my mother-in-law-to-be used to be a flamenco dancer. Her dance is so soulful. She danced yesterday to the music and singing of a young man, Simon."

Veronica interrupted. "I know him! He works part time at the yacht club. I have heard him sing. He has a wide variety of song possibilities. Perhaps he can gather a few more players to offer dance music for the guests?"

Meghan nodded. "I like that idea. Maybe all we need are some bar tables set up and waiters passing food. It would be great to have Sabine's input on this."

Annie said to Veronica, "Would you reach out to Simon? We mentioned it yesterday but have not formally hired him. I have two artist friends coming. One of them is from Bali. The people of her country make spiritualism their highest priority. Perhaps she might have some ideas."

Veronica answered, "As long as we do not have to staff and prepare food for a formal sit-down dinner with full service, I think we can wait a few days before deciding."

That sounded good to all of them. As they wrapped up their meeting, Annie remembered to ask if the local almond cake could be made into a wedding cake. "I heard Greta's Bakery might be able to do it. Should we go by there and ask?"

Celeste commented, "We are meeting Marguerite and Antonio for lunch. Maybe after lunch?" Asking Veronica for a lunch recommendation, she invited her to join them. "Perhaps after lunch, we can all go by the bakery?"

Veronica, pleased with the invitation to join them and have a chance to see Antonio again, suggested a place along the board-walk. "I think you'll like it."

# Chapter 45

Marguerite and Antonio showed up at Veronica's shop to walk with them to lunch. Veronica chattered on about the restaurant they were going to and how much they had accomplished. Annie felt like they had much more to do. Meghan suggested they meet again on Monday, and Annie promised to talk with both Sabine and Mara to get their input on the wedding ideas. She wanted to go with Ramone to the doctor Monday morning to get his stitches out. They agreed to meet again Monday afternoon.

Veronica talked about various activities in the area that might entertain the guests. Of course, the Night of the Pilgrims would be that weekend. The Mallorca pearl factory made an interesting excursion. And another option was an intermediate hike with a beautiful route though the picturesque villages of Valldemossa and Deià that her artist friends might love.

Annie jumped in. "We heard about Valldemossa. I think Sarah and Mara might like to paint there one afternoon."

It was a pleasant lunch, and Veronica was happy to engage Antonio in conversation a few times. The visit to Greta's bakery was a treat for them all. She brought out one of the flat round almond cakes, fresh out of the oven, and divided it between them. When asked if she could use the recipe for a wedding cake to feed twenty-five, Greta answered, "My, yes! I have four sizes and can make layers. I sometimes put a lemon filling between the layers that is quite tasty. Then add a fondant icing. It can be decorated as simply or ornately as desired."

Not ready to make a final decision on the decoration of the cake, they at least got it ordered for the wedding. Celeste was busy making her notes.

When they parted, Veronica confirmed with Marguerite. "Annie said you will be dancing at the wedding. I will contact Simon to confirm him and possibly a combo for guest dancing." Marguerite nodded in agreement. To Annie, Veronica said, "I will work on all the other items we discussed and report at our meeting Monday." With a quick wink at Antonio, she added to him, "I hope to see you again soon!" This time she got a reciprocating wink from him.

Ramone was waiting for them at the villa and could not wait to share about the hike and the village of Fornalutx. To Annie and Meghan, he explained, "There are hikers that come to Mallorca just to see these remote ancient villages with less than 350 residents."

Annie answered, "Veronica spoke of a hike that passes the villages Carmina said were worth painting! I would love to try a hike sometime over the week."

Celeste sat down with her pad. "Have you thought where you are going to put everyone?"

Annie thought for a moment. "I'm not sure when Mara and Jonathan are coming. I plan to call her to find out. Also, I'm not sure if they need two rooms? The casita has three bedrooms, and if we need the extra room at the other villa, it is available."

Annie agreed to go call Mara, who answered right away when she saw the call was from Mallorca. "Hello, Annie? I was hoping you would call! How can I help?"

"Did you speak with Jonathan? What are your plans?" Annie asked.

"I did speak with Jonathan. He told me to tell you he would be honored to come. We are meeting in Capri next Saturday. When is Sarah coming?"

Annie answered, "She and El Amir arrive on the following Tuesday."

"All right, we will try to get there Tuesday, at the latest Wednesday. How can I help with the wedding? I know you have certain ideas."

"First, a quick question. I don't mean to pry, but do you need one or two rooms?" Annie could almost feel her blush through the phone. "We have two villas close to each other. I am sure Jonathan could room with my cousin's friend Robert. Or you could room with Sarah? Either way, you would be in the three-bedroom casita with Sarah and El Amir, right by our villa."

Mara answered then dug in a little deeper. "Jonathan and I are not together that way. Your idea is perfect. I know how much you enjoyed the Balinese wedding when you were here. What type of wedding are you planning?"

Annie knew Mara would understand. "Ever since I decided to accept Ramone's proposal, I have wanted a spiritual wedding. I think we have found the perfect place, but I want the ceremony to be right. I did love that Balinese wedding."

"To have a true Balinese wedding, your religion needs to be Hindu. So a full traditional Balinese wedding won't work. However, you can receive a Balinese blessing that includes a lot of the ceremony you seek. I am qualified to do that blessing if you would allow me to do it for you and Ramone."

"That sounds like a dream come true. I would love it! What should I tell the wedding planner to prepare?"

"Why don't you give me her number? I can explain it better one-to-one," Mara replied.

Annie gave her Veronica's number, feeling better and better about the wedding. As an afterthought, Annie asked, "Mara, do you know anything about Hans Schuman?"

"Sarah's Hans? I haven't heard about him in a long time. He studied art with us in Australia. How do you know about him?"

"He is here in Mallorca sailing in the regatta. He is captain of one of the racing boats. He might be here during the wedding. Is there any reason I shouldn't ask him to come?" Annie's curiosity piqued further.

"They have a history, Annie. That's all I can say." Changing the subject, she said goodbye. "Can't wait to see you!"

Annie thought, *Isn't that interesting? Perhaps I should get to know Hans a little better before Sarah arrives.*

# Chapter 46

By the time Annie returned from her call to Mara, her father and Dom were back from their golf game. They had stopped at the yacht club to check on the regatta. Dom was speaking. "The *Nautilus* finished its second day of racing in third place! We saw Roff, and it sounds like he's having an amazing experience. He seems to really admire Hans as a captain."

Alex added, "Roff asked about Captain Luis and Helene, and we told him what a nice outing we had with them yesterday. He did ask Dom about how his replacement did, concerned he was absent."

Dom said, "I told him Simon did a fine job, but we would be glad to have him back after Tuesday night's awards. He knew they were sailing back to Marbella on Wednesday to help Tomás. Then Roff left as Hans was about to take the crew to an early dinner since the start time on Sunday was a little later."

Inwardly, Annie thought Roff might shed some light on Hans and how he might be connected to Sarah. That line of thought led to wondering about Roff's reaction to a possible romance developing between Helene and Simon. *Hmmm...*

Celeste broke her thoughts with a question. "Have you decided about your wedding party?"

Annie had already thought this through. "For me, I would like to stay with family. Meghan, if you will do me the honor, I would like to have you and Sabine stand up with me."

Meghan had hoped but didn't want to presume. She went over to Annie for a giant hug. "Yes, I would love to!"

Ramone added, "I feel the same about family. Antonio, I could not do any better than to have you and Tomás at my side as I marry this woman."

Antonio rolled his chair over to Ramone. "I wish I could stand next to you, brother, but I will definitely be by your side!" Ramone reached down to hug him.

Ramone had run out of steam. Not a hiker, he had pushed his endurance to the limit and was exhausted. "I'm afraid I am going to say good night early. Muscles I didn't know I had are aching, and I think a good night's rest is calling me."

Annie suggested, "How about a hot bath to soothe those muscles? I'll be along soon. We don't have anything planned tomorrow. Maybe we can relax a little."

"I did commit to lunch with Stephan and Carmina, but other than that, no plans. Take your time, *querida*. I like the idea of a hot bath." With a kiss, he said good night.

Antonio and Alex were playing a card game. Dom was reading the paper. Gennie motioned Annie over to where she was sitting with Meghan and Celeste. To Annie, she said, "You only have two bridesmaids. If I can find someone to loan me a sewing machine, I can make the dresses for Sabine and Meghan. I could start on Meghan's, and by the time I finish, I could start Sabine's and fit it to her when she arrives. Did you decide on your color theme?"

With a sigh, she responded, "I know it is not traditional, but I keep coming back to red. It reflects Spain, and I am marrying a matador! I will also marry the man who presented me red roses tossed from the ring the first day we met, with every note or invitation, on the flight when I decided to come back to Spain, and even strewn everywhere when he proposed. How could we not use red?"

Meghan smiled. "Even with my red hair, one of my favorite colors to wear is red!"

Celeste was stunned. "Red dresses?"

Gennie suggested, "Why don't we see what solid red fabric

we can find that would go with red roses or red orchids? Plus, I need to find a sewing machine!"

Annie added, "Veronica will have spoken with Mara about what she needs for the Balinese blessing part of the ceremony. Having seen a wedding when I was in Bali, bright colors would not be a problem." To Meghan, "Tomorrow, let's look at pictures of dresses and see the style we want that would be easy enough to have ready in time."

Marguerite had overheard and walked over. "Over the years, I have danced in many places and worn red dresses. What about a simple strapless dress with a wrap bodice and tea-length skirt? I asked Tomás to bring one of my gowns that happens to be gold and white with red accents! If we could find black-and-white lace fans, perhaps your florist could add them to the bouquets? I think the effect could be very pretty. The men could wear black and white with a red-rose boutonniere."

Annie's excitement showed in her response. "I love these ideas! It is coming together. Now I am also going to say good night and join my soon-to-be husband."

*****

Annie and Ramone, happy to sleep in, felt no urgent need to move about. Annie's leg draped over Ramone in a possessive spooning position. His arm secured it in place. Before long, with Annie's stomach flat against his lower back, Ramone felt the baby kicking. Adjusting himself to roll over, he put his hand over the source of the movements and whispered, "Rest now, little one." The movements slowed, then stopped. At that moment, Annie didn't think she could love this man any deeper and smiled holding him closer until they all three drifted back to sleep.

It was midmorning before they finally dressed and came downstairs. Dom and Gennie had gone to mass at the Santa Maria cathedral. Celeste offered to bring them a coffee and pastry, so they wandered out to the pool. Antonio was already working with

Meghan. He had the float and weights attached to get back to the vertical position and bounce. She then had him using his arms at the same time. Eventually, she took off the weights and had him hold the side of the pool and try to kick. One leg, then the other. His right leg seemed to show more strength. Meghan kept experimenting with how to strengthen the left leg further. She planned to find someone in Palma trained in therapeutic massage who could come to the villa to work with him on a series of specific stretches and weight training.

Celeste mentioned, "Meghan and I might go back to Port D'Andratx to look for something to wear to the awards dinner at the yacht club. Annie, would you like to join us?"

Annie replied, "Ramone and I plan to meet Stephan and Carmina for lunch, but I could meet you after. Depending on where they are hiking in the afternoon, Ramone might join them."

Celeste nodded. "That sounds good. Marguerite, what about you?"

Marguerite smiled at her younger son. "I am taking Antonio to Old Town. I believe we might be meeting someone."

Annie quickly asked, "Veronica? How did that come about?"

Antonio, distracted from his exercise, said, "Mamà! It is nothing! She called this morning and mentioned she would be on the boardwalk later."

To Annie, Marguerite asked, "If we see Veronica this afternoon, do you mind if I share some of the ideas from last night? If you want to wait until tomorrow's meeting, I understand. I have to admit, I am anxious to know if she booked Simon. His music has such a hypnotic effect!"

Annie realized all they were trying to accomplish in such a short time. Soon there would be guests arriving to be entertained. "Yes, it would be good for her to start thinking about them. Hopefully, we can finalize some of it tomorrow."

Looking at his watch, Ramone told Annie, "It is time to go if we don't want to be late. We will take the scooter to Cala Deià. It is a beautiful beach, and the restaurant is known for its fresh seafood! If we like it, perhaps we can hike the beginning of the Dry Stone Route. From Palma to Cala Deià, it is a fairly easy thirty-minute walk. We'll take the scooter today. If I hike after lunch, you could take the scooter to meet Meghan and your mom."

Annie and Ramone grabbed their backpacks and waved as they left.

# Chapter 47

W hen the scooter crested the foothill nearest the shore, Annie called out, "There are the boats in the regatta. I wonder if we will be able to see them from the beach?"

Ramone pulled over to the side to watch for a few minutes. "Possibly. Stephan told me there are four royal entries—the king, a duke, and two viscounts. I would think they would be enormously competitive."

"Tuesday night should be interesting. You heard my friend Sarah might know Hans. I wonder if it is through his art gallery?" More thinking aloud than wanting an answer, Annie climbed back on the scooter.

When they rounded the last corner, the small rocky cove of Cala Deià stood before them with crystal-clear blue-green water and a small beach filled with pebbles and large boulders. Locals were swimming or perched along the rocks catching some sun. Annie and Ramone found the open-air restaurant up a narrow stone stairway at the top of a cliff overlooking the water. Stephan waved them over to their table with a spectacular view.

They greeted with European hugs all around. Stephan asked if Ramone was sore from yesterday's hike. He answered, "I was sore but in a good way. The hike was amazing! I can't wait to get Annie up in the mountains."

Annie laughed. "He slept like a rock! He talked on and on about how great it was. Especially interesting to me was the village you stopped at."

Stephan answered. "That was Fornalutx. I guess Ramone told you its history dates back over a thousand years?"

Annie answered, "Yes, and that it was originally an Arab farmstead. Our friend El Amir will be here for the wedding next week. He is from Morocco and should find that interesting. We will have to plan a visit." Looking at Ramone as an afterthought, she added, "We should tell Tomás to bring our hiking boots with him and also let the others know to bring theirs if they want to hike."

Carmina said with excitement, "I heard you liked Vista Hermosa as your wedding venue and were able to book it! Isn't it awe-inspiring? I can't wait to hear how you plan to pull this off in just two weeks!" Happy to share, Annie and Carmina began discussing the wedding and some of the ideas they had come up with so far.

Stephan and Ramone were deep in conversation like old friends. Their lunch of salad, fresh fish, and root vegetables was extraordinary.

Carmina confided to Annie, "It was nice to take a break yesterday. It always seems Stephan can go forever, but I sure don't mind a little downtime, or even doing one or two of the easier hikes."

Annie had a thought. "Maybe while our guests are here, we could offer two hikes with you leading the easier one and Stephan leading the more difficult? By the way, will it be hard to finish the pilgrimage hike to the monastery?"

Carmina told her, "We would love to do the hikes for you. Stephan and I are here and training to increase our endurance so we will make it. But honestly, it would be almost impossible for someone new to hiking to make it to the end. It will still be worth going for the spirit of the occasion, as well as the atmosphere. They make it easy to stop wherever along the way and take the shuttle back to Palma."

Stephan had Ramone convinced to join them on their afternoon hike, so Annie shook her head, smiling, realizing he seemed to have found a new passion! She said goodbye and took the scooter to join her mother and Meghan shopping in Port

D'Andratx. Checking the map, she charted her course over the mountain ridge. Along the way, she noted various remote villages that looked deserving of further investigation. Annie had one scare along the road where the loose gravel was particularly thick. The gravel caused the scooter to slide, which led to a moment of panic before she fortunately righted herself and the scooter before falling. Slowing her speed a little, she thought, *That was a close one.*

*****

Annie didn't see the car coming around the curve of the mountain road until it was right upon her. Pure instinct made her swerve in order to miss being hit. Both Annie and the scooter went airborne and landed hard in the side ditch. The car screeched to a halt and pulled over. The driver, a middle-aged man, rushed to Annie's side. "I am so sorry! I didn't see you. Are you all right?"

Annie tried to focus. Was she all right? Then, with a bolt of fear, she muttered, "I'm pregnant."

Another car had stopped and the silver-haired man came over to help. The original driver was assessing whether she could be lifted. "My name is Paulo. The hospital is twenty minutes from here. Does anything feel broken?"

When Annie shook her head, the two men gently lifted Annie into the back seat. Paulo used his jacket as a pillow under her head. Once they loaded the scooter into the trunk, the other man asked if there was anyone he could call. Annie tried to think where everyone was. *Dad should be at home with Dom and Gennie.* Haltingly, she said, "My name is Annie. Please call my father. He is at Don Marco's estate, Casa de Esperanza." Before she could give him the number, Annie faded out of consciousness.

To Paulo, he said, "Don't worry. I will find her father. Get her to the hospital."

*****

186

Celeste and Meghan decided to browse through the fashions at the boutique where Annie planned to meet them. Meghan was looking through a rack of dresses and pulled one out. "Look what I found!" Holding a strapless red dress, Meghan beamed. "Should I try it on? Gennie wouldn't have to make the dresses. Celeste, why don't you check to see if there is one in Sabine's size?"

Meghan came out of the dressing room in the dress. It was the deepest crimson red with a strapless fitted bodice and draped tulip skirt. Celeste looked at Meghan. "You should wear red often. It looks absolutely stunning on you!"

"I know Annie would love it. Did you find a second one?" Meghan saw Celeste hold up the second dress. "Shall I keep the dress on? I want Annie to see it. Shouldn't she be here by now?"

Celeste answered, "Maybe their lunch took longer than expected?" To the clerk, she explained the situation and were told they could purchase the dresses, and if the bride didn't care for them, they could be returned.

Marguerite left Antonio in deep conversation with Veronica at the café by the marina. Veronica seemed to like the idea of the red dresses with the black-and-white fans attached to the bouquets. She suggested a shop a block up the main street that specialized in fans. Marguerite passed a lot of the tourist shops, most with the unique handmade pearls of Mallorca in the windows. Finally, she found the shop with the fans. The selection seemed endless. How was she to pick the right one? She would find one she liked, only to not find a matching one. When she mentioned to the shop owner what she was looking for, she went to the back room and came back with two of the most exquisite black-and-white fans with intricate lace designs. "These are perfect! I will take them."

*****

Alex answered the call from the witness. His daughter had been in an accident and was being taken to the hospital. Alex immediately called the hospital to tell them his daughter was on the way, and he was on his way. To Dom, he hurriedly explained he was heading to the hospital. "Find Ramone and Celeste, whatever you have to do!" Gennie insisted she go with Alex.

*****

The trail ended at the Palma marina in Old Town. Ramone had once again found hiking gave him a sense of clarity that made his thoughts seem less jumbled. He suggested a quick beer to Stephan and Carmina, then spotted Antonio up ahead at the café. He was in an animated conversation with Veronica, and Ramone was happy to see some of Antonio's old confidence restored. The three of them pulled over a table and sat down. Marguerite returned just as they were getting their beers. She slipped her shopping bag to Veronica so Ramone wouldn't see what she bought. Veronica gave her a knowing smile.

The waiter was going to each table. He came to theirs. "Is there a Ramone Sanchez here?"

"I'm Ramone Sanchez."

"There is a phone call for you," the waiter said.

"That's strange. Who would know I was here?" He hurriedly went to take the call. "Dom, what! *O Dios mío!* How is she? Tell them I will be right there!" To the waiter, "How do I get to the hospital?"

# Chapter 48

Ramone rushed back to the table to get his backpack. "I have to go. Annie was in an accident and is at the hospital."

Marguerite quickly said, "Go quickly. We will settle up here and be right behind you!"

Stephan called after him, "Please let us know if we can do anything."

Alex and Gennie entered the waiting room at the ER and looked for someone to ask about Annie. A man about Alex's age came up to him. "Are you Annie's father? I am Paulo, Juan Carlos's son. I was in the car."

"Was she hit? Where is she?" Alex inquired.

"Thankfully, she must have been going slow. She saw my car at the last minute and swerved off the road. She and the scooter landed in the ditch. I checked for any broken bones, then brought her here as quickly as I could. I can't tell you how deeply sorry I am. The medical desk is over behind that door. I'll be right here."

Alex went straight to the medical desk. "My daughter was just brought into the ER. How is she? May I see her?"

"I can only allow one person at a time." Gennie said she would go back to the waiting room. The doctor led the way, explaining, "Your daughter is stable. I understand she is pregnant."

Alex responded, "Yes. Five months."

The doctor continued, "We are monitoring them both. The baby's heartbeat is weak but steady. Annie is drifting in and out of consciousness, giving us a little concern about a concussion. My recommendation would be to observe her and the baby overnight to make certain how the trauma affected them both."

Nodding, Alex went up to Annie, lying so pale in the hospital bed. "Honey, it's Dad." He took her hand. "You were in an accident and are in the hospital."

Annie squeezed his hand with her eyes still closed and asked, "The baby?"

Alex's eyes glistened. "You will both be fine, sweetheart. Get some rest. Ramone and your mother will be here soon. Your grandmother is right outside in the waiting room." Alex pulled up a chair and held her hand until she visibly relaxed. Through the squeeze of his hand, he willed all of his love and healing thoughts into his only child. "Annie, you've got this. You're strong, and so is your child. Rest well." In her light sleep, Annie could hear her father's words. *Wasn't it just this morning Ramone told our child to rest?* A single tear rolled down her cheek.

Alex could hear Ramone speaking with the doctor. He started to release Annie's hand, but she wouldn't let go. After a moment, she must have felt Ramone entering the room. She tried to open her eyes but couldn't. In a flash, he was at her side. Alex transferred her hand to Ramone's and left to go update Gennie. When he got to the waiting room, they were all there, including Paulo, looking distraught.

Alex went to Celeste to give her a comforting hug, then told them Annie and the baby were stable. They would probably be moving her to a regular hospital room for the night to continue to observe her for a possible concussion. The baby's heartbeat had been weak. However, it was getting stronger. With a little lightness to break all the serious concern, he added, "Probably because he or she is the child of a matador!"

Somehow those words made Antonio's heart swell with pride for his profession. He knew his brother felt that same pride deep in his heart. He said a prayer for Annie, the baby, and Ramone.

Ramone held Annie's hand tight and reached up to kiss her, lingering with his lips close to her. "*Querida*, you frightened me. What would I do without you?"

As if to comfort him, Annie moved her arms to his shoulders to bring him close. "We are going to be fine. I know it. Don't worry." Ramone looked at her with wonder. He might have muscular strength, but he knew his *querida* was the strong one.

The nurse came to move Annie to the hospital room. Ramone asked her, "I know her mother wants to see her, but I just can't leave her side. Can she come in?"

"Let's get her moved and I will let her mother know she can come see her as soon as she is settled in her new room." The nurse turned to an assistant to have him share that news with Celeste. Then Annie was moved to a stretcher to transport her. Ramone could see her reach for him when they lost contact. Once secure, Ramone took her hand for the ride to her room.

Without the intensity of the ER surroundings, Annie relaxed in her new environment. Celeste came in with tears flowing to see her daughter hurt. Annie's eyes fluttered open, and she reached up to her mom for a hug. More conscious than before, she attempted to tell them what happened. "I had just run across a patch of gravel. The scooter slid a little but got back on course. I was deliberately going slower when the car came around the corner. That allowed me an extra split second to get out of the way. The driver stopped immediately. He felt terrible and made sure I got here to the hospital."

Celeste told her, "He is still here. His name is Paulo, and he is Juan Carlos's son. He feels entirely responsible and won't leave until he knows you and the baby will be okay."

Encouraged by Annie's new alertness, both Ramone and Celeste felt better about her prognosis. Ramone insisted he would stay by her side overnight. He was not going anywhere. Celeste went to tell the others. Annie said to her, "Mom, tell them I love them. Please don't let that man feel so bad. I know he didn't see me."

# Chapter 49

Celeste went out to the waiting room and announced, "I am so relieved. Annie is conscious and speaking. She and the baby had a jolt, but they both seem to be doing well. The doctors are merely keeping her for observation. Ramone will be here with her overnight." Such good news for all of them, it seemed there was nothing more they could do there at the hospital.

Paulo was sitting in the back corner on the waiting room with his head in his hands. It was Marguerite who went over to him and put a consoling hand on his shoulder. "You heard her. Annie and the baby are going to be fine. Everyone knows it was an accident."

Crushed, Paulo looked at her with an agonized expression. "It was my fault. What if I had hit her?"

Marguerite found herself staring at an older version of Simon! Flustered by this man who had Simon's striking looks, Marguerite struggled to get her wits back. "But, you see, you didn't hit her. She's going to be okay." Not quite sure how to phrase it, she went forward anyway. "I heard you are Juan Carlos's son. He has been wonderful to us during our stay here. I see the resemblance between you, but you look exactly like a young man we just met. He substituted for our first mate on the *Porto Banus* Friday."

"You must mean my son, Simon. We are all sailors. I am manager of the yacht club, and Simon works there part-time. I've seen the *Porto Banus*. She is a magnificent vessel. How are you related to Annie?"

"It is my son, Ramone, who is marrying Annie two weeks from today. It is his child she is carrying. Your son has a soulful sense of music. He played the guitar and sang for us. I think the wedding planner is booking him for the wedding."

"He does have the gift of a true musician. I am surprised he has not pursued it more purposefully. You should hear my daughter, Marcella. She can play tunes on her violin that bring you to tears or lift you higher than ever imagined!"

Marguerite studied this man a little more. "She must be the violinist who played for us the first night. She has a beautiful skill as well. Your children have an abundance of talent. Both of my sons are matadors out of Marbella. Unfortunately, my younger son was injured in the ring." Realizing everyone else was leaving, her final words were "Thank you for your speed in getting Annie here to the hospital and for caring enough to see her safe. Maybe we will meet again at some point while we're here."

Alex and Celeste both came up to Paulo to shake his hand. Alex said, "Thank you for your quick actions and your concern."

"I wish I could have seen her or done more. I am devastated she was hurt." Alex could see his sincerity and was touched.

"Thank you." Alex shook his hand once more.

Meanwhile, Ramone blamed himself. Looking at Annie, he said, "I should never have let you go off on the scooter alone on these roads. How could I have been so selfish?" Caressing her stomach with one hand and the other with fingertips entwined with hers, said, "You and this child are everything to me. How could I exist without you?"

Annie encouraged him to lie on the bed next to her. "We both feel that way. If anything, we have learned there are no guarantees in life that our journey together will be an easy one. Maybe we simply make a habit of enjoying each step along the way. Let's never regret the moments we have together and try to live them with joy, not fear."

There was not much sleep to be had in the hospital sleeper chair, but it was all worth it when the doctor came in and gave both Annie and the baby a clean bill of health. To Annie, the doctor said, "You had a mild concussion and a shock from the fall.

And that baby of yours is a warrior! You are free to go once the paperwork is finished. Take it easy for a few days. By the way, we did an ultrasound of the baby. Do you want to know the sex?"

Looking at Ramone gently shaking his head, Annie said, "No. Either way, this child is a blessing. We don't need to know yet." The doctor nodded and was about to leave when Annie interrupted him. "Doctor, we are supposed to come back here to get Ramone's stitches removed today. Is there a chance we could get that done before we leave to save a trip?"

"That is a good idea. I will have the nurse practitioner come in and remove them." Walking over to Ramone to check the stitches, he said, "Those were some pretty nasty wounds, but they are healing nicely. Another week or two the redness should be gone."

Annie laughed. "Just in time for the wedding!"

The whole family was relieved Annie and the baby were well and coming home. Alex took the car to bring them back to the villa. At the hospital, he found them in good spirits and Ramone's stitches out. A hug to his daughter, then a closer look at Ramone, he said, "The scars look much better without those stitches."

# Chapter 50

A huge bouquet of multicolored flowers was waiting for Annie back at the villa. Attached was a note from Paulo:

'Annie,

*I am so terribly sorry about the accident. I have spoken with my son, Simon, and he would be happy to play at your wedding. My daughter, Marcella, plays the violin in such amazing ways, and she would also like to offer her talent. If you would allow me, I would be honored to cater the food for the reception. I have full-service chefs at the yacht club who are brilliant with their culinary skills. If my family can make it up to you in any way, please let us know. Veronica could fill in the details for us.*

*Most humbly, Paulo'*

Meghan said, "That was so generous! Annie, why don't you get some rest? Veronica offered to come here for the meeting so you wouldn't have to go back out."

Annie was still looking at the note. "I forgot about the meeting with Veronica. Tell her meeting here would be great." Suddenly, Annie looked as if she might pass out.

Ramone caught her and added, "Why don't you make it a little later in the afternoon? Let's let her rest some." He moved her toward the stairs. By the second flight, he thought it would be easier to just lift and carry her. Annie undressed and got into bed, then reached for Ramone. "You didn't get any sleep. Will you rest with me?" All she wanted was his naked skin close to hers. He cringed when he saw the large bruise forming on her hip where she had landed. He got the Moroccan oil and rubbed it gently into the bruise. She had already nodded off when Ramone climbed in beside her cradling her like the treasure she was to him. Before he knew it, he was asleep too.

Meghan lightly knocked on their door. When there was no response, she knocked a little harder. After two more tries, Ramone woke and called out, "Yes, what is it?"

"It's Meghan. You two have been sleeping for hours. I have a tray with various tapas and some sparkling water. I will set it outside the door. Veronica will be here in about forty-five minutes. Alex suggested you men go down to the yacht club while we are meeting."

Ramone answered, "Okay, thank you." Rolling over to gently caress Annie's face, he said, "Wake up, *querida*. Your meeting will start soon. Meghan brought us some tapas."

Reaching to bring his head down, Annie lifted her body up into a most sensuous kiss. Ramone, with a teasing scold, complained. "That is not the way to let me out of this bed!"

"Who said anything about wanting you out of this bed?" Annie purred.

"Oh no, let's go! Hop in the shower and get dressed." Ramone wrapped a towel around himself while Annie reluctantly went to the shower. He got the tray from the other side of the door. Gennie had created quite an assortment. Ramone suddenly realized he was starving and started munching before he could set the tray down. A few bites down, Ramone went to the bathroom door and leaned against the frame as he let his towel slide off. Annie stepped out of the shower to reach for a towel. Ramone said huskily, "Here, let me do that." He rubbed her with the towel, noticing how lush and intoxicating her body was becoming. She leaned into him, hungry for his caresses. When he began to tease her nipples with his tongue, she broke away from him.

"Now who is the seducer? Hold that thought, sir, and don't forget where we left off."

"Oh, I won't, *querida*. I won't," Ramone said with a wicked smile.

Annie enjoyed one last toasted baguette with Iberico ham and cream cheese, then was ready to go downstairs. Celeste saw her and commented with a knowing smile, "I'm glad to see you've got your color back, sweetheart. Did you have a good nap?"

With a slight blush, Annie replied, "Ramone was awake most of the night. Fortunately, we both slept well. When will Veronica be here?"

"She should be here any time. The men are going to the yacht club to see if they can locate Paulo."

Ramone had to admit he was anxious to thank Paulo for his quick reaction to get Annie to the hospital and for his offers about the wedding. He saw Antonio heading for the pool and asked, "Aren't you going with us?"

Antonio replied, "I want to continue my exercises. Also, Veronica plans to bring her swimsuit to go for a swim after their meeting."

That got an *oh really?* look from Ramone, but he said, "Have fun, brother. You deserve it."

Veronica arrived soon after Ramone left with Alex and Dom. She shared with Annie how worried she was about her and was so happy to see her better. She waved over at Antonio, but he was working out. "Shall we get started?"

Moving out to the veranda, Annie looked about. "Where did Meghan go?"

"Annie, we have a few surprises for you. If you like what Meghan has to show you, Gennie won't have to locate a sewing machine!"

Meghan walked out in the red dress they found. "Surprise!"

Annie, stunned, got up and walked all around her. "I love it!"

Meghan twisted and turned. "I feel like I should have a pair of ruby slippers and click my heels three times! Isn't it great?"

Celeste lifted the second dress. "If you approve, we got an extra in Sabine's size!"

Gennie was next to add, "I think these dresses are exactly what you asked for. If you need me to embellish them in any way, that would be my pleasure."

Looking at her mom, Annie said, "What do you think? Is it too much for a wedding?"

Celeste understood her daughter and her second thoughts. "What if Gennie were to wrap a little red mesh over the bodice and one shoulder? That would tame it down a little."

Veronica then interjected, "Marguerite found another surprise!" She opened the bag with the fans.

Annie held one gingerly like she was holding a piece of fine art. "It is gorgeous! I've never seen anything like it." Looking at Marguerite, she said, "Where on earth did you find it?"

"Veronica told me about a store not far from the marina that carried an assortment of fans. I couldn't find a matching pair of anything that would be suitable. Then the shop owner went to the back and brought these two out for me to see. I couldn't resist and bought them on the spot."

Annie took the fan she was holding and asked Meghan to hold it. She envisioned the flowers attached to it and the mesh over the shoulders. "Oh my gosh! You ladies did an incredible job. Thank you!"

Meghan went to change. Her mother said with a heartfelt lump in her throat, "You can't imagine how happy we are that you are here with us. We're here for you, sweetheart."

Annie wrinkled into tears. It was Marguerite who came over to her. "My darling girl, you are marrying a daring young man fit to be a star matador. You are strong too. I think he's met his match in you. I will also be here for you always. You are exactly the right woman for my son." She ended with a hug.

Celeste and Gennie were both tearful at that touching scene. Even Veronica's eyes were glistening.

Composing herself, Veronica took back control of the meeting. "So we have the bridesmaids' dresses worked out. I think Marguerite's idea of white *Guayabera*-style white shirts and black pants for Antonio and Tomás is perfect."

Annie agreed. "Don't tell me what Ramone will be wearing. I want both our outfits to be a surprise."

"Noted!" Veronica continued, "We are set on the wedding cake. After seeing the input of the red dresses, this is what I ordered, with your approval of course. We are doing a three-layer almond cake. Each of the three levels will be two cakes with Greta's lemon filling between them. The entire cake will be covered with white fondant icing. The bottom tier will be covered in large dark-red icing roses. At the seam between the second and third tier, there will be an accent row of small red icing roses. On the top will be genuine red roses."

Annie was beside herself. "So I represent the large red roses, and our child represents the small red roses. Veronica, that could not be more perfect!"

"As you know, Paulo arranged for the catering on the reception. He will provide me with menu options in the next few days. Mara called me and is bringing certain things that I will go over with her once she gets here. For now, our next meeting is Wednesday. We will meet with the florist and go over the menu options with Paulo. Does that sound good?"

Annie answered Veronica. "Perfect. Is it okay if I join you at the pool?"

"Me too!" Meghan added. Veronica's hope of having alone time with Antonio was long gone. There was nothing to do but make the best of it.

# Chapter 51

The yacht club was teeming with activity late Monday afternoon when Ramone, Alex, and Don Marco arrived. The sailors were coming in from the day's sail, and the atmosphere was tense as the next to the last day of the regatta ended. Tuesday's race would be a short one to get the final rankings. There was a dispute between the Viscount's boat captain and another racer with a challenge of foul play. Paulo was over on the dock attempting to settle it.

They saw the *Nautilus* tied up to the dock. Roff spotted them and came over with Hans behind him. Roff greeted them, concerned, "I heard Annie was in an accident. Is she all right?"

Ramone answered, "The doctors kept her overnight as an extra precaution with the baby, but thankfully she seems fine today after some rest."

Hans shook hands and to Don Marco said, "I can't thank you enough, sir. Roff has been an excellent addition to the crew. It looks like we are in the running for one of the top places."

Dom answered, "It was my pleasure. We think very highly of the boy! What is this dispute all about?"

Hans explained, "The *Prisa* came too close to the Viscount's boat when she crossed the bow. I agree it was reckless, but the Viscount pressed his course and did not give way. It could have been a bad accident. If the *Prisa* gets disqualified, that moves the *Nautilus* up a place and would put us in second place behind the duke. The race tomorrow is a short one and will end by early afternoon. The judges will add up the scores and announce the winners by categories at the awards ceremony tomorrow night. I have arranged a large table for my crew. Do you have arrangements?"

Don Marco answered, "Juan Carlos has arranged a table for my family. It was his son Paulo's car that made Annie swerve her scooter off the road. It was an unfortunate accident, but we owe him a debt of gratitude for his quick actions on the scene." Glancing over at Paulo, he added, "It looks like he might be finishing with the Viscount."

Paulo saw them and walked over. "I am so glad you are here. That means either Annie is much better, or you are here to shoot me!" That got a laugh from the three men realizing they might have looked a little intimidating as they arrived together.

Alex answered this time. "This visit is to thank you for taking care of our girl. Your flowers and offers for the wedding were most generous."

"It is the very least I could do." Looking at Ramone, Paulo asked, "Ramone, is it?" When he nodded, Paulo continued, "Your mother was so kind in the waiting room. It meant a great deal. I understand she plans to dance to my son's music. Marcella's violin should also make a great addition. Simon asked me about a playlist. He will be at the awards ceremony tomorrow night. Perhaps they can arrange a rehearsal time." To Hans, he continued, "I heard both the Viscount's version of what happened, as well as the captain of the *Prisa*'s story. I will convey that to the committee, and they will have a ruling before the race begins tomorrow." To all of them, he added, "If there is nothing else I can do, I will go report to the committee."

As an afterthought, Don Marco inquired, "Would it be possible to add two more seats to my table for tomorrow night? I would like to have Captain Luis and Helene join us." He could see that idea pleased Roff immensely.

"Of course! Consider it done. I must go now. See you all tomorrow." Paulo left with a final shake of hands.

Hans suggested, "Why don't you join me in the club for a drink? A cold beer sounds good right now!" That got a round of approval, and they followed him into the club.

The conversation moved from how the regatta was going and how they thought the *Nautilus* would place to Roff going back to the *Porto Banus* to make the round trip to Marbella on Wednesday. Ramone recalled Annie's comment about her friend Sarah possibly knowing Hans. He knew El Amir was bringing her next Tuesday. Maybe he could edge his way into learning more. He asked, "Hans, if I recall, you are staying until after the Night of the Pilgrims hike. Our wedding is that Sunday at Vista Hermosa."

"I have seen that place carved into the mountain. What a magnificent venue for a wedding! Yes, several years ago, I began to close the gallery for the month of August each year. It is the perfect time to travel, do the sailing I love, and find new adventures. Then it is back to reality until the following August. Don't get me wrong. I enjoy what I do, but ever since I lost my wife, I feel I somehow need to remove myself from my rather boring daily life every year. I plan to do a lot of hiking after tomorrow. There is one hike that goes between the old villages that sounds really good to me. If I think I can manage the hike to the monastery, I'd like to try it. I have an open ticket to return to Hamburg."

Ramone told him about Stephan and Carmina and how much he enjoyed hiking with them. "You should meet them. Maybe we can set up a hike later this week? By the way, I like your idea of taking a month off every year. With my fighting, I move a lot from city to city and don't have much downtime. Getting married and having a child might change all that."

Don Marco and Alex knew the struggles Ramone was going through and were happy to see him opening up more. Meeting Stephan and now Hans might be just the thing he needed.

# Chapter 52

Annie thought the awards dinner and ceremony seemed like it would be a most interesting evening. Hans would be there with his crew, which meant Roff would be there. Dom added Captain Luis and Helene to their table. According to Ramone, Simon would be there to work out rehearsal times with Marguerite. He mentioned Paulo would be checking on her to be sure she survived the accident, but he also said he seemed a little intrigued by his mother. And Hans was married? Did Sarah do a show at his gallery? It certainly looked as though he would be here while she was. *Hmmm...*

For the moment, her attire was the question. She gave herself a mental note to try on the wedding dress again. She felt the baby and her stomach seemed bigger every day. For this evening, Annie chose a pair of white linen pants that had an elastic-back waist that should give her some room. She decided to pair it with a bright pink knit tank top, multicolor chunky necklace, and navy blazer. This would have to do. Saturday with her wardrobe replenished could not come fast enough!

Ramone and her father had picked up a few things at the yacht club pro shop the day before. He looked dashing as ever in a hunter-green sport shirt and khaki pants. Having the stitches removed made a big difference to his handsome face, and she thought she better keep a close eye on her man. Laughing at herself when she saw the look in his eye as she walked out to the veranda, she knew she was the only woman he saw. Walking toward her, he put his arm around her and whispered, "There is a new glow about you, *querida*. You have put a spell on me."

She smiled up at him. "The accident was a scare, I'll admit. I am just so happy to be alive and that our baby is healthy."

Ramone jokingly complained, "Last night, our little one must have been building houses in there. It would be nice if we could get on the same sleep schedule."

That got a chuckle. Annie knowingly said, "Just wait. At least we are not yet listening to screaming cries demanding food or to be changed. That will come soon enough. Speaking of little ones, I am a little disappointed we don't have any children for the ceremony. It would be nice to have a flower girl or ring bearer." Just as she said it, they looked at each other and said simultaneously, "We forgot the rings!"

Ramone shook his head. "Guess we're going ring shopping tomorrow!"

Annie thought for a moment. "I have the next meeting with Veronica tomorrow after lunch. There are lots of jewelry stores in Palma. I already have my engagement ring. We just need the bands. That shouldn't take long."

The captain and Helene were at the door when Don Marco and all the family arrived. Juan Carlos had asked if Dom and Gennie would like to join their table, but tonight Dom wanted to be with his own group. As he looked around the table, he felt proud of each of them. Ramone's family was fitting right into theirs. Meghan was a true gem who had won Tomás's heart. Sabine's family would be here soon. He and Gennie had discussed several ideas about guest activities to do after they arrived. They planned to start working on those plans in earnest tomorrow.

Annie commented, "Helene, you look particularly lovely tonight. Are you ready to sail back to Marbella tomorrow?"

Helene was looking around the room, somewhat distracted, but answered, "Of course. I always took forward to sailing, but the time here in Mallorca has been very nice."

The awards portion of the evening would come first, followed by dinner and dancing. Hans's table was across the room. The *Prisa* and the Viscount's boats had both been disqualified for reckless sailing. As far as they knew, the duke's entry was the leader. Roff came over to say a quick hello, then rejoined Hans's table. Paulo sounded the brass ship's bell to get the awards session started. He began by explaining the procedure. They would present the awards by class.

While Paulo continued to MC the ceremony, Marguerite had an opportunity to scrutinize this man who had been on her mind since that evening at the hospital. Observing a little closer, his tall, lean body did not have the breadth of Simon or even her own sons, but he had the same wavy hair as Simon, although with streaks of gray along his temples. There was something about his face that held her attention. The similarity to Simon's was there, but with added experience, wisdom, and even pain. She could see it all. As if he could feel her stare, he glanced over with his eyes piercing hers. Annie noticed and nudged Ramone, who saw it too.

*****

The final class of awards was the fifty-to-sixty-foot classification. Once they announced the third-place position and it was *not* the *Nautilus*, the crowd started cheering. Indeed, the *Nautilus* came in second and the duke's first. Both crews moved to the stage and were shaking hands with each other. Hans and the duke accepted their trophies, and the room was an uproar in applause and cheers. Don Marco's table seemed to lead the cheers. The captain and Helene ran up to the stage to congratulate Roff. Annie was still clapping when she saw Helene hug Roff before Simon stepped up and pulled her away. Ramone got another nudge, especially when they saw Roff watch Helene and Simon leave with a questioning look on his face.

Captain Luis brought Roff back to their table, and everyone was on their feet, offering congratulations. Since Helene seemed to have vanished, everyone asked Roff to join them at the empty seat. He had to go back for photos but promised he'd return. Annie couldn't resist asking Luis, "Is Helene dating Simon?"

The captain gave a deep laugh. "Lassie, I'm an old man. I've learned not to stick my nose where it doesn't belong." Changing the subject, he said to Don Marco, "I heard the chef here at the yacht club is Michelin rated and that he will be providing the food for the reception. I wonder what he has in store for tonight?"

Don Marco was wise enough to see some of the dramatic possibilities surrounding him, but he took heed of Luis's advice. Even Antonio seemed to be looking around for Veronica, who had not made an appearance as of yet. Dom patted Gennie's knee under the table and spoke to her in a low voice. "Love is in the air tonight, my dear. Don't stray too far."

Gennie laughed at the absurdity that she would ever stray. Then she remembered Dom as a young debonair man who stole her heart but raged with jealousy any time another man looked at her. She leaned over and kissed his cheek, giving him the assurance he sought, that she had always been and would always be devoted to him.

Dinner was served, beginning with a light Mallorcan soup containing tomato and garlic. Fresh sourdough bread came straight from the oven. After the soup, the chef offered a *fritanga*, a family-style platter of grilled meats and sautéed plantain. The pan-fried artichokes were the perfect side dish. When everyone thought they could not eat another bite, the dessert that came was the lightest caramel flan with an edible orchid on top.

Helene came back to the table with Simon, who immediately went up to Marguerite. "I very much look forward to working with you. You dance as light as a feather and sway with the wind. I think you will enjoy Marcella's violin as well. Would tomorrow afternoon work for a rehearsal? Marcella and I could come to the villa, or there is a studio here we could use."

"I think the studio here would be best, without interfering with anything at the villa. Was it Marcella who played at the villa the night we got here?" When Simon nodded, she agreed wholeheartedly. Marguerite walked him over to Annie and Ramone. Simon said to Annie, "I am so relieved you are feeling better! My sister and I look forward to playing our music for you. I have found several guys I play with to join us for more lively dancing for the guests during the reception."

Touched, Annie replied, "We know you and Marguerite, and of course your sister, will be a perfect addition to our wedding." By that time, Roff had returned and pulled up a chair next to Helene. Annie could swear she saw the challenging stare Roff gave Simon, warning him to give way. Helene watched Simon leave, knowing she would be sailing for the next four days with Roff. That didn't stop her, however, from the temptation to jump ship.

Juan Carlos stopped by the table, shook hands with Don Marco, and walked over to Annie. "Young lady, you gave us all quite a scare. Are you sure you are recovered? Is there anything more we can do to help with the wedding?"

Annie smiled. "Juan Carlos, your entire family has already done so much! Thank you. Ramone and I did just realize we did not bring wedding bands. Do you happen to know a good jeweler?"

"Skip the tourist stores in the harbor. We like a jeweler in Polensa on the north part of the island." Juan Carlos jotted the directions to the jeweler and gave it to Annie. "That gives me an idea while your guests are here. Have you been to the Caves of the Dragon?"

Ramone overheard. "I went with Annie's father and cousin. It was incredible. That would be a good outing. I'd like Annie to see it."

Juan Carlos continued, "Very close to it is the Mallorca Pearl Factory. We are known all over the world for our handmade pearls. You and your friends can see how they are made and find a large selection in their showroom."

Annie liked the idea. "Can we schedule a tour for a larger group?"

"Oh yes, or they will break you into smaller groups with multiple guides." Pleased Annie and Ramone seemed to like his idea, Juan Carlos wandered off to say hello at the other tables.

The consummate hosts, Paulo was circulating the room like his father, stopping to speak at each table. Music began to play, and guests started to move to the dance floor. Ramone escorted Annie to the dance floor. Alex and Celeste joined them, then Don Marco and Gennie. Roff asked Helene to dance. She looked around, distracted, but smiled and went to the dance floor with him. Hans came over to the table and asked Meghan to dance. Making sure her wedding ring was visible, she accepted. Marguerite patted Antonio's hand. "I guess that leaves us, son."

She didn't see Simon on his way over to her, but Helene did. She also didn't see Paulo move his son aside, saying, "I've got this, son." What she saw was the captivating man who fascinated her. When he asked her to dance, she gave Antonio a quick glance with an apologetic shrug of her shoulders, and she took his hand.

Sitting there alone at the table, all Antonio could do was tap his feet to the music absentmindedly. *What? He was tapping his feet!* He began to experiment by crossing one foot over the other, then reversing them. He was concentrating so hard he didn't see Veronica come up to the table. "You didn't think I would leave you all alone, did you? The awards part is boring to me. I came for the music and to see you!" Antonio gave her that charming and devilish smile of his, and they fell into an easy conversation.

Simon watched his father on the dance floor with Marguerite, glued to each movement of her body. Helene could see where Simon's attention was. She tried to concentrate on Roff, but her gaze kept wandering back to Simon. Roff looked at her. "What is going on? Is something happening between you and Simon? Perhaps we need to talk."

Annie noticed Roff and Helene go outside and did not miss Simon watching Marguerite. Marguerite, however, looked like she had been dancing with Paulo for a lifetime.

# Chapter 53

Annie and Ramone wanted to get an early start on the day. While they dressed, Annie speculated, "It appears your very attractive mother has two suitors, but only one age-appropriate!"

Ramone fairly growled, "I did not care for that young stud from the beginning reducing you and Meghan to schoolgirl giggles! He's younger than me! At least Mamà is giving him no attention."

"Perhaps, but she seemed quite interested in Paulo," Annie said with a smile and a raise of her eyebrows.

Ramone shook his head and rolled his eyes in response. "Let's go. We have rings to buy!"

Explaining to Alex and Celeste, Annie said, "Ramone seems a little overcautious about the scooter, and I understand Polensa is fairly far. Could we take one of the cars?"

"Of course, sweetheart." Alex was glad he had suggested renting two cars after the scooter incident. "Here are the keys."

"We are meeting Hans, Stephan, and Carmina for lunch back in Palma near Veronica's shop. The four of them will go for a short hike for Hans to get to know Stephan and Carmina." To her mother, Annie said, "I will meet you and Meghan at Veronica's at one thirty. Are we walking to the florist from there or should I bring the car?"

While they were working out the plans, Ramone went over to his mother. "You plan to rehearse this afternoon? Be careful. Simon may have designs on you."

Marguerite tried to hold back her laugh. "I danced for a living, son. Do you not think I was propositioned all the time? I know how to handle that. I had eyes for no one other than Salvador."

Ramone put his arm around her. "Mamà, he is gone now. You stood by him through all the years, including the bad times. I don't know how you did it. Maybe it is time you allowed your eyes to wander a bit." As an afterthought, he added, "Except at a young stud half your age!" They both laughed.

Antonio was excited to show Meghan what he had accomplished the night before. He was able to tap his feet and cross one over the other on both sides. When Meghan saw, she was just as excited! "The therapist coming to work with you today will know how to massage and stretch those newly awakened muscles to strengthen them. She should be here soon."

*****

Ramone easily found the jewelry store once they reached Polensa. They walked around the main area of the town and noticed there were lots of Brits there. When they entered the store, the proprietor immediately greeted them. "Juan Carlos said you might be stopping by. Welcome!" Annie asked about the many British people here. "There's a combination of expats and tourists. For some reason they gravitate here, probably to get away from the hustle of Palma. Now what can I help you with today?"

Annie showed him her engagement ring. The proprietor held her finger. "Do you mind?" He asked as he slipped it off her finger. "Such an exquisite blue diamond!"

Ramone told him, "We did not plan to marry here and had not gotten our wedding bands. The wedding is a week and a half away. Can you help us?"

The jeweler pulled out several cases of men's wedding bands and arranged them on the counter. "I have many choices for you, sir. Please feel free to try any of them that appeal to you. But a band for this perfect stone—ah, that is more difficult. It needs to be worthy enough to pair like they belong together, yet not take away from the diamond." Annie smiled at Ramone as he began to try different rings. His hands were large and muscular. Somehow the simple bands did not suit his hand, and Annie would shake her head. He pulled out a heavy eighteen-carat gold band that had a chiseled design around it. Upon further inspection, Ramone thought it looked like two doves.

"Yes," the jeweler explained, "you're correct. Doves symbolize peace, but also, since they mate for life, eternal love and fidelity."

Inspecting it from different angles, Ramone slipped the band on his finger. "I love the design and its meaning. *Querida*, what do you think?"

Annie's eyes glistened with emotion. "It is beautiful, and I love its meaning as well."

Ramone nodded. "Then this is the band for me. And, what about you, my love."

Annie wandered a bit, gazing into the display cases until something caught her eye. "There, may I try that one?"

The band was a platinum gold that perfectly matched the band of her engagement ring. It was delicately embellished with slightly raised roses across the top of the ring. Annie tried it on with her ring. It seemed to her they belonged together. To Ramone, her expression was radiant and said it all. "Roses," she whispered.

# Chapter 54

Stephan and Carmina were already at the restaurant when Ramone and Annie arrived. Hans came in right after them. Once Hans was there, Ramone made the introductions. Stephan, in his easygoing manner, was pleased to meet a potential new hiker. Carmina, on the other hand, wanted to know about the wedding ring choices.

However, Annie's curiosity about Hans took over. "Hans, Ramone told me you spend every August taking time off work to travel. You are such an accomplished sailor. Do you always look for a regatta as part of it? Do you actually close your gallery during the whole month of August?"

"Ever since my wife died, I have to push myself to avoid falling into monotony and solitude. I had a great love once, but sadly it did not end well. The sailing, especially when racing, gives me a great sense of achievement."

Ramone put a hand on Annie's knee to stop her from going forward. "Stephan, where do you think we should hike this afternoon? Let's break Hans in!"

Hans, shaking off his sudden sadness, agreed wholeheartedly! Stephan suggested, "Why don't we maneuver our way to the east and circle back. There are some beautiful views!"

*****

Meghan and Celeste were in a lively conversation with Veronica when Annie walked into the shop. Veronica had a large photo of the pavilion at Vista Hermosa on an easel. A storyboard beside it showed the red dresses with the black-and-white fans.

Next to that were the *Guayabera* white shirts with the black pants. In the middle was a photo of Annie's dress. There were pictures of red roses and crimson orchids, as well as a rendering of the cake with the rose icing design they chose. Annie gasped, "Veronica, this is great! We can really see what it will be like. But I don't see what Ramone is wearing?"

Veronica answered, "Ramone told me he asked Tomás to bring an outfit from Marbella and assured me it was also black and white. Before we discuss the catering or flowers, I have a few photos of ideas Mara mentioned when she called. She plans to do a Balinese blessing, but that would not make the wedding official. Who do you want to officiate?"

Celeste asked, "Would a priest or monk be offended by a Hindu blessing?"

Veronica thought for a moment. "Our local priests might object. However, there is a minister of a little country church in Fornalutx who encourages parishioners from all religions to join his weekly Sunday service. He might be open to the idea."

Meghan looked at Annie. "Isn't Fornalutx the village Ramone told us we would love? We could go to church there Sunday morning before Sabine and the family arrive."

To Veronica, Annie suggested, "Do you mind asking him? If he says yes, go ahead and book him." Back to Meghan. "I would like that, and it would give us a chance to see the village."

Veronica made a note to contact the minister. "When I spoke with Mara, she told me some of the things she was packing, all featuring the color combination of red and gold. She has two print cummerbunds for the men and two headdresses for Meghan and Sabine, if you decide to use them. There should be an offering, usually a decorative tower of fruit. She is bringing two straw skirts for the plate and large fan-like decorative toppers that are the same straw with deep red accents."

"I can have Mara explain the tower to Paulo better once she arrives. I have his catering menu for you to take home to consider. He said as long as he had your requests in by the first of the week, his staff would have plenty of time to prepare. He also said if Mara met with him next Wednesday or Thursday, there would be time to design the stack of fruit however she wants it." Celeste tucked the menu into her notepad, and they walked around the block to the florist.

"*Hola*! Welcome!" The florist greeted them with a warm smile. "Veronica says your wedding will be at Vista Hermosa! It is so beautiful! But we do not have much time. The good news is I have two excellent flower resources in Barcelona, and there is a ferry from Barcelona to Mallorca every day. Now tell me how I can help."

Veronica started. "Annie is marrying a well-known matador. Throughout their courtship, he gave her red roses, even from the bullring. Although it is not traditional white and pastels, we want crimson red to be the feature color."

Annie added, "My mother brought a sample of the bridesmaid's dress with the fans we would like to be part of their bouquets. There will be two of them. I love the idea of sprays of crimson orchids if that will work."

"Yes, those will come from Barcelona. Go on." The florist made notes.

They continued to discuss options. The florist was particularly interested in the addition of the Bali influences and potential headdresses. That would bring golden yellow into the color scheme, which should be perfect at sunset. The florist finished the meeting referring to her notes. "It will take a few days to offer you some design ideas. My shop is open Saturday if you would like to come back then."

Annie was about to say yes but replied, "My cousin, the other bridesmaid, arrives on Sunday. I would love to include her. If we met early Monday, would that give you enough time? I do have a friend flying on his plane from Barcelona on Tuesday. He might be able to bring a shipment of flowers with them if necessary."

"If we meet early enough so I can allow the flower wholesaler to gather the order to package, and depending on what time your friend leaves Barcelona, that could work. The backup would be the ferry on Wednesday." The florist nodded, thinking it through, and they agreed to meet at 9:00 a.m., Monday. Veronica assured them she would be there too. One more step taken! On the way home, Annie smiled at the irony of El Amir bringing the flowers for her wedding. *What a twist of fate!*

# Chapter 55

Hans could see the easy rapport that had developed between Ramone and Stephan. Carmina seemed at ease as well. He thought about his crew. Had he had that kind of rapport with any of them? They worked well together as a team, but would he call any of them a friend? Probably not. Most of them had spread out and were off to their various home ports. Roff had set sail for Marbella. At lunch, he had seen the great love both Ramone and Stephan had for their women. A moment of regret ate at him. He had felt that great love once. No reason to think about it now, though. It only brought him sadness and loneliness.

Determined to shake this unwelcome mood, Hans forced himself to take deep cleansing breaths of this fresh mountain air. When they stopped for a break, Hans asked Stephan and Carmina, "Have you hiked every day since you've been here?"

Carmina answered. "I got one day off thanks to Ramone! Stephan does not know the meaning of the phrase 'take it easy.' Maybe if he has you two to hike with, I can take off a little more. I did tell Annie I would lead some of her wedding guests on the coastal hike along the northern coast of the island that doesn't have the inclines of these mountain hikes. Ramone, I really like her. I hope I can get to know her better while we are all here."

Ramone answered, "I know she'd like that. I am wondering about the night hike to the monastery. Do you think I can make it to the top? What about Annie and the others?" And to Hans, "Are you considering it?"

Stephan responded first. "Ramone, you have the strong physique and stamina of a matador. I have no doubt you have the endurance to make it. Carmina and I could pace ourselves with you. It is not a race. For Annie or those in your party who are not hikers, or haven't recently trained, to be honest, it is doubtful they would make it to the end. But the festivities are lively, and I am sure they will enjoy participating. It is never considered a failure to stop along the way. But I assure you, it is an amazing feeling of accomplishment to see the monastery ahead and realize the distance you have come."

"Hans, you have a week to work on the inclines and your stamina. I think you could make it too."

Hans was caught off guard. "Ramone, I didn't realize you are a matador. Are you planning to fight locally while you're here?"

Stephan realized he might have blundered again, but Ramone shrugged it off. "It's a long story. My reasons for being here have nothing to do with my profession."

Hans thought he understood. "Right, the wedding."

Ramone smiled. "The wedding came together suddenly once we realized we had most of the family together in one place. More family and friends begin to arrive starting Sunday. Carmina, when are you doing the coastal hike?"

Carmina answered, "Annie wants to try for next Wednesday or Thursday. It can be a half-day hike, or through the various villages we can stop a lot and make it leisurely. Stephan and I will be resting during the day Friday to be ready to start Friday night."

Hans said, "I would like to try. Any hikes you are willing to let me join you on would be helpful, and I would love the company."

Ramone added, "If you plan to stay through the pilgrimage, the wedding is that Sunday. Stephan and Carmina will be there. Would you consider staying long enough to join us for the ceremony?"

Hans could feel the beginnings of new friendships and was pleased with the invitation. "I would be honored." They were hiking again when Hans asked Ramone, "What if you did a fight for your guests? I imagine there are those arriving who have never seen you face the bull."

Ramone did not answer. Stephan quickly changed the subject back to the course of the pilgrimage through the Tramuntana mountain range.

# Chapter 56

The next two days were filled with anticipation for Tomás's return on Saturday with all their wish-list items. Each of them seemed to find their own routine. Antonio continued his progress and was now able, with his life jacket, to get into his swimming position and propel himself forward with the help of his arms and small leg movements. Veronica was a frequent visitor at the house and assured Annie everything was moving along as planned. The minister in Fornalutx had accepted the booking and said he would be happy to meet them at his service Sunday morning.

Don Marco and Gennie enjoyed spending time with Juan Carlos and Carlotta. They were also making sure the villa for Sabine and the family was clean, well-stocked, and ready for their arrival Sunday afternoon.

Marguerite continued to rehearse with Simon and Marcella. She was just as entranced with Marcella's musical talent with the violin as she was with Simon's majestic sound of his voice and soulful guitar. She appeared oblivious to Simon's infatuation, but she always had an eye out over his head for the possibility his father might appear. A little chagrined at her wishful thinking, Marguerite made every effort to put Paulo out of her mind.

By the time Saturday morning arrived, Meghan could not contain her excitement about seeing Tomás! She woke up at dawn full of energy so she decided to make breakfast for the family. She rummaged around the kitchen and found all the ingredients for two large Spanish quiches that could each be split eight ways. She paired them with a large bowl of assorted oranges, kiwi, and melon, along with some of the toasted almond pastries from Greta's bakery.

Everyone was looking forward to the *Porto Banus* arriving that morning, and seeing Meghan it was hard not to catch her excitement. Tomás said they would call once they were in sight of the port.

After a delicious breakfast, no one wanted to be left behind when the call came from Tomás. They were at the marina eagerly waiting for the *Porto Banus* to anchor and the Zodiac to start the transfer of packages to the dock. Tomás gathered all the packages marked clearly for each of them and came in with the first group. After a passionate kiss from his wife, he began to pass them out, feeling a little like Santa at Christmas. All the excitement was beginning to get attention and draw a crowd, so they changed tactics. After the third transfer, they put all the packages in a trailer to be transferred back to the villa where they could sort through them. When Tomás caught Ramone's attention and held up the last package, Ramone gave a subtle shake of his head. Tomás nodded and handed the package back to Roff to keep on board.

As they were leaving the dock with Tomás headed back to the villa, Annie looked back at the *Porto Banus*. The captain and Roff were waving, but there was no sign of Helene. *Hmmm...*

\*\*\*\*\*

The rest of the day went by in a whirlwind! They each put away their newfound treasures, planning their attire for the coming week. Tomás went with Don Marco to check on the villa. Although he knew Dom would have everything handled, he still wanted to check for himself. The villa was suitable, not nearly as stunning as Don Marco's, but it would be fine for a week. Mentally calculating the rooms, Tomás allotted a room for Francoise and Marta, one for Claudette, one for Sabine, and one for Robert. If space became limited and they needed a room, Sabine said she could move in with her grandmother. Basic supplies were stocked. Everything looked ready for tomorrow afternoon, and Tomás looked forward to accompanying the family to the church in Fornalutx.

They were planning a festive welcome BBQ around the pool tomorrow night. Yuba worked with Gennie and Celeste to finalize all of the details. The new arrivals would be there. Juan Carlos and Carlotta, Stephan and Carmina, Hans, and Veronica were also invited. As an afterthought, Annie sent an invitation to Paulo. The ladies were all busy cooking and preparing the food to grill at the party. The chef and Maria were making full use of the catering kitchen. Ramone asked Roff and Hans to come by to help set up the tent and arrange the tables and chairs out on the lawn area. Marguerite had found some cheerful tablecloths, which added a festive touch to the welcoming scene that would start the wedding week festivities. Yuba set up tall torches to illuminate the area. It was Antonio who stayed out of the way and felt unable to contribute. Annie, so proud of how hard Antonio was working to strengthen his legs, was the one to notice. She took him a cold beer and sat with him.

"Why are you over here by yourself? There is plenty to do," Annie said gently.

"This feeling of helplessness is so frustrating. I'm trying so hard. These are such small steps forward, and I need big ones." Antonio's frown was so sad.

"Last year," said Annie, "after Sabine's accident, I felt a sense of helplessness that I should have done more to keep her safe. I was frozen with guilt. When I came to help Dom and Gennie at the villa, Dom sat me down with one of his wise lectures. Something like, what really matters is not your situation but rather your attitude about it. You have to make a commitment to allow good things happen. Only then, when you're totally committed to making progress, will you find a way. It takes a great deal of courage to believe in your goal. Antonio, you have made milestones of improvement. It is inspiring to watch. What does Meghan think is the next step?"

"She has certain objectives I have to accomplish in the pool before I can try to walk, or even stand, probably with a walker.

The massage therapist seems to be helping. Meghan always seems to be taunting me to try harder."

Annie laughed. "You know that's not so. Meghan is giving you incentives!" She was about to go back to the kitchen and almost brought up Sabine coming the next day but thought it best to leave it alone.

The conversation made Annie think about her own situation and how her course had altered. Had she seen the island of Mallorca in her future, much less a wedding here? *Impossible*, she would have thought. Yet here she was, surrounded by family and friends, about to marry Ramone! With Stephan and Carmina living not too far away in Barcelona, she was sure they would keep up their new friendship. Ramone seemed to enjoy Hans. Annie had not had much of a chance to get to know him other than a few questions. There was no doubt he was handsome in a Nordic sort of way. Not her specific taste. She leaned toward the dark, and she was certainly all about the eyes. Hans seemed like a nice man who had been through some heartbreak. She hoped reuniting Hans and Sarah was a good thing. As for Antonio, she kept trying to picture him with Veronica but just couldn't get there. Was Sabine a possibility? She wasn't certain that if Antonio regained his mobility that he wouldn't fall back into his gigolo ways.

Annie roused herself out of her speculative mood and determined in the midst of all the activity to come, there was one person who must not be neglected. Suggesting to her mother they have an early dinner, Celeste understood right away. Hans and Roff finished helping and left to go have dinner in Old Town. It sounded like Roff might join Stephan, Carmina, and Hans's hike the following day. Now that everyone had their own hiking boots, they were excited to do more. Even as Annie was ready to go upstairs with Ramone, she thought to herself...*The hikers, including Ramone, seem to be working hard to conquer the pilgrimage. In the midst of planning a wedding and spending time with friends, I don't see how I could do it.*

# Chapter 57

The early morning hours often brought much pleasure to Ramone. Waking to Annie's beautiful face and body was a privilege he never wanted to take for granted. The peaceful way she slept and the sensual way her eyes gazed at him half open as she woke drove him mad with desire yet humbled him to know she would soon be bound to him. He reached over to hold her tighter.

Annie awoke and could see the emotion in Ramone's eyes. "What is it, my love? With the arrival of Sabine and the family, it gets real, doesn't it? Are you having second thoughts?"

"No, *querida*, far from that. It was real for me that first day I saw you from the bullring and tossed my rose to you after I conquered the bull."

Hoping it wasn't too difficult a subject for him, Annie said as gently as possible, "Have you given any more thought to fighting? I don't think I have ever known you to go so long between fights."

Ramone held her and looked up at the ceiling. "I have many feelings about it right now. The training to do what I do was long and arduous. It has been a family tradition for generations. Strangers know me as Ramone Sanchez, the matador. There is great pride in that. Then, there is the death of my father. I now understand better what it did to him to see his own father gored to death when he was so young. It breaks my heart and my spirit to think that could happen to a child of ours. Perhaps it is time for me to be known as Ramone Sanchez, the man? That is what I am struggling with."

With tears in her eyes, she saw his raw emotion. "I have promised to love you and be by your side no matter what your choice. And, my love, I love you both, the man and the matador."

Wiping her eyes, she suggested with a smile, "Why don't we go see this preacher who is said to accept people no matter their religion or their ethnicity? I hope he is a good choice to bind us for eternity. With Mara's help, of course."

As soon as they arrived in Fornalutx, Meghan glanced at Annie, and they both realized they were somewhere meaningful. It was clear the people of Fornalutx strove to keep the ancient tradition of the village, with its narrow cobblestone streets, stone building facades, and Gothic church. Even the town hall included a seventeenth-century defense tower. After dropping Antonio at the church, they parked at the bottom of the hill and walked up the stone staircase. The minister wore the traditional black robe and stood at the entrance welcoming his parishioners. Annie and Ramone introduced themselves, and he seemed genuinely happy to meet them. The service began with a melodic song from the choir. To their surprise, leading the choir was Simon. Marcella stood by the organist accompanying with her violin. Such a bonus to this excursion to hear them, knowing the key role they would play a week from now.

Annie studied the Catalan and Gothic influences that embellished the interior. The next song allowed those attending to join in. It was a soulful version of Steve Winwood's "Higher Love" from the '80s. As they sang the words, she wondered if the song might work for the wedding. Looking over at her mom, Annie could tell she was thinking the same thing. Holding Ramone's hand, she sang with her heart, a tear falling from her eye. Ramone had never heard this version before, and it spoke to him as well about facing fear and the hope for a higher love.

What Annie and Ramone had failed to notice was how the song affected Antonio. The congregation and choir sat, waiting for the minister to begin.

"Brethren, you have all joined us on this beautiful summer day. I want to say welcome. I also want you to take a minute and look around you. Every person in this church made a choice to come here today. For this moment in time, they are your neighbors. Look around, say hello, shake a hand." There was a warmth inside this old traditional church. Greetings flowed in every direction. They saw Paulo in the front pew and waved. Marguerite's eyes caught his, and he smiled.

"Here you all are on your own individual life journey. Many of you might be strangers, but your paths brought you here together. Paths cross. You just took a moment to say hello to a perfect stranger. Once you connected in some way, you were no longer strangers. Pay attention. There is a person's path that might be running parallel to yours. When those paths intersect, there is a reason. Don't miss it. Be aware of those around you and be amazed at new connections."

He went on to talk about tolerance and forgiveness. All of them left the service thoughtful and uplifted. As they exited, Marguerite lingered a bit for Paulo to catch up. He said he was looking forward to the BBQ that night and hoped she had a nice afternoon greeting the new guests. When Ramone and Annie said goodbye to the preacher, he said he looked forward to the wedding ceremony and to let him know if they wanted to request any special words. They said they would and mentioned how much they liked the song "Higher Love."

They gathered for lunch in the main square at an outdoor café, then stopped at a bakery the waitress recommended to get some freshly baked items for the barbecue. Sabine would be here soon, and Annie's excitement could hardly be contained!

# Chapter 58

Sabine could not wait to get caught up in her cousin's wedding plans! She hoped having Robert there would not be a distraction. In the last couple of days, there seemed to have been more awkward silences between them than fully connected enjoyment. In a way, she was surprised he came with them to Mallorca. She knew he wanted to see Annie. He was also an avid hiker in Maine and had heard amazing stories about the hiking on the mountainous island. She was trying to be a good sport, but she desperately wanted to stay in the villa with Annie, Dom and Gennie, and Uncle Alex and Aunt Celeste to get immersed in the plans!

At the airport, Francoise rented a large SUV to carry them and all their luggage. Tomás was waiting for them at their villa with the promise to bring them over to Dom and Gennie's as soon as they were settled. He showed them to their rooms. Sabine tentatively asked if there was space in the other villa. Robert gave her a questioning look but said nothing.

Tomás explained, "The captain, Roff, and Helene have moved back to the *Porto Banus*, and Annie's friends move into the casita on Tuesday, which will fill it up."

"So Robert and I could stay in the casita tonight and tomorrow night if we promise to have the rooms clean and ready for Tuesday?"

Marta and Claudette shared a glance with the roll of their eyes. They recognized Sabine's stubborn steak when she had her mind set on something. She was a lot like Annie that way. Looking around the large villa, Marta said a little wistfully, "There is plenty of room here if needed."

Tomás hugged her. "If Sabine and Robert do this, they will be back on Tuesday. And, really, it is just a short walk to the other villa."

Gleeful for such a turn of events, Sabine got her suitcase. "Which way?" Tomás laughed with a shrug of his shoulders and led the way with Robert lagging behind. Francoise, Marta, and Claudette quickly decided they could unpack later and followed Tomás on the path.

The uproar at the villa where everyone was waiting was deafening when the whole crowd arrived. When Annie saw Sabine and Robert with suitcases, she screamed, "What!"

Sabine excitedly said, "Your friends don't come in until Tuesday. We can at least stay two nights. We promised we would have it clean before we left." Annie and Ramone walked them out to the casita to get them settled in their rooms.

Back in the main living room, Tomás had a thought. He went up to Dom and asked, "Wasn't Helene here at the villa this past week?"

Dom shook his head. "No, we thought she was with you. She didn't sail on the *Porto Banus*?"

"When I got on board, I didn't see her and asked where she was. Luis said she didn't feel well and stayed on the island since it was just for a few days, and there were no passengers other than me for the one way. I thought she was here." Back to the introductions and excitement, they let the subject go.

Gennie and Claudette were just as excited to see each other as Annie and Sabine. The sisters had not seen each other since right after Sabine's accident over a year ago. Annie introduced Ramone and Marguerite to Francoise and Marta, explaining, "My future mother-in-law was a professional flamenco dancer, and she has agreed to dance at our wedding!" She led them over to Antonio. "And this is Antonio, Ramone's brother." That introduction got Sabine's attention, and she came over with Robert in tow to say hello.

After Sabine gave Antonio a kiss on each cheek, French style, she could have sworn she felt a skip of a heartbeat. She quickly introduced him to Robert, and they shook hands.

Sabine and Annie were busy filling each other in and sharing the plans for the next day. Seeing the two of them together, Ramone knew he wanted the close bond with Annie that she shared with Sabine. Giving Robert a pat on the back, he said, "It seems we are now invisible! I hear you like to hike. Would you like to join us tomorrow?" Robert nodded, thankful he was not left out.

Tomás overheard them. "It seems my wife is part of the girl plans too. Do you mind if I join you?"

Seeing the dejected look on Antonio's face that he could not participate, Alex stepped in. "Antonio, how about after your workout tomorrow morning, we go meet them for lunch?"

Nodding in appreciation at Alex, Antonio thought at least it was something. He hadn't shared it with anyone, but that morning's sermon had reached a place deep within him. A split second was all it took to change one's life. That one moment in the ring changed everything for him. But his one-man pity party was not the way to move forward. He needed to change his attitude for the better. He had felt something when Sabine greeted him. Not just attraction for a beautiful woman which she was. It was hard to describe. Thinking about it, he felt it was more like a sense of coming home. He watched the closeness Sabine and Annie shared. When he realized how much Sabine and Annie were alike, he looked over at Robert and knew in his heart Robert would never be enough of a man for her. Was there a chance he could break through his own stubborn walls to a future that included Sabine?

# Chapter 59

Annie couldn't believe Sabine was here and that Sarah and Mara would arrive in just two more days! She was pleased with the extra clothing and accessories she now had thanks to Tomás and the *Porto Banus*. While she pondered what to wear to the BBQ, she caught Ramone staring at her. Caught off guard, she crossed the room to where he was sitting and sat on his lap with her arm around him. She whispered, "What is it?"

"Seeing you with Sabine, it made me realize how busy the coming week will be. I hope we don't get so caught up in the festivities that we lose our focus on each other." Ramone laid her head against his shoulder.

"It's true. It will be busy, and these are friends I haven't seen in a long time. I am hopeful they will be yours as well. Do not worry. I will never have you out of my sight for long. Don't you know I feel the same way when you go off hiking every day?"

"I thought about that. If you do the coastal walk on Thursday, I will plan to join you. I hope to make it to the monastery on the overnight hike Friday, and an easier hike the day before with fewer inclines would be good."

"I'm so proud of you for trying. I know with everything going on this week, it doesn't make sense for me to try. Who else do you think will do the pilgrimage?" Annie asked.

"Definitely Stephan and Carmina, Hans, and myself. Possibly Roff. We'll see how Tomás and Robert do tomorrow, and they can decide. I don't think I see El Amir doing it, do you?"

"Probably not, but I'd bet Jonathan McNamara might join you. He is a strong one with a gentle soul...a little like you." Looking at the time, she added, "Oh, we need to hurry. It's time to get to the party." A lingering kiss sealed their promise, and they quickly finished getting ready.

The chef had set up stations for the various courses, and the aromas guaranteed a wonderful meal. Yuba moved throughout, constantly checking the details. Juan Carlos and Carlotta arrived and immediately took to Georgette. Along with Don Marco and Gennie, they began to plan the activities for the week for the "old folks." Other than the wedding, most of the conversation centered around the Night of the Pilgrims. Juan Carlos mentioned he had booked a flat this year with a balcony overlooking the starting point. Mentally calculating those in the wedding group not participating, being a sizable number, Don Marco inquired, "Do you think it is too late to do something similar?"

Juan Carlos answered, "I should have thought of this before! Let me check. I have a friend who summers elsewhere and who has the perfect apartment with a wraparound balcony overlooking the festivities. He leaves during the event every year because it is too noisy for him and his wife. I will check with him and let you know." Dom and Gennie loved the idea. They planned card games, dinners, a day sail on Thursday, and a sunset sail on Saturday on board the *Porto Banus*.

Gennie and Claudette outlined their plans to Alex and Celeste and Francoise and Marta. Alex wanted to participate in the hike. He suspected he wouldn't finish, but realized there would be access back to Palma if needed. They loved the idea of the apartment for the pilgrimage night if that might work. Celeste was sure, after a good rest from the hike, everyone would love the sunset cruise on Saturday night.

Stephan and Carmina arrived early and got introduced to everyone. Hans arrived with Veronica. He was staying close to her apartment and offered her a ride. Once introductions were made, they also began to make plans. Veronica quickly made her way to Antonio's side while options were discussed. She noticed the boy from Maine, thinking him slightly old-fashioned but nice-looking.

Veronica planned to pick up Annie, Sabine, Meghan, and Celeste in the morning. They would cover the florist and Greta's bakery, as well as decisions on the menu with Paulo. Sabine needed to try on her dress to see if any alterations were necessary, and Annie needed to try on the dress she bought once more. Gennie had found the mesh that would work with the red dresses.

Ramone, Hans, Tomás, and Robert were to meet Stephan and Carmina at the base of the foothills in Palma for the next day's hike. Carmina was used to being the only woman, and it didn't bother her. They would pass the Castle of Alaró and meet Alex and Antonio for lunch in the town there.

Paulo arrived at the BBQ late, making his excuses for some last-minute issues at the yacht club. He made the rounds from group to group, introducing himself. He had naturally seen Marguerite the moment he entered. Something held him back from approaching her. She seemed dangerous to him in a way. It bothered him the way Simon looked at her and talked of how she danced. He knew she planned to go back to Marbella in a little over a week, and he was not looking for a heartbreak.

Marguerite, on the other hand, was used to fending off men's advances but was definitely not used to a man's cold shoulder. Common sense told her he was not interested and that she should steer clear. So she did.

Hans found a chance to have a conversation with Sabine, and they sat down to talk. He knew she was here with Robert, but he could not honestly see a connection between them. "Sabine, you and Annie seem so close. How do you all know each other?"

Sabine easily replied, "Annie and Tomás are my cousins, but they are both more like siblings. I was involved in a boating accident a little over a year ago. Robert was on the boat when it happened. I had a brain injury and was put into an induced coma. Robert wrote me letters every day. Maman read them to me, and I think it gave me the courage to fight harder. I saw him again in Maine at Tomás and Meghan's wedding. I like him so much and appreciate all he did, but I have realized he's not for me. What about you? Are you here alone?"

"Yes, ever since my wife died, I take the month of August to break the routine and go out on my own a little. I have made mistakes. I had a friend too, with a medical issue. Unlike Robert, I didn't stop at letters. I married her. She had just been diagnosed with a terminal disease. She had no family and no insurance. I had just met the most astonishing woman while abroad. She was like no one I had ever known. But I couldn't deny offering my friend a safe haven to battle her last months. It was brutal to watch her decline day after day. Months turn into a year. The woman I met found out about my marriage and disappeared. Once my wife died, I tried to look for her. Much later, I found out she had moved to Africa to paint."

Sabine, immediately on alert, asked, "Was her name Sarah?"

# Chapter 60

Don Marco was up early. Yuba was outside supervising a crew to clean up from the party. He poured himself a cup of coffee and took the paper out to the veranda. Francoise and Marta would be here soon for breakfast. Dom knew Claudette was sleeping in, and he suggested Gennie do the same while she had a chance. His mind wandered over the days to come and all the personalities that would be emerging. It had been his experience over the years that when you had that many strong personalities together for a prolonged time, anything could happen. He said a little prayer that all would proceed well.

He thought about how to react to the piece of information he had gotten last night. Helene did not sail on the *Porto Banus*, and Luis did not tell him. That was not like his old friend. For now, though, he decided to keep it to himself. They were scheduled to be on board the *Porto Banus* for a sunset sail Saturday. He expected to see her there or know the reason why not.

Maria set up a tea cart on the veranda with coffee and tea. Robert poured himself some coffee and joined Don Marco. Seeing the crew, he asked, "Sir, is there anything I can do to help clean up? It was a great party, and the food was outstanding!"

Dom looked across the yard and said, "The crew seems to be finishing. Are you ready for your hike today?"

"I love to hike, and I appreciate Ramone including me. I feel a little guilty being here since I wasn't really invited. Sabine is so caught up with Annie and the wedding, I'm not sure how I will fit in."

"Nonsense, young man. You have known Annie for years and she is happy to have you. It occurs to me I never had a chance to thank you for all you did after Sabine's accident. I know she appreciated it." They were interrupted by Ramone and Tomás coming to get Robert.

Ramone said, "Let's get an early start. We can get a quick bite to eat at the café near the starting point of the hike."

Tomás was in good humor and replied, "Sounds good! My boots seem very well broken in so I will no doubt be leading the pack today!"

Ramone replied, "I never thanked you. They saved me! Now I have to get used to my own." They continued to chat, bringing Robert into the conversation, as they left for Palma.

Dom poured himself another coffee and found Celeste and Meghan planning breakfast with the chef and laughing. Annie went directly to Sabine's room with her wedding dress and the other bridesmaid's dress to try on. This morning would be a good chance for Sabine to catch up on all the wedding plans.

"Hurry, Sabine! I can't wait!" Annie anxiously waited for Sabine to try on the dress.

"Who ever heard of a red bridesmaid dress? *Oh la la*! Look at this!" Sabine stood in front of the full-length mirror twisting and turning. "It is a little big, but I love it!" Annie handed the fan to her. "Look at me. I look very Spanish. I should wear my hair up. The fan is such a clever accent. I love it!"

"Gennie said she could do any necessary alteration. Just try the dress on again for her this afternoon. Who knows what Mara is bringing for her Balinese blessing. I am so nervous to try on mine. This baby is growing every day, and I am not sure the two of us will fit in it by next week!" Annie slipped into the dress, and Sabine zipped her up. When she turned around, there were tears in Sabine's eyes.

"Ah, *ma cousine*, it is so simple, but on you it is gorgeous! It fits perfectly. The subtle draping is perfectly placed. And the deep V-back! It demands something special. In France, it is all the rage to have a pearl necklace, with a single pearl suspended on a chain in the back. That might set it off, *n'est pas*?"

"Well, Mallorca is known for its pearls We were thinking it might be fun to go to the pearl factory later in the week. Maybe we could find one there?" Annie asked.

"I'm sure we can. It is quite a popular style," Sabine reasoned.

They changed back into their clothes for the day and re-hung the dresses. Annie ventured, "You haven't told me how it's going with Robert. You didn't spend much time with him last night. Actually, it seemed you spent a great deal of time with Hans." Annie raised her eyebrows, waiting for an answer.

"Robert is such a nice person, but sometimes he is too nice. Do you understand?" Sabine hoped she did.

Annie nodded. "I came to the same conclusion when I considered him. He is more like a brother. But what about Hans? He doesn't seem like a brother!"

"Oh *chérie*! What a wicked smile! He is a very striking man, but with such a sad story. I think he might have been in love with Sarah years ago before his marriage. Does she know he will be here? I mentioned to him how you and Sarah met and that she will be here tomorrow."

Leaning in for a secret, Sabine said, "While we were talking, I kept peeking over at Antonio. That girl was all over him. What is that all about?"

"That is Veronica, who happens also to be my wedding planner and is picking us up this morning! She seems nice enough, and she has been interested in him ever since we got here."

Meghan knocked on the door. "Breakfast is getting cold. Hurry or we'll be late."

Giggling, they hurried. Then Annie whispered, "Wait until you meet Simon!" That got the raised eyebrows from Sabine.

# Chapter 61

Francoise and Marta were still at the breakfast table. With quick good mornings, Annie and Sabine finished just as Veronica arrived. "*Hola*, ladies, we have a big morning planned! Is everyone ready?" Annie was excited to have Sabine's ideas. Celeste and Meghan were ready to get the day started.

Veronica began the drive away from Palma. "This morning, we shall go back to Vista Hermosa. Sabine, you will be able to see how stunning the view is, and we can make a few decisions. From there, we meet with the florist, then a stop at Greta's bakery. Finally, we meet with Paulo to discuss the menu options for the reception."

Sabine knew if Annie had chosen this place, it had to be beautiful, but she was not prepared for the dazzling dome-like temple that stood at the end of the cliff-side peninsula. They walked out to the end. So high up and projected out from the mountain, the views of the sea and other islands made them feel like they were suspended midair. Rarely was Sabine speechless, but all she could say was, "*Mon Dieu!*"

Annie looked around to envision the final scene. "I think definitely a tall arrangement for the pedestal in the center of the pavilion. With that, maybe just bows for the aisle chairs?"

Sabine was quick to suggest, "You have the red theme going on. What if you chose white bows at each chair on the aisle for a little tradition and red rose petals along the path to the altar?"

Annie turned to Veronica and asked, "When you spoke with Mara, did she give you any requests?"

"Mara would like two arrangements of stacks of fruit with large straw fan toppers decorated with red accents placed on each side at the entrance to the aisle behind the seating. They would serve as an offering. Why don't I have both white and red ribbon, and you can decide which color to use once we see what she brings?" Veronica and Celeste were both making notes.

Veronica walked over to the flat terraced area. "This area makes a good place for the reception." They discussed the seating arrangement and size of the tables, knowing the older group would want to be seated together. More notes were taken.

Meghan was trying to think of the tables. "What if each table had a candle centerpiece surrounded by a spray of crimson orchids?" They all liked that idea.

Celeste then brought up Salvador's ashes to be spread. Tomás had brought them from Marbella, and they were in Marguerite's room in a tall brass urn.

Annie thought out loud, looking around. "There needs to be a transition from the wedding ceremony to the reception when that can happen. It needs to be an important part but separate from the wedding ceremony. Let me talk about that with Marguerite, Ramone, and Antonio to see how they would like it to unfold."

*****

The drawings the florist showed them had lovely ideas, and they decided on an exotic combination of white lilies, red roses, and tall tropical ferns as the centerpiece for the pedestal. The drawing that caught Annie's eye was a Zen arrangement. It was simple in a white square ceramic bowl. Sprays of the crimson orchids climbed up shoots of bamboo tied together, offset by a single accordion-like emerald palm leaf, a deep green carnation, and dark red Sweet William. It gave her a feeling of Bali. They decided to do those arrangements for the reception tables with a tall candle added to each.

The bridesmaids' bouquets used the fans with three large open red roses and a white satin bow. An additional three red roses for the top of the cake would go to Greta. Groomsmen would have the rosebud boutonnieres. Annie wanted her bouquet to be kept simple. It took her breath away when she saw the drawing. Amidst three enormous white lilies, there were miniature clusters of baby red roses, accented with the tropical ferns from the centerpiece and white baby's breath.

Happily satisfied with the flowers, Annie asked the florist whether any would come from Barcelona. She answered that everything but the orchids were available locally. However, her source in Barcelona needed an extra day to gather them. They should be on the ferry Wednesday, so the Tuesday flight transport was unnecessary.

The stop at Greta's bakery gave Sabine a chance to taste the almond cake. Her mouth full and large grin on her face, Sabine gave it an enthusiastic thumbs-up! Annie explained about the design Greta would do with the three tiers and red roses. Veronica looked at her watch. They were just in time for their meeting with Paulo.

Checking the tasting table once again, Paulo thought about the accident that he caused. He would be forever grateful Annie was driving the scooter slow enough to swerve out of his car's way. Providing the food for the reception was the very least he could do. It was not a formal dinner, and the cake would be provided. It should be easy enough. On the table were various tapas, grilled shrimp and mushroom skewers, stuffed eggplant, tarragon chicken salad, and his chef's version of tomato and basil bruschetta.

When the ladies arrived, Paulo introduced them to the chef, who gave them stickers to place on the dishes they liked. It was a delicious assortment. Once they had their decisions made, Paulo offered to take them into the club for lunch, and they eagerly accepted. It had been quite a productive morning! When seated, he asked, "Have you seen any of the rehearsals for the music and dancing?"

Annie shook her head. "No, but I am completely confident in whatever Marguerite arranges. She is such an amazing dancer!

She knows the one song we want included somewhere is 'Higher Love.' Hopefully, Simon will sing it."

Paulo said, "I remember that song from church. It speaks to the heart."

Celeste asked him, "I don't mean to pry, but your two children are such talented musicians. Do they get their talent from you?"

"No, I am afraid I can't take any credit for that. Their mother was the musician. She played a variety of instruments and had the voice of a saint."

"Was? She's no longer with you?" Celeste saw the look of pain that crossed his face.

"Sadly, my wife, Nadia, died four years ago. We were married for twenty-three years."

They were touched by his loss. Annie asked softly, "Was it sudden?"

Crushed by the weight of reliving the accident, Paulo sighed and answered, "She drowned in a boating accident."

That rang home as too familiar to the boating accident in Maine and how it might have ended so tragically. The mood at the table was suddenly somber.

Shaken out of his reverie, Paulo said. "There now, that is enough of such subjects. It is your wedding week. Tell me about your plans."

They discussed options for the week. When lunch was finished, Paulo wished them good luck and hoped he would see them again before the wedding.

Paulo walked toward his office. He could hear the distant sounds of music coming from the studio. It was not the first time he'd heard them, but up until now he had resisted his curiosity. Maybe it was the talk of Nadia that fed his desire to see her dance. He quietly opened the door enough to slip through and stood in the shadows watching. Marguerite's body moved in perfect harmony to his son's music. Paulo watched him quicken then slow his pace, and her body met his rhythm. *My God! No wonder he is enamored with her*. It was as if his musical notes acted like strings to a puppet. But this woman was no puppet. She was flesh and blood. Her dancing mesmerized him, and the idea of her in his arms tantalized him beyond endurance. He slipped out of the room before he could make a complete fool of himself.

# Chapter 62

Ramone smiled to think it was just a little over a week ago he did his first hike. Tomás and Robert hung in there all morning, but by lunch, they were finished. He knew how they felt. These were some intense inclines. The climb up to the Castle of Alaró, at the peak of the southern outcrop, was challenging. But the site dated back to the year 902, and the views were mind-blowing. They met Alex and Antonio at the restaurant in town. Both Tomás and Robert, smiling, pleaded for a ride back to the villa, but knowing the challenge ahead of him, Ramone continued on with Stephan and Carmina.

It was quiet at the villa. Dom and Gennie had gone out for a game of cards. The ladies were still gone. Tomás and Robert went to shower and rest. That left Alex with Antonio. Alex said, "I can help you with a pool workout if you'd like."

Antonio perked up and quickly said yes. He was anxious for someone to see what he could now do. "Great, Alex. I will meet you at the pool." Antonio had greatly improved in managing a change of clothes and personal grooming, so he maneuvered into his swimsuit and joined Alex at the pool. He fastened his float and ankle weights to start his round of exercises.

Alex watched, then commented, "You have been working on your arms! Look how strong they've become." Once Antonio got to his sitting position on the side of the pool, he managed to lift his body weight to slide himself over to the steps and come down into the pool. Sometimes when he sat on the top step in the water with his legs dangling, he actually felt a sense of normalcy.

Antonio explained, "I have a pair of weights in my room. I'm trying to build the strength in my arms enough to carry my own body weight if necessary and compensate for the weakness in my legs." They went through the exercises one by one. Alex continued to be impressed by Antonio's progress and told him so.

Antonio felt the pride of accomplishment but clarified, "This is the result of Meghan and the massage therapist."

Alex added, "And a lot of hard work on your part!" After about thirty minutes, they saw Celeste coming from the veranda.

Celeste called out, "We just got home. The girls are getting on their swimsuits. Antonio, Meghan brought you a surprise! Alex, when you get a chance, I need your help. We found another long picnic table to add to the outdoor table under the trellised area by the veranda. This will help accommodate the group coming in tomorrow."

Antonio looked at Alex. "I wish I could help."

Alex gave him a pat on the back. "Someday, Antonio. Someday. Will you be okay if I go?"

Sabine came out just as Alex was toweling off. Antonio did not think he had ever seen Sabine in a swimsuit, much less in a wisp of a tiny bikini that did not leave much to the imagination. She was very slim, he noted, but well proportioned.

Sabine splashed him. "What are you staring at? Have I grown two heads!" She dove into the pool and swam to the other side.

Oh, he wanted to swim after her. Her spritely carefree spirit could not be more opposite from Veronica's. She actually made him want to laugh and *play*. He opted to laugh. Meghan and Annie got to the pool, and Annie went down the steps next to Antonio.

"Antonio! Look at you all tanned and beefed up. Good thing I'm already taken!" Annie's playfulness reminded him again how alike she and Sabine were. Except Annie's body was ripening, carrying his niece or nephew. He was genuinely happy for his brother and thought the glow about Annie was stunning.

Meghan was busy blowing up what looked like a raft or float. When she finished, Antonio saw it was a floating chair. "Come on, Antonio. You have all of us here in the pool with you. Take off your float and weights." She brought the chair float over to the steps, and with a little help from Meghan, he propelled himself into the seat. There he was, able to use his arms to paddle the chair around and splash the girls, which they heartlessly returned. He learned to steer the chair with his arms, and he could easily make it from one end to the other.

Tomás came out to join them. "Wow, look at you!" He got in the water and immediately dunked Meghan. Antonio could see there was no mercy in this crowd. Sabine pushed off from the wall and glided right by him underwater to the other side, poking his leg as she went by. He swore he felt that.

Meghan watched Sabine and got an idea. "Sabine, try something for me. Everyone get out of her way. Now, don't push off and don't use your legs. Try to get to the other side underwater with just your arms." Sabine sensed this was important, so she concentrated. No pushing off and no legs. It took her a little longer, and she had to hold breath a few more seconds, but she did it. "Antonio, watch her. You're next. Go, Sabine! Do it again." She went underwater and let her legs go limp. She pumped through the water with her arms and popped up on the other side.

Antonio thought Meghan had lost her mind. She pulled the float back over to the steps and got him out onto the step. "You can do this. The four of us will make a corridor for you. You'll be safe. All you have to do is use those arms of yours, hold your breath and get to the other side. Put your head underwater to get yourself oriented." He floated face down for a few seconds. "Now hold your breath for as long as you can." That part seemed easy. Antonio held his breath until Meghan pulled him up. "Sabine is on the other side of the pool. She will be sure you are able to grasp the wall. We are right here. Now go!"

It took a moment under the water to get his legs behind him. Through the force of determination, the strength in his arms, and the knowledge that Sabine was at the other end, Antonio glided under the water feeling like he could fly! He could hear the cheer of encouragement. He saw Sabine ahead and swam right up to her and grabbed the wall on either side of her. Looking face-to-face at Sabine, with his arms touching hers on the wall, the elation he felt showed in his face. He looked at her and the ear-to-ear grin with those dimples let her feel it all with him. It took every ounce of strength he had not to kiss her. Turning around to Meghan, he yelled, *"I did it!"*

They were all amazed and felt like they had just seen a major step in his recovery. It was Meghan who said, "Now do it again. Back to the steps."

With a challenge, Sabine looked at him. "I'll race you."

They went under together, and Sabine did not start until he did. She willed him forward, and they began to move in unison. However, right at the end, he pushed harder and won. He reached the steps and got seated. She pulled up next to him and sat. "You cheated!"

He reached over to pull her legs closer to him. When his hand accidentally touched her inner thigh, Sabine let out a short intake of breath. No one noticed but Antonio. Sheepishly, he said, "Sorry."

Robert came out. "What did I miss? We could hear all the cheers."

Annie hadn't missed any of it. She knew her cousin well. Before it could get awkward with Robert, she called out to Antonio, "Show him, Antonio. I'll be here at the wall."

Sabine encouraged, "You can do it! I'll bring the float." The cheers began again as Robert dropped his jaws in amazement. This time, he grabbed the wall next to Annie. Sabine was right behind him with the float, and Tomás helped him into it. Antonio was exhausted and exhilarated all at once, and the chemistry with Sabine was undeniable, breaking through any barrier he thought he might have. His only regret was that his mother and brother weren't there to see it.

# Chapter 63

Paulo knew the moment Marguerite finished the rehearsal and looked out the window of his office to see her walking toward the marina. He frantically looked around to find some excuse to go by the marina. The pair of dinghy paddles would have to do. He made a dash for the marina but slowed down to a casual stroll when he got close to her. "*Hola*, Marguerite! The ladies were here earlier to select the menu for the wedding. How did the rehearsal go?"

"Your children have incredible talent. You must be so proud," Marguerite answered.

Paulo smiled. "That was all my wife's doing."

Feeling a moment of disappointment, Marguerite said, "Oh, I didn't know you were married."

"I'm not anymore. My wife, Nadia, died several years ago in an accident."

"That's horrible. I am so sorry. Was that why you seemed so sad at the hospital?"

"Just bad memories. May I give you a ride back to the villa? I just have to deliver these paddles."

"Ramone should be finished with his hike. He said he would wait for me to give me a ride." Marguerite wanted to accept but would not leave Ramone not knowing where she was.

"Ah, well then, goodbye." Paulo began to walk away, then turned around. "Marguerite, I don't know if you are involved with all the guests arriving at the villa, but I would love to invite you to dinner tomorrow night if you're free."

"We have four new arrivals tomorrow so I doubt I would be missed. I'd be delighted to have dinner with you, Paulo. How about if I meet you?" Marguerite asked, hoping he would understand.

"There is a nice restaurant about two blocks from here." Taking out a pen and a small notepad, Paulo wrote down the address. "I'll be there at seven o'clock."

Marguerite nodded and said goodbye. She saw Ramone up ahead and went to join him with a couple of butterflies in her stomach about her dinner date. By the time she and Ramone got to the villa, they had to get caught up on Antonio's achievements. She hugged her son tightly. "It sounds like a huge accomplishment! Son, you have persevered and worked hard for this next step."

"Mamà, for the first time since the injury, I felt like I had some control over my life. Gliding through the water gave me a taste of the freedom I've been yearning for."

Sabine could not begin to describe the emotion she felt when she heard Antonio say that to his mother.

The rest of the evening was spent telling stories, exchanging banter, and anticipating the arrival of the new guests. Sabine and Robert promised to be up and have their rooms cleaned early so they would be ready. Dom announced he had arranged for the flat over the festivities surrounding the Des Güell a Lluc a Peu pilgrimage. There would be a group dinner tomorrow night that would be festive but not as elaborate as Sunday, giving everyone a better chance to get to know each other. Yuba and the chef had collaborated with Gennie about the menu earlier.

Ramone had heard so much about Sarah, Mara, and Jonathan, he couldn't wait to finally meet them in person. He was also slightly anxious about El Amir and how he would react to his marrying Annie. He pulled Annie aside, suggesting they retire early to be crystal clear about the delights marriage to him would bring. With a mild blush, Annie quickly said yes.

Tomás and Robert both wanted to join Ramone on a half-day hike in the morning to get in some more training. It wasn't long before the villa quieted. Celeste was locking up when Marguerite approached her. "I do not want to make a big thing of it, but if it would be all right to miss tomorrow night, I have dinner plans."

Celeste smiled. "Paulo?" When Marguerite nodded, Celeste added, "He appears to be a lovely man. He loved his wife very much. It sounds like her sudden death was a huge blow to him. I'm pleased he asked you. Go. I won't say a word."

\*\*\*\*\*

Sleep was impossible for Antonio. In his mind he kept replaying the time at the pool. The swim made him feel alive again. The urge to kiss Sabine when they were face-to-face was overwhelming, and he was certain the gasp she made when his hand touched her thigh meant she felt something for him. He tossed and turned, thinking it over and over. Then, in the late hours, there was a soft knock at his door. He called out to come in.

There was Sabine. She had thrown her robe over her nightgown and stood there. In shock, Antonio asked, "What are you doing?"

She took off her robe, leaving on her sheer nightgown, and Antonio raised the covers. Sabine climbed in and said, "I decided today was going to be the day I stopped waiting for something good to come along. I realized what I was longing for was right in front of me." Antonio's heart melted, and he took her in his arms. She leaned over him and gently kissed him, exploring the possibility. He pulled her closer to deepen the kiss, letting it communicate all the feelings he had been reluctant to express before.

Antonio released the kiss to plead, "Stay with me." Then he kissed her again. Both of them seemed satisfied to lie there together, in no rush to go further. But there was no question they were both pleased that a certain part of his anatomy seemed to work just fine. Their common understanding smile said it all.

# Chapter 64

Antonio awoke alone. Had it been a dream? He didn't think so. He could still feel the curves of her body next to him. She naturally got up early to avoid any whispers about them that would hurt Robert. Sabine and Robert planned to move back to the other villa this morning. Robert would also be on the hike this morning. *I need to get up!*

Marguerite knocked on his door to help him dress for the day. She looked serious when she entered. "There seems to be a problem. Alex heard from El Amir." Antonio listened and could hear Annie's raised, agitated voice.

Annie begged, "Dad, you can't leave! Please!" Ramone stood quietly at her side, trying to comprehend what had happened.

Alex held Annie's shoulders and tried to explain. His leather bag was packed and waiting at the front door. "I got a call from El Amir early this morning. He heard from Ernest, and there is some trouble brewing with the Chinese who stayed in custody in Malaga and possibly the operative who shot Salvador. They need me. Sweetheart, it should only take two or three days. We will be back in plenty of time for the wedding."

Annie began to cry. Sabine heard the noise and went to comfort her, but Annie looked at her dad with sad eyes. "You can't be sure of that! You will be with El Amir? What happens to Sarah?"

Alex answered, "Hurry, get ready to take me to the airport. El Amir's plane is arriving early this morning. Sarah will be on board. Then I will fly back with him to Malaga to meet Ernest. But now I need to speak with your grandfather."

Don Marco excused himself and followed Alex into the library. It was a short conversation because they were back quickly.

248

Going to her mother, Annie pleaded, "Mom, make him stay. Please?"

Celeste, her own eyes glistening, said with a lump in her throat, "Through all our years together, it has never been easy to see your father go. This is what he trained for, and he has to see this through. He has promised, Annie." She looked over at her husband for assurance, and he nodded. "He and El Amir will be back in time for the wedding. Now let's go send him off and pick up Sarah."

Ramone watched the raw pain Annie and her mother had by sending Alex to an unknown fate. This was what would happen, whether she tried to hide it or not, each time he stepped into the ring. Putting that knowledge aside, he stepped up to Alex and asked, "Does this involve the men who killed Papa?" When Alex answered that it was possible, Ramone continued, "Then I should go with you." Ramone tried to close his eyes to Annie's shock and horror at his words.

Alex put his hands on both of Ramone's arms, "Son, trust us to do what is best. We have been trained for military missions, just as you trained to fight the fiercest bulls. If you put me in a ring facing a thousand-pound bull, I would be gone in moments. Let us do what we were trained to do." Reluctantly, Ramone drew sense from Alex's words and nodded. Annie took a deep breath and wiped her eyes, relieved that at least Ramone was staying.

It was decided Annie, Ramone, and Celeste would go with him to the airport and bring Sarah back. Alex shook Don Marco's hand then said his goodbyes around the room to well wishes for a safe and hasty return. Antonio tried to steal a look at Sabine, but her concern for Annie distracted her.

Sabine told Annie, "Uncle Alex will be back. You know he wants to try the night hike Friday. Robert and I are almost finished cleaning our rooms in the casita. We will move our stuff over to the other villa and be back here to greet Sarah. Come on, *chérie*! We have a big week ahead of us!"

No one noticed the serious look on Don Marco's face.

As the group left for the airport, there it was, the moment when Antonio caught Sabine's eyes. The slight smile and warm eyes reflected a mutual confirmation that their time would come. Sabine told Dom and Gennie, "I have changed the sheets, and I think everything is ready. We'll be back soon to help prepare for tonight. I know Annie is taking Uncle Alex's departure hard. She wasn't expecting Sarah until later, and I have to admit I'm looking forward to meeting her."

Meghan looked at Sabine and suggested, "If Annie has to go with Mara and Veronica tomorrow morning to work on the Balinese part of the wedding, why don't you and I take Sarah to Valldemossa? She might want to take her paints and she could paint while we shop and wander around."

Sabine nodded. "That sounds great. I wanted to see that village. It is supposed to be an artistic dream."

Sarah's welcome at the airport was bittersweet. Annie's tears resurfaced as she hugged her father tight, then hugged El Amir, saying, "Please keep both of you safe and try to get back for the wedding. It won't be the same without you both there with us."

El Amir nodded and shook Ramone's hand. Ramone walked over to Alex and hugged him with sincerity. "Stay safe, Alex. Our girl needs you to walk her down the aisle. But get those bastards who killed my father!"

Sarah completely understood the scene in front of her and was determined to help however she could. She greeted Alex, introducing herself. "You have an amazing daughter. I look forward to getting to know you better upon your return." With a final hug to El Amir, Sarah turned her attention to Annie while Celeste said her goodbye to Alex.

They watched the plane take off, and Annie tried to swallow the sob of despair she felt. Trying to lighten the mood, Sarah looked at Ramone and said, "So this is the handsome matador I've listened to you run on about?" That got a chuckle from all of them, and Annie knew her good friend would be the perfect remedy to fill the void left by her father's absence, although she was still reeling from Ramone's willingness to go with her father right before their wedding.

Ramone could already pick up on Sarah's dry sense of humor and rebounded, "I am. And I understand you are the artist who lives in a tent and paints zebras!"

Sarah laughed and simply replied with a sly smile, "Among other things."

Celeste was happy to see the easy banter Annie shared with Sarah, and that Ramone seemed to like her as well. It made her wonder what Mara and Jonathan would be like. So many personalities in one place! She prayed the tense moment with Ramone would pass quickly.

# Chapter 65

Back at the villa, Annie made introductions, and Sarah was glad to put faces to all the people Annie had told her about. Sarah said, "I am so excited to meet all of you! What a handsome family you are." She could see how close Annie was to Sabine and that Meghan was a force to be reckoned with, in a good way. Antonio didn't seem to be as broody as Annie had portrayed. Tomás was obviously entranced with Meghan and seemed to be the business-man of the group. Marguerite seemed very exotic, and she could not wait to see her dance. She immediately fell in love with Dom and Gennie and felt she could sit and talk with them for hours. And then there was Ramone. How dashing and serious on the outside with a warm and sensitive inside. She looked forward to getting to know him better too. The only one that seemed slightly out of place was Robert.

There! She had made her initial assessment, laughing to her-self that she did the same thing when she assessed the subject at the beginning of one of her paintings. Sabine took her to the casita and told her to pick her favorite room since Mara and Jonathan would now have the other two without El Amir. They would figure out the room situation whenever El Amir got back. She got the tour of the villa and immediately guessed the stunning veranda would be where everyone hung out. Everything was beautiful. The trellises, the large varieties of floral scents, and the pool with the large backyard. She would love spending time here.

Tomás went to Ramone. "Robert and I waited for you to do a short but challenging hike. I'm sure Stephan and Carmina and Hans have already left by now." Ramone went to get his gear together.

Curious, having heard Hans's name, Sarah asked about the hiking. "Annie told me to bring hiking boots. Are there a lot of trails?"

Tomás answered, "There is a huge network of hiking trails here on the island. Some go along the coastal villages. I think some of you are planning to do that on Thursday. The trails inland through the Tramuntana mountain range can be quite challenging. Some of us want to participate in the arduous pilgrimage overnight hike to the monastery at the top of a mountain peak. We are trying to hike every day to train. Ramone and Annie met Stephan and Carmina when we first got here. They mostly lead the hikes." Casually, he added, "The King's Cup regatta is where we met Hans. After the regatta was over, he started hiking with us."

Trying to remain nonchalant, Sarah wondered if their paths would cross. As randomly as possible, she asked, "Will they be at the wedding?"

Annie overheard and came to sit on the arm of her chair. "Yes, we invited the three of them along with several others we've met on the island." Annie supposed this would be the point she would find out if there was a problem with Hans being there. Sarah, never quiet about anything, stayed uncharacteristically silent.

Ramone kissed Annie, trying to gauge her mood while assuring her El Amir and her father would be back soon. He then left with Tomás and Robert. Gennie and Celeste were in the kitchen with the chef coordinating the dinner plans. Gennie softly said to her daughter, pulling her aside, "Are you worried about this mission?"

"Oh, Maman, I am always worried when he leaves. The last time he was away over two years, he had been shot and was captured. Every day since he returned, I have said a prayer, thankful he finally came home safe. But I have to be strong for Annie. She needs him to walk her down the aisle. What was not easy to hear was when he told me Dom should be the backup to walk her down the aisle if necessary." She assumed that was the topic in the library.

Gennie took her daughter's hands in hers and raised them to a kiss. "Keep your faith, *chérie*. Do not dwell on what could go wrong. Be inspired by what can go right. Share that inspiration with Annie and will it so."

"Thank you, Maman, I'll try."

Marguerite came into the kitchen to help. "I know I won't be here for dinner, but I would love to help any way I can."

Celeste asked, "Are you not rehearsing with Simon and Marcella today?"

"No, they are both participating in the festivities Friday night, and there is a large rehearsal for them today." Marguerite told them she would be free to do whatever needed until late afternoon.

Gennie asked where she planned to go. Marguerite glanced at Celeste and answered, "Paulo suggested a restaurant on the water down a few blocks from the yacht club. I have to admit I'm a little nervous. I know so little about him."

Celeste remarked, "You know about his wife's tragic accident. What about you, Marguerite? During all those years Salvador was gone, why did you never divorce him?"

Marguerite sighed. "You only saw him a couple of times when we first met. He was a special man, such a loving husband and good father. He would have short bouts of anger, but they were quickly suppressed, and he was always apologetic after. I didn't realize the dramatic impact his father's death had on him. That anger he had mostly kept hidden during those good years surfaced once our sons followed their uncle into the family tradition. I suppose I always hoped he would get past it and come back to us. At the very end, he did. It was simple, really. He just wanted his sons to be safe."

# Chapter 66

On the veranda, Don Marco was sharing some of his own travel stories and expressed his curiosity about Sarah's lifestyle in Africa and what prompted her to go there. Sarah started with, "It was an odd time in my life. I thought I was going in a different direction. Things didn't go as I'd hoped, and it seemed time for a change. At a gallery in London, where I was working during summers while I was in school, I met two men who were instrumental in my decision to go paint in Africa. One was Sam Patterson and the other was El Amir. Sam was a sculptor who was obsessed with lions. His talent with capturing their likeness, especially engaged in battle, was incredible. He was the one with the ambition to do his art among the wildlife in Africa. El Amir was a patron to our London gallery and had bought several of my early paintings. During a fundraising event at the gallery, there was a wildlife exhibit featured. We were demonstrating our painting techniques live at the event. Sam was working on a lion piece, and I had decided to paint zebras. El Amir seemed to admire our work and offered to sponsor us. Sam told El Amir his dream was to go to Africa to produce sculptures."

Annie had never heard how Sarah and El Amir met. Such an interesting story. Everyone was listening. Sarah continued, "At the time, I didn't know it, but El Amir had ties to East Africa and had reached out to a safari lodge to check on the availability for tent camping on their property in Tanzania. Sam was not a boyfriend or anything at first, but he was familiar company, and I was looking for a change. The rest is history. We gave notice to the gallery, and within a week, we were on our way to tent life and art in Africa!"

All of them wanted to know more. It was Annie who asked, "Were you afraid there with animals that might see you as their next meal?"

That made Sarah laugh, remembering. "At first, I was a blithering coward! I am sure my heart stopped a few times in fear. We had a guide whom El Amir paid to get us set up and teach us how to stay alive."

Sabine was awed. "What an adventure!" Always the romantic, she asked, "Did you ever get together with Sam? In those circumstances, it seems inevitable you would consider it." Antonio smiled at her question and wondered if she thought they were inevitable. He, too, waited for Sarah's response.

"There were times when I was scared or lonely that I was particularly happy he was close by, but a love affair was not why I was there. It was the majestic beauty of the animals and their unpredictable movements that enchanted me."

Annie mentioned, so proud of her friend, "I remember once you told me about the zebra stripes, that no two zebras have the exact same pattern. In a way, I think that was what the minister who is marrying us said in his sermon last Sunday about us humans."

They continued for a while, then Meghan offered her suggestion. "Sarah, Annie is going with Mara tomorrow morning to add some Balinese touches to the wedding. Sabine and I thought we might go to this picturesque village, Valldemossa, that has been painted by artists from all over the world. I know it's not animals, but it might appeal to you to paint it."

Annie loved the idea. "Mom could decide to go with you or with us, and we could join you there for lunch. Antonio, we could come back and pick you up to go with us to lunch."

Sabine casually said, "Or he could come with us. I could help with the chair?"

Antonio had read about Valldemossa and was intrigued. "I'm not sure my wheelchair could manage the cobblestones, but if Sarah decides to paint, perhaps I could stay and watch?"

Dom picked up the book he was reading about Mallorca. "Valldemossa dates back to the beginning of the fourteenth century, and there is a distinguished monastery there. It was also home to Chopin and his lover for a short time and inspired him to compose. I will see if Gennie would also like to visit the village."

Annie loved to see her friends and family get along. It sounded like it would be a lovely day. She was trying hard not to worry about her father and El Amir. She determined to maintain a leap of faith they would get back safely and soon. Her father's words comparing his training and Ramone's training kept spinning in her mind as to whether they were meant to do what they were so well trained to do.

As always, she was happy to see Captain Luis arrive and join Don Marco for a whiskey and a cigar. But when they retired to the library for a little privacy, she was barely aware with all the activity around her.

# Chapter 67

Meghan offered to do a workout with Antonio at the pool. Sabine observed, noting where he particularly needed work. He wanted to do his underwater swim, but Meghan wouldn't allow it until they had four in the pool to provide the "corridor." Once Annie and Sarah joined them, Antonio did four laps before tiring. Sarah was amazed how the pool and his weight training had helped him.

Meghan thought out loud to Antonio, "I need to come up with a way to get you semi-vertical to put partial weight on your legs. Maybe when the men get back from the hike, they can help me."

Before long, it was time for Annie and Sarah to change out of their swimsuits for the airport run. Meghan planned to go read and expected Antonio to get out of the pool. He said he would rather stay to work on his leg exercises a little more. Meghan hesitated.

Sabine assured her, "I can stay for a while if he's not ready to go in." Annie and Sarah waved goodbye. Meghan left to read her book.

Antonio ventured, "Did that really happen? We're alone?" Those dimples definitely drove her mad. She smiled the warmest smile he thought he had ever seen. "I thought I dreamed last night when I woke up and you were gone."

Antonio was sitting on the step, and she sat pressed next to him. "It was no dream. But this is Annie and Ramone's time. It was hard enough this morning when Uncle Alex left. I can't imagine if anything happens or if he can't make it back for the wedding. Did you think about me today? Just a little?"

There was his smile that lit up his eyes. "You have never left my thoughts. I remember Sunday when you first greeted me, I had a feeling of coming home. You do that, Sabine. Ever since the injury, I have not felt worthy to pursue you. My life can be a major burden and often requires sacrifice."

"Antonio, do you not see you are doing better every day? You swam four laps today. Meghan is going to have you weight-bearing before you know it."

"I know. I can't believe all she has done for me. Do you honestly think you could be with someone with my limitations?" Antonio asked with trepidation.

"Robert has no physical limitations, but you won't find me lying next to him. I didn't want to leave Marbella. You were nice enough, but I didn't think you were interested in me. When Robert wrote me, I thought I should explore that. It only took a couple of days to know he wasn't the right person for me. Antonio, I want to be with you."

Antonio pulled her to him to kiss her with all the passion he had for her. He wanted to leave no doubt in her mind how he felt about her. Blinded by her feelings, Sabine deepened the kiss with a moan, lying back against the pool wall. It was at that moment the hikers had returned and walked out to the pool.

Robert came over, furious. "Sabine, what are you doing?"

Ramone looked at his brother, not knowing whether he should be angry this happened or deliriously happy. He chose to be quiet. Tomás smartly went to find Meghan. Robert was obviously in an outrage. "You would choose a cripple over me?" The moment the words came out of his mouth, he regretted it. Both Antonio and Ramone were incensed, and Sabine went off.

"Honestly, Robert, I owe you no explanation. I am sorry you are hurt, but this man is far from a cripple, and I will never allow him to be spoken about like that." Inside, Ramone was screaming his praise for Sabine.

Antonio, in amazing calmness, broke in. "Robert, we never set out to hurt anyone. This feeling that we have has been building

259

since we met."

It was time for Ramone to step in. "Okay, we are all here for a wedding, mine and Annie's. She has already gone through a lot with her scooter accident, then her father leaving. Robert, will you stay with us and do the night hike and wedding, or do I need to help you find a flight home?" There was the ultimatum. Robert could either stay and enjoy the week or go home.

Robert answered, "I understand, and I can't say that I didn't see something like this coming. Let's don't put anything else on Annie today. Let me think about it tonight and let you know tomorrow."

# Chapter 68

At the airport, Annie couldn't help the memory of her father leaving that morning. Sarah put her arm around her with comfort. "It will be okay. Let's focus on now. I was trying to remember the last time I saw Mara. I think I have only seen her once since we did the art course in Australia. You told me a little about Jonathan, but what do you remember most?"

"Jonathan is different from these other guys. He is a cattle-roping, crocodile-fighting cowboy with his dog Roscoe by his side. He is brawny and rough around the edges, yet he is a serious environmentalist and marine biologist."

Sarah, curious, asked, "How could someone like that end up with someone as dainty and delicate as Mara?" Annie remembered thinking when she met him that he would be a great match for Sarah. Guess she missed that one. The plane was about to land.

"There they are," Annie said, waving. "Let's meet them at baggage."

Sarah stopped Annie. "This is a joke, right? That hunk of gorgeous man is not with Mara! No way!" Annie burst out laughing, but she had to admit he did look ruggedly handsome. Scruffy facial hair, ball cap with careless dark blond curls springing out from underneath, blue work shirt with rolled-up sleeves over bulging muscles and unbuttoned far enough to display a mass of chest hair, all over well-worn khakis. Altogether, Jonathan gave off an irresistible nonchalant manner, and when he smiled, his whole face lit up. Next to Jonathan, Mara was a total contrast. Beautiful China-doll-like facial features with perfectly coiffed hair, a tailored print sundress, and tiny frame. There had to be a good story behind them as a pair!

Annie ran up to both of them, so excited, and gave each a giant hug. "I am so happy you could make it. Mara, I can't wait to see what you are planning to add to the wedding. And, Jonathan, gosh, it is good to see you again! Meet our friend Sarah."

Sarah, who was hugging Mara, turned to Jonathan. "Hi, oh, what the heck! We're like family." Sarah gave Jonathan a hug too and was rewarded with his bright smile.

They put the bags in the car. This was their first time in Mallorca, so Annie, having been there for a while, told them about the regatta, finding Vista Hermosa, the night hike to the monastery, and the gorgeous beaches. Jonathan explained a big part of how they could pull off adding Mallorca to their Capri trip. "Here in the Balearic Islands, there is a unique species of sea grass, *Posidonia oceanica*, that is crucial to our ecosystem. The underwater meadows where it grows are considered to be the most important habitat of the entire Mediterranean Sea. The Palma Aquarium is committed to ocean preservation and especially protecting its Balearic Sea habitat. I contacted them explaining I would be here, and they offered to pay for our tickets if I worked with them for one day. It is up to you, Annie, which day."

"How do you feel about hiking here in the mountains? The guys are hiking tomorrow. Mara, you and I are meeting with Veronica to finalize details. Sarah and another group are going to this village by the sea where Chopin lived."

"I could hike with the mates tomorrow. I'll see how I do before deciding on the overnight hike. Why don't I tell them Thursday? Is that good with you, angel?"

Mara said, "Yes, of course, Jonathan. I will love spending time with Annie and Sarah. Looking at the scenery, I can tell there will be much to paint. Annie, is there a hike that doesn't have the paths high in the mountains?"

"My new friend Carmina is here hiking with her boyfriend. She offered to lead some of us in a lower elevation coastal hike on Thursday." Both Mara and Sarah liked the idea of that hike.

Annie told them about the monastery and the annual tradition to make the overnight hike to the monastery. "It is said to be quite challenging. There are several in our group planning to do it. For those of us who don't, my grandfather has booked a flat with a balcony overlooking the festivities."

The tension around the pool had eased. Antonio went to change. Sabine suggested she and Robert go to the other villa to have a talk, then change before coming back for dinner. Ramone went to the refrigerator to pull out two beers for Tomás and himself. Tomás took his beer and sat on the veranda. "I did not see that coming. I feel bad for Robert. What do you think he is going to do?"

"I honestly don't know, but the truth is he has spent more time with us than with Sabine on this trip. I know he is looking forward to Friday night's hike with us. Hopefully, it won't be too uncomfortable. Annie has enough to worry about wondering if her father will be back in time for the wedding."

Tomás asked, "Did you hear from either Alex or El Amir if there was danger involved where they were going?"

Ramone answered, "Not that I could tell. If it involved the men who caused my father's death, I offered to go help." He nodded toward the door and let the subject drop when he heard Annie and Sarah arriving with Mara and Jonathan.

When Annie saw there was just Ramone and Tomás, she said, "Thankfully you don't have to be bombarded by the whole crowd! I was hoping you would get a chance to get to know Ramone."

She made the introductions and loved the typical Aussie greeting from Jonathan. "G'day, mates! Pleasure to meet you two."

In contrast, Mara was warm but more reserved. Ramone observed these three friends Annie had met on her journey last year and thought they could not be any more different from each other. As he looked at Jonathan, his gut instinct was he could hike with the best of them. He was pleased Jonathan said he planned to join them on tomorrow's hike. So far, Ramone got along with all the men, and he looked forward to the time on the hike to get to know Jonathan better. Mara was certainly more exotic, and Ramone was curious what she would add to the wedding.

Sarah joined Ramone and Tomás while Annie gave Mara and Jonathan a short tour of the villa. When Annie showed them each to their own room, it was Mara who spoke up. "I thought you said Jonathan would stay at the other villa."

Jonathan added with a smile, "I am fine wherever you put me." To Mara, trying to make it light, he added, "Are you already tired of me?"

Annie heard it but didn't think anything of it. Instead, she explained. "The plan was that El Amir would have one of these rooms. However, he and my father had an urgent mission back in Spain. They are hopeful they will be back before the wedding. If we have to figure out rooms when he gets back, let's just stay flexible, all right?"

# Chapter 69

Not having any obligations for the day, Marguerite took time to walk around the city and allow herself time to mourn the death of her husband in solitude. In the end, he had made the ultimate sacrifice to save their son and father of their grandchild. She would always love him for that. Was she ready to let go and consider a relationship with another man? The thought of it was intimidating to her so soon after Salvador's death. She had not been with a man in so many years. What would he expect? How was she supposed to act? The questions ate at her to the point where she was close to canceling the dinner. It was so tempting to simply avoid or deny the possibility of a life with someone else. Should she remain alone or accept and deal with the opportunity to find love in her future? It was one dinner. She supposed the sooner she gave it a try, the sooner she would discover if it was something she wanted. There was something about Paulo that appealed to her. *Maybe it was time to find out what that was.*

\*\*\*\*\*

At the villa, Sabine and Robert rejoined the group. Their conversation went as well as could be expected, and Robert reluctantly admitted he knew Sabine did not have the same feelings for him that he had for her. However, Robert was thoroughly enjoying the hikes with the other guys and was looking forward to Friday's challenge. Sabine promised to slow things with Antonio down at least through the wedding to make his presence a little easier.

She found a moment to share her promise with Antonio. He could see the wisdom of it but quietly said to her, "We are not done yet. Our paths are intertwined now." She smiled in agreement. Once she moved away from Antonio, she subtly nodded to Robert they had an agreement.

Robert moved into an easy conversation with Tomás and Jonathan. Jonathan was telling them about the marine projects in Australia as well as here in the Balearic Islands. As he explained, "These meadows are what helps maintain the cleanliness and transparency of the seawater."

Meghan was thoroughly enjoying getting acquainted with Sarah. Antonio quietly let Ramone know Robert planned to stay and that he and Sabine would go easy until after the wedding. Ramone patted his brother on the back, pleased they were avoiding any disruption. They joined Meghan and Sarah to hear some of the stories of her life among the animals. "I think the biggest thing I learned as soon as I got there was not to take any food into your tent! If the animals smell food, they're coming in, and you become the main course! Otherwise, they see the tent as just another object to walk around. At night, though, the sounds get much louder, and it took me quite a while to be able to sleep without one eye open."

Ramone excused himself to make the plans for the hike the next day. Now that Jonathan wanted to join them and Robert was staying, there would be four of them. He spoke to Stephan first to get the route for tomorrow. Next, he called Hans who seemed curious about all the new guests that arrived. "Who all is hiking?"

Ramone answered, "It will be our regular three, plus Jonathan McNamara from Australia. The girls are going to Valldemossa tomorrow morning. I think Sarah plans to paint. Dom and Gennie might go tour the monastery there. It is supposed to be quite impressive." Pausing a moment, he added, "Do you feel ready for Friday's hike?"

Hans hesitated. "I am signed up, but I think I will take a break tomorrow and do another big one Thursday. I saw Roff in town, and I think he would like to join you."

Ramone gave him the starting information to pass along. "If you change your mind, come join us." Ramone finished the calls then wandered over to Annie and sat next to her, draping an arm around her.

Sabine loved some of Mara's ideas! "Yesterday, I went to see the wedding location. The views and feeling of being suspended in air are extremely inspiring."

Mara was excited to see it. "I think we go there tomorrow, right, Annie?"

"Yes, you are bringing all your accents and ideas! Veronica will pick us up, and we meet with a lot of the same vendors Sabine saw yesterday. We will add your touches and agree on any final details." Looking at Ramone, she asked, "Are you doing a full-day hike? Mara and I plan to come back here to get Antonio to meet the others for lunch in Valldemossa."

Ramone answered, "I plan to do a full day hike tomorrow, then join you for the coastal walk on Thursday. Probably rest Friday."

Holding Ramone's hand, she looked up at him. "I am praying Dad and El Amir will be back safely by Friday." They filled Mara in on what happened in Malaga and that her dad left for an emergency that morning. Mara took Annie's hands and said a silent prayer.

Marguerite came out to get introduced. She was dressed for the evening. They were all happy to meet Ramone and Antonio's mother and agreed she looked sensational. Ramone pulled her to the side. "If you need anything at all, call me. I'll be right there."

*****

Paulo was waiting for Marguerite at the entrance to the restaurant. He fought to calm his nerves purposefully, trying to give her the warmest welcoming smile he could, having no idea her nerves were as taut as his. At the beginning, they were trying so hard that every attempt at conversation seemed awkward. The waiter poured them a glass of wine. Paulo made the toast. "To new friendships and being at the right place at the right time."

That helped Marguerite smile and relax a bit. Little did they know at that moment, Simon and Helene walked into the restaurant. When Simon noticed his father with Marguerite, he was furious and insisted to Helene that they leave. Even after they left and got to another restaurant, Simon could not shake the thorn of jealousy that was stabbing at his gut. Helene realized she had been so focused on Simon, she had missed that he was not sincerely into her. It was that dinner that convinced her to move back to the *Porto Banus* and Roff and the captain before they gave up on her.

# Chapter 70

Today's hike was to be a long one, and Ramone was pleased to feel the light breeze from the sea. He assured Jonathan that he could abort at any of the villages they went through and find it easy to get a ride to Valldemossa. Before they set out, Annie wanted a few minutes with Ramone and his mother and brother. They went out to the seating area around the pool to talk freely. After the expected questions about Marguerite's dinner with Paulo and her assurance it was quite nice, Annie began, "I am working to finalize details with Veronica this morning and wanted to have an idea how you would like to handle Salvador's memorial. I thought we should probably finish the wedding and move to the service between the wedding and the reception. Do you have preferences? Would you want to talk?"

Marguerite answered, "I like the idea that it would be separate. Everyone will be seated for the wedding ceremony. How about after the ceremony is over, we gather at that side of the cliff with the peninsula in the background? Ramone, I know you want to say words. What about you, Antonio? I will think about what I want to say."

Antonio suggested, "The minister is there. Do you think he might add some comforting words?"

Annie nodded. "I'll find out. I know Dad will probably want to say something." Ramone cringed for her inside, hoping he would make it back in time. "Okay, I think I have it. Veronica will be here soon to pick up Mara and me. Marguerite, would you like to join us? I think Mom is coming."

"My rehearsal is not until the afternoon. I overheard you say you'd come back and pick up Antonio. You could drop me off back

269

here. If that works, I would love to join you."

Ramone gathered his backpack and got the hikers on their way. Sabine was chatting with Meghan and Sarah like long-lost friends. They did not seem to be in any hurry this morning, just enjoying their coffee and each other's company. Sabine was not good at keeping secrets, especially from Annie, so it seemed best to be around Meghan and Sarah, who did not know about Antonio.

Mara had a large bag at the door, and they were ready when Veronica arrived. Marguerite adored being included in the plans. Once her nerves had settled down at the table, she had very much enjoyed the evening with Paulo. At the end of the evening, he had asked to see her again, and she explained she would be rehearsing the next afternoon. They planned to go have a cup of tea after the rehearsal.

The first stop of the morning was back at Vista Hermosa. It was the first time being there for Marguerite and Mara, and they were as enchanted as each of them had been upon seeing it. Veronica explained the seating on either side of the aisle. She put a piece of tape down where she calculated the end of the rows would be. Mara pulled out two large straw fans with deep-red embellishments. She wanted two pedestals about four feet tall, and Veronica made a note to find them. Mara told them to envision an elevated cake stand that would sit on the pedestal. She pulled out two short grass skirts that would attach to the plate. An eight-inch stack of fruit and almonds, now that she knew they flourished here, would layer up with the inverted fan and bamboo shoots springing from the top. The two pillars would greet the guests as they arrived and serve as the offering.

"I will be dressed in full Balinese attire. When the service is about to start, I will ring this large bell, showing it to them. Veronica, can you provide a large basket with red rose petals? Preferably metallic gold. I will come down the aisle first and scatter the petals along the path. I will then take my place to the side of the minister. The wedding party will arrive. I will do the blessing, then the minister takes over."

Annie was so pleased. "It sounds wonderful. Once we move from here, what do you think about this spot to do the spreading of the ashes?"

Marguerite loved the location. "What if we had a third pillar and had the urn on top?"

Mara suggested, "Let's do some palms and bamboo on the pedestal under the urn." Everyone seemed to love that idea, but Veronica suggested the urn be placed to the side during the wedding and on the pedestal for the memorial.

Veronica recalculated the tables for the reception and pointed out where Simon and Marcella would play. It was a natural raised terrace area that looked like a natural stage. Marguerite thought it would be perfect, then said, "Marcella plans to do the intro as guests arrive and bridal march with the violin. Why don't we have her to the side of the altar with the minister before we start?"

They spent the rest of the morning reviewing flowers, then meeting with Paulo. He wasn't expecting Marguerite, and he lit up when he saw her. It took every effort he could muster to focus on the additional items Mara asked for. She had to draw the design and show him how to hold the stacks together with a series of toothpicks. As they left the yacht club, Paulo smiled at Marguerite. "I will see you in a few hours!"

# Chapter 71

M eghan, Sabine, and Sarah left Palma behind, heading to the lower slopes of the Tramuntana mountain range. They passed through agricultural land filled with almond and olive trees and could imagine the delights the hikers found on their various routes. Once the valley loomed below them, they looked up in the distance to see the tower of the Carthusian Museum with its turquoise tiles gleaming in the sunlight. Looking at the stone houses that descended the hillside in a haphazard series of terraces with the backdrop of the higher mountain range, each of them found themselves speechless.

It was hard to imagine the thousands of years of history in this single place. Meghan said she was looking forward to finding any Arab elements left from their time of occupation in the tenth century. They left the car near the bus stop. Sarah pulled out her easel, paints, and canvas and tucked them under her arms as they made their way through the stone village. Terracotta clay pots ornamented the stone walls along the narrow streets. They were filled with everything from fresh herbs and trailing ivy to blooming flowers. They passed open markets displaying fresh fruit and vegetables and outdoor cafés. The monastery was indeed impressive as the focal point of the village, and they knew Dom and Gennie would enjoy their tour.

At every crossroad, Sarah scrutinized the scene. She did not want to decide too soon for fear of missing that perfect spot. Shaking her head, she told Sabine and Meghan, "I could paint here every day! Even the stones of the facades vary in color and dimension. It is magnificent in such an authentic and charming way!" Eventually, Sarah noticed an area where various other artists were set up. She moved over to their angle and saw the most interesting narrow street with its vivid colors. She found a location where she could have an unobscured view and unfolded her portable chair. She murmured, "This is it."

Meghan and Sabine told Sarah they would climb up to the monastery to see the view and possibly run into Dom and Gennie. Someone told them about a pearl museum, so they planned to look for a pearl necklace to give Annie for her wedding dress. They said they would come back and check on her in about an hour. Sarah waved goodbye and settled down, chewing on the tip of her paintbrush while studying the scene before her. Finally, she knew her angle and pulled out her charcoal pencil to rough out the design.

The walk up the hill held surprises at each terraced level along the way. Whether the picturesque scenery, the fragrant aromas of fresh baked goods in the open-air bakeries, or the interesting window shopping, Sabine and Meghan were enjoying the village and their time together. They found the pearl museum and went inside. Sabine had loved pearls since she was a little girl when she would see her grandmother, Claudette, wearing hers each time she dressed up. She looked closely at these man-made pearls in the case, and it was almost impossible to tell them apart from authentic pearls that naturally come from an oyster.

The salesperson explained how each of the pearls had layer after layer of pearly liquid that gave it the final luster and iridescence. They can be made perfectly round or slightly oval. Meghan described that they were looking for a bridal necklace for a dress with a deep V-back. The clerk asked, "Are you looking for ivory or would you consider this shade of grayish blue which gives a rainbow of iridescence?"

Looking at Sabine, Meghan questioned, "Should this be something new or something blue? You know her best. What would Annie like?"

Sabine answered, "Annie likes simple, but she also likes unusual. Depending on the piece, I think she would like the blue if the shade leans toward silver. If we do that, we should also get simple drop earrings to match."

From inside the case, the clerk pulled a silver-hued necklace. The larger pearls that went around the neck in a single strand had a white gold chain suspended in the back with three smaller pearls about four inches down. Between each of the pearls was set a small sparkling diamond. It was stunning, and both Sabine and Meghan decided to splurge and buy it together. Satisfied with their purchase, they continued up to the monastery.

*****

Sarah had begun to lay the first layer of paint onto the canvas. She chewed on the tip of the brush deep in thought, trying to get the dimension of the narrow street in front of her. From behind, a voice startled her reverie. "Hi, Sarah. Long time." Sarah swirled around, and standing there, with his chiseled face and slicked-back blond hair, was Hans Schuman.

# Chapter 72

Sarah let out a large sigh. "Hans...aren't you supposed to be hiking?"

"Ahh, so you knew I was here on the island. Ramone mentioned you might be painting here this morning." Looking at the frayed paintbrush tip, he added, "I see some old habits die hard."

Sarah self-consciously put the brush down. "What do you want, Hans? It has been years. Let's just leave our past in the past where it belongs."

"Sarah, I simply want a chance to tell you my side of what happened. I never meant to hurt you."

That last statement stoked her anger. "Listen, let it go. I have a good life and don't need you to stir it up. I know you have become friends with Annie and Ramone, and we will likely run into each other this week. Let's just call a truce, okay? We can certainly be civil to each other."

Quietly, Hans persisted. "I searched for you after Camille died. It was like you vanished into thin air. When I finally found out you were in Africa, I kept trying to contact you, but every message came back undeliverable."

"Look, I don't want to hear it! Now please let me get back to my painting."

Hans could tell Sarah's stubborn streak had set in and he was getting nowhere. Looking at this watch, he tried to estimate where the hikers were and reluctantly left her to go join them. Before he left, he added, "I hope you will reconsider and allow me to explain sometime this week. Bye, Sarah."

All the old emotions and hurt came flooding back. Sarah remembered the strength of the love she had for that man, her first and only true love. Or so she had thought. When she lifted her brush, her hand was shaking. She needed to keep this to herself. There was no need for Annie to worry about her. She could force herself to be indifferent.

Sarah finally calmed herself enough to start painting again and began to explore some unique blends of colors to portray the subtle variances in the stones. When she took the brush tip to her teeth, she remembered Hans's words and jerked it out. After a while, Sarah found the groove she sought where she knew her strokes were having the impact she wanted.

She could feel someone looking over her shoulder. Sure that it was Hans coming back to bother her, she turned around ready for a fight, and saw Jonathan, just as rugged as before and a total contrast to Hans's perfect, put-together look. There was something wild about him that reminded her of Africa. He was gazing at the beginning of her painting. "*Blimey*, you can paint, cobber!"

Whatever that meant, it seemed like a compliment. Sarah smiled. "You decided not to do the whole hike?"

Jonathan casually sat down on the short stone wall next to her. "I had a good walk, but I'm not as serious about it as they are. Tomorrow I will work with the aquarium all day, so I won't be trained enough for Friday night. You and Mara have so much talent. I admire it. She told me you both took one of your early courses from an art teacher in Australia. She said it was an international scholarship competition. I can tell there is a similar style in both of your paintings. Did you pick it up from that teacher?"

Sarah was intrigued how Jonathan would notice the similarity. On the surface, the end result of their paintings were vastly different, but the fundamentals were the same. Interesting. Then with a quick change of subject, Jonathan asked, "Where do we meet for lunch?" She told him the family-owned restaurant up on the hill. "Okay, I am going to wander a bit and see you there." Off he went with a confident swagger, and Sarah couldn't help thinking, *Now there goes trouble. How did Mara get involved with him?*

Having a few minutes with Mara alone, Annie wondered the same thing. "Mara, what is going on between you and Jonathan? You two seem like total opposites!"

"It is true Jonathan has a large personality and can be loud and overbearing. I am usually quiet and reserved and cherish my alone time. I am not sure what happened. I guess I had seen him for such short visits I thought it possible. But after the time in Capri, he was just too much for me. I haven't said anything yet. We will be fine this week. You and I had this morning, which I loved. He is working tomorrow. But what about you? There are lots of personalities surrounding you. How are you holding up?" Mara watched as Annie ran through her thoughts.

"It is great to have you all here. I love that. I am terribly worried about my father, not just his getting back in time but also about his safety. I learned firsthand how ruthless those Chinese renegades can be when they shot Ramone's father point-blank. And that leads me to my future husband. Mara, you should have seen him when he realized his father was killed in front of him saving his life. It has shaken his pride about his profession. He is a really good matador. The local commission invited him to fight here anytime he'd like. He did not turn it down but neither did he say yes. I feel like he's brooding about it, and it's easy to hide that with all the people around. I do think the hiking has been good for him and has given him space to work out what is going on in his head."

Mara sighed, "It has to be hard to plan a wedding, entertain everyone, and have these worries all at the same time."

Annie, with glistening eyes, hugged Mara, "I am so glad you are here!"

*****

Veronica dropped them off after they finished. Annie suspected she had finally realized Antonio was not interested in her since she decided not to join them for lunch. Soon they were on their way to Valldemossa with Antonio, leaving Marguerite to rehearse. Annie was able to navigate the car up to the monastery. The problem quickly became evident they couldn't manage the wheelchair down the cobblestone street to the restaurant. Antonio felt that familiar rush of helplessness come over him. Annie looked at him, "Hey, I get it. But we are not giving up, okay? Just a minor setback. Mom, will you wait here? Mara and I will see who is at the restaurant and if anyone can help."

The restaurant was not too far down the street. The group was seated at two large tables. When Annie told them about Antonio, the restaurant owner overheard them. "There is a narrow alley in the back that is smooth. A car won't make it, but a wheelchair might." Jonathan got right up. So did Francoise, both ready to help. Sabine wanted to come too. Mara sat down in the vacant seat next to where Jonathan had been seated, and Annie proceeded back up the hill with Jonathan, Francoise, and Sabine.

They got to the top and found the small alley that led to the restaurant. Francoise and Jonathan, on either side of Antonio, supporting him, slowly moved to the alley while Annie moved the wheelchair. Jonathan said, "Come on, mate. We've got you."

Antonio was in a standing position. Instead of simply being dragged, he tried to move his feet with them. He felt something. Asking the two men to let him bear a little weight, they both shifted him a little lower so his feet were on the ground. Watching in amazement, Sabine called out, "You can do it, Antonio! Walk with them!" Jonathan and Francoise were still carrying the bulk of his weight, but Antonio began to move his legs in time with their steps!

The ladies were screaming with clapping and cheers. In the alley, they got him into the chair and into the restaurant, feeling as though they had just witnessed another breakthrough! Looking up from the table, it was clear something big had happened. Sabine couldn't help herself and directly to Meghan gleefully said, "Antonio bore weight with the two men supporting him!"

Meghan was ecstatic! "Antonio, this could mean you are ready to try a walker, especially with your arms so strong. Excellent job!"

Jonathan, glad to have been a part of it, patted Antonio on the back and said, "Well done, mate." And Francoise agreed too. Everyone raised their glass for a toast. Don Marco got up and shared a short story.

"Valldemossa happens to be the birthplace of its own saint, Santa Catalina Tomás. She was born here in the 1500s. From the time she was a young girl, she had visions of angels and saints. She had an aptitude for prophesy and miracles and spent a life of prayer and humility in a convent in Palma." Looking at Antonio, "Possibly Santa Catalina smiled upon you today in this ancient city by the monastery. Cheers!" Annie suddenly remembered the note she pinned to the wall at the monastery of Lluc and sent a thankful prayer upward.

# Chapter 73

Marguerite entered the room for the rehearsal only to find Simon irritable and in a foul mood. Marcella shrugged her shoulders, not knowing what the issue was. Having two sons, Marguerite knew their moods. This definitely had to do with a woman. "Simon, your musical talent is a gift. Whatever is bothering you right now needs to be put aside to let that talent shine. Just imagine letting go of any frustration, anger, resentment, or envy. Let yourself feel the freedom and power of not being held back by any negative feelings. That is how I can dance with abandon. It will work for you. Take a deep breath, then another. There, now play."

Simon moved into the rendition of "Higher Love" they had worked on. He reined in all his feelings and let them flow through the music, his eyes never leaving Marguerite. Marcella smiled as he played and joined him with her violin. This song would have no dancing. The showcase would be Simon's voice and the soulful words of the song.

Paulo was waiting for Marguerite at the door after the rehearsal. Simon came out in time to see them leaving together. He clutched his guitar case tighter. He glanced over at the *Porto Banus* to see Helene waving. Without a response, he tucked his head and walked the other way.

Paulo and Marguerite walked for a while with no particular destination in mind. He asked her about her dancing days in Barcelona. Paulo ventured, "I imagine men fell madly in love with you every night when they saw you dance."

Marguerite smiled in memory. "Perhaps one or two, but no one touched my heart like Salvador. We were happy for many years. It was after the boys and I left Hong Kong and Salvador's brother, Pedro, convinced them to train to be matadors that Salvador's anger pushed him into a dark place. My heart broke to see my sons lose their father, knowing he was out there somewhere. At the end, once he knew Ramone was in serious danger, I was convinced he would do whatever it took to get his son to safety. I never expected that ultimate sacrifice."

Paulo reached for her hand. "I know it must have been impossibly painful. When we pulled Nadia from the sea, we did everything we could think of to resuscitate her. I prayed to take me instead of her. By the time we got her to the hospital, I knew she was gone, but the doctors insisted I wait for her passing to be 'declared.' That is why it was so difficult to be in the hospital waiting room. Her gift of music melted my heart. For weeks after, I would think I heard notes coming from the piano, and I would go expecting her to be there playing but instead found an empty bench. I think in some way that is why your dancing moves me like it does."

Marguerite's sympathy showed on her face. "Her sudden death like that must have been dreadful. There was something in your face there in the waiting room that drew me to comfort you."

Stopping her inside a narrow alley, Paulo drew her to him, looking into her eyes. Softly, he asked, "Do you think you might ever love again?" She looked up at him and felt that same magnetic pull as the first time she met him. Before she could answer, he kissed her. The chemistry they both felt was undeniable, and the kiss deepened.

Their conversation continued over tea, and time flew by. When Marguerite realized it was time she got back to the villa, she could not hold back her invitation for him to return to the villa with her. However, upon their arrival, she had second thoughts about whether it was reckless to begin a relationship just as she was about to scatter her husband's ashes.

Paulo noticed her hesitation. "If you would prefer, I don't have to come in."

Marguerite looked at him, hoping he would understand. "Our timing is probably not the best."

"As you wish, but let me ask you a question. How long has it been since you and Salvador were together as husband and wife?"

Marguerite thought a moment and answered, "Over eight years."

Paulo spoke softly. "Don't you think it's past time?" Marguerite finally gave in, and eventually they went inside, agreeing to keep things simple and platonic.

Gennie was the first person they ran into. She eagerly came to greet them. "There was exciting news today! You might want to find Antonio so he can share it. All the young people are around the veranda and pool area."

"Gennie, I hope you don't mind. I ran into Paulo after rehearsal and asked him to join us."

Gennie hugged Paulo. "Heavens, no, he is always welcome. We have a house full, and one more just adds to the festivity." Gennie then went back to supervise all the activity in the kitchen and side catering area.

Marguerite and Paulo passed Dom on their way to find Antonio. He greeted both of them, happy to welcome Paulo, and said he was looking for Gennie. They spoke for a few minutes, then Dom left, knowing she would most likely be in the kitchen.

When he found her, he gave her a big kiss on the cheek and a pat on the behind. "Do you realize we have a backyard full of unattached young adults? You can literally feel the electricity in the air out there! It would seem lots of paths are crossing this week. Take a break from kitchen duty and come with me to see." He took her hand and led her to the veranda.

Hans had joined them. Ramone had invited him when he showed up for the second half of the hike. Sarah was doing her best to ignore him. The cluster of all the various conversations caused a low-pitched buzz. Dom looked at Gennie. "See! I've been trying to keep up. Antonio had such a big day, and Sabine seems to be most excited. However, Robert hasn't given Sabine much notice and is spending time with Mara. Mara came with Jonathan, but he has been in deep conversation with Sarah. Hans is obviously trying to speak with Sarah, but she doesn't seem to want to leave her conversation with Jonathan. And now we have Marguerite here with Paulo. Let's go over to the double swing to watch."

"Dom, this is not like you. Leave these young people alone. Did you notice Celeste sitting over by herself? I can tell she is worried about Alex. I am going to get Claudette to help me assist the chef. Why don't you talk to your daughter?" Gennie signaled to Claudette to come help her, and Dom, now concerned, went to Celeste to join her.

"Hi, sweetheart, may I join you?"

Celeste welcomed her father as always. She hadn't shared the news, but there had been a message from Alex while they were gone earlier. She pulled it out of her pocket and unfolded it, then handed it to Dom.

'Dearest Celeste and Annie,

The British were supposed to take the Chinese renegades involved in the incident, but apparently they did not. We have not gotten to the bottom of why. The authorities in Malaga had them and just released all of them, except the one who actually pulled the trigger to kill Salvador. It was not the wisest of things to do. Unfortunately, the released inmates turned around and broke their comrade out of jail, so they are now all on the loose. We have tracked them from Malaga to Barcelona, where they seem to be searching for someone. Our pursuit is taking a little longer than we hoped. We will try to be there with you by end of day Saturday.

Love always, Alex'

While Dom read it, Celeste reminded him, "You know you are the one to walk Annie down the aisle if Alex does not make it back for whatever reason. She will be heartbroken if her father is not here. It is up to all of us around her to help her accept that if it should happen."

"Let's not get ahead of ourselves. We have several days until the wedding. Let's choose to see a positive outcome at the end of this." Thinking how to bring this up, Dom just started, "Did you see that Marguerite brought Paulo tonight? She is about to scatter her husband's ashes. Have you thought about the rough time she might be going through?"

Celeste thought about Marguerite. "There is no question she loved Salvador. But they had so many years apart, I can't imagine her devotion to have stayed faithful all that time. She is a beautiful woman. She should be open to someone new. I need to spend more time with her to help her see the opportunity that might be right in front of her."

On the other side of the pool, Hans casually got up and walked over to where Sarah was in a conversation with Jonathan and Meghan and Tomás. To Sarah, he asked, "May I speak with you?"

Sarah had so far avoided him, but she didn't want to make a scene. "Sure." Hans led them over to a small garden area on the side of the house.

Before Hans could start, Sarah firmly said, "I told you I don't want to talk about it."

Trying not to show his frustration, Hans replied, "Just hear me out. I know what happened seemed heartless. You left in such a hurry, I never had a chance to explain."

"What, that you embark on a love affair in a faraway country and all the while you are married? Nicely done." Sarah got up to leave.

Hans pulled her back down and softly asked, "Please, Sarah. Let me tell you. I wasn't married when we were in Australia. The feelings we shared there were real. The love I felt for you was beyond anything before or after that time together. I had a close friend back in Hamburg, Camille. She was like a sister to me. When I got the opportunity to take the course in Australia, I knew she was ill. She didn't have any family. I was selfish, and any remorse I felt about leaving her with no one was overshadowed by this amazing opportunity. Then I met you. From that first day, you captivated me with your spirited eagerness to hone your skills as an artist. I never saw your shyness you often spoke of except around me during those early days, and all I wanted was to protect you and show you how I felt."

Sarah choked back an unwelcome sob at the memory. Hans continued, tears in his own eyes. "By the time I returned to Hamburg, Camille had just been diagnosed as terminal. She had no insurance and was facing death alone. I knew I could not live with myself as a human being if I did not do something to help her. I didn't think through the impact it would have on you finding out before I could explain what happened. When I discovered you came to Hamburg, I tried to find you, but you seemed to vanish."

It was Sarah who begrudgingly added, "I went to the South of France for a while. Later I found work at a gallery in London where I interned in my youth. I felt sick and betrayed. Then the chance to go back to Africa to paint happened. I didn't think I had anything to lose, so I went."

Hans shook his head sadly. "It wasn't easy seeing Camille suffer through the end, but I won't ever regret being there. After she passed, I desperately tried to find you. Through the London gallery I learned you went to Tanzania. I wrote you numerous letters. Each time they were returned unanswered."

"I thought you were still married," Sarah said quietly.

His frustration showed. "If you had read the letters, you would have known differently. When I found out you were planning to be here for the wedding, I could not believe that fate had allowed us to cross paths again. Don't you think we should at least try to get to know each other after all this time to see if that connection might still be there?" Hans looked at her and reached over to put his hand on the side of her face. There was that hint of shyness resting just below her strong facade. He wanted to hold her and assure her it would all work out. He understood Sarah was processing it all. Hans stood up, pulling her into an embrace. "There is no pressure and no agenda. It gives me enormous happiness you finally know the truth."

Stunned by all Hans told her and how wrong she had been about him, Sarah returned his embrace, ready to look at him anew, with fresh eyes.

# Chapter 74

The following morning, Annie awoke to the caressing hands of her very amorous matador. Ramone loved that his simplest of touches could bring a response in Annie. He seemed to never tire of exploring what their bodies could enjoy together, and this morning was no exception. When they were both well satisfied and spent, Annie snuggled in tighter and brought up the subject of her father. "Last night, Mom showed me the message from Dad. I know he wants to be back before the wedding. There is no way to postpone it this late. I might have to accept that Dom might walk me down the aisle."

"Well, that man has done so much for you, he is like a second father, *querida*. You are lucky to have him here with us. My grandfather died in the ring."

Since he brought up the subject, she asked, "Did it ever frighten you that death or injury could be so close?"

"Honestly, I never thought about it until recently. I loved the adrenalin that supercharged me when I became face-to-face with the bull. I keep thinking about it. I know if I plan to go back into the ring, I need to do it soon."

Annie couldn't help but ask, "Would you seriously have gone with Dad right before the wedding?"

Ramone shook his head, not really knowing the answer. "These men murdered my father. I did not want to sit by while your father put himself at risk on my behalf. His reasoning was sound. I was not properly trained."

Annie nodded and thought it best to change to a lighter subject. "I believe my cousin is quite smitten with your brother! I know Sabine well. She may be trying to keep it quiet, but I can see it all over her face."

Ramone knew eventually Annie would find out about the pool and Robert's decision to stay. He told her they had walked in on the kiss in the pool. "I offered to get Robert a ticket home if he was uncomfortable. In the end, he decided he wanted to stay. Sabine and Antonio will keep it quiet for now."

"So Antonio feels the same way? I thought you said he would not pursue her as long as he remains in the chair."

"He seems to have gained a great deal of confidence working with Meghan and increasing his upper-body strength. But it is crystal clear to me he is in love with her. Hopefully, our families will become even more entwined in the future." With a pat on her bottom, he said, "Let's go, *querida*. We have walking to do."

Breakfast was a bustle of activity. Dom planned to drive Jonathan to the aquarium for his day of working out in the meadows of seagrass. Sarah had not mentioned her conversation with Hans, and thankfully he, too, was keeping it quiet. She wanted a little time to digest it and debated whether to spend the morning painting or going on the walk. She debated it with Mara, and they eventually decided to do the walk in the morning and go back to Valldemossa in the afternoon to paint.

Tomás and Robert planned to get their last day of hiking in with Stephan and Hans before the long pilgrimage walk the next night. Carmina would take Annie and Ramone, Sarah and Mara, and Sabine on the hike along the north coast. Celeste thought she would like to try it too. Meghan, elated about Antonio's progress, decided to stay home and continue to work with him. Francoise was poking around in the storage unit at the other villa, looking for a tool, and found an old walker that he brought over. He and Marta had caught Antonio's excitement the day before and were ready to help.

Dom and Gennie were hosting an outing on the *Porto Banus* with Claudette, Juan Carlos, and Carlotta. In the back of Don Marco's mind was the curiosity to see if Helene was on board and if all was well. At the last minute, seeing that Marguerite did not care to do the walk, Dom invited her and suggested she invite Paulo.

There was anticipation in the air for all the plans as each group set off, eager for the adventures ahead. Seemingly at the last minute, Roff decided to join the coastal walk which would begin in Son Serra de Marina. Carmina was waiting for them.

After introductions to Sarah and Mara, they all set off. The relatively flat trail would take them along a stretch of pristine beach with its protected sand dunes. Once back on the rocky path, they moved on to the headland of S'Estanyol. They would work their way past a parade of privately owned villas along the coastline and rocky coves. Carmina said they would check their timing but thought they would end around noon. She explained they would take an easy pace, and if anyone tired, shuttle buses frequently came by to take them back to Palma. Ramone was fine with slowing his pace and holding hands with Annie and watching her see the beauty of this island up close. Roff joined Carmina in the lead.

Mara had her sketchpad with her and every now and then stopped to rough out a sketch of a scene that caught her fancy. Sabine kept pace with Celeste, easily chatting about a variety of subjects mostly centered around the wedding.

That gave Sarah breathing room to sort through all that Hans had explained the night before. She'd rashly judged him over the years and never gave him a chance to explain. Was that a result of her feeling of abandonment from her father? Thinking about that time he spent watching Camille wither away made her cringe on the one hand and guilty she let him go through it alone on the other. They were not young students anymore. Both of them had experienced so much during these past years. Was it even feasible they might rekindle those feelings and carve out a life together? It seemed so unlikely. She held on to his words that there was no agenda. Possibly the best thing was for her to stay open to the idea to see if they might rekindle those feelings.

While she spent this time of reflection, Sarah had to admit she was no longer that shy and timid girl that Hans knew. She found herself fiercely drawn to Jonathan. His burly rough exterior could not be more opposite from Hans. Maybe it was her time in the wilds of Africa that made him appeal to her? And their mutual love of conservation was very enticing. She was convinced Mara didn't have strong feelings for Jonathan but was unsure how he felt. Sarah took a deep, relaxing breath and convinced herself to simply enjoy the ride and not fight against the paths that opened in front of her.

# Chapter 75

The *Porto Banus* was under sail, and Captain Luis had caught the wind in the sails perfectly to go rushing along the surface of the water. Don Marco felt good to be under full sail. He was particularly pleased to note Helene was on board. Luis had still not mentioned her absence on the trip to Marbella. After considering whether to bring it up, Dom decided it was best to leave it alone. If Luis had chosen not to tell him, there was most likely a reason.

Juan Carlos got out the cards, and a competitive game of *conquian* began with periodic cheers coming from the main cabin. Marguerite and Paulo, however, were content to sit up at the bow and talk. They enjoyed the time getting to know each other, and their mutual affection grew by the hour. So did the attraction between them. Marguerite was the one to finally acknowledge it. "This is crazy. We are not teenagers! And your parents are here on board!" Both of them laughed at the irony of possibly "getting caught by the parents."

The intensity in Paulo's eyes grew more serious. "Go out with me tonight, Marguerite. Alone?" Although Marguerite knew where the evening might lead, she could not find it within her to decline his invitation.

*****

From the trail, Annie could see the *Porto Banus* under sail out on the horizon. She felt a moment of envy toward those on board and looked forward to spending the last night before her wedding on the *Porto Banus* for a sunset sail. She told Ramone the baby must like hiking, too, because her belly seemed very active in there! She pointed out the *Porto Banus* to the group. Mara was the first to respond. "I can't wait to be on board! Annie, remember the Greek Islands and the *Majestique*? I never imagined you trying the rock climbing. What a wonderful time we had!"

Ramone teased Mara, "I found the picture you drew and about had a heart attack! Seriously, I was so worried something could have happened to her."

That had them all rolling their eyes, knowing Annie had the same fear about him. Sarah joined in. "I should have been on that trip with you! I was so disappointed I couldn't go."

Annie took Ramone's arm and said, "Mara, it was after you went home and I met Ramone in Karpathos that this child was conceived. Such an unforgettable experience. And here we all are together!"

Curious, Sarah asked Mara, "Were you already seeing Jonathan by the Greece trip?"

Mara answered, "No, I had just heard from him. Annie and I were both surprised. He said he would like to visit Bali." Looking at Annie, "While we were with him in Australia, I never noticed his having any interest in me. Did you?"

Annie reflected. "I remember trying to think back. I know he loved watching you paint."

"I sometimes feel I must be like one of those precious sea creatures he loves to collect. He sees me as unique because I am different looking. But am I different on the inside?"

Sabine looked at Annie. "Didn't you say the minister said something similar in his sermon?"

"You're right!" To Mara: "So why are you still with him?"

"We hadn't spent much time together. We are so far apart. I knew in Capri, though. He thought the relationship would take a different path, but obviously it did not. Annie, I know you didn't invite him, and now he is here. I do not want our situation to cause any conflict this week." Sabine and Sarah paused, knowing they were both experiencing the same dilemma.

Ramone jumped in to assure Mara. "Jonathan is welcome. He fit right in on the hike yesterday. The work he is doing here is fascinating. Don't worry. Are you uncomfortable in any way?"

Sabine quickly said, "Mara, you could come over and stay at our villa with me."

They were close to a village, and Carmina could see they were more interested in conversation rather than hiking and offered, "There is a seaside restaurant just ahead. Why don't we take a break?" Celeste had to admit she was ready to stop and after lunch would probably catch a ride back to the villa. Carmina continued, "Once I get you settled, Roff and I will probably find where the guys are and go join them. Ramone, do you want to come with us?"

Ramone was quick to answer, "I promised today to my *querida*."

Now it was Annie who shook her head with a smile, knowing he wanted to get back to "real" hiking and that there was obviously girl-talk that needed to happen.

"No, my love, go ahead. I don't often get this opportunity to have my favorite friends around me together. We will be fine and make our way back to the villa." Annie looked at her mother carefully. "You look tired. Will you stay with us for lunch?"

"Sweetheart, I would love that as long as I won't hold your conversation back." Celeste had no idea how this conversation would unfold.

# Chapter 76

Ramone and Roff left with Carmina after appetizers were served. Sarah ordered a bottle of champagne, and the waiter brought five glasses. Annie had not had any alcohol other than a sip here or there since finding out she was pregnant. She looked at her mom to see if just this once would not harm the baby. "Sweetheart, it is three days before your wedding. Why don't you have one with your friends today and another on your wedding day? You and the baby will be fine."

Sabine started. "Annie, I haven't been quite honest with you. Robert and I are not together, and I hate being separated from you over at the other villa. I am just thankful he has found hiking with the guys so enjoyable."

Annie, most interested and knowing what Ramone shared with her, said, "Are you thinking of pursuing things with Antonio?"

The most genuine smile came over Sabine's face. "I think it might be mutual. We didn't want anything to take away from you and Ramone. We can wait."

Before Annie could respond, Mara looked at Sabine and asked, "You and Robert aren't together?"

Celeste looked over at the waiter and said, "You should probably bring us another bottle of champagne." She had the phone and called Meghan to come join them. "This could be your bachelorette party!" Before too long, Meghan arrived, ready for a glass of champagne.

Meghan quickly asked, "What have I missed?"

Annie seemed to be keeping score and with a smile, loving all of this, responded, "Well, Sabine is not with Robert and is now with Antonio. Mara is not into Jonathan. Sarah, what about you?"

Sarah, still trying to think things through, hesitantly answered. "I have a past with Hans. After speaking with him last night, I know I misjudged him. He wants another chance, and I am very tempted." Looking at Mara cringing, she added, "But, for whatever reason, I am drawn to Jonathan. I think it is the time I have had in Africa. But if he is looking for a specimen to put on a shelf, that is not for me either." Mara agreed.

Meghan, always the rational one, said to Sarah, "Why don't you take the time to find out if that spark you felt for Hans is still there?"

"I have been self-sufficient for so long, I'm not sure I even want to enter into a relationship at this point. I hate the thought of putting all my trust in one person again. And I could obviously not have young children tent camping in Africa."

Celeste, with her usual understanding advice, said, "You don't know what you are capable of when you find your true love. Alex leaves for each mission, and my heart sinks not knowing when or if he will return. He is gone now. Annie feels the same about her father and does not know what will happen when Ramone goes into the ring. These are choices our men have made. We can choose to accept them or not. Sarah, you can choose to live somewhere else other than Africa among the animals."

Annie's mother once again made her realize Ramone's choice was his own, just like her father's. Whether they liked it or not, they loved these men. If they chose them, they have to accept the risks. Annie knew marrying Ramone meant that accepting those risks would be essential. Looking around at her mother and closest friends, she said, "I made a choice the day Ramone proposed to me to accept the chances he takes when he goes in the ring. But I would not trade one day I have with him. The depth with which I love him is beyond any words I could find. You are each on your own journey, and I do not want you tiptoeing around because of me. True, we are all here together on the surface because of the wedding. But there are interesting paths crossing this week. Please take advantage of this time to explore them."

Meghan added, "Annie is right. The past is past, but it has brought each of us together at this place and for the opportunity that exists now and for the future. My decision to marry Tomás seemed to happen quickly, but that doesn't mean it was easy. We were from two different countries with vastly different backgrounds. Sadly, my family was gone, possibly similar to Hans's Camille. I got so lucky to find not only a man I love but a beautiful family who has accepted me as their own. Had it not been for a chance meeting in Capri on summer holiday, Tomás would not have make a last-minute visit to Ireland to see me, and none of this would have happened."

Annie thought about it. "That's true! If I hadn't come to Marbella after Sabine's accident, I might never have met Ramone, which means my father might still be imprisoned or worse."

Sabine added, "And if I hadn't had my accident and Antonio his, would he still live the life of a Casanova with no care of a woman's feelings? As bad as his injury was, it has caused him to mature and strengthen his character tremendously. I think I am falling in love with him because of that."

The conversation at lunch stayed with each of them realizing life's journey was unique but amazing for each of them. Instead of acting like they'd seen it all and knew the outcome, they needed to look at opportunities that presented themselves with curiosity to see what unfolds.

# Chapter 77

Upon arriving back at the villa, Celeste found another message from Alex.

*Dearest Celeste and Annie,*

*We have run into unexpected issues that might take some time to unravel. Believe me, I want nothing other than to be with you both Sunday, but I wouldn't be here if it wasn't important.*

*Love to you both.*

When Annie saw the message, she tried to put on a brave face. "Mom, at least we are hearing from him, and he is, so far, safe. It was brutal not knowing last time. He didn't mention El Amir. Surely Dad would say something if anything had happened to him." She joined Sarah, Mara, and Meghan on the veranda to tell them about her father's message. Sabine had gone to look for Antonio. They all offered comforting words about his mission, his safe return, and how the wedding would proceed if he couldn't make it back in time. Meghan wanted to cover any last-minute details needed for the wedding, so she went to check Celeste's list.

Sarah and Mara abandoned their plans to paint that afternoon. Instead, they were content to be in each other's company with Annie. The time flew by catching up and speculating about the future. They agreed to all meet again when the baby came, and they each designated themselves official aunts. Mara even offered to paint a mural on the baby's wall. Annie told them about the house they found in Mijas. It had been perfect, and they were on the verge of buying it, but with all that happened with Salvador's escape and Ramone's abduction, they hadn't had the chance to secure it. She tried not to sound disappointed and was hopeful they would find another.

Meghan returned and saw the three girls deep in conversation so she decided to join Sabine and Antonio at the pool. She noticed, now that she knew, how at ease Sabine and Antonio were together. Antonio especially no longer seemed to have that pent-up depression. It made Meghan genuinely happy to have helped in a small way. The walker was too much at this point since it required his full weight. She knew there were set ups in the therapy office at home that would begin his progress to walking with partial weight-bearing. She was very hopeful and knew Antonio was as well.

Jonathan returned from the aquarium and joined the girls. When they asked about his day, Jonathan answered, "We went out to the sea-grass beds looking for sharks. I was able to share with them the important role that sharks play in the ecosystem, along with the work we are involved with in Australia protecting the shark population. The sharks create a balance by removing the weak and sick to maintain a healthy ocean."

Sarah was fascinated. "It is like that on the plains of Africa with the predators like lions, leopards, cheetahs, and hyenas. They prey on the weak, quickly eliminating them. When I'm there, I often marvel at an early morning kill of a gazelle, or some other weak animal, that sets into motion the hierarchy of animals who partake in it so by nightfall all that is left is a slight dent in the grass. Nature is magnificent with all its intricacies."

Jonathan answered, "I agree. At the aquarium, they told me about their Species Protection Plan. I was asked if I would stay another week to collaborate with them. They also asked about tomorrow." Looking at Mara, "I don't plan to do the hike tomorrow night. I wanted to check with you to see if we have any plans during the day. I know your flight leaves Monday, but I think I might stay through next week."

Mara glanced at Annie for confirmation. Annie quickly said to Jonathan, "What a fantastic opportunity! You should definitely do it. Some of us might go to the caves and pearl factory, but none of that should keep you from whatever you choose."

Mara shrugged and said, "Sarah told me of a picturesque village nearby where we could paint. That sounds good to me, so I would be glad you had something interesting to do."

Looking over at Annie, Mara asked, "I have certain things about the wedding that I'd like to clarify. Do you have time?" Annie glanced at Sarah and Jonathan and immediately understood what Mara was doing. She quickly nodded and went to Mara's room to talk.

When they left, Sarah was amazed the opportunity had presented itself and thought it time to take full advantage of it. "When you are home in Australia, are you out in the wild with your work?"

Jonathan shook his head. "Not in the sense like Africa with its long list of predators. Our gators and crocs give us a little trouble. The kangaroo can be a bit bothersome when they go *troppo*, but for the most part they are quite easygoing."

"Sorry...*troppo*?" Sarah smiled at the accent.

Jonathan laughed. "When they go crazy or get aggressive. I travel around a great deal. I am a naturalist. That means I do a variety of projects designed to improve the environment and, in certain instances, preserve sacred lands."

His last comment sounded similar to Meghan's passion. "Have you spoken to Meghan about her work as a historian and preserving the old Gaelic ways in Dingle, Ireland? I find her work captivating. It sounds like yours is too."

"Ha, that is ironic. I haven't seen any of your paintings, but an artist's talent is an amazement to me. That is what drew me to Mara. To see her make a scene come alive with a few strokes of a brush and some paint is an extraordinary sight to witness. Do you have any photos of your work?" Jonathan's curiosity about Sarah was piqued.

"I just came from an exhibition of my work at a gallery in Barcelona. I have one of the pamphlets that was sent to collectors prior to the event. It has a few pictures of different paintings that were displayed there. Would you like to see it?" Sarah knew her recent collection of birds of prey was one of her best.

# Chapter 78

The hikers came in tired and hungry. To be ready for tomorrow night, their plan was to eat then get to bed early for a solid night's rest, take it relatively easy tomorrow, and get plenty of hydration. They had to be in the starting location, Plaça des Güell, by 9:30 p.m. During the following hour, all the roads to the monastery would be cleared of cars, and the sound of the horn at 11:00 p.m. would signal the start of the trek.

The flat Don Marco rented for the night would be open beginning at 6:00 p.m. for anyone who planned to participate. If any of the hikers did not make it all the way to the monastery, they could shuttle back to Palma and stay at the flat until morning.

Ramone, Tomás, and Robert would begin with Stephan, Carmina, Hans, and Roff. They would be among thousands attempting to make it to the top to be blessed by the sacred Black Madonna. The course was an ambitious trek of fifty kilometers through the Tramuntana Mountains that would take between nine and eleven hours, so it was certainly not for the faint of heart.

Annie, Meghan, and Sabine spent Thursday evening preparing essential backpacks for the seven of them. Marta had brought the backpacks she found in town. Mara and Antonio also helped. Helene dropped off four boxes of groceries earlier. Each pack would contain nuts, seeds, protein bars, hard-boiled eggs, and dried meats, along with the water bladders Francoise had found to keep them hydrated along the way. Antonio filled them each with fresh water and loosened the long straws so they could drink while they walked. There would be rest stops along the way where they could relieve themselves and refill. Everyone was helping in whatever way they could.

While on board the *Porto Banus*, Dom arranged with Paulo to have a huge buffet ready at the flat so the hikers could get a good strong meal before they started. It would also serve as dinner for the rest of them later. The anticipation was building within the cheering team for the hikers. They would be hiking among young and old, locals and tourists, uniting a wealth of people gathered for this pilgrimage.

The day of the hike finally arrived. There were various plans scheduled. Jonathan left for the aquarium and promised to return early. Hans would pick up Sarah and Mara to go to Valldemossa. It had been a long time since he had picked up a brush and thought it the perfect place to give it a try. Antonio wanted to somehow participate in the night's festivities. Don Marco was working with Juan Carlos to find something for him. So far, he could be on the shuttle and offer water and fruit to weary travelers, position himself along the way to support the hikers, or go to the top to greet the pilgrims who made it. If he did the latter, he wouldn't be needed until the morning. Dom planned to take him to the event coordinators to discuss his options. And Mara suggested Sabine move in with her in the casita, which she eagerly accepted.

Hans picked up Sarah and Mara with their canvas and paint ready. Mara did not have a fold-up chair like Sarah, so she brought a couple of stools from the villa for Hans and herself. Sarah noticed Hans looked a little different this morning, not so polished and perfectly put together, with tousled sandy-blond hair, unshaven face, and white shirt rolled at the sleeves and partially unbuttoned. He noticed her looking at him and apologized. "Sorry, I plan to clean up better for tonight."

Mara glanced at Sarah, who shrugged and said, "You look okay to me. Right, Mara?"

With a smile, knowing Hans had done the exact right thing, Mara said to Hans, "This morning, you look more like you did when we were all back in Australia!" Arriving in Valldemossa, Mara squealed, "Oh my! This village is breathtaking. We aren't the only artists here. I can certainly understand why."

Sarah found her spot from before and began to unpack her bag. Sarah handed Hans an extra canvas she brought, as well as a makeshift easel. He pulled up his stool to sit next to her. Mara looked at the scene and thought she might wander a bit to find a scene that suited her taste a little better. "I think I will go a little farther if you don't mind. No sense us all painting the same picture."

Sarah laid her paints out so Hans could use them as needed. She was curious and asked, "What made you give up painting and open a gallery instead?"

Studying the scene in front of him, Hans answered, "I was so honored to have been accepted for the course in Australia, but I had to admit even then I never had the talent you and Mara did, although I did feel like the glass blowing had potential. But life turned around so suddenly back in Hamburg with Camille. Between the wedding, securing insurance, and doctors' appointments, there was hardly a moment to think about painting. I was offered a position as assistant manager at a local art gallery and decided to take it. They offered me flexibility when Camille needed me, and they offered great insurance. I found I enjoyed discovering new talent and helping young artists become better known. After Camille passed, the owner of the gallery retired, and I decided to buy it. It seems to pay the bills pretty well." He smiled at her. "You should do an exhibition there. I think my collectors would love your work."

Sarah asked, "You've seen my collections?"

"As a dealer, I received materials on a couple of your exhibitions. I saw your zebra series and lion series. They looked incredible. I thought about coming, but the timing wasn't right. Also, I wasn't sure about how I would be received since my letters came back unanswered."

Sarah took a deep breath. "I owe you an apology, Hans. It must have been horribly difficult for you." Sarah was looking at the scene but without focus, chewing on the tip of her brush.

Hans, thoughtful, put a few more brushstrokes on his canvas, then looked over at her in time to see that old habit he so affectionately remembered. "I will never regret being there for Camille. It was the thought of how I hurt you and how betrayed you must have felt that put a dagger in my heart. Sarah, please believe me when I tell you from my soul, you were the love of my life. There has never been anyone close before or after you."

Sarah thought about the choices she had made. She, too, had locked herself into a romantic solitude. Sure, she had gotten close to Sam, but was it true love? "If things had been different, I would never have moved to Africa and had my amazing experiences there. El Amir's sponsorship has paved the way for my success. That probably would never have happened either. The paths we took moved in different directions. Perhaps it was destiny we did not end up together."

Hans stared at her seriously. "Then why do you think we are here together now? Do you not think this is destiny? Shouldn't we allow ourselves another chance, a new beginning?"

He leaned over and pulled her to him. His kiss was gentle at first, willing the memory of their blissful days of kissing in the past to come forward. Slowly, as if awakening, Sarah felt her own response. Hans felt it, too, and deepened his kiss, willing her to give him a chance. They couldn't change the past. Was it possible to go into the future inspired by the past, not burdened by it?

# Chapter 79

Annie watched Robert's easy banter with Ramone and Tomás and was happy he decided to stay for the wedding. All those hours hiking together seemed to have created a bond between them. Ramone and Tomás were much closer too. All three hoped to complete the trek to the monastery and were comparing strategies.

Annie loved the idea of getting to Lluc the next morning to cheer on the successful participants. Meghan said she would go with her. Ramone overheard the discussion. "Antonio is looking for a way to participate. Maybe he could go with you?"

Sabine offered with a chuckle, "I can ask him, but I think he wants to prove he can stay up all night like you!"

Tomás asked, "Are we still planning to go to the caves?"

Meghan, getting a nod from Sabine about their plan, said, "Why don't you guys go? Sabine and I want a little alone time with Annie. We could meet you at the pearl factory."

Robert rolled his eyes. Oh yeah, the pearl factory. Can't wait."

That got a snicker from Ramone and Tomás, and a laugh from the girls. Annie, curious about what Meghan and Sabine wanted, felt she should give everyone the option about the pearl factory. "This tour is definitely not set in stone. If anyone would rather not go, it is perfectly fine." Looking at their doubtful faces, she added, "Seriously." She took Ramone's hand. "If you skip it, you can take longer at the caves."

"Are you sure, *querida*? I will come if you want me to. You might find something you like."

Smiling, she answered, "And if I do, I certainly know how to go to a cash register." Ramone laughed, handled the check, and left with Tomás and Robert.

Annie said to Sabine and Meghan, "You two don't want to go to the caves? I hear they are a breathtaking result of nature's course over the millennia. I don't want you to miss anything important!"

Sabine started. "Annie, we are your bridesmaids, and the wedding is day after tomorrow. YOU are what is important to us. We want to be sure you are okay. What if Uncle Alex isn't back in time? Will that spoil the wedding for you?"

Annie sighed, raising her chin slightly. "I plan to keep my hopes high until I start that walk down the aisle. I know he is doing everything he can to get back here. And how lucky am I to have Dom as a backup? I need to keep my focus on starting a life with Ramone. And now that we have Mara's additions to the ceremony, they will only add to how incredibly special it will be."

Meghan nodded in agreement. "I can't wait to see them. But how do you feel about having Salvador's ashes spread at your wedding? Honestly."

"Considering he is the reason I have Ramone here with me, I think the timing and the setting will be perfect. My concern is Ramone and how he has buried his role as a matador deep within him. I do not know if I am marrying a matador or not. I keep thinking he will let me know, but so far nothing. If I bring it up, he changes the subject. I don't know if I am secretly hoping he has given it up. I want to stay supportive."

Sabine took Annie's hand. "*Ma cousine*, he will let you know in due time. For now, before we go to the pearl factory, we have a gift for you. When we were in Valldemossa, we found a pearl museum. We looked for a necklace that would feature the beautiful back of your wedding dress." Meghan took out the wrapped gift. Annie looked at both of them in amazement.

Annie unwrapped the small box to lift out the most exquisite silver-blue pearl necklace! The three pearls in the back with the diamonds had her teared up and unable to speak. Finally, words came. "You didn't have to do this. It is gorgeous!"

Meghan said, "We first thought we should get ivory, but Sabine mentioned you like unusual. Plus, we thought it covered the something new and something blue. And the three pearls represent the three of us! So now you just need something borrowed and something old. We love you, Annie."

Later, on the tour, learning how unique and special the pearls that are made on this island are, Annie felt a moment of pure gratitude to have Sabine and Meghan in her life.

# Chapter 80

Paulo's assignment for the evening required both Don Marco's and Juan Carlos's buffet tables and adequate seating set up by 6 p.m. Catering would bring the prepared food at seven. Marguerite offered her help. Since disembarking the *Porto Banus* the afternoon before, she had not left his side except for a couple of hours in the morning to freshen up and get a change of clothes for later. Paulo paused to stare at the woman whose sensuous moves had hypnotized him from the moment he saw her. Their intimacy had exceeded all his dreams, and sometime during the night, she reached deep into his heart and captured it forever.

Marguerite could instinctively feel his stare and turned to gaze at him in return, feeling the heat of the evening's memories. Never had she imagined after all those years hoping for a miracle with Salvador that this miracle would find her here on the island of Mallorca.

Francoise and Marta were the first to arrive. Claudette would come later with Dom and Gennie. Paulo had the cases of wine Francoise had shipped from his vineyard in Bordeaux for tonight and the wedding reception. There was a mix of reds and whites. Francoise opened the cases and checked the temperatures to be sure they would be served appropriately. Marta helped with the setup.

The flat had an enormous open layout and large wraparound balcony with additional seating thanks to Paulo. Down below in the square, Plaça des Güell, a stage ready for music and the choir had been placed over to the far side. Tables were now ready for hikers to sign in and get their bib numbers that would identify them. Ramone, Tomás, and Robert dropped off their backpacks at the flat and went down to sign in early to avoid the crowds. At the table, they ran into Roff who said the captain and Helene had already gone up to the flat. He waited and walked upstairs with them.

Hans came in with Stephan and Carmina with their numbers and immediately went to find Sarah. Antonio had arranged to take one of the shuttle vans to the village where the hikers would arrive after about an hour so he could help the other volunteers. Sabine agreed to go with him. They would then decide whether to go further along the trail to help or head back to Palma.

The discussion among the young people was whether to go to Lluc in the morning to be at the finish line. Stephan spoke up. "For those hikers who make it, count on it being unlikely anyone will make it under nine hours, the slower around eleven hours. The seven of us will split into small groups that set their own pace. Knowing our group, I would say to expect us at the monastery closer to ten hours. That means you would want to be there to watch by eight-thirty. You might have to wait a while."

Carmina was smiling. "Or not!"

Annie, Meghan, Sarah, Mara, and Jonathan all planned to go. Sabine and Antonio said they might be more supportive to cheer along the way and thought they would leave it open.

The hikers ate a healthy meal with time for it to settle. From the balcony, they watched the crowd gathering. There had to be thousands spread out in the large square. The starting time was quickly approaching and soon they could hear the organ music begin. That was the signal for the hikers to move to the square. Each of them got multitudes of hugs and well wishes. Annie held Ramone tight. "Don't do anything foolish, my love. We have a big day coming up!"

"This is amazing! What inspiration with all these partici-pants! I will be fine, *querida*. I will see you at the end. I love you."

"I love you too." Annie sent him off with one final kiss.

Robert had his shares of hugs, but there was one surpris-ing one. He had not met the wedding planner yet, but she had stopped by the flat to wish everyone luck. Veronica gave him a wink and a hug and actually saw Robert blush!

The choir started their song, the "Song of the Sybil," and Simon's shining voice over the loudspeaker lit up the night. The monk overseeing the pilgrimage walked up to the microphone and began:

"Good evening. You are gathered for the annual Des Güell a Lluc a Peu, Night of the Pilgrims. Pilgrimages have been made here since the fourteenth century to honor the miracle of the Virgin of Lluc and Patroness of Mallorca. I want each one of you here tonight to make a commitment as to why you are making this walk. This is a spiritual journey for each of you. It is not an easy one. You need a purpose to succeed. Look deeply into your soul and commit yourself to that purpose. Do that and you will find the endurance to persevere. Blessings to each of you. Godspeed."

The group on the balcony watched as the hikers began their journey. In the distance, they could see their group waving up at them. As soon as the final hikers got on the road, Antonio and Sabine made their way to the shuttle to get to the first stop along the way. After the musicians packed up, Simon and Marcella stopped by the flat to say hello. They wanted Annie to know they were ready for the wedding. Helene quietly walked out of the room without Simon seeing her. Marguerite stood next to his father and smiled over at him. That familiar pang of envy was still there, but Simon shrugged it off. He was sure Helene would be here. He looked around and finally asked Captain Luis if she had come tonight. He replied, "That's odd. She was right here a moment ago."

# Chapter 81

Antonio and Sabine asked the shuttle driver where they should stop first to volunteer. He suggested Marratxí. "The hikers should start arriving there in about two hours. The journey to that point will be in the lower foothills so the difficulty will lie ahead. However, there will be many in the crowd dropping out at this village who do not believe they can manage the mountain range. Santa Maria would be the next major resting stop." He and Sabine agree to be dropped off at the first stop. The driver turned the shuttle around to slowly return to Palma, picking up a few hikers along the way.

There were tables filled with water jugs and small cups, coffee and fruit. The villagers who were not participating were out in full force to support the hikers. The head of the volunteers greeted them, happy to have the help. "Since our village is the first stop along the route, we get the most traffic. Your help is much appreciated! The village of Santa Maria is another hour by foot from here. Most people will try to make it there before stopping. That means we will be handing out thousands of cups of water. We have large trash cans spaced on each side of the road ahead to encourage them to dispose of trash in the cans. Just find a position along the road. We have various hoses hooked up to the well to help refill the jugs. Offer your encouragement. They have a long journey from here."

He continued, "Even here, there will be those who fall short and decide to quit. Maybe they are simply here for the experience. You will see. Those who push themselves steadily and persistently will make it to the next plateau. Ah, here come the first hikers!" The mood among the front line was solid and determined. Sabine and Antonio offered cups of water and a supportive comment to each hiker they touched. They looked for their hikers. They arrived in groups starting about twenty minutes later. Stephan, Ramone, and Roff were in the first group. Antonio saw them and waved them over. Antonio asked if they needed anything. Stephan said they intended to stop in Santa Maria for a break. They appeared to have their stride and a determined pace. Antonio called out as they walked on that he would see them farther up the route. The next to come by were Hans and Carmina. They were walking at a slightly slower pace, but they were surrounded by hikers, making it a little more difficult to maneuver their way through the crowd. "The group ahead of you said to look for them in Santa Maria. You're doing great!"

Carmina laughed. "This is the easy part! Wait until we get into the mountains."

Sabine called out, "See you along the way!"

By this time, some of the hikers had come off the course. Robert and Tomás saw Sabine and Antonio and came over for water. Sabine asked, "How are you two holding up? The others are stopping in Santa Maria for a break."

Tomás responded, "We are taking it slow and steady, not trying to win the race, but we are determined to make it to the monastery."

Robert added, "We want to maintain our momentum and not use up all our energy. We are not thinking about if we can do it but rather how we can do it! The higher mountains are ahead."

Antonio looked at Sabine to confirm. "We thought we might move on to Santa Maria, where you all plan to take a break, but I think we could help better if we moved farther up into the mountains to Consell or Binissalem, in the wine country. Those villages are beautiful, but the course becomes much harder, and we want to be there for support."

Sabine nodded. "Look for us in Consell. You've got this! Get some coffee and fruit in Santa Maria, and we will see you ahead in Consell!"

Tomás and Robert cut back in among the other hikers to continue on. Sabine and Antonio flagged a shuttle down on the return trip from Palma on its way up the trail to take hikers back to town. On their way to Consell, Antonio asked Sabine, "Do you think they will all make it to the end?"

Sabine considered their determination during their training to stretch themselves beyond what they knew or even thought they could do. "So far, their confidence and capability seem strong, don't you think?"

Antonio agreed and was reflective about whether he would have pushed to do this daunting hike himself even with strong legs. Would he have pressed his endurance? They reached Consell and checked in at the volunteer desk. The leader greeted them, thanked them for coming, then said, "You are here at an important part of their journey. By this time, those who make it will have mastered several difficult inclines, and their stamina is being tested. Their calves will be burning. Our job is to get them to stop and stretch, be sure they are hydrated, and feed them some nuts and dark chocolate for a boost of energy. Every year, we've lost about a third of the hikers by the time they get to Consell, and it gets even harder from here."

Unlike before, when many of the early hikers did not stop, here they all stopped, becoming a different experience for both Sabine and Antonio. Many of them were drenched in sweat, aching and exhausted. Many of those, once they stopped, decided to call it quits. Down the road, they saw the first of their hikers. Their groups had shifted slightly. Stephan and Ramone appeared first. Roff had fallen back. They were both winded when they stopped. Sabine encouraged them to stretch out their calves and hydrate. Antonio handed them nuts and dark chocolate.

Stephan asked, "Please check with Carmina. If she does not feel she should go on, tell her it is perfectly fine to go back and that I am so proud of her for making it this far."

Ramone added, "It is great that you are here, brother. It gives me the push I need to press on." Antonio shook his hand in support, smiling.

# Chapter 82

Hans and Roff were next to arrive about a half an hour later. Hans had developed a cramp in his leg, and Roff helped him over to where Sabine and Antonio were stationed. The doctor on call came to check on Hans and deeply massaged the area on his calf that was the issue. Antonio asked, "Do you plan to go back?"

Looking at him in amazement, Hans said stubbornly, "There is no way I am stopping! I can stretch this out. If I am going to succeed, I have to make my way through these challenges to get to the more difficult achievements ahead." He drank close to a quart of water and kept working his calf. Looking up at Roff, he said, "Buddy, you don't have to wait for me."

Roff simply smiled. "I've nowhere else to be. Besides, look at the opportunity you gave me on the *Nautilus* during the regatta. It was all for one, remember? You and I are a team, and we will make it to the finish together." The cramp eased up about ten minutes later, and they moved back to the road. To Antonio and Sabine, Roff suggested, "You might want to go to Selva next along the route. Any hikers making it there will most likely make it to the monastery."

Antonio answered, "We'll be there. Good luck!" Admiration for these two men swelled in Antonio. Instead of being weighed down with regret about his injury, he needed to embrace the achievements he had already conquered and look at the woman by his side who cared for him no matter what his infirmities were.

Sabine got coffee for them both. Antonio expressed a little of what he was feeling. Sabine was touched by the hikers' determination too. To Antonio, she said, "I am convinced you can accomplish whatever goal you set for yourself. Just like Roff said, we are a team now. I will be here for you and help in any way I can." He reached to kiss her, knowing in his heart this woman was home to him now.

It was about thirty more minutes before they saw their next group. They were busy giving support and refreshments, as well as encouraging the stretching. Tomás, Robert, and Carmina saw them and walked over. In this group, Tomás was the one struggling. They sat down to rest. Sabine scrutinized Carmina as she had promised. "Stephan wanted me to tell you how proud he is of you! How are you? It is fine if you stop. You have already accomplished so much."

Carmina, slightly indignant, responded, "Just like Stephan, I am here to do this pilgrimage, and I have trained for it. That doesn't mean I have to keep the same pace as him, but I am just as determined."

She got up to stretch, and Sabine quickly said, "I didn't mean to offend you, Carmina. Stephan cares about you and wanted us to check on you."

Immediately contrite, Carmina explained, "I might be tired and aching right now, but without commitment, my hope and goal would simply end up a frustrating disappointment." Antonio overheard her and absorbed her words.

Robert smiled at Carmina. "You are doing great. We will make it!" Looking at Tomás, "Take your time, friend. We're here with you."

Sabine felt an undeniable sense of pride in Robert to see the man he had become and gave him her most genuine smile. "Robert, I am terribly sorry if I hurt you, but I am so proud of you for all the work you put into this night and the support you give the others."

Tomás got up, had more water and some chocolate. "I'm good. Let's go."

Antonio told them they would now move on to Selva and see them there. "Stay strong. We believe in you!"

The shuttle to Selva struggled along the higher inclines.

Sabine and Antonio could only imagine how difficult this part was for the hikers. They checked in at the volunteer desk to ask how they could help. They were now many hours into the journey and had seen hiker after hiker give up in defeat.

The leader said, "The air is much thinner at this elevation. You will see. Only the extraordinarily strong and determined will get to this village. The last part of the route to Lluc remains arduous, but usually those who make it this far and move on will endure to the end. Again, hydration is key. A piece of fruit will give them a surge of energy. Offer a cup of coffee since they have now been hiking most of the night."

The number of hikers on the road had dwindled significantly. It was not long before they spotted Stephan and Ramone coming up the incline. They were breathing hard when they came over to sit and rest. Sabine offered bananas and apples. Stephan asked about Carmina and the rest of their group. Sabine answered, "As of Consell, everyone in our group is still hiking. Carmina seemed good at their pace. Hans was dealing with a cramp in his leg, and Tomás seemed to be struggling with the steep inclines. No one seemed willing to quit."

Ramone and Stephan nodded in unspoken agreement between them. "Stephan and I plan to wait for the others. It makes sense about Tomás. He didn't have as much time to train. If we can't all finish together, we don't finish at all." Sabine had to hold back the tears in her eyes and took Antonio's hand. They waited.

Roff and Hans arrived. Roff was extremely winded, having borne some of Hans's weight supporting him. They couldn't believe Ramone and Stephan were there with Antonio and Sabine. Stephan immediately went to work massaging Han's leg. "There is a shuttle waiting if you need it, buddy. You can be proud. Very few hikers make it here to Selva."

Ramone patted Roff on the back. "You did well, Roff. That last part was difficult enough on its own, but supporting someone else must have been brutal."

Catching his breath, Roff said, "It's the least I could do. He had my back throughout the regatta." They were both able to stretch and hydrate. When they heard Ramone and Stephan's plan, they heartily agreed.

Stephan had Hans lie down on the ground and do a series of stretches while they waited on the last group. They all breathed a sigh of relief when they saw Carmina, Robert, and Tomás coming up the hill. When they observed closer, though, it looked like Tomás was about to pass out. The hikers expected to see Antonio and Sabine but were shocked to see the other hikers waiting on them. Stephan called the doctor over to check on Tomás then went to embrace Carmina and look her over carefully. Ramone talked to Robert to check on him.

Antonio observed all of them making the same journey but each coping with it differently. All of a sudden, he felt like he was on the journey with them, and he wanted to cross the finish line with them. They all knew now that they each had to make it. The doctor gave Tomás a natural supplement to bring his heart rate down. Stephan was the one to say, "We have accomplished so much on this night. Are each of you prepared to go the distance?"

Without hesitation, they all said yes and moved back to the path. Antonio could almost feel the struggle each one of the hikers was dealing with to cope with their own courage, strength, and endurance. Witnessing them, he knew this night had changed him and could not wait to get to Lluc to see them cross the finish line. He and Sabine caught the next shuttle moving up to Lluc.

They arrived to find Annie, Meghan, Sarah, Jonathan, and Mara waiting at the finish line. Antonio and Sabine took turns telling them about the challenges of this course and how many had quit in frustration and pure exhaustion.

As of Selva, their group of hikers were determined to stay together. For that reason, it might take them a little longer. Antonio estimated the time they should arrive, but the time passed, and there was no sight of them. They all kept glancing at their watches as the minutes rolled by and hiker after hiker crossed the line into Lluc.

Thirty minutes later, there was still no sign of them. Meghan and Sarah, knowing about Tomás's and Han's struggle, began to worry. Then, far in the distance, all seven rounded the corner, and Jonathan called out, "There they are!" Walking slowly, Hans supported by Stephan and Roff and Tomás supported by Ramone and Robert, they crossed the line together and collapsed. Full of emotion, everyone rushed to them. It was then without thinking Antonio stood up out of his chair with his arms up in victory! He had crossed the finish line with them.

Annie, crying with joy, remembering the wish she had placed on the basilica wall, ran to Antonio. "It's a miracle!"

# Chapter 83

The mood at the villa was total euphoria! Not only had all seven hikers made it to the top but Antonio had stood on his own. Celeste, Marta, Gennie, and Claudette had prepared a huge breakfast. The hikers were starved but wanted to shower first. Then they would eat and try to sleep for as many hours as they could. Marguerite came home in time to hear the news, and her excitement could not have been greater for both of her sons and all the achievement that night.

A bond had formed overnight, working together to accomplish such a feat, and it was shared with Antonio and Sabine, who had been there to see them through. The only shadows at the villa were the regrets of those who didn't participate and that there had been no word from Alex since Thursday.

The rest of the day was free until the sunset cruise on board the *Porto Banus*. Everyone needed to be at the marina by four. Jonathan offered to take Mara and Sarah to lunch in Fornalutx since they hadn't seen it, and possibly stop by the caves or pearl factory. The girls eagerly accepted, and Sarah, knowing Hans went back to his apartment to rest, looked forward to getting to know Jonathan better.

After that morning's dramatic finale, Annie was satisfied to stay home and take it easy. It was clear Ramone and Stephan were the strongest of the hikers, but what they did for the others confirmed the generosity they both shared. Ramone had conquered the strongest of bulls, and he had trained hard to conquer this hike to Lluc. She was so proud of him. Annie somehow knew whatever decision he made about his role as a matador, she would accept it and give him her full support. When she went to their room, he was already sleeping soundly. Annie removed her clothes and snuggled next to him. In his sleep. Ramone instinctively drew her closer. She had not slept much thinking about his journey, so she drifted to sleep beside him.

Tomás chose to soak in a hot tub after breakfast. Every muscle ached, but he couldn't be happier. Meghan could not believe he hadn't quit, realizing her respect and love for him grew stronger that day. She got tremendous pleasure from getting in the tub with him to give his back a sensual massage. After the tub they, too, soon fell asleep.

Once Robert left for the other villa to rest, Sabine slipped into Antonio's room. Sleep for the moment was out of the question. The adrenalin flowing between them thanks to the night they shared and his bearing his full weight was over the top! Antonio took Sabine into his arms and kissed her over and over until their breath was ragged. He wanted this woman in his arms to know she was meant for him, and he set out to prove it. After a time well spent, they fell into a deep sleep within each other's arms, happy to have rediscovered each other on this magical island.

The villa now quiet, Celeste finally had a chance to talk with Dom and Gennie about Alex. Gennie brought tea out to the veranda. Celeste began. "Dom, I am worried. I haven't heard a word in two days. I know he would be in touch if he could. Something must have happened. I am becoming more doubtful he will be at the wedding, and I don't want Annie's special day to be ruined."

Dom said, "Don't underestimate Annie, sweetheart. She is not that same woman as a year ago. She has a strength about her now. Sure, she would be disappointed, but I do not expect it would ruin the day. It has been many years since I walked you down the aisle, but I imagine I still know how to do it." He said it with a chuckle but he turned serious. "We have to do all we can to give tomorrow the spiritual meaning Annie is looking for. Mara told me a little about the blessing. It sounds exceptional." Patting his daughter's hand, he added, "Celeste, Alex will be fine. Keep your faith. I am glad he has El Amir by his side. You can be sure they will look out for each other."

*****

Fornalutx turned out to be just as charming as they had been told. Sarah regretted not bringing her paints and watched Mara so easily sketch out some of the scenes. "Mara, you have such a gift to have the ability to quickly sketch out a scene that has its ambiance come to life on the page. I, on the other hand, think and ponder, often chewing on the tip of my brush to figure how to create the layers that give the final effect I look for."

Mara smiled and shook her head. "Don't you understand? It is those layers that add up to paintings worthy of exhibition and desired by collectors. It is brilliant."

They wandered through the village for a while before they found a café for lunch. Jonathan asked, "What did you think of the hike? And Antonio?"

Sarah replied, "Personally, I feel bad I didn't go with Sabine and Antonio. I am just getting to know Hans again. It would have been nice to be there for him."

Curious, Jonathan asked, "Do you think you can rekindle a love that happened so long ago?"

"I don't know, honestly. I did misjudge him, and he seems sincere." Sarah tried to envision a life with Hans.

"Well, on another subject. The aquarium confirmed their marine project manager wants me for another week. They have a waterfront two-bedroom apartment available for me to use. Do either of you want to stay a week longer?"

Mara was quick to respond, "I already took extra time off to be here. I am on a plane back to Bali Monday afternoon."

Sarah was slower to respond. "Possibly. I just finished the exhibition in Barcelona. Who knows if El Amir will be here to fly me back? Then there are the countless breathtaking venues here to paint. Can I think about it?"

# Chapter 84

Captain Luis arranged with the dockmaster to dock for the night since many of the boats that were in the harbor for the regatta were now gone. The *Porto Banus* was waiting, polished and ready, for the sunset cruise scheduled as the last activity before the wedding tomorrow. Roff stood at the gangplank to greet them. Helene had flutes of Spanish cava to hand out as they boarded, and Captain Luis was there to welcome them. Most of the guests had never been on board, and the vessel was quite an impressive site!

Francoise and Marta naturally knew about the *Porto Banus* but had never sailed with her. It was a first, too, for Mara, Jonathan, Sarah, and Hans. Robert asked Don Marco if he could invite Veronica, so it was her first time as well. For that reason, Captain Luis insisted they do a safety drill prior to getting under sail. Once that was complete, with the help of Roff, the lines were released, and they motored out of the marina.

Annie looked around her at all the people gathered to celebrate her marriage to Ramone. She felt an abundance of gratitude but also a pang of loss that her father and, yes, El Amir weren't there. It had to be bittersweet for Ramone to have his father's ashes at the wedding and not Salvador himself. She was overjoyed for Antonio and his amazing miracle. Was it too much to ask for another?

Ramone came over to her and put his arm around her. "What is it, *querida*? You seem lost in thought. Is it your father not being here?"

"Mom hasn't received word from him in two days. If he could make it, we would have heard from him by now." Annie looked at him with sad eyes.

"Come on, *querida*. This is a time for celebration! We defied the odds this morning, and Antonio is recovering. You and I will marry tomorrow and start our lives together." After a moment, "Look, they've hoisted the sails!"

Annie took his hand. "Hurry!" They went up to the bow so she could look back and see everyone's face when the sails caught the wind for the first time. *Whoomph!* There it was, and off they went, gliding through the water. Such an incredible moment, and everyone seemed to love it!

Ramone led Annie over to where Hans was in conversation with Sarah. His leg cramp was soothed over, and he had rested. His focus had certainly turned toward Sarah for the evening. Ramone started. "What are the odds you two would meet again so randomly on this tiny island of Mallorca? Do you have any plans from here?"

Hans answered, "I would love to have her come to Hamburg to do an exhibition at my gallery. Beyond that, we have agreed to take it one day at a time."

Right as he said that, Jonathan came over to join them. To Sarah, he asked, "Have you given any more thought to staying next week?"

A startled and questioning look crossed Hans's, Annie's, and Ramone's faces as they waited for her response. Sarah finally answered, "I said I would think about it, and I am. But I am leaning toward staying." Hans searched Jonathan's face to see his intentions, but he couldn't find them on his noncommittal face. Looking back at Sarah, all he saw was a shrug. Evidently, she was keeping her options open!

Veronica broke away from her conversation with Robert to find Annie and discuss the plans for tomorrow. She wistfully glanced over at Antonio, who was smiling and in deep conversation with Sabine. Once she found Annie, she pulled her aside to tell her she had seen the floral arrangements and they were spectacular! She had arranged for a stylist to do hair and makeup for Annie, Sabine, and Meghan. She asked, "Would you like the stylist to come to the villa or directly to the museum at Vista Hermosa? The proprietor said he would close to the public about thirty minutes before you need it, so I need to give him a time. Also, who plans to bring the ashes?"

With no hesitation, Annie answered, "Vista Hermosa is such an inspirational place, I would love to get ready there. About the ashes, I believe Marguerite is bringing them. However, I do not want the urn on the pedestal during the wedding ceremony. I will ask Mara if she would move them onto it once the ceremony ends. If you are closer, would you?" Veronica nodded in agreement.

Captain Luis planned his course to round the northwest side of the island in time for the sun to turn a crimson red and start its descent. The sunset did not disappoint; it projected an abundance of varying hues of reds, yellows, blues, and pinks into the sky with the sea reflecting all of it. The feeling was similar to being suspended in a prism, and no one was left untouched by the experience. This set the stage for tomorrow's ceremony at sunset. The difference would be the colors would cover the surrounding mountains. Nature's beauty surrounded them with extraordinary richness as it would tomorrow. Annie smiled, knowing that was exactly what she wanted.

# Chapter 85

The wedding day arrived at last. Today was about Annie and Ramone. Jonathan and Robert joined the groomsmen, Tomás and Antonio, to take charge of Ramone after breakfast, then have him back in time to change and get to Vista Hermosa. Only Antonio and Tomás knew of Ramone's plan for the wedding and promised to keep it quiet. The last several weeks had been an intense inner struggle within Ramone. He knew in his heart it was only fair his new bride knew the conclusion that had come to him. She said she would support him either way, which made the decision easier for him. When the monk, at the beginning of the pilgrimage, said to look deep for a purpose, Ramone had hours during the night to decide what that was. He knew now he had the strength to move on with his life with Annie by his side. That night had changed him, and he had witnessed the change in his brother, who actually made the journey with them. Antonio had found the strength to move forward, and Ramone knew with certainty he would not stop until he was fully recovered. The two brothers had a strong bond before, but the pilgrimage dug their respect for each other even deeper.

Mara outlined a little of what the Balinese blessing would require, and Annie loved it. She hadn't realized she and Ramone would participate, but the idea appealed to her. Sarah understood she was not directly involved with the wedding, but she asked if she could spend the day with them helping in any way she could. Annie gave her a giant affirmative hug. Annie had Sabine, Meghan, Mara, and Sarah by her side. It was then she remembered the night Sabine and Meghan were with her when she took the pregnancy test, and her mom came in to share the news and the joy. Celeste had been a constant in her life. Their special mother-daughter talks and her wisdom had been a guiding force to her. She also realized Celeste would be missing her father today as much as she was.

Annie found her mom alone, sipping a cup of tea on the swing out on the veranda. She sat on the swing, silent for several moments before asking, "Mom, if you aren't busy with other things, I would love nothing more than to have you spend the day with us girls. It will be hard with Dad not here, but at least you and I will have each other."

Celeste put down her tea and embraced her daughter with all the love she had. "Annie, I cannot begin to tell you how proud I am of the woman you have become. You have found the strength to not let fear overcome your sense of joy. I have grown to love Ramone as a son and accept his family as our own. As difficult as the road to get here sometimes was, you have learned to weigh each crossroad you come to and make good choices. Just remember, you won't always make the right choice. That is okay, you're human. When that happens, do what you can to fix it and make a different choice. I love you, sweetheart, and I would love to spend the day with you and the girls!"

Veronica stopped by to give them the schedule. The cleanup crew from the wedding the night before was almost finished, then Veronica's crew would begin. All the furniture would arrive first. Veronica, the florist and the stylist, planned to arrive at three. That was also when the girls needed to be there. Sarah offered to help Veronica with any setup needed with the florals, and Veronica knew that her artistic eye would be valuable. Gennie brought in Sabine's altered dress for her to try on. Celeste got the steamer out to freshen Annie's dress and both of the bridesmaids' dresses. When Mara shyly brought in her authentic Balinese outfit to steam, they were all in amazement. Mara quickly asked, "Is it too much?"

Annie had seen Mara dressed to perfection during her visit to Bali, so she smiled, knowing it was excellent and would add cultural authenticity to the wedding. Annie grew excited. "Will you put it on, Mara? Please! I would love to see it!" Mara went to change and came back to *oohs* and *ahhs* from all of them. She wore a full-length sheath of the palest gold hue. Her empire-waist cape was an Endek fabric with an intricate blend of crimson and gold with a three-inch border of gold lamé at the ruffled sleeves and bottom of the bodice that tied in back with the ribbon. There was a slight V at the neck. She brought her headdress that spread like a fan across her head attached similar to a headband. The base was a crimped red fabric with gold fabric balls attached along the outside frame. Annie squealed, "That is gorgeous!"

Mara explained she would wear her gold ballet slippers and had requested Veronica to bring a basket painted metallic gold to carry the red rose petals. Veronica retrieved the basket from her car, and the golds were a perfect match! Mara tentatively asked, "Annie, normally I would wear the full makeup like you saw in Bali. I can tone that down if you'd like."

"Absolutely not! As a matter of fact," smiling over at Sabine and Meghan, "if my girls are up for it, would you make up our eyes to give us a bit of the exotic?" When they both wholeheartedly agreed, Annie continued, this time to Veronica, "Do you think the stylist would mind if Mara did our eyes? Also, I would love Mara's input on my hair. I don't want a headpiece, but perhaps the way it is arranged with the flowers we ordered?"

Veronica quickly smiled and answered, feeling a little like a fairy godmother, "You are the bride! I am here to make wishes come true. Mara also gave me the matching cummerbunds for the groomsmen. Do you like that?"

Annie nodded, then asked Sabine and Meghan, "Hair up or down for you both? Mara, what do you think?"

Mara thought for a moment and went to her room to get something. Their red dresses had given her an idea. When she returned, she held out two of the most gorgeous ceremonial hair combs they had ever seen. They were a burnished gold that moved in a horizontal S-curve. A carved design of small red roses surrounded by gold filigree trailed its way along the center, and the comb was bordered by gold beads. Annie's tears flowed to see such beauty with perfect meaning. Sabine and Meghan took the treasures in awe. Annie took Mara's hands. "Thank you for being here, my friend. You have added so much to this day!" So caught up in the moment, no one saw the frustration Sarah had with not having done more.

# Chapter 86

Sarah thought about it. She did know one secret El Amir shared with her on their flight over. With him not here, should she disclose it? She told the others she needed to work on a little something in her room and would catch up with them later. Annie shared a glance with her mom. *Oh my gosh, did she feel left out? I never wanted that.*

Celeste said, "You girls continue. I'll go check on her." She went to Sarah's door and knocked softly. When Sarah called to come in, Celeste entered to find Sarah searching for something. "Sarah, are you all right? You know no one is trying to exclude you. Annie is so happy you are here."

Sarah answered, finding the picture she was looking for. "Annie is so lucky to have you, Celeste. I lost my own mother when I was young."

Celeste, with a sympathetic tone, said, "Let me help. What is going on? Is it Hans?"

"There was such an awkward moment on the *Porto Banus* last night. Jonathan is staying another week to work with the aquarium, and he asked if either Mara or I wanted to stay. Mara has to get back to work and can't. But I just finished my exhibition in Barcelona, and for once I don't have El Amir pushing me." That got an exchanged smile between them. Continuing, "I find this island an artist's dream. I can see why Chopin composed splendid works while here. I am considering staying. When Jonathan came up to me to ask if I had decided to stay, it caught Hans by surprise, and he misunderstood. It seems misunderstanding is a pattern with us. I tried to explain that I was not staying for Jonathan, but in my deepest heart, I wonder if that is true. So many years and so many experiences have passed since I was with Hans. I question whether he is chasing a dream of the past."

Celeste, talking to Sarah like she was her own daughter, said, "Sweetheart, you do have a lot going on with these two men. Unfortunately, you can't save today for later. It is here, and the things you do and the choices you make can either create the future you deserve or regrets that might be hard to overcome. Think about the choice you made when you left Hamburg, not giving Hans a chance to explain. How different would your life have been? Take time to choose wisely to get the future you envision for yourself."

Sarah hugged her and thanked her from her heart. Then Celeste asked, "What is the picture?"

"It is something I want to paint for Annie. I think I can finish in time to give it to her as a wedding present. Will you just tell her I am working on a surprise? Tell her I will be there later to help Veronica and the florist." Sarah smiled at Celeste and set up her easel by the window.

Celeste went back to the girls to find Dom asking, "How are my girls doing?" He now considered Mara one of his "girls" too so the question was all-inclusive.

Annie answered and lightened the mood, "Everything seems to be coming together. Are you ready to be one of the stars of the show?"

"I suppose this old man can get you to the altar. Although that cliff is pretty high, and I've never done well with heights." Dom chuckled.

Celeste shook her head. "So not true! I have seen you on the highest of mountaintops!"

"Well, okay, you got me." Dom put his hands on the sides of Annie's face and said earnestly, "You will be a most beautiful bride, Annie, a loving wife, and nurturing mother. You begin the next part of your journey today. Just remember, you don't have to go somewhere special to be somewhere special. What will continue to make your life exceptional is your choice to live it fully."

Gennie brought in a tray of tea sandwiches. "So I understand you have something new, and blue. Sounds like you need something old." She handed Annie a small velvet bag. Inside was a delicate gold bracelet inset with small rubies and interspersed with diamond accents. "When I discovered you were doing a red theme, I asked Tomás to bring it from home. It was my mother's, your great-grandmother's." Gennie glanced at Celeste for her approval and received a smile and a wink.

Annie was overwhelmed. "Oh Gennie, it is beautiful! You and Dom are so special to me. What would I have ever done without you?"

Claudette piped in, "I think that leaves something borrowed, *n'est-ce pas*? I am loaning you this embroidered handkerchief. I wore it on my own wedding day, and I will want it back to loan it to Sabine one day at her wedding." Annie's tears were now joined by Sabine's.

Meghan piped in, "At this rate, the stylist will have nothing to do with us with our puffy eyes and blotchy faces! I think we need a little toast."

Gennie smiled, pulling out a chilled bottle of champagne. Celeste began pouring half glasses. "We don't need you all wobbling down the aisle, do we?" That got a laugh that lightened the spirit in the room.

Meghan lifted her glass. "To a most beautiful bride and my amazing sister-in-law. To you, Annie." Annie was overwhelmed with emotion and did not hesitate to drink to the toast.

# Chapter 87

Before they knew it, the time had come to take the dresses and go meet the stylist at Vista Hermosa. Sarah left her room to tell them she was just finishing something and had called Hans to ask for a ride to the venue. She would not be too long and promised to be there to help the florist. Going back to her easel, Sarah looked at the picture once more and added some additional detail. Scrutinizing it, she realized it was not a noteworthy painting, but it would suffice, and the subject of the photo was recognizable in the painting.

Sarah changed into her dress, hoping the painting would dry by the time Hans got there. Realizing that wasn't happening, she did something she never did and got out the hair dryer. Laughing at herself for this desperate move, on the cold setting it at least got the painting dry enough to put a cover over it. She still wondered if she should give this without El Amir present. Hopefully, the answer would come to her, and at least she'd have it with her.

Sarah had dressed but had been so caught up with her painting she hadn't added all the touches she would have liked. You would never know it by the appreciating look Hans gave her. He kissed her on the cheek and noticed the canvas she held. She explained, "It was a last-minute gesture. I'm still not sure whether I'm going to give it to them after the wedding. May I keep it in the car?"

Hans said, "Of course." As she knew he would, Hans again brought up last night. "Sarah, are you really considering staying with Jonathan for the next week?"

She had not made up her mind until that moment. "Yes, and I very much want you to understand. Now that El Amir has found my work marketable, he often keeps me on a tight leash to paint more. What has happened is that there are times I feel like I am doing formula painting simply to get a piece sold. I don't think he realizes how I miss the freedom to paint landscapes. This island is a mecca of breathtaking scenery to let my imagination go free to paint what I want. I have this week off anyway, so I have decided to stay. Jonathan has given me no indication he wants anything more than companionship. He will be working all day anyway. If I can't maintain a platonic week with Jonathan, then you certainly don't want to rekindle a meaningful relationship with me. We don't know what the future holds for us, Hans. What we do know is that we didn't handle the past so well. I am willing to take the time to see what is in our future. Are you?"

Hans looked at the road ahead. "I can't say I like the idea. It was a surprise and a shock seeing each other again here in Mallorca. If we do find a future together, I want it to be like what Annie and Ramone have and know with certainty we are meant to be a couple. Will you sit with me at the wedding? When I found out I would be there early, I offered my help to Paulo getting the catering organized."

Sarah gave him her most genuine smile and, once he parked, gave him a sincere kiss that left them wanting more. "I would love to sit with you." She left the painting in his car and went to check in with the girls. The stylist had already started with Meghan. Annie said she loved the combs, and the stylist planned to do low waterfall buns with the combs ornamenting the side. Sarah said she would be back in a while to touch up her own hair and makeup.

Mara got herself ready. She wore the sheath, leaving the cape and headpiece for last minute. She concentrated on her eyes with a deep layer of charcoal lines pointed out at the sides. She would wait on the lips. Annie asked the stylist, "What do you think? Can she go ahead and start on my eyes?"

The stylist looked closely at Mara, then Annie. "Annie, with your being blonde, I would suggest more of a chestnut. Sabine's can be charcoal like Mara's, but I would use a deep hunter green for Meghan with her red hair." To Mara, she added, "Why don't you do everything but the points on the side until I get their base makeup on. Then you can add those."

Mara agreed and started to work on Annie's eyes. None of the girls was used to wearing heavier makeup and they couldn't wait to see the result. Then with a sudden worry, Annie asked, "Ramone will still recognize me, right?"

Mara quickly answered, "Let's start light, and you can decide if you want more."

Outside, Veronica and the florist brought the carts of flowers out to the peninsula. Veronica gave the gold basket with the rose petals and the two bridesmaids' bouquets to Sarah. They were magnificent! But when she looked at Annie's bouquet, something seemed off-center. "Let me take these in first. I have an idea about Annie's bouquet." The florist exchanged a look with Veronica, who nodded to not offend her.

Sarah went in with the basket of rose petals and two bouquets, then had to sit down in shock when she saw Annie's eyes. "Annie, you look like a goddess! Your blue eyes stand out like sapphires!"

Mara took the rose petals, nodding her approval. She showed Meghan and Sabine how to hold the fans rather than the stems of the flowers. Sarah took one more approving look at them and went back out. Tablecloths had been put on the round tables, and Veronica began placing the centerpieces. The florist was checking some last-minute details on the arrangement in the pavilion. Hans brought out the offering arrangements one at a time to go on the pillars at the front on each side of the aisle. They were exquisite! Paulo had worked with the chef to create layers of oranges, green apples, lemons, kiwi, and almonds with Mara's fans at the top. Sarah asked if she could add red bows at the handle of the fans, and Veronica loved the idea. Even the florist thought they had done an authentic job. The pedestal was set up where the ashes were to be scattered. Marguerite arrived dressed as the Spanish dancer she was, and Paulo almost dropped what was in his hands when he saw her. She brought the urn of ashes to place beside the pedestal. The ferns and bamboo were already arranged.

Simon and Marcella arrived to set up the music and stage area. Sarah turned back to Annie's bouquet, studying it. The white lilies were stunning, along with the baby's breath, but the baby red roses seemed to get lost. She suggested to the florist, "I just saw Annie's eye makeup and it is exotic. Do you happen to have another sprig of the crimson orchids?" When she brought one from the box, Sarah twisted and turned it to weave through the lilies and moved the roses to a more prominent location. Trying to get confirmation, she looked at Veronica and the florist. They both nodded and said she had created a masterpiece.

Sarah took it inside to Annie and started to do her own makeup and hair. Annie loved the bouquet and the addition of the sprig of orchids. "When was that planned?"

Sarah smiled. "Just a few moments ago, actually. I thought it needed a little tweaking." Annie was radiant when she smiled, and Sarah knew she had done the right thing.

# Chapter 88

During lunch together, Ramone asked Robert and Jonathan to usher the guests to their seats while he and Tomás and Antonio went inside to dress. He wanted there to be no bride's or groom's side. Each person was there because they both wanted them. Robert checked in with Veronica to be sure they knew what to do. She showed them how to take the women's arm and lead her to a seat. If it was a couple, the man was to walk behind and take the aisle seat. Family should be in the front rows. Veronica winked at Robert and asked if he would sit with her. He smiled and answered, "That would be great!" That got a nudge in the arm from Jonathan.

Guests began to arrive. Marcella moved up to the altar and stood to the side of the pavilion. While the guests arrived, she brought her violin up to her chin and did a slow and soothing background rendition of "Higher Love."

Don Marco decided he was more comfortable in a suit to walk Annie down the aisle and looked more debonair than ever! Robert and Jonathan took their usher roles seriously and Robert seated Celeste in the left front row. Jonathan did the honors seating Marguerite with Paulo on the right.

Gennie was next, followed by Francoise, Marta, and Georgette. Captain Luis walked up to Georgette. "May I join you?" Georgette was flattered and said yes. Sarah had left Annie with a final hug of encouragement and went to find Hans to get a seat. Stephan and Carmina arrived, then Juan Carlos and Carlotta. Helene and Roff took a seat together and that left Robert and Veronica as well as Jonathan, who wasn't quite sure if Mara's role would allow her to join him or not.

The venue was spectacular and it was obvious every detail had been beautifully handled. Robert looked appreciatively at Veronica. "You've done an amazing job!"

Smiling with her inside knowledge, she answered, "Just wait."

Antonio looked proudly at his brother as they left their room to arrive at the ceremony. "You've got this!" Tomás gave him a hug with a pat on his back. Ramone took a deep breath and began the walk down the aisle that would lead him to his wife and their future destiny together.

As he walked, he heard the gasps he was expecting. When he turned around to face friends and family, he was there in full splendor in his black-and-white *traje de luces*, or matador's suit of lights! The fully embellished short jacket, and ornate black waistcoat, white shirt, black knotted tie, and skin-tight trousers of silk and satin, richly beaded in silver with embroidered black silk was flawless. His heavily embellished *capote* or cape wrapped over his shoulder and around his waist completed a most resplendent ensemble. Ramone could not have looked more dashing. He saw them staring and realized he was proud of the man he was.

Mara was the first of the girls to see him and realized he must have made his decision. She walked up to stand between the two pillars with the offerings, appreciating their authenticity. Marcella stopped playing the violin. Mara put the basket down and stood with the golden bell in hand, pausing for a moment. The guests were still reeling over Ramone in his suit, and she wanted their full attention.

The sound of the bell as Mara firmly rang it resonated with an echo produced by the surrounding mountains. The hypnotic sound held the attention of the guests when she, in full Balinese garb, walked down the aisle tossing red rose petals along the path. Seeing her, Jonathan almost fell out of his seat. She had always dressed Western around him; he had never seen her like this. Inherently, he realized this was a major part of her identity and heritage which was so very different from his own.

After the rose petals were scattered along the aisle, Mara put the gold basket and bell to the side and stood next to an impressed minister. Mara was satisfied to see the things she had asked Veronica to provide were close by.

Antonio wheeled his chair down the aisle to maneuver it next to Ramone. He looked exceedingly handsome in his white Guayabera shirt and narrow black pants with the ornate Balinese cummerbund. Next was Tomás. Equally striking, these two with their toned-down attire made Ramone stand out even more.

Sabine was next, and she saw Antonio's reaction just a moment before registering what Ramone was wearing. She swallowed a gasp, knowing she could not turn around to warn Annie. She focused on holding her bouquet correctly and smiling at the guests while she took her place. Meghan was next, and she, too, was stunned by Ramone's decision. But she had to admit he was a striking figure to behold. Looking at her husband, smiling to herself, she thought, *he's not too bad either*.

Dom held out his hand to Annie. "You are ravishing, my dear. Shall we go?"

From behind her, Alex said to Dom, "Sir, may I have the honor to cut in and walk my daughter down the aisle?"

Dom answered, "You are a sight for sore eyes, son. We're happy to have you back."

Annie could not believe her eyes! "Dad, you came! If I cry, I will have all of Mara's eye makeup rolling down my face."

"We can't have that! Let's go get you married!" The joy inside her was overwhelming.

There was a surprising pause after Meghan walked down the aisle. Guests, and particularly Ramone, wondered where the bride was. When they saw Don Marco walk down the aisle toward Ramone, it had everyone whispering. He couldn't let the boy look so forlorn, so he smiled and gave him a wink, then took his seat next to Gennie. El Amir slipped into the chair beside Jonathan. Sarah turned and smiled when she saw him, but Jonathan mistook the smile for him and winked. Hans turned in time to see the wink, struggling to understand what that meant.

Marcella began the wedding march on her violin, and they all saw Alex walking Annie down the aisle. Celeste was beside herself with happiness! Annie had another surprise waiting when she looked up and saw Ramone in his full matador regalia. She realized at that moment he had made his decision to continue as a matador. Her father, also in a dangerous line of work, was standing next to her. The stern face of the matador was there until it saw her and softened. He had never seen any woman so beautiful. When she saw that look, Annie knew she would follow wherever he led. Alex turned his daughter over to Ramone, then Mara stepped up and began.

"The wedding couple requested a Balinese blessing for their ceremony so before our minister begins his service, I would like to have the bride and groom stand before me." To the guests, she explained, "The sounding of the holy bell summoned the good spirits and announced the wedding to the Balinese deities."

Mara picked up three stalks of bamboo and handed them to Simon to light the ends. She reached for her open coconut and her tied corn broom. She dipped it in the coconut water to sprinkle a few drops onto Annie's and Ramone's heads. "These drops of holy water will begin your cleansing as a couple." Simon held the bamboo with smoke rising. "See the holy smoke? Turn and pull it toward you to cleanse your souls from evil spirits and past sins."

Mara asked them to turn back toward her. "We have a purification ritual that asks you to both drink the same water from the young coconut with your hands." She poured a little in each of their hands, and they drank. Mara brought out two slices of banana and asked them to feed each other. "This is a symbol of how you will nurture and provide for each other. And finally, please put your hands up in prayer." Looking up, Mara continued, "On behalf of this couple, Ramone and Annie, we beseech the blessings of the benevolent Divine. Please ask your hearts to receive their grace for your life together as a married couple. Amen."

# Chapter 89

A spiritual silence had come over all who witnessed the blessing, including the minister. Eventually he stepped forward. "What an inspiring blessing, Mara. It shows how religions can stand side by side with prayer so similar and unified in cleansing wishes for a new couple to start their lives together. As Annie and Ramone both know, my calling is to follow a different doctrine, which is very accepting. We are all traveling this same journey called life, side by side, whether we know it or not. It is the blessed ones who realize cultures do not have to have boundaries. The one next to you might be worth a second look of acceptance." His last sentence caused a series of glances and hand-holding. Sabine and Antonio, Meghan and Tomás, Celeste and Alex, Dom and Gennie, Marguerite and Paulo, Hans and Sarah, and even Robert and Veronica. His words touched them all. And, even more to the point, his next words rang true.

"A purposeful toss of a matador's rose, the enticement of a woman's dance, the feeling of coming home, a chance for a new beginning, chances to be taken...there is so much to value, appreciate, and enjoy about life. Miracles do happen. Don't miss what is right in front of you. It really makes no sense to fight against it. And why should you? Annie and Ramone, you have received a most spiritual Balinese blessing holding you united. Do you promise to never let the miracle between you fade and to love, respect, and honor each other throughout your lives together as a family?"

In unison, they both answered, "I do."

"In the name of the Father, the Son, and the Holy Ghost, please bow your heads in silent prayer for the future of this young couple and their child to come. God bless you both. Amen. As a servant of God and by right of the island of Mallorca, I pronounce you husband and wife. Ramone, you may kiss your bride!"

Ramone, touched deeply by the ceremony, kissed Annie like she was giving him life. Whispering, he added, "*Querida*, please make up your eyes like that for me again and again!" He kissed her once more, and the two of them turned to walk down the aisle.

As the guests left their seat and followed the bride and groom, naturally everyone wanted to know where Alex and El Amir had been. El Amir was in an arm sling. The two had talked on the flight over about what they would say and had signals set up between them to determine their course of action. Veronica looked at Robert playfully and said, "Told you!"

He held her hand. "I never saw any of this coming!"

"I have to go set up the urn for the scattering of the ashes. Save me a dance?" Veronica smiled at him.

"Absolutely." Robert had been so inspired by the ceremony he decided it might be worthwhile to pay attention, considering who seemed to be right beside him.

The guests made their way to where the urn now stood on the pedestal. Alex saw the way Paulo and Marguerite looked at each other. He caught El Amir's eye and nodded toward them. Understanding, they nodded in accord to keep their findings silent for a while.

Paulo led Marguerite up to the pedestal. Annie stood beside Ramone. Jonathan had brought the walker, and although Antonio had the chair as backup, he made the effort to stand with the bulk of his weight on his arms.

Ramone began, "First, I want to thank each of you for being here to witness me marry the woman I love. This might be unexpected for some of you, but we are also scattering my father's ashes here today from this magical place high in the mountains. He died several weeks ago saving my own life." Alex and El Amir glanced at each other once again.

"It might be hard to understand. I do not wear this suit of lights to defy my father but instead to honor him. He might have followed this family tradition had he not seen his father mortally gored at an early age. No one should have to experience that. I personally have more scars than I can count, and my beautiful bride loves me in spite of them. I saw my brother injured and bound to a wheelchair. I pray every day for him, and yesterday, he stood for the first time as he is standing before us today.

"I will never forget the moment my father lunged at me. I honestly thought he was trying to harm me and tried to defend myself. Instead, he gave the ultimate sacrifice to save me from the brutal captors he knew so well. We spread these ashes off this rocky cliff down into the sea to send him to safe harbor. And I wear this suit with pride and honor. But this is the last time I shall wear it."

Annie, astonished after having so misread the meaning of his wearing the suit, looked at him with fresh eyes, knowing what it took to make this decision. Antonio stood up on the walker while Marguerite and Ramone scattered the ashes.

Later, as the reception began, Sarah went to El Amir to see if he planned to unveil the surprise. He nodded, and she went to Hans's car to get the painting. When she returned and showed him the painting, El Amir clanged on a glass for everyone's attention. "Annie and Ramone, your sudden departure from Marbella caused you to leave behind something important to you both." Both Annie and Ramone looked at each other with a combination of question and hope in their eyes.

"I know how important this was to you both and to the child you will soon bring into this world. Please allow me to hand you this key and all that it opens for your future together." Sarah stepped up and handed them the painting. El Amir had just handed them the key for the house in Mijas!

*It's Annie's friend Sarah's time to tell her story!*

*https://books2read.com/Finding-Sarah-A-Phoenix-To-Behold*

## About the Author
## Nina Purtee

Nina Purtee is a worldwide traveler, philosopher, and award-winning adventure romance novelist. Growing up in Atlanta, Nina's father ignited her travel obsession with lavish family trips to exotic locations. Some of those experiences have found their way into her writing. Island-hopping with her family through the Greek islands on a 95-foot sailboat, the *Eleni*, gave Nina the inspiration for Don Marco's vessel, the *Porto Banus*.

While on safari in East Africa, she met a woman artist with her companion, a sculptor, living in tents, immersed in their artwork. They inspired the character's of Annie's friend, Sarah, and the sculptor, Sam, that we meet in Sarah's book.

Nina draws from her travels to embrace multicultural characters and couples seemingly from different worlds and allow them to compromise, co-exist, accept each other's traditions, and even find love.

READER VIEWS describes Purtee as "a natural storyteller, with the ability to transport readers into realms of imagination and possibility."

Nina now lives in Florida surrounded by family and friends when she is not traveling the globe seeking new experiences to write about.

## www.ninapurtee.com

# FINDING SARAH

## A PHOENIX TO BEHOLD

Sarah Wilkinson's Gripping Story Joins The *Annie's Journey* Series

Sarah Wilkinson has found passion as a painter whose skillful talent was shaped and influenced by many, including two past female artists who came from different worlds and different centuries, yet both defied the odds against women becoming successful artists.

Evolved from the Annie's Journey series, Sarah was living in a tent painting the wild animals of the Serengeti in East Africa when Annie met her. They quickly became close friends, but what Annie was unaware of is the heartbreaking childhood Sarah experienced before she struggled to find her way into the competitive art world. As a result, it was Annie who would force Sarah to confront her destiny and make a choice that would forever change her life.

Her father, in a letter written just before his death, referred to Sarah as a phoenix that rises from the ashes to new heights. Follow along as Sarah surpasses one pitfall after the other, painstakingly getting closer to the potential for the phoenix to soar.

*****

*"Finding Sarah is the kind of book that breaks your heart, then mends it, and you will finish it with a smile and a long, satisfied sigh. I recommend it to anyone who loves to paint and enjoys coming-of-age stories, romances, and books with fierce female protagonists."*

**--READERS' FAVORITE**

Milton Keynes UK
Ingram Content Group UK Ltd.
UKHW032039180324
439698UK00001B/179